DEAR
LITTLE
CORPSES

DEAR LITTLE CORPSES

A JOSEPHINE TEY MYSTERY

Nicola Upson

CROOKED
LANE

NEW YORK

Private letters written by Margery Allingham and an extract from The Oaken Heart by Margery Allingham reprinted by permission of Peters Fraser & Dunlop (www.petersfraserdunlop.com) on behalf of Rights Limited.

Published in the United States by Crooked Lane Books, an imprint of The Quick Brown Fox & Company LLC.

Crooked Lane Books and its logo are trademarks of The Quick Brown Fox & Company LLC.

Library of Congress Catalog-in-Publication data available upon request.

ISBN (hardcover): 978-1-64385-902-6
ISBN (ebook): 978-1-64385-903-3

Cover design by Nathan Burton

Printed in the United States.

www.crookedlanebooks.com

Crooked Lane Books
34 West 27th St., 10th Floor
New York, NY 10001

First Edition: August 2022

10 9 8 7 6 5 4 3 2 1

For my mum and dad.
This one is from the heart.

The children were gathered halfway down the garden by the apple trees, their heads bowed in mock solemnity, playing out the ritual as they remembered it from the funeral. The dolly—Maisie or Prudence or whichever one had been chosen this time—lay in a box at Edmund's feet, wrapped in a pillowcase that doubled as a shroud, and she watched from the nursery window as he picked it up and carefully placed it in the shallow grave, dug earlier that morning. Lillian—quiet, earnest little Lillian—had taken her Sunday school bible out with her, and she read a passage from it, then crossed herself and held the book close to her chest, as if it were the most precious thing in the world. Not to be outdone, Florence glanced slyly at her siblings, gave a theatrical sob, and buried her face in the handkerchief that she had stolen from her mother's drawer. The three of them stood together in mourning next to the square of freshly dug earth that was waiting to be planted, then Edmund took up the spade again and filled in the grave. When he had finished, they ran, laughing, across the sunlit lawn, the dolly and their grief for her all but forgotten. There must be four or five of them there now, she thought. Dear little corpses, all in a row.

31 AUGUST 1939

I

The full moon made a nonsense of the blackout. Josephine pulled her front door to and walked out into the garden, where a mischievous, scavenging breeze chased the first fallen leaves of the year. The uneven path felt hard and dry at her feet, and the countryside around the cottage had tired visibly in the late August heat; even now, on the cusp of midnight, the breeze could do little to banish the day's stifling humidity. In the distance, a low rumble of thunder promised some respite from the tension in the air, and she wondered if the run of good luck which had blessed the Suffolk harvest was about to come to an end. The fields were half cut now, the ratio of stubble to thick yellow corn growing steadily by the day, but in the sharp, silvered light, everything seemed suspended in time, as if the fields—like the men who worked them—were holding their breath, waiting to see which way the world would turn.

Stopping at the garden gate, she looked back towards the cottage, hoping to take satisfaction from the darkened windows which she and Marta had worked on all afternoon, diligently lining the curtains with black, as though for a funeral which had yet to take place. She stood here often in the evenings, finding happiness in the home they had made for each other, in the scent of the flowers or the remnants of a meal on the table—all evidence of a simple, shared existence amid lives that were otherwise separate and complicated. Tonight, without its cheerful lamplight, the cottage already looked forlorn and derelict, as if it sensed a period of desertion and had decided to strike the first blow. The small transformation of something so cherished shocked Josephine—more so, even, than the dramatic reconfiguring of London in preparation for war; changes that made her feel like a stranger to the city she loved. She stared at the cottage's featureless anonymity, but the security she craved didn't come; instead, she had the sense of slipping into an abyss.

An oblong of light from the doorway broke into her thoughts, and Marta joined her by the gate. 'We did a good job,' she said, passing Josephine a nightcap and looking approvingly at the windows. 'Nothing to tempt an eagle-eyed Jerry there.' The thunder came again, closer this time, and in the context of their conversation it felt like an ominous rehearsal for the uncertain months ahead. 'We'll get through it,' she said quietly, taking Josephine's hand. 'No matter how long it lasts or how bad it gets, we'll get through it.'

The sound of the telephone challenged the comfort of Marta's words; whenever it rang these days, even at a more sociable hour, Josephine found herself fearing the worst. 'It might be Archie,' she said, as they went back inside. 'Perhaps something's cropped up at work and he can't come for the weekend after all.'

But it was Hilary Lampton, the vicar's wife, and one of Josephine's closest friends in the village. 'I'm so sorry to call at this time of night,' she said. 'Did I wake you?'

'No, we're still up. Is everything all right?'

'Yes, fine—at least, I *hope* it will be. The man came over from Hadleigh just after nine. They'll be here in the morning.' The words would have sounded absurdly cryptic if evacuation hadn't been the main focus of Hilary's conversation for months. Ever since the false alarm of the year before, when the prospect of war had loomed and then retreated in the wake of Chamberlain's fated visit to Munich, she had been preparing the village for an influx of children from the cities, spearheading a band of local women who—in Josephine's opinion—might profitably have been put to handling the war in general. Considerable time and effort had been devoted to the enterprise—reconciling the hopelessly out-of-date census cards provided by the authorities with the reality of the village; visiting households to scout for suitable accommodation—and Josephine had listened sympathetically to her friend's concerns, relieved that a part-time status in Polstead exempted her from an obligation to do anything more practical about them. 'We're getting twenty in the end,' Hilary announced triumphantly, as if the allocation had been a prize for the taking rather than the bane of her life. 'The bus should be at the school by half past eleven, and I wondered if you might be able to help? I'd be so grateful.'

Josephine's heart sank. 'I'm sorry, Hilary, but I did explain the last time you asked—I really can't have anybody here. I'll have to go back to Scotland soon, and it wouldn't be fair to take someone in and then leave you in the lurch when—'

'Oh, I don't mean that. No, we've got them all fixed up—on paper, at least—and they're going where they're most *wanted*, even if the facilities aren't ideal. That's the least a child deserves, and things will be difficult enough for them as it is, away from home for the first time. I'm not having any of that "five rooms, three in family, two billets" nonsense—you can't do mathematics with people's lives, can you?' Hilary invariably talked as if she were partway through a never-ending to-do list, and Josephine guessed correctly that the question was rhetorical. 'The village has been very good, on the whole. Of course, it makes it easier that we're not having any adults. Most of the wives I know would want more than five shillings from the Post Office to let another woman anywhere near her kitchen. I really can't see that working. But children are different.' Josephine smiled, but she knew what Hilary meant. Even in her limited dealings with the community, she had been aware of a general eagerness to welcome some youth into the village—a subconscious compensation, perhaps, for the casualty lists that were bound to follow. 'I'm confident that we can soon make them feel at home,' the vicar's wife continued. 'Stephen's just been out on his bike to tell everyone to make their households ready, bless him, and they're all doing their bit.'

There was no judgement in Hilary's words; still, Josephine couldn't help but feel that her personal war effort hadn't got off to the most laudable of starts. 'So what can we do for you?' she asked.

'Well, I want us to put on a really good show when they first get here. They'll have been travelling since the crack of dawn, so I'm having a ring-round to get a few friendly faces to make them welcome while we fix them up with their people. Just a bit of tea and sympathy, really, and only for a couple of hours or so. I'll completely understand if you haven't got time, and I'm already taking up your Saturday afternoon with the fete, but I thought I'd ask on the off chance that you and Marta were at a loose end.'

It wasn't exactly how Josephine would have described the precious few days that they had arranged to spend together before another separation, but she couldn't think of a way of explaining that without sounding selfish, and the silence on the line was becoming awkward. 'Yes, of course,' she said eventually, shrugging defensively as Marta glanced up from her book. 'We'd be happy to help. What time do you need us to be there?'

2

He could never have spoken the thought aloud, but Penrose found the body oddly reassuring. So far, it was the only normal thing about the day.

The man lay in the corner of the second-floor stairwell, curled in a foetal position around the pair of tailor's scissors that someone had pushed with force into his stomach. This was obviously not where he had been stabbed: there was nowhere near enough blood, and Penrose glanced back at the stairs, wondering where the victim had come from, and if he had staggered here on his own or been helped on his way. There were no scuff marks or telltale trails of crimson to enlighten him, and that in itself was interesting.

Whatever had happened, finding the person responsible promised to be a thankless task, full of closed doors and tight lips. Castlefrank House, on the east side of Hoxton Street, was a large block of workers' flats, erected before the war—the last war, he supposed he should get used to saying. These days, the flats were still occupied by people from all walks of life—railway employees, shop workers or staff from the nearby bacon factory—but they all had one thing in common: an ability to keep their mouths shut when it suited them, and a knock at the door from a policeman was unlikely to loosen their tongues.

It was another airless, muggy day, and Penrose put his gloves on grudgingly, already finding the staircase unbearably claustrophobic. He squatted beside the body to take a closer look at the dead man's face, catching a stale, unpleasant whiff of alcohol as he did so. The victim was middle-aged, with mousy brown hair that was starting to grey at the temples and a dark shadow of stubble. A creased shirt with a layer of grime around the collar added to an unkempt, down-at-heel appearance, and yet the clothes weren't cheap, merely worn with very little care. With cautious fingers, Penrose lifted the man's jacket lapel and removed the contents of his inside pocket—a thick wad of notes, with a pocket book and a pencil stub. He flicked through the pages, noting a list of names and flat numbers, some with a tick and a date next to them, others left blank. At least they would have no difficulty in tracing where he had been that morning.

He heard his sergeant coming back up the stairs, breathing heavily and muttering something about people never being murdered on the ground floor. 'I'm afraid we're not going to be short of suspects, sir,' Fallowfield said, when he had got his breath back. 'The bloke was a—'

'Rent collector?' Penrose waved the notebook before Fallowfield could credit him with too much flair. 'It obviously wasn't money they were after, though. There's more here than most people earn in a year.'

'Perhaps someone just ran out of tick on the rent, then. Saw a way out, and took it.'

'Yes, perhaps. What's his name?'

'Frederick Clifford, and he's here every other Friday, regular as clockwork. The woman who reported it lives on the ground floor, but she was on her way upstairs to return a saucepan she'd borrowed from a friend of hers, and she got more than she bargained for. That was at about half past nine, and she called us straight away.'

'I'm guessing she didn't see anyone, hear anyone, or think of anything else that could possibly help us?'

'Course not, sir. He'd already been round to collect her rent this morning, but she didn't notice anything different about him. "Same miserable bastard as usual", apparently. No love lost there, as you'd expect. Spilsbury and the team are on their way. I've left Robertson downstairs to bring them up as soon as they get here.'

'Good. Next of kin?'

Fallowfield shrugged. 'Nothing personal yet, sir, but we've got a telephone number for his boss, so we'll start there.'

'So he didn't own the building.'

'No, he just did the dirty work. The owners are—'

The rest of Fallowfield's words were lost in a sudden clamour from above, a barrage of slamming doors and raised voices as the constable stationed on the next floor tried in vain to follow his orders. 'You can't use these stairs at the moment, ladies,' he shouted, but he was no match for the number of tenants who seemed determined to leave their flats at the same time; the clatter of footsteps grew louder, and Penrose braced himself for an altercation as a group of women and children rounded the turn in the staircase. The ringleader—blonde, and in her early thirties—clutched a little girl's hand and stared at him defiantly as he and Fallowfield did their best to shield the body. Penrose was suddenly glad of the lack of light on the stairs. Except for one of the older boys, no one showed much horror or even curiosity about what had happened on their doorstep, and he found that unusual.

'We've got to get this lot to the station,' the woman said. 'They're shipping them out for real today, and they can't be late. Anyway, you've got no right to keep us here . . .'

'And I've no intention of doing so.' Penrose was as keen to move them on as she was to leave, and he saw that he had wrong-footed her by conceding the battle before it had started. He looked at the children, each carrying a small bag or pillowcase, and tried to imagine what was going through their minds; it was asking a lot of them to understand this strange new world, when even the adults found it difficult. 'My sergeant will see you downstairs now,' he said, 'but please give him your names and addresses before you go. We'll need to talk to you as soon as you get back.'

'Why? This hasn't got anything to do with us.'

'I'm sure it hasn't, but we'll be speaking to all the residents as a matter of course.' He ushered them on in single file, preserving as much space around the body as he could, and was struck by how quickly it had become impossible to avoid the shrapnel of war; the fighting had yet to begin, but still the reminders were everywhere. On his way here he had been caught up in the chaos at Liverpool Street, and the thousands of evacuees flooding into and out of the station had shocked him, even though he was briefed on the plans and knew the scale of the operation only too well. London had hardened its face to the small changes—cars crawling through the streets with one headlamp hooded to a ray of pallid light; the cultured tones of a BBC announcer telling motorists what to do in an air raid—but this was different. This felt like a fracturing of all that was familiar and dependable. He watched the children leaving their homes now with a deep and desperate sadness, as if any hope of a different outcome was leaving with them. Only a matter of days ago, they had still been a peace-loving nation. 'Good luck,' he called after them in a rare moment of sentimentality. 'Let's hope they're not away for too long.'

The mother bringing up the rear turned and looked back at him, obviously surprised by his kindness, and he saw the distress in her face, one of thousands of parents left behind to wait for someone to tell them where their sons and daughters had gone. It touched him, and he realised with a shock that he was no longer an impartial observer. There were children he cared about now, a woman he was growing to love. He didn't just sympathise with the fear and uncertainty that he saw in a stranger; he understood it. The woman glanced down at the dead man and seemed about to say something, but a boy whom Penrose assumed was her son pulled her on.

He turned back to the body when the staircase was quiet again, depressed by the idea that someone could leave the world with so little sorrow. Perhaps he would find more compassion amongst those close to the victim—if such a person existed—but somehow he doubted it; too many years and too many bodies had given him an instinct for the deaths that brought more grief to the killer than to the victim, and although he hoped he would never let it affect the investigation, he knew that this was one of them. The answer, he was sure, lay behind one of these closed apartment doors, and a part of him would have been relieved not to find it.

Conscious that he was doing the victim an injustice, he checked the rest of Clifford's pockets, finding a driver's licence and the home address he was looking for, a few streets away in Hackney—rather more comfortable, as Penrose recalled, than the flats he was collecting from. Fallowfield was probably right: debt and desperation could easily be what had brought them here, although he would have expected that sort of spontaneous, last-resort killing to manifest itself in a blow to the head or a shove down the stairs. From what he could see in the half-light, the wound that had killed Clifford was a deep one, and he couldn't remember anything similar that hadn't turned out to be personal and rooted in either anger, fear or resentment. Spilsbury would be able to tell him more, but at least the scissors were a distinctive weapon, much easier to trace than a razor or a common kitchen knife; he wondered why whoever was responsible hadn't thought to remove them.

Downstairs, he heard familiar voices again, and left the police photographers to get on with their work while he went outside to find Fallowfield and outline a plan. Every other vehicle that passed down Hoxton Street now seemed to be an army truck, and he marvelled at how schizophrenic the city suddenly appeared—some roads quiet and civilised, while others looked like France, with convoys waiting under trees. 'Feels different this time, doesn't it, sir?' Fallowfield said, reading his thoughts with an accuracy that Penrose had come to find reassuring over the years. The two men were nothing like each other, polar opposites in class and temperament, separated in age by several years, but they had both fought in the last war and that simple fact alone gave them a shorthand whenever they were together, a shared past and a mutual understanding of what their work asked of them.

'Yes, Bill, very different,' Penrose said. One of the trucks was caught at the traffic lights, and he stared at the brooding, faraway look on the faces of the soldiers, unsure of whether to be relieved at a lack of the jingoistic eagerness that had characterised his own call-up, or in mourning for its ignorance. The men putting on uniforms this time had been brought up in distrust of war and were wise to the phoney romance of the battlefield, and he sympathised with their uncertainties. Twenty-odd years ago, there had been no doubts for him and very few choices; now—at forty-five, and four years beyond the current conscription age—his duties were more blurred than they had ever been, in war or in peace, and he hated this sudden lack of purpose. 'God knows where we'll all be this time next year,' he said with feeling.

'Talking of which, shouldn't you be getting back to the Yard? I thought you had a briefing with the governor at eleven.'

'I do. Why do you think I'm here?'

Fallowfield grinned. 'You'd better get off then, sir. I'll sort out the door to door here and bring you up to speed when I get back. You're cutting it fine now that Pied Piper's closed some of the streets.'

Penrose nodded reluctantly and went back to his car. As he followed a circuitous route to Embankment, avoiding the cars and buses that were now pouring steadily out of the city, he wondered who had had the bright idea of naming this evacuation procedure after a fairy tale in which children were spirited away from their families and never seen again.

3

Maggie Lucas sat on her daughter's bed and checked the haversack one last time against the instructions sent by the school: spare socks and a change of underwear; night clothes; two clean handkerchiefs; plimsolls to wear indoors; and a toothbrush, comb and towel. It wasn't a difficult list, and she must have been through it a hundred times already, but she wanted to make sure that Angela had everything she needed when she went away. She fastened the bag with a sigh and adjusted the shoulder strap, wishing they had been able to afford the rucksack recommended in the letter, but this one would do the job well enough, and other children would be packed off with worse. Bad enough that she had to go at all.

If she had to go.

There it was again, the doubt that kept her awake at night and plagued her during the day. She and Bob had talked it through until they were blue in the face, but still she wasn't sure if they were doing the right thing—and she could tell that her husband felt the same, even if he was better at hiding it. Every instinct she had said that surely, if war came, it would be better for families to stick together and not go breaking up their homes? But the advice had been persuasive, couched in that brown envelope that sat behind the clock on the mantelpiece until Bob got home from work: a better chance outside the towns, they said; no guarantees—they wouldn't go that far—but safer for the kids than the homes they were leaving behind. Then came the meetings, sitting in the school hall with rows and rows of bewildered parents, listening to speeches about knockout blows and casualties per ton until you'd think that the bombs were already falling. She could scarcely believe that there was a time when the word 'evacuation' had never crossed their lips; it was all they talked about at home now, sucking the air from the room whenever they were together, and eventually the decision was made. Bob had stormed out to the pub that night, even though it was only a Monday, while she retreated to the kitchen to make the tea, banging the pans and plates about in case Angela could hear her crying.

The haversack felt absurdly light as she took it downstairs, absurdly inadequate to keep her child safe. Angela sat at the table, her breakfast untouched, and the smell of bacon that filled the small kitchen turned Maggie's stomach; it had the air of a prisoner's last meal about it, although she wasn't entirely sure which one of them was condemned. 'Come on, sweetheart, eat your breakfast,' she said brightly, hating the false note in her voice. 'You've got to keep your strength up, and I've made you your favourite.'

'It's not my favourite. I hate it.'

'Of course you don't hate it.' She sat down and tried to take her daughter's hand, but it was pulled roughly away, and the bacon and eggs that were supposed to have been such a treat sat congealing on the plate between them. 'You need something inside you, love. It might be a long day.' Suddenly, the idea that Angela would leave the house hungry was more than Maggie could bear, and she fought back tears. 'Please, Angie. What about a bit of toast?' She reached for the pot of jam, but Angela shook her head, her young jaw set with all the bolshiness peculiar to a five-year-old. She pushed the plate to the edge of the table, not quite brave enough to send it crashing to the floor, and Maggie scooped it up and scraped the food into the bin. 'All right, then. Please yourself. Now go and wash your hands and face. I don't want them to think you've been dragged up.'

She saw the hurt and fear pass fleetingly across her daughter's face and instantly regretted her impatience, but Angela ran from the room before she could do anything to soften it, much as she had done on the night they broke the news that she was to go to the country without them. They had put it off as long as possible—selfish, in hindsight, because it gave her no time to get used to the idea—and her reaction had been all that they dreaded, and more. Their nerves made them clumsy with words, and once the phrase 'sent away' had been uttered, it couldn't be taken back; there was no other way to put it, she supposed, but still it sounded like a rejection. That night, and every night since, they had tried to explain to Angie that it was for her own good; that she would be with lots of other girls and boys in the same situation; that it wouldn't be for long and they would all have to make the best of it; that it would be worse for her parents, left behind without her—but she didn't believe a word of it, and Maggie doubted that their daughter would ever trust them again. She didn't blame her. It was all so sudden, and what was she supposed to think of these faceless, nameless people they were sending her to? Strangers were far more sinister to a five-year-old than bits of metal falling from the sky, and there was nothing they could say to reassure her. Even now, they couldn't tell her where she was going or whose roof she'd be living under or how kind they'd be. And *why*—those were the hardest questions of all. *Why do I have to go? Why don't you want me any more? Why don't you love me?*

The clock struck the half-hour, dragging Maggie from her thoughts, and she knew she couldn't put it off any longer: there were sandwiches for the journey to make, and then it would be time to leave. The bread was nice and fresh, and she sliced more cheese than she would normally have used, then gathered together some biscuits and an apple, hoping that Angela would be tempted by those, at least. They had said no liquids, so she added a stick or two of barley sugar instead, just in case Angie was thirsty or felt sick on the train. When she had finished, there was still no sign of her daughter, so Maggie packed the food into the haversack and called up the stairs. 'Come on, sweetheart. We mustn't be late.'

She gave her two more minutes, then went to fetch her. Angela was sitting on her bed, surrounded by all the favourite toys that she had gathered together to take, and Maggie's heart broke for the hundredth time that morning. 'Sweetie, they can't all go. We talked about that. Just choose one.' Angie gave her a look which suggested that this latest betrayal was the worst of all, then got up and walked past her, still empty-handed. Obviously it was all or nothing, so Maggie grabbed Polly, a cloth doll with bright blue eyes that had been a constant companion since Angie's third birthday. She could send some others on, perhaps, once she knew where her daughter was staying, and there would be toys there already, no doubt—that's what *she* would do to welcome an evacuee, if the boot were on the other foot. Somehow, the thought became a magnet for her deepest fears, bringing to the surface all the worries that she dare not share, not even with Bob, in case it made her seem selfish. She prayed that the family would be kind, of course she did, but most of all she prayed that Angela would miss her and long to come home. As she lay awake at night, the sadness of being parted from her child was blurred by something more complicated; by the idea that a surrogate mum and dad would be able to give Angie things that were beyond the scope of her real parents. In her mind's eye, she could still see the joy on the little girl's face when they took her to Victoria Park for her last birthday; she had loved the flowers and the birdsong, and she would love the countryside, too. They hadn't taken her out enough, she thought bitterly, and now someone else would be doing it, someone who could teach Angie far more about nature than they ever could. Why hadn't they found more time? In hindsight, it seemed such a simple thing.

Downstairs, she helped Angie tie her shoelaces and fasten her coat. Each small detail that had been a source of pride a couple of days ago now seemed shabby and second-rate: the mackintosh was too big for her, the carefully polished shoes would soon be too small, and she wished again that they could have afforded a better bag, or even a small suitcase. Still, she was clean and tidy, and her thick blonde hair smelt freshly of soap; at least they would know she was loved. Before her daughter could resist, Maggie drew Angie to her and held her tight little body close, breathing in the scent of her, memorising the touch of her skin and the rhythm of her breathing so that she would have something to see her through the weeks and months apart. She felt her relax, a child's anger suddenly no match for her mother's love, but there was no comfort in that; somehow, her daughter's vulnerability—hope, perhaps, for a last-minute reprieve—was worse than her defiance, and it was all Maggie could do not to pull away in shame. Forcing a smile, she slung the cardboard box over Angie's shoulder. There was no argument—gas masks were still a novelty for kids—but the smell of rubber and disinfectant made it easier to imagine the dangers ahead, and Maggie was glad it was safely stowed away.

She opened the front door, trying to pretend that this was just like any other school day, but she had barely stepped out onto the pavement before that illusion was shattered. Obviously she wasn't the only mother to have left the inevitable until the last possible moment, and she saw her own despair reflected in her friends and neighbours as she was swept along with them to the school. The playground swarmed with people. Teachers were marking names off on a clipboard and handing out armbands and labels, working cheerfully to the tempo of 'Ten Green Bottles', an over-excited refrain from children who had been dealt with and were keen to get on their way. Maggie looked at their happy faces, and wondered what trick their parents had thought of to make this an adventure rather than a punishment. She held Angela's hand tighter, asking herself if it was too late to change her mind, and she must have stood there by the gate for some time, because the next thing she knew a teacher whose name she couldn't remember was gently touching her arm; suddenly, she was aware of tears pouring down her cheeks. 'You can leave Angela with us now, Mrs Lucas,' the woman said, and Maggie stared blankly at her name badge; Place that was it—Angie adored her, so it shouldn't have slipped her mind. 'We'll keep her safe, I promise. We'll keep them all safe.'

Maggie knelt down and kissed her daughter. 'You've got to be a brave, grown-up girl now,' she said, conscious of the hypocrisy when she was hardly behaving like an adult. 'Mummy and Daddy will come and see you as soon as we can, cross my heart, and you'll be back with us again before you know it.' Angela began to cry, and Maggie spoke more urgently, as if words could speed things up and get them both through this awful moment. 'Try to have lots of new adventures, then you can tell us all about them when we visit. You've got Polly to look after you, and we'll write to you every day, I promise.'

'But I don't *want* to go. Why are you cross with me? I haven't done anything wrong, and I'll be good if you let me stay.'

'Of course you haven't done anything wrong, sweetheart, and we're not cross with you. It's just . . .' She tailed off, about to say that they *had* to do it, but of course that wasn't true, and she couldn't bring herself to lie to her daughter when she had no idea how long it would be before she spoke to her again.

'Best not to prolong things,' Miss Place said briskly. 'She'll forget all about it with the excitement of the train, and we'll be there to keep her company.'

It was meant in kindness, but the last thing Maggie needed to hear was that she would soon be forgotten. Before she had a chance to argue, the teacher shepherded her daughter away to the waiting lines of children. She waved and waved, but Angie didn't look back, too involved now in her teacher's instructions. Maggie glanced round at the other mothers, embarrassed to think they might have noticed how quickly Miss Place had been proved right. With an ache of regret, she realised that she hadn't even told Angie how much she loved her.

Another teacher handed her daughter a brown luggage label, and Maggie watched as Angie pinned it awkwardly to her coat, looking intently at the writing on it. Then a whistle blew and they were off, leaving the playground in one long, winding crocodile, flanked by teachers and volunteers and following a large white placard, held aloft at the front of the queue with the number of the school painted on it. Maggie followed, pleased to see that Angie had been paired up with a friend of hers; at least they could stick together. She watched in amazement as the line of children quickly merged with more of the same, coming from other schools in other streets until the whole district seemed to be shedding its future; it was almost overwhelming, and she couldn't help but wonder what sort of life would be left behind. Their ages and uniforms varied, but the children marched as one, past the houses and shops that they knew so well, waving to the crowds who came out to watch and cheer them on, as if they were an army leaving for battle. There was a carnival atmosphere in the streets and it seemed so wrong, somehow, so at odds with the warnings and gloomy predictions that she questioned again why they were putting themselves through this. The congested pavements became harder to navigate, but she battled on, encouraged by how many other mothers were doing the same. They had all been given strict instructions not to go to the station unless they were helping with the arrangements, but no woman in her right mind would take any notice of that, and a few she recognised had banded together in small groups for solidarity. They caught her eye occasionally, but she kept herself to herself, needing to be on her own today. She didn't want any distractions from her last glimpse of Angela.

At Liverpool Street, the station forecourt was packed with buses, coaches, taxis and ordinary cars, all dropping off children and their escorts. Angry horns and raised voices took over from the cheerful cries of encouragement, and there was a bad-tempered, desperate feeling in the air. Signs to the evacuation trains were everywhere, and she fought her way through the crowds to the designated platforms, panicking as she lost sight of her school's placard and envying the women with toddlers in their arms: if only Angela had been six months younger, Maggie would have been allowed to go with her. The noise was almost unbearable now—hundreds of bewildered children, anxious parents, stressed teachers, and railway workers under pressure, all trying to make themselves heard or keep some sort of order, and the further into the station she got, the more everyone seemed to be milling around with no clear sense of purpose. Next to her, the string on a young boy's parcel broke, scattering his belongings all over the floor; his face crumpled and she tried to stop to help him, but the crowds carried her relentlessly on and there was nothing she could do. Above the hubbub, a little girl screamed to be taken to the toilet.

The crush grew more suffocating still in the bottleneck to the platforms. Maggie pushed and jostled her way through, worried that Angela might be separated from her classmates in the chaos and packed onto the wrong train, but then she saw her up ahead, standing at the side of the platform and miraculously still glued to Lizzie, the child she had been paired with in the line. She made a final effort to get close enough to shout goodbye and let Angela know she was still there, but a policeman began to stretch the concertina gate across, barring their way. 'That's far enough now,' he called, although his words were barely audible. 'No parents allowed on the platform. Stand back, please.' There were cries of protest all around her, but the crowd receded a little and Maggie lost sight of Angela as she was pulled back with it. Desperately, she caught hold of the barrier, scouring the platform through the diamond-shaped holes until she spotted her again, nearer the train this time. Rather than being excited by the prospect of the journey, Angela looked more terrified than ever, and Maggie wished for the hundredth time that her daughter could be more like the daring kids, the ones hanging out of the windows or plaguing the railway staff with questions about the engine; she would willingly be forgotten if it meant that Angela was happy. A man crouched down with a bag of sweets, someone Maggie didn't recognise, and as she watched, he took a handkerchief out of his pocket and wiped Angela's face where she had been crying. Suddenly she smiled, and Maggie tried not to resent the fact that a stranger was allowed to comfort her child when she could not.

A scuffle broke out to her left and she turned to see a mother break through the barrier onto the platform, calling her daughter's name. The noise died down for a moment as everyone watched the woman scoop up a frightened little girl and run sobbing with her from the station. Maggie turned back to the train, half tempted to do the same herself and cursing her own weakness for allowing things to go this far, but Angela had disappeared. She glanced up and down the platform, but her little girl must have boarded the train while she wasn't looking. A cloud of steam engulfed the platform, frustrating her efforts to see as carriage doors were slammed shut and the shrill sound of a whistle pierced the air. The train was full long before the platform had emptied, and it pulled slowly out of the station, tiny arms waving frantically. In vain, Maggie looked for Angie among the faces leaning out of the window, but her daughter was gone, headed God knows where.

She lingered a while, just to make sure that Angie hadn't been left behind with the kids bound for the next train. Eventually, she had no choice but to go home and wait for the postcard that would tell her more. As she turned into their street, the terraced houses looked smaller and more vulnerable than usual, the bricks and mortar ill equipped to survive the onslaught that everybody seemed so sure was coming. God forbid that anything should happen to them, she thought: if the street was bombed and they were the unlucky ones, she would never have the chance to convince her daughter that she was wrong, that she *was* loved and cherished, the most precious thing in her parents' life. The thought was unbearable, and she tried to shrug it off as she put her key in the door, dreading the silence of the house. They would just have to make a pact, she and Bob, a solemn promise to make sure that nothing happened to either of them until they'd had a chance to put things right.

4

The last time she left this room, she had been twenty-one and so full of hope. Lillian Herron took the small suitcase off the bed and smoothed the counterpane down, then pulled the curtains back as far as they would go to let in the early morning sun. It had always been a dark room, even when she was a little girl and the cedar tree outside the window had fifty years' less growth to throw at the sky, but the shadows had lengthened with age, and now it was hard to distinguish them from the ones that lived only in her mind.

And hope really wasn't something that women should rely on. Back then, she had never considered that, not when she was young and in love, leaving this house and all that it reminded her of. For a while, the unexpected happiness of her marriage had convinced her that she deserved it; ten years later, when Richard was killed at Gallipoli along with most of his regiment, she realised that she had always been looking over her shoulder. Inevitably, she had moved back to Polstead, joining her sister and brother in the family home to see out the rest of the war. It made sense, or so she told herself at the time, and it was only temporary, but somehow she had never left, and once again the Virginia creeper was making its presence felt along the crumbling garden wall, turning everything a deep blood red, while in her mind it had barely faded from last season. How could it be, she wondered, that the years passed so quickly when the days seemed so long?

She turned away from the window, trying to see the room through the eyes of a stranger and wondering whose head would lie on her pillow that night. It was the right thing to do, and really they had no choice, but still she felt that uncomfortable sense of intrusion—and she questioned the wisdom of having a child in the house, even now. The WVS visitor had come when she was out, though, and her sister—gentle, naive little Florrie, always so eager to please—had committed them wholeheartedly before Lillian could argue. Perhaps it would turn out to be a good thing: the house had lived without laughter for so long, and a child might bring them closer again, succeeding where years of living the same life, eating the same meals, avoiding the same conversation had failed. A part of her longed for that, and she looked wistfully at the box of old things that Florrie had dusted down with such enthusiasm for their visitor: the handful of dolls that had survived their own childhood; one or two harmless oddities from their father's medical collection—shiny, esoteric objects that had always seemed more fascinating than the toys they were supposed to play with; books that she still knew by heart. She hesitated, then bent to pick one out, her brother's much-loved edition of *The Three Musketeers*, the book that had given them the motto of their childhood. They still lived by it, but out of necessity now: the day that bound them inextricably to one another had simultaneously driven them apart, and she doubted that this new adventure would change that—not for the better, at least.

With a sigh, Lillian put the book back unopened and straightened the crucifix over the bed, then picked up the suitcase that was so rarely used and walked across the landing to her sister's room. She paused at the door, struck by how little it had changed since her parents slept there: her father's Audubon prints still on the wall above the beds; her mother's trinkets cluttering the dressing table; the perfume bottle with the familiar scent of freesias that Florrie insisted on wearing. In Lillian's mind, even the dust was the same, disturbed every now and then by the breath of memory but never entirely eradicated. She took the bed nearer the door—Florrie hated a draught—and put her clothes in the bottom drawer that her sister had emptied for her, tempted to heave the ugly mahogany chest over to the right, where it wouldn't block half the window, but it was bad enough that they should be thrown together like this without looking for niggling little resentments. She put her copy of *Middlemarch*—read each year without fail—on the bedside table, knowing that it was an optimistic gesture: the peace of the evening would be lost to her now, and with Florrie's chatter chasing Lillian to her dreams, poor Dorothea was likely to stay trapped in her unhappy marriage for some time to come, doing her bit for the war effort along with the rest of them.

Upstairs, she could hear Edmund ringing the bell that he kept on his desk. Before she had counted to ten, Florrie bustled past the door with the tea that their brother was perfectly capable of going down to the kitchen to fetch for himself. He would never have dreamt of doing so, though, and in that—if in nothing else—Ned was his father's son. They could have afforded a maid of all work by cutting back on other things, but none of them wanted the gamble of another stranger in the house, and Florrie was happy to do it; looking after them was her role, just as Ned's was to take her for granted and Lillian's was to pay the bills and eke out the money that Richard had left her. She knew that was why they had begged her to come back all those years ago: without her small legacy, they would lose the house—and there were so many reasons why that could never be allowed to happen. One of them must see out their days here until the others were too dead to care what might be found in their absence, and Lillian prayed self-ishly every night that the role wouldn't fall to her. It would be kinder if fate left Florrie on her own with the past. Of the three of them, she was the happiest there.

Before her thoughts could take hold, Lillian went down-stairs to the kitchen that overlooked the garden at the back of the house. Florrie had been up since the crack of dawn, as giddy as a child on Christmas morning, and the smell of fresh bread and stewed blackberries filled the room. 'How many children are we taking in?' she asked, looking at the array of dishes lined up along the dresser. 'You've made enough to feed the village.'

'Well, dear, she's bound to be hungry when she gets here,' Florrie said with disarming familiarity, as if the stranger they were taking in were a niece who had been coming to them for years. 'I want everything to be nice for her.'

She glanced up from her baking, her face flushed from excitement and the heat of the stove, and Lillian had a sud-den pang of conscience for the wife and mother that her sister might have been had she herself not been first to escape down the aisle, away from the responsibilities of ageing parents and a brother who had no intention of fending for himself. 'It all looks lovely,' she added more kindly. 'No one could ask for a better welcome.'

Florrie smiled, gratified by the praise, and cleared a pile of freshly laundered tea towels from one of the kitchen chairs, making space for Lillian to sit down. 'Are you all settled in upstairs?' she asked, just as she had a quarter of a century ago, seemingly oblivious to her newly widowed sister's grief.

'Yes, thank you. I've left the toys and books where you put them. I wasn't sure what you wanted me to do with them, but I can pop up and put them out if that would help?'

'No, no, no. I'll do it when I've finished here. I've been looking forward to it. Now, dear, what would you like for your breakfast? The hens have been good to us today. I think they must be as excited as we are.'

'I'm really not very hungry, Florrie. Some toast will do, but I'll make it. You've got enough to get through.'

'Nonsense, dear. It's all under control, and you need something more substantial than toast.' She took the bread knife out of Lillian's hand and cut two thick slices from the middle of the loaf, then broke an egg into a pan on the stove and added some bacon. 'It'll be just like it was when we were younger, sharing a bedroom again,' she said, and Lillian realised with a start that Florrie actually thought that this was something to be welcomed. 'Do you remember how we used to creep into Mummy and Daddy's room when we thought they were too busy to notice? And that time they caught us going through Rosie's things? Daddy was so angry, but I still don't see what harm we were doing. It seemed such a shame to have all those beautiful toys hidden away like that, and they spoilt her dreadfully.' She paused with her spatula suspended over the frying pan, staring out into the garden while the fat from the bacon spattered her hand, and Lillian wondered for the thousandth time how two people could have such different defences against the same memory. 'We'll have some fun again now,' Florrie said, shaking herself back to the present and arranging the unwanted food lovingly on a plate. 'I'm looking forward to the company, aren't you?'

'Yes, I suppose so.'

Lillian reached out to take the breakfast, if only to change the subject to some harmless niceties about her sister's cooking, but Florrie looked intently at her. 'Sometimes I hear you, dear, pacing up and down in the middle of the night. You can always talk to me if you need to. You do know that, don't you?'

'Of course I do, but it's nothing to worry about. I'm a light sleeper, that's all—I always have been. If you're concerned that I'll disturb you while we're sharing, though . . .'

Florrie waved the suggestion away dismissively. 'Nonsense, dear. I'm happy to have you. Neither of us needs to be alone at a time like this.' That was a matter of opinion, Lillian thought, but she kept her silence, hoping to distract her sister with an appreciation of the hens' efforts on their behalf. 'I just want you to know that I'm here for you, that's all I'll say,' Florrie continued, beginning to shell a colander of peas. Her silence was thoughtful, casting doubt on the truth of the last few words, and Lillian found herself waiting anxiously to see what line the conversation would take. 'Mummy would have been so proud of us, wouldn't she? Doing this, and giving a home to someone who needs it. Making a family again.'

Exasperated, Lillian put down her knife and fork. 'Florrie, you mustn't become too attached. Who knows what will happen next in the world? Things are so uncertain at the moment, and any child we take might not be with us for long. They might not like us, and they might be unhappy here, no matter how hard you try. If we're going to do this, I don't want you to be hurt by it.'

'I'm not stupid, Lillian—and I was the one who dealt with the authorities about it, if you remember, so I know what's expected of us.' Florrie's temper flared suddenly, as it always did when she thought her siblings were treating her as the baby of the family, but it subsided just as quickly. 'It feels like a chance to put things right, though, doesn't it? Don't you believe that?'

'No. I believe we're doing our duty, just like everyone else, and if I had any choice in the matter, I'd bar the door until Hilary Lampton had found a home for every one of her blessed evacuees.' The idea that their mother was smiling beatifically down while they took care of someone else's child angered her with its irony, although perhaps shamed would have been a more accurate word; shame, tinged with another emotion that felt very much like fear. 'We're doing our bit, Florrie, nothing more. Please don't try to turn this into some sort of miraculous redemption—and anyway, how could we even begin to make up for what . . .' Lillian tailed off, seeing the expression of pain on her sister's face and reluctant to compound it with common sense. 'What time are we due at the school?' she asked, trying to sound less fatalistic than she felt.

'Eleven thirty onwards, but Edmund needs the car this morning, so I've warned Mrs Lampton that we might be a little late getting there.'

'What's Ned up to that's so urgent?'

'Oh, I don't know. He didn't say, but he's promised to be back here to pick us up by quarter to.'

Lillian hesitated before introducing another red flag, but it really couldn't be left unsaid. 'We *are* going to be careful, aren't we, Florrie? Ned and a child in the house . . . He's so set in his ways.'

It was as if she hadn't spoken. 'Fifteen minutes will give us plenty of time, and we might even be there before they are,' Florrie continued. 'It would be nice to see the bus arrive. I imagine they'll be so excited. Now, dear, if you've finished, would you be a love and go and fetch some more apples? I didn't pick nearly enough yesterday.'

'Of course. I'll do it now.'

'And you might want to tidy the orchard up a bit while you're down there. I thought it would be a nice place to play while the weather lasts, but there are lots of windfalls that I haven't had time to collect, and we don't want anyone to get stung. There's a trug on the terrace you can use.'

Lillian changed into the communal wellington boots that were always left on the mat, and went out into the garden, glad to feel the air on her face after the heat of the kitchen. The ivy that covered the back of the house was dense with flies, which rose in a noisy, buzzing swarm as she closed the door behind her. A new September sun was gathering its strength for the day, but the grass was still wet underfoot, and frogs leapt for cover in the borders as she made her way over the lawn to the little group of apple trees that her family had always rather grandly referred to as the orchard. The garden was narrow but long, sloping down to a thicket of woodland, and eventually to the stream that separated their property from the neighbouring fields. As Florrie said, it had once been a magical place to play.

The air smelt sweet with the scent of rotting apples, their bruised and hollow shells now home to the sleepy, dangerous wasps of late summer. She stooped to collect the fallen fruit, stopping every now and then to rest her aching back, feeling every minute of her fifty-nine years. One day, the house would be too much for them, and then what would they do? A jay's wing feather, barred with blue and white, drew her eye—a marker, just like in the old days—and she tried to remember whether the bird was good luck or bad. The other markers were long gone, suddenly not as innocent as they once had seemed, but the names were still fresh to her: Prudence; Maisie; Violet; Matilda, each mourned but soon forgotten as the next one came along. It had all seemed so harmless at the time. Phoebe hadn't been given a marker, of course, but there was never any question of her grave being forgotten. As if it were yesterday, Lillian saw her brother's dirt-streaked face as he forced the spade deep into the sodden ground, lifting it again and again as the rain poured down, sobbing uncontrollably like the child he still was until that day. Somehow in her mind the memory had become fused with an image of Richard, the wet, dark earth filling his mouth as he lay dying on the battlefield—all of her horrors rolled into one endless, deafening scream of pain. Well-intentioned they might have been, but—as much as she loved them—the men in her life had all let her down.

5

September had arrived lazily in the pattern of its predecessor, with a bold, determined sun that made the overnight rain feel like an improbable dream. Josephine and Marta decided to walk into the village for their appointment at the schoolhouse, taking the narrow woodland path that led from the pond next to the cottage. In a matter of yards, a dense canopy of leaves—the shadow-filled greens of the oak in late summer—offered a very different world from the parched earth and tinder-dry grasses that filled the garden. Josephine led the way across the pond's wooden footbridge, careful to avoid the parts where it was rotten, and they walked in single file through the damp nettles and ferns. The woods were quiet except for the occasional scurrying of a rabbit or the clap of pigeon wings, echoed and magnified by the enclosed space. In the stillness, away from the heat of the day, the faint presence of autumn was unmistakable, and a vein of yellow appeared here and there in the trees, heralding the soft melancholy of a new season.

A sharp turn to the right took them out into the open, and it was a relief to see the sky. The hedgerows were a tangle of blackberries and wild roses, but the sun had dried the grass sufficiently for them to ignore the path and walk side by side. Marta took Josephine's hand. 'You promised to tell me more about the woman that Archie's bringing to the fete,' she said. 'I'm afraid I've forgotten her name.'

'Virginia.'

'That's right. Why were you so coy about it on the phone? I think it's lovely that he's met someone.'

'Oh, so do I. I wasn't being coy, just surprised.'

'Why?'

'Because of *how* they met.' Josephine paused, choosing her words carefully, but the news was sensational whichever way it was delivered. 'Archie hanged her first husband,' she said eventually.

Marta laughed, then realised that Josephine was serious. '*Hanged* him?'

'Yes—at least, he made the arrest that led to the execution. Somehow that doesn't feel like very fertile ground for romance.'

'No, I see what you mean. When did all this happen?'

'A couple of years ago now. You were away at the time. It was while I was house sitting for you.'

'Those murders in Cambridge?'

'That's right.'

Marta shook her head, taken aback by the news. 'I remember you telling me about it,' she said. 'I just didn't realise that Detective Chief Inspector Penrose had his eye on the grieving widow.'

Josephine laughed, then came to Archie's defence. 'It wasn't quite like that.'

'Of course it wasn't! Have you met her?'

'No, but he told me about her at the time.' She thought back to those dark November days, when Archie had been as unsettled as she had ever seen him, frustrated at every step of a murder investigation and fighting the sadness in his personal life. 'He was still with Bridget back then,' she said. 'I think they both knew it was over, but neither of them wanted to be the first to admit it—and Archie felt guilty. Nothing happened, but he liked Virginia, even then. I remember telling him that he was confusing attraction with sympathy. Obviously, I was wrong.'

'It's taken him long enough to do something about it, though. Two years is more than decent.'

'He didn't have any choice. Virginia took her children back to Chicago before the trial started—she didn't want them affected by the scandal, for obvious reasons. Archie thought she was going to stay in America with her family, but apparently not. She looked him up as soon as she got back to England, and she's decided to settle in London.'

'How romantic.'

'It is, isn't it? That was three months ago now. I gather things are going well.'

'They must be if we're finally allowed to meet her. How many children has she got?'

'Two. A boy of ten and a girl who's nearly three.'

They climbed the stile by Flaggy Pond, one of the many small pools that gave the village its name, and took their time through the final stretch of trees, which—with its ancient, gnarled branches, entwined overhead like something from a fairy tale—was always Josephine's favourite part of the walk. 'I'm so pleased for Archie,' Marta said. 'I bet he's marvellous with those kids. What an awful thing to have to cope with at that age. And nice for *him*, too, to have some family life after missing out on Phyllis's childhood.'

'He's loving it.' Josephine raised an eyebrow and looked sideways at Marta. 'I know I shouldn't presume, but there's plenty of time for him to have more children of his own, as well. Virginia's fifteen years younger than he is.'

The path came out at the village green, and the peace and quiet of the walk gave way instantly to a sense of expectation and carefully measured excitement. Everyone, it seemed, was focused on the imminent arrival from London, and Josephine wondered if the children boarding those trains and buses could have any idea that evacuation was just as big an adventure for their hosts as it was for them, awaited with equal amounts of enthusiasm and trepidation. Several people were standing at their doors, looking out for the first sign of the visitors; others were engaged in last-minute preparations—scrubbing steps or sweeping paths, anything that might contribute to a favourable first impression. Jars of sweets and biscuits filled the window of the village stores, replacing the usual bread and vegetables, and Josephine could only admire the shopkeeper's commercial shrewdness: any child who was miles from home, frightened and unhappy, was unlikely to be refused a treat.

'I could do with some cigarettes,' Marta said, making a detour. 'Can I get you anything?'

Josephine was about to ask for chocolate when she was nearly knocked off her feet by a whirlwind that tore through the open shop door. She grabbed Marta's arm to steady herself, and looked down at the little girl who was clinging to her legs and squealing with delight. 'Annie! Where on earth did you come from? You should be playing rugby with a tackle like that.' She bent down to pick the child up, if only to save her stockings from further damage. Annie giggled shyly, then thrust a toy in Josephine's face. 'Who's this?' Josephine asked, looking at the rag doll with its cheerful smile and nut-brown hair tied in pigtails, a miniature version of its owner.

'She hasn't got a name yet. Granny made her for me. She said it was an early birthday present, but I think it's because I've got to share my room with a girl I don't know and she wants me to be nice.'

The child's face showed such disdain for the transparent duplicity of adults that Josephine had to laugh. 'Well, with a bit of luck, the two of you will get on like a house on fire, and then you can cause trouble for the grown-ups.' The idea of treating the stranger as an ally rather than a threat was obviously new to Annie, and she considered it carefully, frowning as she tugged at the doll's buttons.

'Do you think I'll like her?' she asked earnestly.

'I'm sure you will. And if I were you, I'd get your granny to give you a bag of those sweets from her window as well. It'll give you something to bargain with.' Annie Ridley's grandmother, Elsie Gladding, owned the village stores. She had made Josephine work hard for acceptance in the small community when she first came to Suffolk, but the two women had gradually come to enjoy a mutual respect, and it didn't take Josephine long to realise that Elsie's Achilles heel was her granddaughter. The little girl was often sitting on the counter when she went in to order her groceries, and Annie's obvious fascination with all that was different about her—her Scottish accent, her well-cut clothes, her liking for tinned asparagus—had suddenly transformed the very things that Elsie viewed with such suspicion into unexpected assets. Josephine was not above taking in a storybook or a postcard to hammer home her advantage, and anyway, Annie was an easy child to like: she had a curiosity and a streak of wilfulness that were very appealing to those not responsible for her welfare, and she reminded Josephine a little of herself at that age—independent, and drawn to adults who hinted at a world beyond the family home.

Today, though, her strategy worked against her. Elsie waved when she saw them, and beckoned them both inside. She was with a younger woman, whom Josephine recognised as Annie's mother, although she didn't know her well. The Ridleys were fruit farmers—tenants on one of Polstead's few remaining cherry orchards—and they lived out on the Stoke road, away from the heart of the village. Now, as she loaded some groceries into a bag, Josephine was struck by the family resemblance—the same strong features and determined jaw, the same directness of gaze—and found no mystery in where Annie got her character from.

'Morning, Miss Tey,' Elsie said, nodding to Marta. 'Has Annie been showing you her birthday present? She'll be five next week, but I hated waiting at that age, so I don't see why she should have to.'

'Yes, she was just telling us,' Josephine said, winking at the little girl. 'I gather she's looking forward to meeting her new friend.'

Elsie looked surprised, but decided to err on the side of optimism. 'Of course she is. We reckon they'll be the best of pals, don't we, Kathy?'

Kathleen Ridley just smiled and raised an eyebrow, obviously less rose-tinted about Annie's generous nature than her grandmother. 'They'll have to be,' she said, ruffling her daughter's hair. 'Otherwise, I'll be thinking long and hard about which one to keep.'

Annie didn't miss a beat, already old enough to spot an empty threat and turn it to her own advantage. 'I could always stay at Granny's,' she said, with an innocent charm that made Josephine fear for her parents in later years. 'She lets me do what I like.'

'Shh, sweetheart—that's supposed to be our secret.' Elsie turned to her daughter, still laughing. 'If you want me to have her tonight, though, while you're settling the youngster in, it's no trouble. You'd like that, wouldn't you, Annie? We could try your costume on, ready for tomorrow.'

'I don't know, Mum. They've got to get used to each other sooner or later, and they may as well start right away.'

'Well, if you change your mind, just send her over and I'll look after her until the fete. Will you be judging again tomorrow, Miss Tey?'

'I certainly will,' Josephine said, with more enthusiasm than she felt. 'I wouldn't miss it for the world.'

'Then I won't spoil the surprise, but Annie's outfit for the fancy dress competition is the prettiest she's ever had. I finished making it last night, and though I say so myself, she's going to be a knockout in it.' She lifted her granddaughter from Josephine's arms and sat her on the counter. 'Miss Tey's in charge of that one, sweet pea, so don't forget to flash her an extra big smile when you're up on that stage.' She gave Josephine a meaningful nod, and—should the significance of it have been lost—followed up with a bribe that was impossible to misconstrue. 'I meant to say, Miss Tey—those almond biscuits you're particularly partial to have arrived. I haven't unpacked them yet, but I'll set some by for you, just in case we run out before you come in again.'

Josephine smiled awkwardly, and heard the laughter in Marta's voice as she asked for her cigarettes. Abandoning all thoughts of chocolate, which might have been used as another inducement in Elsie's quest for a rosette, she waved goodbye to Annie and left the shop.

'Fancy that,' Marta said provocatively when they were on their own again. 'Bribery and corruption alive and kicking in an English village. I'd take the hint, if I were you. When the war comes, posh biscuits will be few and far between and we could do with Mrs Gladding on side.'

Josephine glared at her. 'You thought I was exaggerating when I told you what an ordeal the fete could be, didn't you? It's impossible to keep them all happy, and Elsie Gladding's harmless compared to the perils of the flower and produce tent. If I escape from there tomorrow without a knife in my back, it'll be nothing short of a miracle.'

'Well, that little girl obviously idolises you. I think you should milk it for all you can get.'

They crossed the green, heading for the small Victorian schoolhouse that adjoined the village allotments on the Heath road. Cars were parked along the verge, with Hilary's beaten up old Morris at the head of the line, and several families were already milling around in the playground, passing the time of day in the sunshine while they waited for the evacuees to arrive. 'I bet it was a sleepless night at the vicarage,' Josephine said, quickening her pace a little as the school clock began to chime. 'It's hard to keep track of all the things that could possibly go wrong in a scheme like this.'

'I can't believe there's a scenario they haven't planned for, though,' Marta said wearily. 'It feels like we've lived through them all these past few months.'

Everything certainly seemed calm and orderly as they approached the requisitioned school; still, there was something about hurrying across the playground, about the smell of polish and bleach that hit her as soon as she walked inside, that made Josephine's stomach tighten, even though her school days had been mostly happy. She had never been one to live in the past: it seemed such a waste of time when life was short and the days passed so quickly, but the unexpected familiarity of the assembly hall—the desks and the books, all the timeless trappings of childhood—sent her scurrying back through the decades to her five-year-old self, nervous and shy in her first week at school. 'I feel just like a child again,' she admitted to Marta. 'Isn't that ridiculous?'

Her anxiety only grew worse when she saw the gaggle of women grouped around the refreshments table at the other end of the hall, setting out teacups and pouring squash into glasses. As ashamed as she was to acknowledge it, she found them formidable at the best of times, and did all she could to avoid them, making sure that her only contribution to the collective life of the village was to officiate at the summer fete each year and to have dinner with Stephen and Hilary at every third invitation. She had only agreed to help out this morning because Hilary had put her on the spot, and because she still felt guilty that her cottage was one of very few in the village not to have displayed the small, white postcard in the window, offering beds to children who needed them. That, and the fact that she had begun to snatch at anything which might take her mind off Marta's impending departure; already, before it had even started, loneliness was the feature of the war that frightened her most—and there were no safety precautions in place to guard against that.

A desk just inside the door had been set up as a registration point, and Hilary sat behind it, going through the list of households with an older woman whom Josephine recognised as Miss Bloomfield, the school's headmistress. An air of impatience hung about the room and everyone looked up eagerly as they entered, then resumed their tasks, disappointed by the false alarm. Josephine was touched by the collective determination to make things as easy as possible for the evacuees. Anyone looking at the thoughtful preparations that had been made for them—the books, toys and crayons laid out to keep them occupied, the homemade cakes and biscuits—would have found the scene hard to reconcile with the alleged enmity between town and country that was gathering momentum on the letters pages of the national newspapers. 'I didn't know there were that many houses in the village,' Josephine said, looking at the enormous folder in Hilary's lap and the meticulously composed records of accommodation. 'Are there whole streets I've never seen?'

Hilary smiled, obviously glad to see them. 'It looks worse than it is,' she said. 'We're acting as the drop-off point for Bower House Tye and Polstead Heath as well. There are only a few extra children, and it seemed easier than sending the bus round all the neighbouring villages. It's clearly having enough trouble finding *us*.'

'We certainly should have heard something by now,' Miss Bloomfield agreed, looking anxiously at her watch. 'They promised faithfully to telephone a message through to the Cock Inn when the bus left Colchester Station. The train was due in well over an hour ago, and it's only ten miles away.'

'Perhaps the train was late,' Marta suggested, 'or perhaps they've just forgotten to call. If they're busy shepherding bewildered children onto buses, all the best laid plans could easily have gone to the dogs.'

Miss Bloomfield looked horrified by the idea of an unheralded arrival, although Josephine failed to see how they could have been more prepared. 'What part of London are they coming from?' she asked.

'They're all from schools in Shoreditch.'

'Isn't that your old neck of the woods?' Hilary nodded. She had met her husband in the East End, volunteering at a hostel for unmarried mothers where he was a curate with pastoral responsibilities—an unlikely encounter, Josephine had always thought: the vicar's wife certainly wasn't a do-gooder by nature, and she was surprised that Hilary had been involved in charity work before it was thrust upon her by marriage. 'That's a stroke of luck, though,' she added. 'The children are bound to be homesick, but I'm sure it will help tremendously if they can talk about where they've come from with someone who actually knows the place.'

'Yes, you're probably right.' Hilary sounded unenthusiastic, and Josephine wondered if she was simply distracted or if that time in her life had been an unhappy one. Dinner conversations had led her to believe that the couple's move to a country parish was an obligation rather than a choice, and that they sometimes missed their life in the city, but perhaps she was wrong. 'I don't suppose you and Marta could pop out to the green and keep watch for the bus, could you?' Hilary asked. 'Let us know as soon as you see it coming, and we can get the kettles on and make them all feel really welcome.'

They did as she requested, pleased to be out in the sun again. 'If Hilary pulls this off, it'll be nothing short of a miracle,' Josephine said. 'Any village event is usually so competitive, but for once they're all united. Things must be serious.'

'If the vicar's wife can't put in for a miracle, then I don't know who can.' Marta smiled. 'It's nice to be involved, though, isn't it? I thought it would take years to be accepted in a community like this, if we managed it at all, but they don't bat an eyelid now when we come and go. Sometimes I feel more rooted here than I ever have in Cambridge or London.'

'Yes, I know what you mean. I can't imagine being without it these days.' She thought about the godmother who had left her the cottage so unexpectedly a few years earlier, an actress whom she had never known but who had been a childhood friend of her mother's, and who—as Josephine discovered after her death—had shared many of her own priorities, not least a need for independence and a lack of convention in the way she lived her life. 'Hester would have been thrilled that we love it so much,' she said. 'I wish we could spend more time here.'

They sat on the bench outside the pub, with a good view down the hill towards the first telltale splash of colour that would signal the arrival of the bus. 'Perhaps that's what we should do,' Marta suggested wistfully. 'Dig in at the cottage, I mean, and sit the war out here. We could take one of those allotments back there and grow vegetables until it's all over. I've always wanted to make jam.'

Josephine laughed. 'You've kept that very quiet, and as much as I wish you were serious, I'd like to see you explain your decision to Alfred Hitchcock when he asks why you haven't turned up for work next week.' To her surprise, Marta didn't even smile. 'What's wrong?' she asked, concerned by the sudden change in her lover's mood.

'Honestly? I don't want to go.'

'But you were so excited about it. Six weeks in Hollywood, working on Hitchcock's first American film and a book you love . . .'

'I know, I know, and I *am* excited about the work. But I don't want to leave *you*. How do I know you'll be safe? And going abroad when it's all about to kick off here . . . well, it just doesn't feel right. It doesn't feel very patriotic, and I'm not a coward.'

'Of course you're not a coward.'

'So why am I leaving?'

'Because you have a job to do. It would only be cowardly if you weren't coming back—and you are, aren't you?'

'Of course I am.'

'Well, then—it's hardly running away. There'll be plenty of time for patriotism when you come home. We'll all still be fumbling around and getting used to it.'

'So would you go if you were me?'

Josephine hesitated. In truth, she understood exactly what Marta meant and very little would have persuaded her to leave the country, but to harness those arguments now in the service of her own selfishness felt hypocritical. 'What's brought all this on?' she asked quietly, choosing the question over a lie. 'I hate it when you're away, but it doesn't change how much we love each other. We've learnt that by now, surely? We trust it, and it's not like you to dither. If anything, that's my department.'

'Oh, I don't know. It's been coming on for days, but this morning's just about finished me off.' Marta nodded back

44

towards the school hall. 'It's quite something, isn't it, what they're doing in there? And that's going on all over the country. It must be the most selfless response to anything since Kitchener.'

'Yes, it probably is. We're brilliant at doing what we're told as long as we can call it volunteering,' Josephine said, sounding more cynical than she had intended.

'But the country's united for once, just like this village, and it doesn't feel like a time when you and I should be apart.' It seemed churlish to point out that the separation wasn't of her making, so Josephine said nothing, hoping that her silence might encourage Marta to talk herself into a decision that she scarcely dared hope for. 'I suppose under different circumstances we might have been tempted to help out more,' Marta added. 'Perhaps it's what you said about Archie having a second chance at a family. It struck me back there that this would be a fabulous opportunity to do something positive for a child, just for a while. We could have made a difference.'

Josephine was sceptical, knowing herself to be far too selfish to take on that sort of responsibility, but Marta had been denied the chance to bring up her own children, and it was a void which nothing could fill, not even their love for each other. She understood why a period of caring for a vulnerable child might have offered some sort of redemption for the guilt that Marta still felt, and—while she had no desire for it herself—she would have supported her; fleetingly, for the first time, she found herself relieved that their individual lives made that sort of stability impossible.

Marta must have sensed her awkwardness because the subject receded, replaced by a simple enjoyment of the day. Hilary had done them a favour by soliciting their help; the pressure of making every moment count before Marta's flight the following Sunday meant that a lot of time was wasted on deciding what to do instead of actually doing it, and it was a relief just to sit in the sun and talk. One by one, the volunteers from the hall took it in turns to go home for something to eat, and Marta fetched a scratch meal of bread, cheese and fruit from the Cock Inn while Josephine kept an eye out for the bus. Eventually, Hilary came to find them, looking apologetic. 'Still nothing?' she asked despondently. 'We'll barely have time to get them settled in before the blackout at this rate.' She glanced at the remains of their lunch. 'And that's another thing. They'll be ravenous when they get here, and there's nothing more fractious than a hungry child.'

'Surely they'll have been sent with something to keep them going?' Josephine said.

'Oh yes, but even so. That'll have gone in the first half an hour if they're anything like I was at that age. I remember when my parents took us to the Lakes during the summer holidays one year, and we'd barely left the suburbs when—'

The rest of Hilary's story was lost as the landlady hurried out of the pub and called over to them. 'I've had someone on from the station, Mrs Lampton. The buses are on their way at last. They've just waved them off, so they'll be here in half an hour or so.'

'Thank God,' Hilary said with feeling. 'Mrs Wilson can get the water boiling again.'

The temperature of the water seemed to be a gauge for the day's success in general, and Hilary headed back to the school to resume her last-minute preparations. 'I thought we were having twenty children, plus a few stragglers,' Josephine queried, thinking over what the landlady had said. 'Why would they need more than one bus?'

'She was probably over-excited, or perhaps the buses left the station in convoy, then went their separate ways.'

46

'Yes, perhaps.' In due course, the throaty sound of an engine on the air settled the matter for them. 'Good God,' Josephine said, staring down Polstead Hill. 'Hilary will have a nervous breakdown.'

'They can't *both* be coming here.'

'Don't you think so? This is hardly a natural through-road. Come on, we'd better go and warn her.'

They turned back to the hall, quickening their pace as the noise of the vehicles grew louder behind them. 'White smoke?' Hilary said, but her excitement faded when she saw their agitation. 'What on earth's the matter?'

'There are *two* buses,' Josephine said breathlessly, looking to Marta for support.

'And they're both double-deckers.'

Hilary was obviously doing the calculations in her head. 'That can't be right,' she said, but a shadow fell across the window as the vehicles pulled up outside, challenging her words. 'Still, even if it is, they might not be *full*. They might have made drop-offs on the way?' She grabbed her list, as if it could defend her against the catastrophe that threatened four times as many children as she had planned for, and went outside to see for herself. Marta and Josephine followed, together with the rest of the welcoming committee, suddenly less worthy of the name.

It was evident at first glance that both buses were packed to the gills, and that the passengers were by no means all schoolchildren; weary-looking mothers were letting toddlers scramble across their laps to take a look at their strange new surroundings, and Josephine could see one or two women holding babies. Someone had pasted a large, hand-painted 'Goodbye Hitler' banner to a window, and various other bits of paper were being waved from the top deck, their messages a scrawled hotchpotch of patriotic defiance. Long before the doors opened, she could hear tears and a collective, high-pitched chatter, as tiredness and over-excitement got the better of those on board. 'There really must be some mistake,' Hilary repeated, as if she could will it to be true, and Josephine hoped she was right: it would take a lot more than Stephen and a sturdy bicycle to make these arrangements go smoothly.

The driver stepped down from the first bus, and Hilary rushed over to him before he could give the signal for everyone else to follow. 'Just a moment,' she said, with a slight note of panic in her voice, 'we weren't expecting quite so many of you. I've got a list here. Everything should tally.'

The words sounded naive, even to the most optimistic ear, and the driver shook his head cheerfully. 'Sorry, my love, there's not much chance of that. It was chaos back there.'

'But did no one try to sort it out?'

He shrugged. 'What can you do? The kids want to stick together and the women won't be parted from their friends. They got on the bus they fancied, and it's not our place to stop them—we're only volunteers. I'm used to delivering jam jars for a living, not kids. We promised to get them here in one piece, and that's what we've done. Now, if you could just help us get them inside, we'll leave you to it. We've got the same again coming in later this afternoon, and we mustn't keep them waiting.'

'The same again?'

'That's right. Not for here,' he added hastily, when he saw the despair on Hilary's face, 'but we've got a timetable to stick to, and anyway, the wife'll give me an earful if I'm not back for supper.'

'Yes, of course. Even so, Mr . . . ?'

'Davis. Ronald Davis.'

'Mr Davis, yes, I wonder if you'd mind hanging on for a couple of minutes while I telephone our contact in Hadleigh, just to make sure? The children must be tired already, and they don't want to get off and start making themselves at home, only to discover that there *has* been a mistake. I'm sure you could do with a cup of tea as well before you set off again? It sounds like you've got a long afternoon ahead of you.'

It would have taken a very hard heart not to sympathise with Hilary's predicament, and Ronald Davis relented. 'We have got a bit of time, as it happens,' he said, glancing at his watch, 'and I doubt the next lot will be any more punctual than this one was, so go and make your phone call.' He grinned. 'Throw in a biscuit, and we'll even help you get them settled in. We've got some supplies to leave with you, too.'

Hilary thanked him gratefully and set off briskly to the Cock Inn, while someone else fetched refreshments for both drivers. The villagers who had been gathering in the playground were suddenly quiet, waiting to see what would happen, and Josephine noticed one or two men on the allotments stopping their work to watch events unfold. She glanced at the faces staring expectantly out from the buses, and wondered if the latent prejudices between town and country—troublesome, dirty and ungrateful on one side; hostile, selfish and insular on the other—were about to be laid bare. Five uncomfortable minutes passed before Hilary returned, looking completely defeated. 'Apparently, we're the least of the problems in this area,' she said. 'Hadleigh has got six times its allocation, and it seems the whole county is bracing itself. Essex is even worse, I gather, so we'd better not make a fuss in case they decide we've got off lightly and send us some more. We'll just have to get on with it, but what on earth are we going to do with them all?'

'Perhaps some of them could bed down in the school room,' Miss Bloomfield suggested tentatively. 'At least until—'

'And there's a gypsy camp in the woods by Polstead Hall,' Hilary snapped, 'so perhaps we could farm the youngest ones out there.' She took a deep breath and glanced apologetically at her friend. 'I'm sorry, Edith, but we promised these people a proper home and that's exactly what we're going to give them, no matter what it takes. As it is, the welcome we were planning has fallen rather short of the mark. Let's get everyone inside and make up for it, then we'll see what we can do.'

The buses were emptied eventually, and Josephine—remembering what Hilary had said about women sharing a kitchen—was relieved to see that the children outnumbered the adults by about four to one, a ratio which might ease the burden of finding extra homes; most of them were mothers of toddlers or babies, but there were a few older men and women, whom she guessed were teachers from the schools in Shoreditch. Hilary was watching one of them intently, briefly distracted from the task at hand until the man glanced up and caught her eye; they stared across the children's heads for a moment, as if trying to place each other, and it was Hilary who looked away first.

'Someone you know?' Josephine asked.

'What? No, of course not. That really would be a very small world.' Her irritation was uncharacteristic, and Josephine put it down to the pressures of the day, but not before she had noticed the faint flush on Hilary's cheeks.

The new arrivals swarmed about the playground, their emotions ranging from exhaustion to fear; in some, the anxiety manifested itself as a blank stare, in others as a barely suppressed antagonism, and Josephine wondered what sort of impact the arrival of so many strangers would have on a small, close-knit village, and how they would feel about their new home. She remembered her own first impressions of the Suffolk countryside, how reassuringly gentle she had found it after the more dramatic beauty of what she was used to—but *she* hadn't been wrenched from everything and everyone she knew; she had made a choice to come here. These people already seemed defeated, as if the war had been raging for weeks. The initial excitement quickly died down, and they shuffled dejectedly into the hall and collapsed on the floor, looking to their hosts for direction.

Their weariness seemed to galvanise Hilary into action, as if she realised that all hope of a reprieve was shortly to vanish down the road with the empty buses. 'Right, I need some volunteers to go off round the village and let everyone know what's happened,' she said. 'If we explain the situation, I'm sure people will find they have room after all. We're in this together, and it won't be for ever. If most people take in one more child, or even a mother and toddler, then we're home and dry—and just to encourage them, say that we're taking another *three* at the vicarage. Actually,' she added, almost as an afterthought, 'whoever's passing the vicarage might call in and let Stephen know that's what we're doing. He can get the attic ready when he's finished Sunday's sermon. I left him deciding whether to err on the side of war or peace. It's so difficult when you don't know quite where you stand, but at least this will give him something to get his teeth into.' The volunteers she had asked for were quickly found. 'Make sure you call at *every* house,' Hilary shouted after them. 'Except the Bumpsteads, of course. That simply wouldn't be right.'

Everyone seemed to know what she meant, and the volunteers dispersed to work their miracles. 'I wonder what's wrong with the Bumpsteads?' Marta mused, and Josephine shrugged.

'They lost their daughter last month,' Miss Bloomfield explained, overhearing the comment. 'Little Ada. She was only five, and about to start school. Scarlet fever.'

'How terrible for them.'

'Yes, it was.'

'And it's history repeating itself, I'm afraid,' Hilary said with a sigh. 'They lost another one when she was just a baby, so it's far too soon to expect them to take on someone else's children. Now, I'm going to talk to the host families who are already outside and see what extra room we can find there. Josephine, Marta—can I leave you in charge of the refreshments?'

'Yes, of course.'

'They're going to be looking to us, you know,' Marta whispered, as they waited yet again for the kettle to boil. 'We'll be the only house in the village with a spare bedroom by the end of the day.'

'It's impossible, and Hilary knows that.' Josephine returned Marta's look, challenging her to disagree. 'Anyway, as far as they're concerned, we haven't *got* a spare bedroom. I'm rather hoping that most of the village thinks you're sleeping in it.'

They spent the next hour dispensing tea and cheerful encouragement. As she moved round the room, Josephine noticed how little of their lives people had been able to bring with them: mothers of babies or very small toddlers contained all that their children needed in a brown paper carrier, and the schoolchildren seemed to have bare essentials like nightwear or a toothbrush, but—other than the obligatory cardboard box slung around their necks—that was it. Most of them had a luggage label pinned to their coat, on which was written their name, school and evacuation authority.

At last, she found a moment to take a cup of tea over to Hilary, who had seated herself back at the reception desk to haggle relentlessly over the evacuees. Josephine hovered in the background, waiting for a break in the current conversation and wondering how the children's parents would feel if they could hear what was going on. 'So how much will I get if I take more?' asked one of the villagers, whom Josephine knew by sight but not by name.

'You'll be paid ten shillings and sixpence a week for the first child, then eight and six for each one after that. It's a fair amount.'

'I don't agree.'

'Then you must take that up with the Post Office, Mrs Barker, not with me.'

'And you said I could have two lads,' chimed in someone else. 'What use is this slip of a thing going to be around the farm?'

Josephine could barely bring herself to look at the bewildered little girl by his side, and Hilary obviously felt the same way, because she slammed the folder down on the desk and stood up, raising her voice so that most of the room could hear. 'This is a national crisis, Mr Evans, not a miraculous solution to the labour shortage. How do you think these children feel, wrenched from everyone they love through no fault of their own, from everything that makes them feel safe? There are parents out there now who've waved their children off on a train or a bus without any idea of where they're going, parents who are probably crying their hearts out at this very moment because they don't know if they've done the right thing. They're trusting a faceless stranger with all that's most precious to them, and they're relying on us not to let them or their children down. It's up to us to *earn* their trust. It's our job to be as selfless as they have been in sending their children away, to make every girl and boy feel safe until they can go home again, to be worthy of the task that our country has asked of us—and I will *not* have you treating this operation like a cheap labour exchange. So—will you help us, or won't you? Because if you won't, I'd be grateful if you could stand aside and let me talk to the people who will, and who do so gladly out of nothing but kindness and a sense of duty.'

A spontaneous ripple of applause broke out around the hall—led, Josephine noticed, by the bus driver and the other volunteer chaperones, who had made good on their promise and stayed to help settle the evacuees in, taking some of the more distraught children to play on the bus as a distraction from their homesickness. Hilary's speech had the desired effect; shame-faced, if still a little tight-lipped, the complainers dropped their arguments and took what they were given with good grace, offering their new house guests the sort of gruff affection that passed for an apology.

'That seems to have done the trick,' Josephine said, passing over the cup, 'and you've obviously got an admirer.'

'What do you mean?'

Once again, Hilary seemed uncharacteristically on edge. 'Mr Davis,' Josephine explained. 'Didn't you see him clapping?'

'Oh, I see! Yes, he's been marvellous, hasn't he? They all have. And thank you for this. It's just what I need until I can get my hands on something stronger.' She sipped the tea gratefully. 'I wish I hadn't had to say all those things, though. Why can't everyone be like Kathleen Ridley? She's taking two more without a second thought, and she's already got her hands full with Annie.' As if to prove Hilary's point, there was a petulant cry of protest from the other side of the hall, where Mrs Ridley was cheerfully trying to bring some sort of harmony to her new family arrangements. The real bone of contention seemed to be the boy, and Josephine looked at Annie's troubled expression, a complicated blend of suspicion, indignation and worry which a doll and a bag of sweets were unlikely to pacify. 'I don't often hold with Stephen when he insists on seeing the good in people,' Hilary continued, 'but perhaps he's got a point. That woman really is a saint.' She grinned at Josephine, and held out some paperwork. 'Would you do me yet another favour and run this across to her? I'd do it myself, but I don't want to give her the chance to change her mind before we've made it official.'

'Yes, of course.' It hadn't been Hilary's intention to apportion guilt, but her appreciation of another family's selflessness made Josephine more conscious than ever of her own shortcomings, and she was glad of something useful to do, no matter how small it seemed. 'Mrs Lampton sent you these,' she said, handing over the forms. 'I gather they're the point of no return.'

'Is that right? God knows what Tom will say when he gets here.' Kathleen Ridley smiled, but seemed remarkably unflustered by the upheaval that was about to take over her home. 'Still, it's in a good cause, and doubtless there's a lot worse to come.'

'Yes, I suppose there is.'

'Madam here will just have to get used to it and muck in with the rest of us.' She brushed Annie's cheek but her daughter pretended not to notice, devoting all her attention to a discarded luggage label that she'd found on the floor. 'Still, she's got her way over going to Granny's tonight, just while we get the other three sorted. They've *both* got their way, I suppose I should say. I don't know who's worse, Annie or my mother. Thick as thieves, they are.'

'That sounds like a good idea, though—and it'll be fun, won't it, Annie?' Josephine knelt down to say something conspiratorial to the little girl, but for once her charms failed her and Annie refused to be mollified. 'Would you like me to take her over to the shop?' she offered.

'No, you're busy, and it's only across the green. Mum will be keeping an eye out for her, just in case I change my mind—you can put money on that. Anyway, I think Mrs Lampton needs you.'

Josephine looked round and saw Hilary gesticulating vigorously towards the far corner of the room, where a minor disturbance seemed to have broken out amongst the children who were still to be allocated. She found Marta at the heart of it, looking after a small, dark-haired girl of four or five who had obviously just been sick, while an older boy—her brother, if the resemblance was anything to go by—nursed his right hand. Looking quickly round the group, Josephine traced the injury to a bloody nose on another boy's face. Neither she nor any of the other volunteers had the remotest idea how to deal with a brawl, and it was left to the teacher who seemed to know Hilary to intervene. 'Come on, you two—is this really the impression you want to make when we've only been here five minutes? These people are doing their best to make us feel welcome, and this is how you repay them. How do you think that reflects on the school?'

'It's not my fault, sir. I don't know why he hit me.'

'Liar! He was calling my sister names, Mr Madden. Said we were slum kids, just because we don't have a stupid suitcase like him.'

'All right, Stebbing—calm down. Whatever he said, there's no excuse for using your fists.'

'But he's always picking on us, you know he is.' In the procession of strange faces, Josephine had forgotten that many of the children knew each other, and that old foes and long-held grievances wouldn't simply disappear just because they'd been picked up and moved to the countryside. As the teacher took the injured boy to one side to wipe his face, she looked at the darned pillowcases that held the Stebbings' handful of possessions and hoped that they would find someone kind to look after them, someone who noticed how brightly polished the little girl's shoes were, how her hair shone from brushing. Back in Shoreditch, there was obviously a mother who was desperately missing her children. It was a pity that the Ridleys were oversubscribed already, she thought, glancing back to where Kathleen was gathering up her new arrivals and preparing to take them home. Annie had gone, she noticed; by now, she would no doubt be entertaining her grandmother with tales of injustice and looking forward to her triumph in the fancy dress competition.

'This is Betty,' Marta said, as Josephine went over to join them. 'She was over-excited after her journey, but she's feeling much better now. We were just talking about the fun she's going to have while she's here.'

'Hello, Betty. I'm Josephine.' She squatted down and pointed to the knitted dog that Betty was clutching. 'Who's this?' There was no answer, only a shy shrug and a half-smile. 'Well, perhaps you can introduce me when we know each other better. It's nice to have you here, and Marta's right— you're really going to enjoy yourself once you've settled in. We'll make sure of it.'

'And that's such a pretty dress you're wearing,' Marta said. 'Did your mummy make it?'

Betty nodded. 'Mum makes all our clothes,' her brother explained, and there was a pride in his voice that touched Josephine. 'She's clever like that. People are always after her to do stuff.'

'And what's your name?'

'Noah.'

'Well, Noah,' Marta said, lowering her voice, 'I think you've been quite a hero already this afternoon, sticking up for your sister like that.' He looked at her suspiciously, ready to think that she was making fun of him. 'I heard that boy teasing you, and it was much worse than you told the teacher.

I reckon you gave him what he asked for, but don't do it again, will you? He's not worth getting into trouble for, and Betty needs you to look out for her, so you mustn't hurt anyone else. Do you promise?'

Noah nodded, and Josephine was just admiring Marta's diplomacy when a couple of Hilary's ladies appeared with a mop and bucket to clear up Betty's travel sickness, making such a song and dance over it that eventually Marta put Betty in Josephine's arms, took the mop out of their hands and efficiently restored the polished parquet floor to its former glory. 'Don't think I wasted that spell in prison,' she whispered in Josephine's ear as she sat down again. 'You should see me with a scrubbing brush.'

She could joke about it now, but the humour was brittle and self-protecting, and Josephine was under no illusion about the pain that Marta's past still brought her, and always would. She watched her lover playing with the little girl on her lap and tried to imagine what must be going through her mind; already, she had spent more time with Betty than with her own daughter, who had been taken away at birth by a jealous husband and raised with no knowledge of her mother; already, she knew more about a stranger than her own flesh and blood—and this unexpected moment of tenderness on one side and trust on the other made Josephine more conscious than ever of all that Marta's life had cost her, of all that she had missed.

Marta looked up and caught her eye. 'You needn't worry. I know what you're thinking, but these two are taken. A nice home, apparently—they're just late getting here.'

'That wasn't what I was thinking at all. Quite the opposite.' Marta's face darkened a little, as if a chance had opened up that she didn't dare consider. 'So who's having them?' Josephine asked.

'The Herron sisters. Do you know them?'

'Only by sight.' The sisters always reminded Josephine of something from a fairy tale, and not necessarily on the side of happily ever after, but it wasn't the time to mention that. She had often seen them about the village—at the shop or in church, chauffeured by a man whom she gathered was their brother, and who never seemed to get out of the car. 'They live at Black Bryony,' she said, but Marta looked blank. 'The old doctor's house, halfway down Marten's Lane—lots of red brick and a big cedar tree? It's not far from us. You covet their walled garden whenever we go past.'

'Oh, I know where you mean. A bit different from what these two are used to, I imagine.' She smiled at the children. 'You've got a lovely house to go to, and we're practically neighbours, so you'll be able to come and see us.'

Hilary had put on her welcoming smile again, and Josephine followed her gaze across the bustling room. 'Talk of the devil,' she said. 'Here they are now.'

The two women announced themselves at the desk—one tall and thin, and dressed as always in black; the other a cartoon opposite of her sister, with a round, florid face, and an excitability that belied her years. Once again, Josephine found herself reluctantly casting Noah and Betty as Hansel and Gretel, and she saw Marta's face fall. 'They're older than I expected,' she said. 'Do you think they'll cope?'

Josephine shrugged, but shook off her doubts when she noticed Noah staring at them. 'Let's go over,' she suggested brightly, taking his hand, 'and you can all get to know each other.'

She realised her mistake as soon as they were in earshot, but it was too late to turn back. 'We can't possibly take two,' the taller woman was saying. 'That is absolutely out of the question. My sister agreed to have one child, Mrs Lampton, and you and your committee will stick to our arrangement or we'll be forced to withdraw our offer altogether.'

She sounded as though she meant it, and Hilary looked helplessly at the Stebbing children. 'But as I was trying to explain, we've been sent four times as many evacuees as we expected, and wherever possible we're trying to keep families together.'

'Then find us an only child—preferably a girl—and let someone else take—'

'No, no, Lillian,' her sister interrupted. 'We must take little Betty now we've seen her.'

'But Florence, as long as we take someone . . .'

'Just *look* at her, though. She's the spitting image, Lillian. This is fate, didn't I tell you so? Betty is *meant* for us.' She held out her arms and Marta hesitated, looking hopefully at Hilary for an alternative, but nothing was forthcoming; reluctantly, she handed Betty over, and Josephine gave up one of the pillowcases, wondering whom the little girl resembled so strongly. 'Now, Betty, we've got a lovely room ready for you, and I hope you're hungry, because I've been busy baking all morning. We're going to have such *fun*, the four of us!'

'What about me?' Noah tugged at Florence Herron's sleeve, but she was too absorbed in Betty even to notice, so he turned his attention to her sister and repeated the question. 'Mum said we had to stick together, Betty and me. She said it's my job to look after her.'

'I'm sorry, young man, but there's nothing to be done. Mrs Lampton will find you somewhere, I'm sure.'

'But you've got to have me, otherwise you're not having Betty,' Noah insisted, and the look of indignation on the woman's face would have been amusing had there not been such a plaintive urgency in the child's voice. 'Mum said I was the man of the house now that Dad's gone, so I won't let you take her.'

It was Florence who responded this time. 'Well, you're not the man of *our* house, my boy,' she said brusquely, 'although it wouldn't hurt you to come and be taught some manners. Betty will be perfectly well looked after with us, I assure you—better than she's used to at home, probably.'

'Bitch!'

Noah said the word uncertainly, as if repeating something that he had heard but didn't really understand; it was convincing enough for the Herrons to feel vindicated, though. 'We couldn't possibly take a boy like that,' Florrie said, and Josephine looked at her, struck by the strength of feeling in her voice. 'What on earth were you thinking of, Mrs Lampton? I'll take Betty out to the car, Lillian. Edmund will be waiting, so don't be long.'

Betty was whisked from the hall with no chance even to say goodbye to her brother, and Hilary went half-heartedly through some formalities with the remaining Herron sister, looking as if she would dearly love to abandon the whole scheme there and then. Noah wiped away tears of anger and Marta tried to take his hand, but he shook her off and went to sit with some of his classmates, utterly disillusioned by this new place, and by everyone who was encouraging him to call it home.

'Those poor fucking kids,' Marta said under her breath, barely able to contain her anger. 'I can't watch this any more. I'm going to do some washing up.'

The crowds in the hall began to dwindle as Hilary's volunteers returned with the villagers they'd shamed or strong-armed into helping. Good news came from Polstead Hall, with an offer to house the visiting schoolteachers for as long as they were needed, and up to six mothers and babies. As more floor space emerged, the crates of supplies were unloaded from the buses: biscuits, tinned milk and bully beef, all issued by the government to be distributed throughout the village; and a generous donation of jams and chutneys from Wilkin & Sons, the Essex company which had provided the transport and volunteers. When the last box was unloaded, the drivers were thanked and waved on their way, ready to begin the whole process again.

Josephine gathered up some more crockery and went to join Marta in the school's tiny kitchen. 'Thank God we'll be able to leave soon,' she said. 'There aren't many children left now.'

'What about Noah? Is he still here?'

'Yes. There's a dozen or so waiting, although that includes Hilary's three and a few others who are already allocated.'

'God, what *do* we sound like? You'd never know we were talking about children, would you?' Marta sighed, wiping her hands on a tea towel.

'It just reminds me of school again, and waiting to be picked for the hockey team. It was always the same girls who were last to be chosen, and there's a lot more at stake here than humiliation in front of your friends.'

'I've been racking my brains, thinking of how we could help Noah, but you're right—it's impossible.'

'Perhaps we could twist someone's arm?' Josephine suggested. 'People are still coming in, so if there's anyone we know, we could put in a good word for him.'

'And hope that they haven't heard about the bloody nose or the abusive language?'

'It's worth a try.'

There was an atmosphere in the hall when they returned. A man and a woman whom Josephine didn't know were standing awkwardly just inside the doorway, and conversations faltered as the attention of each small group was drawn to them. Hilary, the last to notice, eventually looked up from the form she was filling in, and her face fell. 'Mr and Mrs Bumpstead,' she said, recovering quickly, and Josephine recognised the name of the couple who had lost their little girl the month before. 'It's nice to see you. How are you both?'

'You haven't asked us,' Mrs Bumpstead said, ignoring the question. 'We heard how many had come and waited for someone to tell us what to do, but nobody has.'

Hilary had obviously been bracing herself for trouble, but the words were more a question than an accusation. 'We thought it was too soon,' she said. 'You've both . . .'

'Did you? Is that really what you thought?' The woman looked to her husband for support, and he put his hand on her shoulder. 'It wasn't our fault, you know. The doctor said there was nothing we could have done, so if that's what you're worried about, there's no need. We'll take good care of her—or him.'

'Of *course* we weren't worried,' Hilary said, looking horrified. 'We were only thinking of you, I assure you. Nothing else crossed my mind. It was very wrong of me not to ask you, though, and I apologise.'

'So is there someone? We don't mind who we have, but we'd like to help, wouldn't we, George? There's a nice room sitting there empty, and that seems such a shame if it's needed.'

'Come with me.'

Josephine held her breath, hoping that Hilary might try to make up for the last scene by encouraging the Bumpsteads to choose Noah, but the pull of what they had lost was obviously too strong for the couple, and they were quickly united with the last remaining girl. A glance around the hall revealed to Josephine that the only people left were volunteers like themselves. 'Well, that's it,' she said despondently to Marta. 'What are they going to do with him?'

The same thought had evidently occurred to Hilary. 'Thank you so much for your help today,' she said, bearing down on them with what Josephine had come to recognise as her desperate look. 'I don't suppose you could just do one more thing for me, could you? Noah's still with us, and I was wondering if you could help by putting him up at the cottage for a bit? Just for a few days, until we can find something more permanent.'

Josephine hesitated, guilty of the very prejudices she had been so critical of in others. If this had to happen at all—and as much as she felt for Noah—she would have preferred a girl; she had no idea where to start with a boy's needs. Marta began to explain to Hilary why it was impossible, but Noah had ideas of his own and no hesitation in sharing them. 'I don't need any of you,' he shouted. 'I can manage on my own, and I'll get Betty back an' all. Neither of us will be here long. Mum said she'd come and get us as soon as it was safe.'

His bravado was heartbreaking when he looked so vulnerable, and Josephine suddenly heard a voice that sounded suspiciously like her own. 'He could sleep in the study, I suppose,' she said, looking tentatively at Marta. 'We must have something to put him up on.'

'And I don't have to leave until next weekend, so that would give Hilary enough time to arrange something permanent?'

'Oh, more than enough!' Hilary said gleefully. 'And we've got an old camp bed that you're welcome to borrow. Stephen can drop it off later this afternoon, when we've got our lot settled.'

6

Winnie Chilver had spent most of the day at her garden gate, enjoying the sunshine and watching as the village gradually began to stir and respond to its new lease of life. She had seen the buses labouring up the hill, the rough noise of their engines as alien to the still country air as the German planes they had all been warned about, and she had predicted the flurry of activity that followed. She had looked on—a little resentfully, truth be told—as Elsie Gladding waved her daughter and grandchild off to the school to meet their new playmate. And later, she had seen the familiar black car driving back through the village to Marten's Lane, the three grey heads now joined by a brunette one; even at a distance, the little girl had seemed so full of life, perched on Florrie's lap in the back seat, her smiling face at the open window. At that point, Winnie had had to go inside.

Now, with the sun losing its strength, she peeled the vegetables for tea and set off to meet Cyril on his way back from the allotments. Next door, the shop had been a hive of activity, and she had enjoyed watching the comings and goings as the next best thing to company of her own; only now were the blinds coming down for the day, and Winnie waved as she passed, envying Elsie her full life and her place at the heart of everything. There was a new sense of purpose in the village, a hopefulness that was both painful and precious in this sudden flood of youth, reminding them all of something forever lost. Winnie would dearly have loved to take a child herself, but it wasn't practical—not with her brother to consider and no spare room in their tiny cottage, and not at her age, when even a stray cat seemed a big responsibility and a job she might not finish. Still, it would have been nice.

More often than not, Cyril met her on the green and they walked back together, but the fete was a big day for him—the culmination of a year's planning and hard work—and it didn't surprise her to have to go all the way to the allotments to fetch him home. The school was finally empty, and she paused in the playground to catch her breath, struggling with a longer distance than she was used to. She could see him now, standing by the dahlia bed, and she waved, hoping that he might save her the last hundred yards, but he was too absorbed in his work to notice, so she walked slowly on and sat down on the bench at the vegetable end of the plot. How he had the patience she would never know, but the hours he spent here seemed to have paid off: to her amateur eye, everything he touched seemed worthy of a best in class.

She watched him for several minutes, noticing how tenderly he handled the plants and smiling to herself when she heard him talking to the Jersey Beauty variety that was his particular pride and joy; it was a sentimental habit that he had had since he was a boy, but one to which he would never admit. Eventually, he glanced up and saw her, and Winnie was relieved by how relaxed he seemed. The tension of the last few days had built steadily, as it always did, but now the moment had come, he seemed at peace with the world, content with his achievement and happy to let fate take its course. He stretched and rubbed his back, then picked up the flask that she had filled for him that morning and brought it over to the bench. 'Everything all right?' she asked anxiously, still prepared for a disappointment that would cloud the day and destroy his mood, but he nodded and smiled.

'The best yet, I reckon. She's an absolute beauty.'

Winnie breathed a sigh of relief. 'I'm pleased for you. So have you done all you need to do? Are you ready to come home?'

'Yes, for now, but I'll have to pop back later. I'm not taking any risks after all this work.' He raised his cup by way of a toast and drained the last of the tea. 'Here's to a good day.'

'You deserve it.' She paused, reluctant to bother him with troubles of her own, but the resentment had been building steadily and there was no one else she could share it with. 'The Herrons are having one of the evacuees, you know—a little girl. I saw them taking her home with them, bold as brass. I don't know how they've got the cheek.'

'Mind what you say, Winnie. They've been good to us over the years, and you don't want to go stirring up trouble, especially not at the moment.'

'Good to us?' She looked at him in astonishment. 'How can you say they've been good to us? You might as well say that Hitler's been good to us by saving the bombs until now.'

'Don't be daft.'

Unusually for him, Cyril wouldn't meet her eye. 'I was hoping for a bit more support from you,' Winnie grumbled, 'but you don't even seem surprised.'

'I'm not,' he admitted. 'I saw the car parked up by the school. What else would they be here for?'

'It's not right, though. Somebody should say something.'

'But not you.'

He stood up, the subject closed, and Winnie bit her lip. 'Did you deliver that jumble to Mrs Lampton for tomorrow?' she asked instead.

'I left it with one of the women at the school. Mrs Lampton was busy, but she promised to pass it on.'

'Well, I hope she does,' Winnie said. 'Would it really have hurt you to stay and make sure? I don't ask much from you, Cyril.'

It was petty of her, a fuss about nothing to distract from what was really bothering her, and he ignored it, his mind back with his flowers again as he stood up and looked proudly down the allotment. 'Do you want to come and see what I'm entering, Win?' he asked. 'It'll knock their socks off.'

She shook her head. 'No, all that can wait until tomorrow. We'd better go home now. I need to get the tea on.'

7

It was just after six when Henry Maitland left Colchester Station, his duty to a philanthropic employer finally done for the day. He climbed gratefully into his car, bone tired and hoarse from calling out instructions, but the clamour of frightened children and bewildered parents still rang in his ears long after he had closed the door and driven away, and he was glad of the half-hour journey back to the factory to clear his head. It was a beautiful evening, gently lit by the promise of autumn, and he used it to draw a line under the events of the day: the peace of the countryside—the calm, man-made order of the fields at this time of year—was a soothing contrast to the chaos of the station platforms, and he drove more slowly than usual, in no particular hurry to be home.

All too soon the outskirts of Tiptree were in sight, and he pulled into the gateway of a farm for a moment to appreciate the small seasonal changes in the landscape that he loved. The farm was one of several that belonged to the Wilkin estate, and most of its extensive acreage was devoted to fruit, with cereals, potatoes and sugar beet grown as rotation crops. Henry looked with satisfaction at the straight lines of plum trees—row upon row of heavy, ripened fruits, leading his eye to the horizon and flanked on one side by an abundance of raspberry canes, and on the other by freshly cut fields of corn. The track that led down to the yard and barns was harvest worn now, and as Henry wound down the window, smelling the scent of ripeness in the air, he found himself envying the men who worked the land, although they would have laughed at him for doing so. In another life, he would have liked to be born to this, but his father was an office man and Henry had followed in his footsteps, working his way up until he was the most senior employee outside the Wilkin family. He liked his job and the respect it gave him, but occasionally he craved something different.

There were new challenges ahead, though, that was for sure. It was before he joined the firm, but the factory had been in the direct flight line of Zeppelins to London during the last war, and there was much talk amongst the older members of staff about the increased risks they would be facing this time round. Temporary bolt-holes now stood at various points in the factory—odd, passage-like structures creatively fashioned from boxwood and covered with heavy bags of sugar—and a larger shelter had been purpose-built in a nearby sandpit; the firm would look after its workers as it always did, but there would be lean times ahead, particularly if they were unlucky. Try as he might, it had proved impossible so far to get insurance cover against damage by enemy aircraft, and more of the fruit plantations would no doubt have to be sacrificed for corn and potatoes. Still, the summer had been good to them, as if nature had sensed the troubles that lay ahead and decided to be kind. The crops were plentiful, the quality of the fruit never better, and—thanks to his own foresight—the company had stockpiled sugar, jars and wood for the packing crates; with luck, they should be able to keep the prices low on most of their signature lines, maintaining sales to offset any government restrictions that came into play. In time, manpower might be an issue, but Wilkin & Sons was a reserved occupation for all but the youngest of men, so there was little point in worrying about that until he had to. In work, just as in life, Henry had learnt that it was best to concentrate on the crisis in hand.

Reluctantly, he started the engine again and continued on into the village. The factory gates were still open, and Henry parked in his usual place, outside the extension that had been built onto the original farmhouse. One of the double-decker buses that he had hired to help transport the evacuees stood next to the boiling room, its doors wide open, and he wondered what it was doing there. Annoyed that his instructions had been ignored, he got out to investigate, then caught sight of his wife's face, watching him intently from his office window. It was becoming a habit of hers, turning up here at the slightest excuse in an attempt to catch him out, and he resented it; God knows what the rest of the staff must think.

She got up to greet him, with Cissy running out ahead, and he wished for the thousandth time that their little girl didn't take so strongly after Dorothy; it was far too easy to let his feelings for one spill over to the other. 'I thought you were going to wait for me at your mother's,' he said, unable to keep the irritation out of his voice. 'We agreed that I'd collect you from there. You can't just hang around here whenever you feel like it. I've got work to do.'

Dorothy looked hurt. 'I was only thinking of you,' she said. 'I wanted to save you some time. You've had a long day, and I can't imagine it was easy, dealing with all those children. It was good of you to volunteer at all.'

Her tone was soothing, and the gesture would have been thoughtful had he not been all too aware of why she had really come. 'Well, I didn't have much choice about that,' he said. 'Mr Wilkin expects us all to do our bit. He's made that quite clear.'

'And how was it?'

'Chaos. Absolute bloody chaos.'

'Henry!' She put her hands over Cissy's ears, too late—as she often was—to prevent the harm she had imagined. Cissy giggled and Henry winked at her, challenging Dorothy with his silence to play her hand. She didn't disappoint him. 'You're back much later than I thought you would be,' she said casually. 'Did you stop off somewhere on the way home?' There was a time when the difference between what his wife knew and what she thought she knew had bothered Henry, but he had wearied of the game even before it ceased to matter. Now, all he had to confess was a craving for a few minutes of solitude, but he refused to dignify the question with an answer, no matter how harmless it would have been. 'Anyway, Cissy was missing her daddy,' Dorothy continued. 'You know how much she loves being here with you. Surely you don't begrudge her that, even if you'd prefer me to stay at home.'

She stroked Cissy's tow-coloured hair, and Henry frowned as the child turned and pressed her face affectionately against her mother's leg; he hated the way that Dorothy used their daughter as a weapon in their marriage, although he knew he was guilty of it too. Sometimes he wondered if that had been her prime motive in wanting a child, the conviction that it would one day be the only thing that tied them together; certainly, there had never been much chance of their having any more. He reached over to the back seat for his briefcase. 'I've got some things to sort out for tomorrow,' he said. 'You'll have to wait now you're here.'

She trailed behind him as he walked across the car park to the bus, and only Cissy's presence prevented him from making a scene. 'Davis, you should have had that bus back to the depot well over an hour ago,' he called, as one of his delivery drivers stepped down from the vehicle. 'What the hell's it doing back here?'

Davis glared at him without a hint of deference, and Henry cursed himself for letting his annoyance get the better of him. The last thing he needed was to give the man any more ammunition than he had already, especially while Dorothy was listening. 'I had to clean it first,' Davis said insolently, holding up the bucket and scrubbing brush that he was carrying as if explaining something obvious to an imbecile. 'I doubt they'd have wanted it back if I hadn't given it a good going over.'

'Why? What on earth's been going on?' He looked at the stain on Davis's shirtsleeve. 'Is that blood?'

'It's nothing, just a cut from one of the crates—but you try carting a hundred and fifty over-excited kids about without some of them being sick on the seats. It's hard for them.' He sighed and nodded towards Cissy, now in Dorothy's arms. 'It's hard for us all, actually—the sort of day that makes you want to cling to your kids and not take your eyes off them for a second. Anything can happen when your back's turned.'

The comment had very little to do with evacuees, and succeeded in its aim of making Henry uncomfortable. He glanced anxiously at Dorothy, but she seemed oblivious to any tension between the two men. 'How is Charlie?' she asked, and Henry could have hit her for the patronising tone in her voice. 'It must be so difficult for you, now that Mrs Davis has had to give up work.'

'It's a struggle, Mrs Maitland, I'll admit that.' Again, Davis directed his words meaningfully at Henry. 'It's brought us closer together, though, so we've got to count our blessings. And Charlie's a gift, just like this little one here.' He held his arms out and Dorothy obliged by handing over their daughter. 'I bet she means the world to you, doesn't she?' He tickled her chin, and gave her a toffee out of his pocket. 'It's hard to imagine what those parents in London must be feeling tonight. I wouldn't want to be in their shoes for all the money in the world.'

'We'd better be going, Dorothy,' Henry said, more anxiously than he had intended. 'Mr Davis needs to get this bus back to where it came from, and we don't want Cissy to be late to bed before the fete tomorrow.'

'I thought you had things to do?' she said, determined to be as unhelpful as possible. 'Why don't you go and get on with them? We'll wait here for you. Cissy's perfectly happy, and Mr Davis might even let her explore the bus if she's a good girl. You'd like that, wouldn't you, darling?'

Cissy nodded enthusiastically, but Davis stepped in hurriedly. 'I haven't quite finished scrubbing it yet, Mrs Maitland, and the floor's still wet. Safer if the little one plays out here. I've got a few toys on board if she'd like them?'

'That would be very thoughtful.' Davis put Cissy down and went to fetch them, and Dorothy stared at Henry. 'What are you waiting for?' she asked. 'The sooner you finish your work, the sooner we can all go home.'

He had no choice but to leave them together. 'I won't be long,' he called back over his shoulder.

'Good—and I've left a basket on your desk with some things that Mum made for us. Bring it out, will you?'

Henry did as he was asked, abandoning any hope of getting through the outstanding paperwork. He dumped the papers on his desk for another day, and lifted the tea towel on the basket. Just as he had feared—another batch of the chutneys and preserves that his mother-in-law insisted on giving them, as if she had no idea what he did for a living. With a sigh, he took the unwanted gift outside and beckoned Dorothy over to the car. 'You'll have to take this on your lap.'

'What's wrong with the boot?'

'It's full of the stuff for tomorrow. I packed everything this morning because I knew I wouldn't feel like it now, and it's all organised. I don't want to have to do it again.'

'Don't be silly, Henry. What can you have in there? Most of what we need will go over on the van, so I'm sure I can make room for one tiny basket.'

She went to open the boot, but he grabbed her hand, holding it tight. 'I said, take it on your lap. For once in your life, do as I tell you.'

They stared at each other, and for a moment he wondered if she was trying to goad him into hurting her in front of their daughter, another battle won on the domestic front, but the crisis seemed to shame her as much as it did him, and he was relieved when she gave in. 'Very well, have it your way. You usually do.' She put the basket on the front seat and settled Cissy in the back. 'I'll go and say goodbye to Mr Davis.'

She clearly wanted to know if Davis had witnessed the scene between them, but to Henry's relief, the driver was back inside the bus. 'He's busy, Dorothy, and we've wasted enough of the firm's time by holding him up. Get in the car and let's go home.'

8

Josephine woke early on Saturday morning, drowsily forgetful of everything that had happened the day before until she felt the empty space in the bed beside her. She pulled on her dressing gown and drew the curtains to let in more of the day, then went quietly next door to the room that had so suddenly become Marta's. She lingered in the doorway, taking a bittersweet pleasure from the familiar contours of Marta's body beneath the single sheets, and did her best not to resent the little boy now sleeping downstairs.

Every floorboard seemed to creak as she tiptoed over to the bed, and Marta stirred from her sleep. 'I missed you last night,' Josephine whispered, sitting down on the edge of the mattress.

'Me too. This isn't turning out quite as we'd planned, is it?'

'No, and I could cheerfully murder Hilary. It's petty of me, I know, but I spent every waking moment hoping that her children are the most troublesome of the lot.'

Marta smiled and sat up, rubbing the sleep out of her eyes. 'And there were plenty of waking moments, if your night was anything like mine. At least it's all quiet now, so he must still be asleep.' Despite Noah's obvious exhaustion, it had taken alternate bouts of firmness and cajoling to persuade him to retire to the bed that had been made up for him in the study, and even then they had heard him tossing and turning long into the night. 'Get in for a minute, before our peace is shattered,' Marta said. She pulled the sheet back and moved over to make room. 'Perhaps we'll be able to find out more about him today. He wasn't really in the mood for talking last night.'

'I suppose that's to be expected. This must be even stranger for him than it is for us.'

'Yes, I suppose so.'

'I never thought I'd hear myself saying this, but I'm quite relieved we've got the fete later. It'll give Noah the chance to relax and have some fun, perhaps even spend a bit of time with Betty if she's there.'

'I'm not sure I can imagine the Herron sisters indulging in anything as frivolous as a fete.'

'I know what you mean, but don't let anyone on the church committee hear you call it frivolous. It's planned with military precision.' As Josephine had grown more familiar with the competitiveness of village life, she had often wondered if the church's feast days actually meant anything, or were merely convenient pegs in the calendar for the parishioners to hang their achievements on. 'At least if Noah enjoys himself, we'll have some common ground to talk about afterwards with him. I don't mind admitting that I haven't got the faintest idea what might make a ten-year-old boy happy at the moment.' Without replying, Marta leant over and kissed her. 'What was that for?'

'Because I know why you're doing this, and that makes *me* happy. Very happy.'

Josephine smiled. 'I'm glad, as long as we both understand that you're in charge. I just want to spoil him now and again like a doting aunt. You can handle all the difficult bits.' Marta was about to reply with a counter offer, but Josephine put a hand on her arm, listening intently for a noise from the room below. 'I thought I heard something. I'll go down and make us some tea, and see if he's all right.'

Already, she had undermined the terms of her own deal, but Marta was good enough not to point it out and Josephine left her in bed. There was a staircase at either end of Larkspur Cottage, although she had never quite fathomed why: the house wasn't the type to have had servants, and she was familiar enough with its history to know that it had been built as a single dwelling. Today, though, she was glad of the privacy it offered and took the narrow, awkward stairs that led down from her own bedroom into the parlour, as far away from where Noah slept as it was possible to be in the small two-up, two-down cottage. The door to the study was firmly closed and there was no sound of movement, so she left him in peace and went about her business as quietly as possible, filling the kettle and placing it on the range, then adding cups and saucers to a tray and fetching some milk. The scullery was tiny, more an extension of the parlour than a room in its own right, and crammed with the detritus of living—the only part of the cottage in which comfort and aesthetics gave precedence to the practicalities of space. Everything here was much more basic than the home comforts she enjoyed in Inverness, and yet the cottage seemed to provide everything that she and Marta could ever want or need. There was a lesson to be learnt in that, she thought—a lesson about priorities and simplicity, and she remembered what Marta had said the day before. Perhaps the silver lining of these difficult times would be an appreciation of things that were too often taken for granted, and she found herself wondering if there really might be a way to make a more permanent life here possible, at least for the duration of the war. The prospect excited her more than she dared admit, and she found herself hoping guiltily again that Hilary would find an alternative home for Noah sooner rather than later. She desperately wanted Marta to herself for a while before they were forced to separate; she wanted to be brave enough to hope.

She took the milk next door, noticing that the parlour was unusually draughty; on all but the coldest of days, the range and a solid thatched roof combined to make the cottage warm and welcoming. The curtain across the front door drew her attention, billowing slightly in a breeze that should not have been there, and she realised instantly what had happened, even before she pulled the heavy velvet back to check. The door was off its latch, and Josephine didn't have to try very hard to work out why.

Noah's makeshift bed was empty, and there was no sign of any of his clothes, only the pyjamas that his mother had so carefully folded, still untouched in the pillowcase. A piece of paper was sticking out of the pyjama jacket pocket, a note from his mother that she had obviously intended him to find when he went to bed, frightened and homesick in a strange house that she couldn't even begin to picture. Josephine unfolded it, touched as much by the thought as by the briefest of messages.

It'll be all right, I promise. Trust me to protect you and do what needs doing, and look after your sister. You can't come back till it's safe. Love Mum x.

It was strange to feel such a sudden and overwhelming sense of responsibility to a woman she had never met, and Josephine tried to imagine herself explaining to Mrs Stebbing that they hadn't even been able to keep her son safe for one night. Panicking now, she hurried upstairs to break the bad news. 'Noah's gone,' she said, throwing Marta her dressing gown and all but dragging her out of bed. 'The front door's open and he's nowhere to be found.'

'What do you mean? He can't have gone.'

Josephine bit her lip, infuriated by the English inclination to face a crisis by denying it. 'Well, he's not downstairs,' she repeated, 'and God knows how long he's been missing.'

'Have you checked outside?' Marta asked. 'Perhaps he's just gone to the lavatory.'

It was an obvious place to look, and Josephine felt foolish for not having thought of it herself. She went back downstairs and out into the garden, happy to laugh about her overreaction if Marta proved to be right, but her relief was short-lived: Noah was nowhere to be seen. Marta joined her outside, and together they searched the rest of the garden, the garage and the sheds. 'We'd better get dressed and look for him properly,' Josephine said with a sigh. 'He might have gone back into the village, and if he's not there, we could at least get some help to search the woods. We'll never cover it all with just the two of us. And what if he's got some idea into his head about going back to London? Anything could happen to him.'

'My money's on Black Bryony,' Marta said calmly. 'I bet he's gone to see Betty. We probably shouldn't have pointed the house out to him until he was more settled. Let's make ourselves decent and go and find out. If he's not with the Herrons, one of us can try the village while the other looks a bit further afield round here. He really can't have got far.'

A voice backed her up before they had even reached the house, and Josephine turned to see Noah coming sheepishly down the grass track from the road, accompanied by the younger Herron sister. 'I found this in my kitchen this morning,' Florence Herron called, much as she might have done about a mouse or a cockroach, or any other sort of vermin that needed dealing with. 'I presume it's what you're looking for?'

As they got nearer, Josephine saw that the woman was actually leading Noah by his ear, something she had thought only happened in pantomime or comic strips, and never to real children in real life. 'Thank goodness he's all right,' she said, 'and thank you for bringing him back to us. Noah, we were so worried about you. You shouldn't have gone without telling us.'

'He shouldn't have gone at all,' Florence snapped.

She looked them up and down, and Josephine was suddenly conscious that her favourite dressing gown was past its best, and that Marta's silk pyjamas looked absurdly out of place in a village which had almost certainly never seen one woman outside in her nightclothes, let alone two. Noah was released with a gentle shove and took refuge behind Marta, leaving Josephine to offer as gracious an apology as she could manage.

'Will you be going to the fete later?' Marta asked.

'We certainly will. I've been baking all week for the cake stall. Mrs Lampton relies on it.'

'Then perhaps Noah could spend some time with Betty there? It might help them get used to this new situation.'

'And allow *us* to establish some rules,' Josephine added. 'We don't want Noah running off every five minutes any more than you do, but we've got to try and understand how hard this separation is for him, and for Betty. If we make arrangements for them to see each other when it's mutually convenient, then there's less chance of his taking things into his own hands, surely?'

The argument was persuasive, and Florence Herron nodded. 'Very well. He can spend some time with us this afternoon. I hope you'll smarten him up first, though. The bombs haven't dropped yet, so I'm not quite sure what his excuse is for looking as if he's just been dragged from the rubble.'

Josephine felt Marta bristle beside her, but she had to concede the point. In the unforgiving sunlight, when she was less distracted by the shock of having Noah at all, she had more time to notice how dishevelled and peaky the boy looked, with dark shadows under his eyes and no colour at all in his cheeks. He had obviously been crying, too, but none of this was likely to improve under constant criticism, and she was unable to keep the edge out of her voice when she replied. 'We'll make sure he's presentable, Miss Herron. He won't let you down.'

'Then we'll see you this afternoon. You know where to find us.'

Without another word, she turned and strode back up the hill. 'We'd better buy some cakes,' Marta said, watching her go. 'There are obviously fences to mend.' She grinned at Noah and winked conspiratorially.

Encouragement was the wrong tack to take. The anger that had got the boy into trouble when he first arrived flared again, sudden and indiscriminate in where it fell. 'Betty shouldn't be with those horrible people,' he yelled. 'I hate them, and it's not fair.'

'Noah, they're not horrible,' Marta said patiently. 'They just haven't been used to children. I'm sure they mean well.'

'You don't know that. I was watching them through the window, before they knew I was there.'

'And what did you see?'

'It was mean, what they were doing. Betty looked . . .'

He tailed off and Marta took his hand, obviously concerned by what he was suggesting. 'What *were* they doing, Noah?' she asked. 'You can tell us, whatever it is, and we'll try to help.' He said nothing, and Marta crouched down, forcing him to look at her. 'They weren't hurting Betty, were they?' Reluctantly, Noah shook his head. 'So what *were* they doing?'

Josephine studied the boy's troubled face. He seemed hurt rather than angry or frightened, and she could only think of one thing that would make him feel that way. 'Were they having fun, Noah?' she asked gently. 'Is that what's upsetting you? Betty looked happy, and that's not fair when you're missing her so much?'

He didn't answer, except to bury his face in Marta's shoulder and sob. She waited until the worst of the tears had subsided, then took him inside to wash his face and smarten himself up while Josephine made breakfast. She broke some eggs into a bowl and cut bread for toast, glad to have something practical to concentrate on rather than the more abstract task of cheering Noah up. They would need to go into Bury to buy him some clothes, she thought, but there was no time to do that before the fete, so the Herrons would have to be satisfied by whatever Marta could achieve with a flannel and an iron. In hindsight, arranging for him to spend time with his sister might make things worse than they were already, but hopefully Betty would be pleased to see Noah and not give him any more reasons to be jealous. Upstairs, she could hear Marta sharing the first harmless nonsense that came into her head, wisely avoiding anything to do with his home or the reasons for leaving it; eventually, Josephine detected two voices in the conversation, and when Noah came back downstairs, she was relieved to see that he looked happier.

She followed Marta's example, chatting about the village and the fete as she dished up a hearty plate of scrambled eggs and bacon, but the practicalities of evacuation couldn't be avoided for ever. 'Have you got your postcard?' she asked when Noah had eaten everything that was put in front of him. 'We need to let your mother know where you are. She'll be worried until she hears you're safe.' He shook his head, as if he didn't know what she was talking about. 'Your school should have given you a postcard with a stamp on it,' she explained, but still Noah looked blank, and when Josephine thought back to the day before, she realised that he hadn't been wearing a label, either. 'You finish your milk, and I'll go and check your bag to make sure. If it's not there, we can easily find you one. You'll just have to tell us your address.'

There was nothing with Noah's things except the note she had already found, so she took some paper and an envelope from her desk and wrote the address of the cottage in the top right-hand corner, then put it on the table next to Noah, resisting the temptation to look over his shoulder at the message he was sending home. When he had addressed the letter to an apartment building off Hoxton Street, Josephine made a note of the details in case they needed to contact his mother themselves, then found a stamp and put the envelope by the door, ready to post on their way to the fete. It would be nice, she thought, if it said that he was safe and well, at least—and even nicer if they could make sure that he stayed that way.

9

The annual summer fete was held in the grounds of Polstead Hall, next to St Mary's Church. 'Am I driving right up to the house?' Marta asked, pausing at the end of Marten's Lane.

'Let's park at the bottom and walk the rest of the way. If we go in by the church gate, they might not notice how late we are.'

A line of cars along the verge added an appropriately festive dash of colour to the deep greens of late summer, testifying to the fact that the event was well underway. Marta drew up behind them, near the large village pond that stood at the foot of the hill, separating the lane to the church from a triangular green where most of the houses were clustered. The water was still and clear in the sunlight, offering a perfect reflection of the nearby cottages, and Josephine was struck as always by the misleading image of tranquillity that Polstead's summer facade presented; she had arrived here at exactly this time of year, and it had fooled her then as it fooled her now, seducing her with its beauty and in no way preparing her for the harshness of a rural life in other seasons.

Noah had brightened considerably as the day went on, although every now and again Josephine noticed him curb a response or an instinct, as if suspicious of his own happiness, and the worry returned to his face, making him seem old beyond his years. There had been no opportunity to ask Marta if she had learnt anything more about him during their brief time together, but she was grateful that the tension had eased, at least for now—and she hoped that the Herrons wouldn't be too hard on him this afternoon, undoing any progress that they had begun to make at home.

He ran ahead of them, and the cheerful sound of a brass band drifted down through the woods. For a hundred yards or so, St Mary's and the Hall shared a narrow, grassy lane that climbed steeply beneath a canopy of oak and ash and elm; as the ground levelled out, a driveway split off to the right, curving out of the trees into ornamental parkland and leaving the path ahead for the sole use of those bent on worship. The distinctive shape of the church's medieval spire was visible through the leaves, marking it out as a maverick amongst the perpendicular architecture that Suffolk was more famous for, and Josephine headed for the simple five-bar gate at the entrance to the churchyard. 'This should scupper any welcoming party that Hilary might have organised at the Hall,' she said. 'With a bit of luck, they'll think we've been here for ages.'

They followed a weedy gravel path round to the north side, where children were playing hide and seek between the gravestones, a reminder of the time when feast days were celebrated in the church itself. Marta—who had always been conveniently busy on fete weekends in the past—stared in surprise at the array of stalls and stages that had transformed what was usually a peaceful deer park. 'It's much grander than I expected it to be,' she admitted, 'and I've always fancied a nose round the big house. It looks so unapproachable for the rest of the year.'

That was true, Josephine thought. Polstead Hall was an attractive, Georgian-style manor house, rendered in a soft honey colour that shone warmly in the sun. Despite its close proximity to the church and an open facade, uncluttered by trees, the Hall remained stubbornly detached from the rest of the village, aloof and unapproachable, as Marta had said, as if—without wishing to cause offence—it preferred its own company. They entered the grounds through a gate in the boundary hedge, close to the magnificent Gospel Oak, one of the oldest trees in England and a site for preaching long before the church was built; today, it had a pagan feel, with bunting and wicker stars hanging from its branches, and lanterns placed in the hollows of a vast trunk, ready for the evening festivities. As always, the fete had attracted visitors from neighbouring villages as well as locals, harking back to the days when Polstead's annual Cherry Fair—held on the village green—was famous throughout the county. The venue might have changed but the spirit of celebration had an age-old feel to it, and in spite of her protestations, it was a day that Josephine had come to love.

'Do you know what time Archie's getting here?' Marta asked, as they picked their way through the nearest collection of stalls and sideshows.

'They were hoping to come up last night. Virginia knows the people at the Hall—something to do with horses and Newmarket.'

'Young *and* well-connected. Archie really has had a lucky strike.'

'Yes, although if they were hoping for a quiet evening, that will have gone out the window the moment the double-decker buses rolled into town. Six mothers and babies was a *very* generous offer.'

'I'm sure they've got the staff to cope with it,' Marta said wryly. 'At the moment, anyway.'

A makeshift sports track had been painted onto a level patch of grass to the side of the Hall, and they paused to allow the current race to pass, a competitive battle involving balloons on sticks and a lot of shouting from the sidelines. The winner was one of the Ridleys' evacuees, and Josephine hoped for the peace of the household that it wasn't the only prize that the family would go home with. There was no sign of Annie anywhere. With a bit of luck, she was currently being clothed in something worthy of a fancy dress first place; it would make life so much easier. 'They seem to be having a good time,' she said, watching as Tom Ridley pinned a red rosette onto the boy's pullover. 'Speaking of which, we'd better get this young man to the cake stall, just in case the Herrons sell out early and take Betty home.'

Marta looked round, shading her eyes against the sun. 'I wonder where it is?'

'Let's try the marquee,' Josephine suggested. 'Even if it's not there, someone will know.' She cut across the track in that direction, but the sight of a familiar figure distracted her. Archie was standing by the coconut shy and she caught Marta's hand and stopped, taking advantage of the chance to watch him for a moment before he noticed them and became self-conscious. He was holding a toddler in his arms, a fair-haired little girl who giggled as the woman with them tried in vain to wipe ice cream off her bright blue sundress, eventually giving up with a good-natured shrug.

'So that's Virginia,' Marta said, a note of approval in her voice.

'Yes, it must be.' Even if Josephine hadn't known that the woman standing with Archie was American, she might easily have guessed. It wasn't the Katharine Hepburn-style trouser suit that gave her away, and they weren't close enough yet to hear her voice, but there was something in her attitude—a quiet confidence which didn't need to announce itself—that stood in sharp contrast from everything around her. Intrigued, she watched the couple for a moment, curious to see how they behaved in each other's company. The age gap that she had mentioned to Marta seemed scarcely noticeable, and not because Virginia Moorcroft looked older than her years; in all the time that she and Archie had been friends, Josephine couldn't ever remember seeing him quite as relaxed as he seemed now. From their very first meeting, during the early months of war, she had been aware of a restlessness in Archie, a disappointment with the world which, despite his warmth and compassion, was an essential part of his character. It was a state of mind that his job did very little to dispel, but it was more deeply rooted than that: even in the untroubled early days of his love for Bridget, it had still been there—a mistrust of his own happiness, which in the end had proved justified. Now, she would have expected him to be more wary than ever of a new relationship, but there was nothing to suggest that in this brief, distant snapshot; on the contrary, Archie looked as if he had everything that he had ever wanted, finally at ease with himself. It felt wrong but somehow inevitable to Josephine that she should already be comparing Virginia favourably with the woman who had preceded her.

'They look happy,' Marta said, distilling Josephine's thoughts into one refreshingly simple observation.

'Yes, they do.' A young boy ran up to his mother, dressed as St George, and Josephine's heart sank when she saw that he, too, obviously had high hopes for the fancy dress competition. 'I could lose all the friends I have in one afternoon,' she said with a sigh. 'I'll either get off on completely the wrong foot with Archie's new family, or everything I want in the village shop will be forever out of stock.'

Marta laughed. 'There are other shops, even if we have to drive to them. Let's go and say hello.'

She put an arm round Noah's shoulder to encourage him, but he shook his head and refused to move. His face was pale, and he seemed shy to the point of panic as he stared at Virginia laughing with her children. Josephine wondered if the reminder of his mother and the family he had left behind was suddenly too much for him. 'Come on,' she said gently. 'I hate meeting people for the first time, too, so let's get it over with together.'

'No, I want to find Betty.'

He remained stubbornly rooted to the spot, and Josephine tried again. 'We'll take you in a minute, I promise, but first we need to talk to our friends.'

Archie glanced up and waved when he saw them, struggling simultaneously to detach himself from the small girl in his arms. It proved a messy endeavour and, as he came over to greet them, Josephine laughed at the streak of vanilla on his lapel. 'You look as though you're having fun,' she said.

'We are, actually. I haven't been to a fete in years, unless it was to arrest someone.' He smiled, and kissed them. 'It's wonderful to see you both. Virginia's been looking forward to meeting you.'

'We've got someone for you to meet, too. We're just getting to know each other, and we . . .' She looked round for Noah, but he was no longer by their side.

'Where the fuck has he gone now?' Marta muttered under her breath, drawing a sharp glance of disapproval from a passing couple. 'He was standing right here just a minute ago. I swear that boy can disappear at the drop of a hat.'

Archie looked bewildered, and Josephine explained. 'We'd better go and find him,' she said apologetically. 'I'll come back when we've got him safely to the cake stall.'

Marta glanced at her watch. 'No, you stay here and talk to Archie, otherwise you'll be late for your judging. I'll go after Noah. He really *can't* have gone far this time.'

'If it helps, the cake stall's next to the marquee,' Archie called after her.

Josephine laughed. 'Spoken like a true local.'

'Ah well, let's just say that Teddy's a very enthusiastic fete-goer. We must have been round everything at least three times already.' He glanced back towards Virginia's son, and Josephine was touched by the affection in his voice. 'It seems we've both had changes to get used to. Should I even ask what happened to the romantic week you were planning with Marta before she has to go?'

She raised her eyes. 'I'm hoping this is just going to be for a couple of days. The village got rather more than it bargained for yesterday, but you'll know that if you spent the night at Polstead Hall.'

'Yes, there was some hurried shaking of sheets, and a fair bit of crying in the night. Come and meet Virginia.'

They walked across to the coconut shy, Josephine a little less enthusiastically than Archie. At times, she had found herself uncomfortably at odds with Bridget, and she didn't want to make the same mistakes again. For Archie's sake, and whether she liked Virginia or not, she was determined to strike the right note between warmth and the sort of over-familiarity that might be intimidating. To her relief, the other woman made it easy for her. 'Josephine, I'm so happy to meet you at last. You're such an important part of Archie's life that I don't feel I can know him properly without knowing you.' Her voice was attractive, the American inflection soft and distinctive, but it was the sincerity of the words that appealed to Josephine. 'This is Evie,' Virginia continued, and the little girl immediately buried her face in her mother's shoulder, shy to be singled out, 'and you might *think* that this is St George, but actually his name is Teddy.'

'It's just as well you told me,' Josephine said. 'I would have been fooled. That's a very smart costume, Teddy.'

Her words must have carried a note of reservation, because Virginia smiled at her and added: 'Don't worry—I've already explained that he won't be able to win the competition. That would be too fishy when the judge is a friend of the family, and as long as he can wave the sword all day—well, that's the main prize as far as Teddy's concerned. We'll have to prise it off him.'

The boy grinned and nodded enthusiastically, dislodging his helmet and revealing the same striking red-gold hair as his mother. 'What a coincidence that you should know Polstead Hall,' Josephine said.

'Well, I know David and Francesca. They were the only friends of my husband's that I didn't hate the sight of, but we always met at Newmarket or the Priory, so this is my first time here.' Her frankness was refreshing, and Josephine admired the unapologetic way in which she had mentioned her husband, refusing to be touched by his shame. 'It's a beautiful village. You're lucky to have such a peaceful place to run to—well, I assume that it's *usually* peaceful.'

'Most of the time, yes.' They were still talking about Suffolk when Marta came back, carrying a Madeira cake, several slices of fruit loaf and a plate of butterfly buns. 'This is as much bribery as I could carry,' she explained, when she had been introduced, 'but it should be enough to buy Noah a warm welcome. I've left him taking the money with Betty, so let's just hope that he behaves himself. And I've met the Herrons' mysterious brother,' she added, turning to Josephine.

'Oh? What's he like?'

'Quiet. I introduced myself and Noah, and he mumbled something into his moustache that sounded like "Ned", then went as red as a beetroot and walked off in the other direction. But at least we know that he does occasionally get out of the car.'

In a move which Josephine suspected had been deliberately orchestrated by Archie, she found herself suddenly alone with Virginia, while Marta was persuaded to try her luck at the coconut shy with Teddy. 'You know how we met, don't you?' Virginia said. Josephine nodded, hoping that she was right to read it as a statement of fact and not a test of Archie's discretion. 'If somebody had told me back then that something so precious could come from the darkest time of my life, I'd have called him a fool.'

Perhaps that was something else that had brought the couple together, Josephine thought; as close as she and Archie were, she had never been able to console him for the violent death of his lover, but that was something with which Virginia was tragically able to empathise, even if the circumstances were different. 'Sometimes it's good to be proved wrong,' she said, with a wry smile. 'We're our own worst enemies, and if we saw the joy coming, we'd find a way to avoid it.' The comment was as relevant to her own life with Marta, something which Virginia seemed instinctively to understand, and Josephine wondered how much Archie had told her. 'Have you met Phyllis yet?' she asked, curious to know how Bridget and Archie's daughter had reacted to her father's new relationship.

'We've had a few awkward dinners and we're taking it slowly, one step at a time. People have full lives already, don't they, when they get to our age? It's important to respect that.' There was a cheer from the coconut shy as Archie hit his target, and Virginia smiled when she saw the look of pride on her son's face. 'Things are less complicated when you're a kid, thank God, but I know I'm not out of the woods yet. There'll come a time when it all catches up with them. Not Evie, perhaps, but I'm frightened for Teddy. His father was such a hero to him, and he's not old enough yet to understand that there are different sorts of strength.'

Josephine didn't envy Virginia those conversations, but at the moment they seemed a long way off, and the hard-won prize of a coconut was more than enough to hold Teddy's attention. 'We'd better go,' she said reluctantly, as Archie and Marta rejoined them. 'Wish me luck with the judging. Most parents in this village aren't content with a sword—unless it's in my back, of course.'

They made arrangements to meet again later by the fancy dress stage, and Josephine and Marta set off to look for Hilary. 'What do you think?' Marta asked, as soon as they were out of earshot.

'I like her very much.' She glanced back over her shoulder and saw Virginia reach up to take a piece of straw from Archie's hair. 'They've got a lot of history to cope with, though. I just hope it doesn't overshadow everything else.'

'We've managed to get through that. I don't see why they shouldn't.'

'No, you're probably right.'

A sizeable marquee dominated the beautifully kept lawns immediately in front of the Hall. Tables and chairs had been arranged outside, all covered in crisp white cloths that rippled in the breeze, and an army of aproned women, sweating gently under the arms of their cotton dresses, served sandwiches, cream teas and jugs of lemonade to an appreciative audience. A 'Wilkin & Sons Ltd' banner ran the length of the trestle tables, celebrating the link between the company and some of the local farms, and a separate stall had been set up to sell both fresh fruit and the preserves that had graced the world's breakfast tables for more than fifty years. Josephine nodded to one or two familiar faces in the queue for refreshments, struck by how deceptively harmless the scene was: one glance inside the tent—stall after stall of crafts, flowers and home baking, not to mention every variety of fruit or vegetable that could be grown in English soil—revealed the competitive atmosphere that threatened the peace of the day. 'It's going to be a long afternoon,' Marta sighed, following her gaze. 'I'll go and check on Noah while you're busy with the judging.'

'Of course you will. Actually, it might save some time if you—'

Whatever suggestion she had been about to make was lost in a shrill cry from behind the marquee. 'Josephine! Marta!' Hilary beckoned them over to join her. 'Thank the Lord you're here. I heard that Noah did a bunk this morning, and I was worried that you'd never forgive me. I hope he's not causing you too much trouble?'

'He's no trouble at all,' Josephine said, imagining the relish with which Florence Herron must have relayed the morning's events. Had she laid them at the door of a boy who couldn't behave, she wondered, or two women who didn't know the meaning of the word 'discipline'? Probably a combination of the two. Hilary seemed both surprised and pleased by her response, and Josephine continued hurriedly, in case her warmth was creating the wrong impression. 'He's just missing his sister and feeling a little unsettled. He'll be much better when you've found him somewhere more permanent.'

'Yes, of course—leave that with me. In the meantime, I've brought a box of the boys' old toys over for you, and a few clothes. They're in the car, so don't forget to fetch them before you leave. Now, shall I run through our plans for the afternoon?'

'I suppose you'd better.'

'Well, we'll start with the judging in the marquee—flower arranging, knitted items, crochet and woodturning on one side, then straight back down for cut flowers, fruit and veg, sweet and savoury pies, homemade cordials, cakes and bread, then finishing off with jams and chutneys. How does that sound?'

Gruelling, Josephine thought, hoping for an appropriate moment to mention that she detested chutney. 'Absolutely lovely,' she lied. 'What about the pageant and the fancy dress?'

'Ah yes. Well, the theme this year is "Tales of Olde England", as you know.' Hilary rolled her eyes, giving 'olde' two syllables, as if to show her contempt for the unoriginality of the subject matter. 'We thought it would be nice if you said a few words first. You know the sort of thing—the power of a good story, the importance of holding on to the old traditions. That should go down well in the current climate, especially if you can throw in a sprinkling of red, white and blue along the way. Then get the kids up on stage for their big moment while you make your deliberations, and we can all go home for another year.' She clasped her hands together and raised her eyes to the heavens, and Josephine wondered if there was a vicar's wife in the country who did the job under more sufferance. 'God, I could do with a drink, couldn't you?' Hilary added, apparently reading her thoughts. 'Still, I suppose we'll get through it. We always do.'

'Isn't Stephen here?' Josephine asked, thinking it strange that the vicar should miss his own fete. It was usually something that he and Hilary gritted their teeth through together, and she realised quickly that she had hit a nerve.

'Well, that's the other problem,' Hilary said with feeling. 'Mr Mortlock simply will not die! Poor Stephen was called to his bedside in the early hours on the understanding that he was taking his final breaths, and now he's stuck there. He sent a note a while back to say that the old boy keeps rallying and fading, so nobody knows quite where they are. I wouldn't mind, but he hasn't been to church in years.'

'It looks like Mr Mortlock has decided one way or the other,' Marta said, nodding towards the Hall as Josephine hid a smile. 'There's Stephen now.'

The vicar hurried across the grass in response to Hilary's frantic waving. 'Has he gone yet?' she asked.

'False alarm, I think. I left him sitting up in bed, eating a cheese and pickle sandwich. Hello, you two.' He smiled at Marta and Josephine and removed his bicycle clips, then bent to kiss his wife. 'Rosalind asked me to let you know that Mrs Carter is here.'

'What?' Hilary looked at him sharply, as if he had announced that Jesus himself was paying tuppence at the gate to get in. 'What did you say?'

'Mrs Carter. She and her brother have just arrived.'

'*The* Mrs Carter.'

Stephen nodded. 'That's right.'

'But she *can't* be here . . . she never replied to my letter.'

'I'm afraid she is. Her brother's parking the car, and Rosalind has taken her to powder her nose. Excuse me for a moment, will you? I'm ravenous.'

He headed for the refreshments and Hilary stared after him, still trying to digest his news. 'Who's Mrs Carter?' Marta asked.

'I'm so terribly sorry, but there's been a dreadful mix-up.' Hilary drew them to one side, away from a group of chattering women. 'Please believe me—this *wasn't* my choice, Josephine. I always wanted you to do the honours again for us this year, but I was outvoted by the committee. Rosalind said that as you hadn't had a book out for a while, and as Mrs Carter is so well known and lives just over the border, we should invite her to come instead—to stop things getting stale, or some such nonsense. I argued that we couldn't possibly have an Essex woman judging a Suffolk fete, but there was no reasoning with Rosalind once she'd got the bit between her teeth, and you know how two-faced the others can be—they won't stand up to her, no matter how often they bitch about her behind her back.' She paused, biting her lip in frustration as another horror obviously dawned on her. 'This is bloody awkward. It must be terribly competitive, writing books. You're probably daggers drawn with the woman, if you'll forgive the pun, and you shouldn't have to be snubbed in your own village. You live here, for goodness' sake—well, some of the time, at least.'

The 'misunderstanding' was beginning to explain itself, and Josephine did her best to reassure Hilary. 'Whatever great offence you imagine I'm about to take, you're wrong,' she said, scarcely daring to believe her luck. 'If you've asked someone else to do the judging this year, leaving me to enjoy myself, then so much the better. And I don't even know a Mrs Carter, so why would we be daggers drawn?'

'Oh, that's her married name. You'll know her as Margery Allingham. She lives in Tolleshunt D'Arcy.' Josephine stared at her in surprise, instantly recognising the professional name of the author who was indeed more famous than she was, and certainly more prolific. Margery Allingham had penned a string of idiosyncratic, beautifully written crime novels, whose hero—Albert Campion—was himself a celebrity. Josephine admired the books tremendously, even if the plot occasionally eluded her somewhere around page seventy: their sense of place was exquisite, the characters real and individual, and the voice that sprang so vividly from the page had always struck her as belonging to someone whose company would be a pleasure; clearly she was about to find out if she was right.

'This *is* a bit awkward,' Marta whispered. 'I haven't read any of her books, have you?'

'Yes, most of them. The last one was a riot. I don't mind if you want to go back to Archie and Virginia, though. I'll come and find you when I've handed over my duties.'

Marta slipped gratefully away, and Josephine turned back to Hilary. 'Here she comes now,' she said, nodding to the gaggle of women who had just exited the Hall. The focus of their attention was a plump woman in her mid-thirties, who hid her figure well with a long, flowing dress, and whose movements were lively and graceful. Her face—which might have been familiar to Josephine from the photograph on her book jackets—was obscured by a wide-brimmed hat, but it was Hilary's Machiavellian committee who conspired to confirm her identity, trailing behind their celebrity like ladies-in-waiting at court, pointing out this feature and that as they accompanied her over to the marquee.

Hilary seemed more flustered than ever. 'What an embarrassment,' she repeated, making Josephine long to shake her into a different train of thought. 'I can't imagine how this will—'

'Listen,' Josephine said firmly, 'this really doesn't have to be a disaster. If you didn't get her letter, what were you supposed to do? And anyway, she might not even find out that you've brought in a replacement. I certainly won't tell her.'

'Thank you, Josephine. I'll make this up to you, I promise.'

Hilary's relief was short-lived, and any hope of discretion disappeared as soon as the introductions were made. Margery held out her hand to Josephine. 'Miss Tey, how nice. I gather that only one of us should actually be here, but it's a fortunate mistake for me because at last I have the pleasure of meeting you. I love your work.'

'Likewise,' Josephine said, pleased to be able to return the compliment sincerely.

'Mrs Carter *did* reply, Hilary,' Rosalind said, interrupting anything that Josephine might have gone on to add. 'Are you *sure* you never got her letter?'

The vicar's wife looked as if she were facing a sniper's bullet, but Margery was gracious and seemed as keen to play down the incident as Josephine was. 'It's just as likely to be buried under a pile of papers on my desk at home, still waiting to be posted. Pip and I have been helping out with the billeting arrangements, and he's Chief Warden for the village, so the house doesn't feel like our own any more.' She smiled, and Josephine assumed that she was talking about her husband. 'And anyway, there's an obvious solution. Miss Tey and I should judge everything together—if that suits you?'

Josephine nodded her agreement. 'It suits me very well, especially if you like chutney.'

Margery gave a peal of laughter. 'Then that's sorted. Perhaps we could make our battle plan over a cup of tea?'

'Yes, of course,' Hilary said gratefully. 'What about your brother? Can we get him something, too?'

'Oh, don't worry about Phil. He's got friends of his own here, so he's not at a loose end.'

They were shown to a table, and the committee disappeared to fight over the honour of fetching their refreshments. 'This is priceless, isn't it?' Margery continued, still chuckling as she watched them go. 'I wonder which one of us will put it in a book first? *A Fete Worse Than Death*.' She took a handkerchief from her bag and wiped her eyes. 'Mind you, they've missed a trick. Dorothy Sayers lives just down the road—they could have had all three of us. Do you know her?'

'No, we've never met.'

'Ah, she's a good sort when you get used to her. A bit schoolmistressy at first. I always used to feel that she was about to tell me off, but she's grown on me.'

'I'm afraid I don't really go to those celebrity lunches,' Josephine admitted. 'I live in Scotland most of the time, so it's hard to keep up with—'

Margery raised an eyebrow and interrupted her. 'You mean you avoid them like the plague and use distance as an excuse. Don't apologise for it. I'd do the same if Essex weren't so damned convenient for London.'

'Guilty as charged. How long have you lived there?'

'All my life, really. I was born in Ealing, but my parents left the city when I was a few months old and we had a handful of places in Suffolk and Essex while I was growing up. Pip and I took a flat in Holborn when we first got married, but we often swapped houses with my parents so they could spend some time in town. Eventually, we got sucked back in and ended up buying a house I've known since I was a child. We couldn't afford it and we still can't, really, but Pip was determined to have it and it keeps me working while we hope for the miracle.'

Josephine wondered what Pip did for a living and whether Margery loved the house that her books were obviously written to support, but both questions seemed impertinent after such a short acquaintance. She was mindful, too, that her own output of work might be more respectable if she were less comfortable financially; writing came easily to her but security made her lazy, and she was still smarting from the fete committee's judgement on her recent absence from their bookshelves. 'How did you end up in Suffolk?' Margery asked. 'It's a long commute from Scotland.'

'If I'm honest, the distance is part of the attraction,' Josephine admitted. 'It's nice to be someone different occasionally.' She saw her own blend of curiosity and reluctance to pry reflected in Margery's face, and found herself hoping for a time when they might know each other better; already, the other writer interested her. 'My godmother left me a cottage here three years ago, completely out of the blue,' she added, by way of explanation. 'I had no intention of keeping it at first, but I've come to love it, just as she did. It's connected to a murder that took place in the village . . .'

'The Red Barn Murder?'

'That's right. The cottage used to overlook the barn, before it was burnt down. It comes with its own ghosts, but we suit each other.'

'Really? How fascinating. I've always thought that Suffolk was much darker than Essex. I'm not sure I'd want to live here again, although I love it. All that superstition and folklore lurking below the prettiness. Did you know that more than half the people hanged as witches were hanged in Suffolk?'

'Even if the witchfinder who hanged them was from Essex?'

'Ah, touché. You must tell me about your ghosts, though. I'm afraid the ones in my house are all in living memory, and some of them have left their furniture behind.'

She was distracted by someone over Josephine's shoulder, and Josephine turned round curiously, expecting to meet the brother and his friends, but the recipient of Margery's greeting was a blonde girl of four or five, immaculately dressed in a pink summer frock embroidered with daisies. She was approaching their table, accompanied by her mother, who had obviously been charged with delivering their tea. 'Friends of yours?' Josephine asked.

'Mrs Maitland? Yes, a neighbour from the village. Her husband works over at Tiptree,' she explained, nodding to the Wilkin banner. 'She mentioned that they were coming today. They're a nice family. Dorothy's been helping out with the arrangements for the evacuees, and I'm not sure what we'd have done without her.'

The introductions were made as Dorothy Maitland laid out the tea. 'Is Henry not with you?' Margery asked, looking over at the stall. 'Surely he's not left you two to do all the work while he's off enjoying the Punch and Judy.'

She winked at Cissy, and Mrs Maitland smiled at her daughter. 'Daddy wouldn't do that, would he, darling? He knows how much you love it.' She put the teapot in place, then lowered the tray so that Cissy could add the finishing touches to the table. 'No, he's just gone to have a word with one of our farmers while he's here. He said he'd be back half an hour ago, but he must have lost track of time.'

'These are Mummy's homemade scones,' Cissy said proudly to Margery, pushing a plate across the table. 'She's hoping you'll give her first prize, and she's made some cakes, too.'

Her directness was disarming, and could have taught Elsie Gladding a thing or two. Mrs Maitland blushed and apologised, then led her daughter away before she could say anything more. 'Out of the mouths of babes,' Margery said, laughing. 'This is obviously going to be trickier than I thought.'

'I'll happily take the flak for the food if you'll judge the fancy dress,' Josephine suggested. 'Unless you have a conflict of interest there, too?'

'No. As far as I'm aware, I can take a clean swipe at that one without any risk of offence. You're on.'

They shook hands on the deal, and Josephine poured the tea. 'This is nice, isn't it?' Margery said, cutting into one of the scones. 'I suppose it really is the last gasp, though, before it all kicks off.'

Josephine followed her gaze across the park and knew instantly what she meant: the small group of service and recruitment stalls that had become a feature of summer occasions from Empire Day onwards, the square cardboard boxes hanging ominously at everyone's side—there was no masking the signs that had slowly and imperceptibly become part of their lives, and she couldn't decide whether this stoic acceptance of things that had once seemed horrific was a blessing or a curse. 'Yes, I suppose it is,' she said quietly.

'The evacuation was a bit of a shock, I must say. Judging by the number of children here, I'm assuming you had the same surprises as we did?'

'Yes, they arrived yesterday. Four times as many as we were expecting, but we found the extra beds somehow.'

'Same here. It was extraordinary, really. The village turned up like the fire brigade, even people who'd said they wouldn't stomach a child in their house for ten minutes. I don't suppose you were able to take anyone if you're not here all the time?'

'We've got a boy called Noah, but only for a few days. He was evacuated with his younger sister, but her family wouldn't take more than one.'

'That seems very hard-hearted.'

'You might understand if you'd met them. A little old-fashioned and quite formidable. In a different age, they'd have been knitting at the guillotine.'

Margery laughed. 'It sounds as if Noah has had a lucky escape. It was kind of you to step in, though.'

'Well, as you're finding out, it's difficult to refuse Hilary when she's got the bit between her teeth—and she *was* bowled a nigh-on impossible situation.'

'I dare say it will all settle down, although I'm not sure how much more chaotic our house can get. We're the Warden's Post, being right in the centre, and I wasn't exaggerating just now—sometimes you'd think the war was actually being fought in our dining room. Medical supplies, fire-fighting equipment, we've got it all—and have you any idea how suffocating the smell of new wellington boots can be?' Josephine smiled and poured more tea. 'Having the children to think about might actually take the horror out of everything, at least for a while.' It was a sobering thought and they were quiet for a moment, watching the distractions going on around them with a new appreciation. 'We organise a cricket match on

August Monday every year,' Margery continued, a little wistfully. 'We've done it for years—friends over for the weekend, a fancy dress ball on the Saturday night, then a feast for the whole village after the match. Everyone mucks in.'

'It sounds lovely. Exhausting, but lovely.'

'It is usually, but this year it just wasn't the same.'

'I imagine that's a phrase we'll find ourselves using a lot before too long.'

'Yes, I'm sure you're right.' Josephine looked at Margery, struck by how quickly her features moved between gaiety and sadness, and how equally well suited they seemed to each mood. 'We went through the motions this year, but nothing more. I don't think I realised until then how serious things had become.'

'You don't, though, do you, until you get to a marker in the calendar and find yourself looking back ten months.' Josephine thought for a moment, remembering all the occasions recently when she had felt a similar longing for things to stay as they were. 'It hit me first on my birthday, I think. I was here at the cottage with a friend, just like we were the year before, but it seemed so different, as if we suddenly had the cares of the world on our shoulders. There was no joy in it, because it only existed in relation to the happiness of last year and the uncertainty of next.'

'That's it exactly, and it comes as such a shock, like growing out of something you've always loved.' Margery smiled sadly, shaking her head at the thought. 'Everything that could possibly go wrong with the cricket match did. Someone lost a tooth in the first over and nobody got any runs to speak of—and do you know, it's the first year I can remember the weather letting us down. A friend of mine kept saying, "When this war is over, we'll all be old." I could cheerfully have strangled her.'

'I'm surprised you didn't,' Josephine said. 'The trouble is, we know how it goes this time. No more fooling ourselves that it will be over by Christmas.'

'And Pip will sign up,' Margery said with weary resignation, but Josephine saw in her eyes the same fear that she felt about Marta's departure, followed quickly by the same attempt to put it to one side. She realised suddenly that Archie's new-found happiness had brought home what she was losing with a force that was all but physical; the thought of weeks without Marta played in her head like an unwanted piece of music, and there was no hiding from it. 'What will you do during the war, Josephine?'

The question came abruptly after the more pensive turn that their conversation had taken. Josephine hesitated, surprised by how exposed it made her feel—not because it was something she hadn't considered, but because it reminded her of how little purpose her life now held without the person she loved. 'I'll have to go back to Scotland when it starts,' she said reluctantly. 'I have family responsibilities there, and I'll have to put those first while we wait to see how things go. There'll be very little travelling, I suppose, but I've got my work.' She stopped herself, aware that the future was sounding as desperate as it felt, then tried to make light of it. 'I might even steal a march on *A Fete Worse Than Death*.'

'Speaking of which . . .' Hilary was striding purposefully over to fetch them, and Margery struggled to her feet. 'I should be more mobile, I know, but so should grand pianos. Let's get this over with, shall we?'

They were escorted to the far end of the marquee and Josephine waved to Noah as she passed the cake stall, relieved to see that he seemed to be enjoying himself without causing any more trouble. 'That's Noah?' Margery asked, and clapped her hands gleefully when Josephine nodded. 'What a priceless description of the Herrons!'

Josephine stared at her in horror. 'You know them? I'm so sorry. I should never have been so rude.'

'Nonsense, you were absolutely right. Florence is the very spit of Madame Defarge, and there's no need to be embarrassed on my account. I don't know them very well, but their father was a doctor and a protégé of John Salter, the man who owned our house for years. Dr Salter was friends with my parents—a remarkable man, actually. My mother was devoted to him. If you've read *Dancers in Mourning*, you'll have met him as Dr Bouverie.'

Josephine remembered the character from a book of Margery's that she had particularly enjoyed, a strict, authoritative figure who seemed to belong to a different age—exactly the sort of cloth that she would have expected the Herron daughters to be cut from. 'So that's how you've known your house for so long,' she said.

'That's right. We only lived a few miles away, so we spent a lot of time there as a family. I remember the Herrons vaguely from various parties. Not so much Lillian—she was married at the time, and lived away—but Florence, certainly, and there was a brother, too, although I don't know if he's still with them?'

'Yes, but I haven't met him.'

'Well, I was only a little girl at the time, so my impressions of the grown-ups are probably exaggerated, but I recall thinking that the whole family seemed to be perpetually at a funeral.'

'And now? Have you crossed paths more recently?'

'Oh, here and there, but it's really one of those historic connections that lives on in a Christmas card. We invite them to the cricket match every year, but they very rarely come.'

Josephine would dearly have loved to find out more about her neighbours, but Hilary was standing purposefully at the entrance to the marquee, already impatient with their dawdling. 'There's a lot to get done,' she said through gritted teeth, when another round of introductions had been made. 'Would you like to split up and take a side each?'

'No, we've decided to stick together and adopt a more diplomatic approach,' Josephine said, drawing a smile from her fellow judge. 'Shall we start on safe ground with crafts?' They made swift work of the first line of tables, and Josephine couldn't help wondering why Hilary and her committee went to such lengths to find a celebrity each year; as far as she could tell from the conversations, none of the competitors had read either her books or Margery's, and didn't seem remotely bothered who judged their efforts as long as they had a fleeting moment in the limelight. 'There's something very levelling about village life, isn't there?' she whispered to Margery, after a particularly close call between knits. 'I'm beginning to wonder if I've been wasting my time all these years.'

'I know exactly what you mean. It's bloody some days, isn't it? I found myself wondering recently if I shouldn't take in washing for a profession instead.'

Hilary cleared her throat, and Josephine resisted the temptation to stand to attention. 'Flowers and veg next, please, ladies,' she said. 'Then you can reward yourselves with some cake.'

The fairest judge in the world would have found it hard to consider more than one winner in any of the growing categories, and Josephine looked admiringly at the familiar stall, which had been designed and arranged as lovingly as any stage set. The custom of anonymity was preserved, but everyone knew who was responsible for the most eye-catching entries, and, as always, the displays had drawn quite a crowd, with children looking on in wonder at the size of the exhibits, adults in envy at their perfection. 'It's been another good year, then, Mr Chilver?' Josephine said to the elderly man who—for as long as anyone could remember—had walked away with every horticultural prize that he aspired to. 'I think you've surpassed yourself with these.'

The dahlias she was referring to might have been sculpted rather than grown, a joyous explosion of colour and form that dwarfed the other flowers and made them seem drab and ordinary. 'Well, Miss, the weather's been kind, that's for sure. Plenty of sun and plenty of rain, that's what they like.' He drew her attention to the biggest bloom of them all, a true pink flower that must have been five or six inches across, with an exuberant mass of petals arching back from the centre like hundreds of tiny flames. 'More flowers than you can find a vase for, she's given me, all summer long.'

'Your garden must be a picture,' Margery said. 'I envy your neighbours.'

'Ah well, these are all grown on my allotment, Miss. We've only got a small garden, and my sister likes to keep things a bit more regular there, don't you, Win?'

'Yes, dear, I do.'

Brother and sister were remarkably alike, with the same lively kingfisher-blue eyes, and Josephine wondered if they were twins. 'There's certainly nothing regular about these vegetables,' she conceded. 'What's your secret?'

'Horse manure, that's my magic ingredient. Horse manure and patience.' He picked up an onion that measured twice the size of a cricket ball. 'These were all grown outside, you know, and I just bring them into the greenhouse to ripen off. They're very mild.'

'But do they taste as nice when they're that big?' Margery asked.

'That's a fallacy, Miss, if you don't mind my saying so—a load of nonsense. If it looks nice, it'll eat nice.' His enthusiasm was infectious, and Josephine noticed that it combined with the benefits of an outdoor life to give him the energy and vitality of a much younger man. 'You never know what's below the ground until you lift it,' he said, selecting a carrot and looking proudly down the shaft, then lifting it to his nose. 'Perfect in all ways, see, and not just for show. That smell is real carrot.'

'Extraordinary,' Josephine said, sensing that Margery was struggling to contain her laughter, and resisting the temptation to meet her eye. 'Well, congratulations, Mr Chilver. I don't think there's any doubt that the glory is all yours again this year.'

'Thank you, Miss—that's appreciated. Makes it all worthwhile when you see your hard work coming to fruition, and you can feel you've achieved something.'

'My gardener's just resigned, Mr Chilver,' Margery said, placing the best-in-show rosette next to the pink dahlia. 'I don't suppose you'd fancy taking on a few hours a week for me?'

'That's kind of you, Miss, but I'm happy with my allotment, thank you. It's my little bit of heaven, and I'm out there every day, aren't I, Win?'

'You are, dear, yes.'

'I like to give it everything I've got, and Win here is magic. She supports it all, don't you, Win?'

'Yes, Cyril—for my sins, I do.'

'It's a long time since I've gardened for a living. It used to take me all over the place, but I was a much younger man then. Anyway, it's not the same as when you do it for love.'

'Well, I quite understand,' Margery said with a sigh, 'but it was worth a try. Tell me the name of this dahlia, though. That's something I simply *must* have.'

He took two of the stems from the display and gave them one each. 'She's a Jersey Beauty, Miss,' he said, and Josephine doubted that there could have been more affection in his voice if he had been introducing them to his favourite grandchild. 'I don't talk to my plants'—his sister raised her eyes to the heavens, good-naturedly challenging his words—'but they do understand me. Everything's got a soul, and if you're nice to Mother Nature, she'll be nice to you.'

'That sounds like excellent advice, Mr Chilver.'

A photographer from the local newspaper moved in to record the gardener's triumph, gathering together the obligatory group of children and committee members, and Josephine noticed Hilary's star begin to wax again as the presence of two notable judges became an asset rather than an embarrassment. 'What a remarkable man,' Margery said, when they were finally ushered on to the next category. 'Just for a moment, I thought I'd found the answer to all my prayers.'

'Have you got a big garden?' Josephine asked.

'Yes, but it's not just the size that's killing me. Dr Salter, God rest his soul, was a keen amateur—his alstroemeria won a gold medal at Chelsea, I believe—and there's an unspoken expectation in the village that I'll keep it that way. Expensive plants, wages for a small army, that sort of thing.' She brightened suddenly. 'Ah, chutney! Do you mind if I take this one, Josephine? I do so love it.'

'Please, be my guest.' Josephine saw Hilary looking at her watch again and moved on to the cake stall, keen to repay the favour by saving Margery from any embarrassment with the Maitlands. She noticed Cissy watching intently, but there was no sign of her mother. Here, there was none of the transparency that years of the same result had brought to the horticultural categories, and she had no idea who had baked the Victoria sandwich that she awarded first prize; when she looked round to see if Cissy's face registered pride or disappointment, the little girl was gone.

Margery and Josephine were reunited at the final table, and they applied themselves efficiently to the cordials and homemade wines, sampling the winner with a relish that reflected what a long afternoon it had already been. Hilary joined them, in much better spirits now that the day was going well. 'We're into the home straight now, thank God,' she said, pouring herself a second glass of elderflower. 'Would you mind making your own way over to the stage for the pageant? Stephen's already there to greet you, but I just want to thank Mr Davis again for his help yesterday. He's here with his wife and son.' She gestured back to the vegetable stall, where the Chilvers were packing their prize exhibits back into crates, ready to go home, and Josephine recognised the bus driver from the day before. He was standing with an attractive woman in a floral-print dress—presumably the wife he had been so anxious not to rile—and he had his hand on the back of a wheelchair, which was occupied by a boy of around twelve. The cheerful demeanour that had been so welcome in the chaos of the school hall was entirely gone; now, he looked tired and strained, years older in the space of just twenty-four hours, and there was no conversation amongst the family as they watched, no hint of pleasure or enjoyment. Instead, all of them seemed isolated by their own thoughts, even the child. 'It must be exhausting, mustn't it, that sort of caring,' Hilary said quietly, and Josephine nodded. 'Now, you know where to go for the stage, don't you?'

'Yes, if it's in the same place as last year. We'll make our way over there now.'

'So what's your conflict of interest in the fancy dress?' Margery asked as they headed out of the marquee. 'Is Noah taking part?'

'No, nothing like that, but the woman who runs the village shop absolutely dotes on her granddaughter—and she's made the costume for her.'

'Ah, say no more.'

'At the moment, she's holding me to ransom over a tin of biscuits, but hostilities could easily escalate if I don't deliver the right result.'

'Do you know what she's coming as? I'll do my best for you.'

'Thank you, but the costume was a closely guarded secret. I'll tip you the wink, though, if I—'

Josephine's ruse was interrupted by the sound of raised voices coming from the refreshment area. Conversations faltered at the nearby tables, replaced by an embarrassed silence which only made the heated argument more obvious. The atmosphere was suddenly excruciating, as Dorothy Maitland shouted her grievances, and Josephine glanced at Margery. 'Is that her husband?' she whispered.

'Henry, yes.'

'Somehow I think this is about a bit more than missing the Punch and Judy.'

'Yes, so do I. Poor Cissy—look at her. Whatever it is, they might at least have kept it from her.' The little girl was standing at the entrance to the marquee, watching her parents' very public display of anger. The expression on her face was desolate, but it wasn't so much the sadness that made Josephine's heart ache for her as the hint of a weary familiarity; this was obviously not the first time that she had witnessed such an outburst. Without another word, Margery hurried over to her. 'Come on, ducky,' she said loudly, enveloping the child in an enormous hug, then sweeping her over to the Maitlands in the folds of her long dress like a protective mother hen. 'It's time for you to go and have some fun with Mummy and Daddy.'

Her words were comforting, but they held a note of steel that was meant for adult ears, and they served to break the tension. Dorothy Maitland seemed to come to her senses as suddenly as if she had emerged from under water. She looked round at the crowd, obviously horrified by her loss of control, then nodded gratefully to Margery and picked up her daughter.

'I would have bet my house on that being the happiest of families,' Margery said, as she and Josephine headed back across the park. 'It just shows, doesn't it? You never know what's going on behind a front door once it's closed. People's lives are so complicated.'

The stage had been set up on the other side of the park, and the woodlands behind formed the perfect natural back-cloth to the pageant's theme of ancient England. Marta was waiting there with Noah, and Josephine introduced them. 'Did you have fun with Betty?' she asked, and Noah nodded enthusiastically.

'We sold all the cakes except the chocolate ones, and Miss Lillian said that Miss Florence always makes those too dear on purpose because they're Mr Herron's favourite and she doesn't want to sell them. She said she spoils him.'

'And what did you think of Mr Herron?' Josephine asked, relieved to see that some sort of thaw had obviously occurred over the course of the afternoon.

Noah shrugged. 'He's all right. He keeps dead things under rocks in his study. He said he'd show them to me when I go to see Betty.'

'He does what?'

'I think what Noah means is that he's a palaeontologist,' Margery explained, laughing at the look of horror on Josephine's face. 'The dead things are *part* of the rocks, Noah. They're called fossils, and Mr Herron has quite a collection, by all accounts.'

'I don't care what he's got in his study if it means that Noah can see his sister,' Marta said, brushing some icing sugar out of Noah's hair. 'Sounds like you've really charmed them if you've been invited over already. Good for you.'

Josephine began to tell Marta about Margery's long connection with the Herrons, but she was interrupted by a breathless Elsie Gladding, who hurried up to them carrying Annie's costume—a medieval-style gown and headdress in a vivid shade of green. 'You haven't seen Kathy, have you, Miss Tey?' she asked. 'I thought they'd all be here by now, and I need to get Annie into her costume. They'll be getting started with the pageant in a minute.'

Children and their parents were beginning to gather by the trees, a motley collection of knights and queens and dragons, but there was no sign of the Ridley family. Josephine looked at Elsie in surprise. 'I saw Mrs Ridley earlier, over by the races, but I assumed that Annie would be with *you*. Did you have fun last night?' She nodded to the costume. 'Maid Marian, I presume?'

Elsie ignored the second question. 'Last night? What do you mean? And why would Annie be with me? Kathy said she'd bring her here.'

'But she changed her mind when she was allocated more children. She told me she was going to give in and let Annie spend the night with you while she settled them in.'

'Well, she must have changed it back again. I've not seen any of them since they left the shop yesterday. I thought they'd have enough on with the new girl, so I left them to it. It's true what Kathy says—I know I spoil Annie, and that's not right at the moment, not when there are kids who've lost their homes.'

Josephine hesitated, certain that Annie had been waved off to her grandmother's but reluctant to worry Elsie in case there had been a change of plan that she wasn't aware of. In the end, the dilemma was taken out of her hands. 'Ah, Kathy, there you are!' Elsie said. 'Thank goodness. Where have you been?'

'Sorry, Mum. Tom's had words with a bloke from the factory about the last lot of cherries we sent them. He said they weren't up to scratch, but that's nonsense—I picked a lot of them myself, and they were as good as they always are. Anyway, Tom's in a right state about it so I've sent him off for a drink to calm down. This lot's enough without a full-grown man having a tantrum.' She gestured to the three evacuees, and Josephine's heart went cold when she saw that Annie wasn't with her. Kathy Ridley looked at the dress in her mother's arms. 'Isn't Annie changed yet? You're cutting it a bit fine. Don't say she's playing you up again. You've got to be firmer with her, Mum.'

'But Annie's with you.' The petulance in Elsie's voice came from fear, and Josephine looked at Marta, scarcely daring to consider the scenario that was playing out in front of them like a terrible dream. 'You said the kids had to get used to each other.'

'I know, but then Mrs Lampton wanted us to take two more and Annie wasn't happy about it. You'd already said you'd have her and she wanted to go, so it just seemed easier to let her.' Kathy glanced back across the parkland, as if willing her little girl to appear from nowhere. Her voice was low and even, but Josephine could see disbelief mingling with panic in her eyes, and she had gone dreadfully pale. 'We were going to drop her at the shop on the way home but Tom was late to pick us up and the other kids were getting restless, so I waved Annie off across the playground.'

'By herself?'

'What do you mean by that?' Kathy turned on her mother, her anger fuelled by guilt. 'She's been across that green *hundreds* of times on her own, and everybody knows her. If you'd told me that she never arrived . . .'

'But I didn't know she was coming!'

Josephine stepped in, keen to put a halt to the recriminations before they got out of hand. 'I'm sure there's an explanation,' she said, although she couldn't for the life of her think what it might be. 'Mrs Ridley, perhaps you should go and find your husband and let him know what's happened, and then we can make a plan to find Annie.' She scanned the growing crowd, hoping that Archie might have arrived with Teddy for the competition, but there was no sign of him. 'A friend of mine is at the fete today, and he's a policeman—he'll know what to do. I'll go and look for him now.'

She had meant the promise to be reassuring, but her words had the opposite effect. 'A policeman?' Kathleen Ridley stared at her almost aggressively. 'Why do we need a policeman? What do you think has happened to Annie?' Even as she spoke her defiance, the reality of the situation began to dawn on her. 'Oh God, Mum, she's been out all night. Why didn't I check with you? I'll never forgive myself if something has happened.'

'Go and find Tom.' Elsie spoke more calmly now, and the familiar mother and daughter roles began to re-establish themselves. 'Miss Tey will fetch her friend, and he'll tell us what to do. There are plenty of folks here who'll help us look for Annie, and she'll be back home in no time, safe and sound and full of her adventures like she always is.'

Josephine didn't know if the picture that Elsie had created was for her daughter's benefit or her own, but either way she was grateful. 'Let's go and find Archie,' she said to Marta, 'and we should tell Hilary what's happened, too.'

'What can I do to help?' Margery asked.

'Would you keep an eye on Noah until we get back?' Josephine asked. 'I've no idea what Hilary will want to do about the fancy dress competition now, but if they go ahead with it . . .'

'I'll hold the fort. Don't worry about a thing. We'll be fine, won't we, ducky?'

She shooed them off, and Marta and Josephine hurried back across the grass to the main cluster of tents and stalls. 'It's busier than ever now,' Marta said pessimistically. 'Finding Archie in this is going to be like looking for a needle in a haystack.'

That was nothing compared to the task of finding a missing child, Josephine thought grimly, but she didn't waste her breath by speaking the thought aloud; one glance at Marta's face was enough to know that the same horrors were occurring to both of them. As it turned out, Archie solved their problem by emerging from a crowd of people gathered around the Morris dancing, followed by Virginia and the children. 'Thank God,' Josephine said. 'At least something's gone our way.'

'There's Hilary, too.' Marta pointed in the direction of the jumble stall. 'I'll go and tell her while you speak to Archie. Let's meet back here in a bit.'

'We were just on our way over,' Archie called apologetically, thinking she had come to fetch them. 'Sorry we're a bit late.' As he got closer, he noticed the expression on her face. 'Josephine, what on earth's the matter?'

'One of the village girls has gone missing.'

'Oh my God, how terrible,' Virginia said. 'Her poor parents.'

From anyone else, it might have sounded hollow, but Josephine recalled that Teddy had been abducted around the time that Archie and Virginia met, and she appreciated the sincerity. 'Will you come and help?' she asked.

'Yes, of course, but try not to worry. I'm sure she can't have gone far, and nine times out of ten when a child—'

'No, no—you don't understand,' Josephine said, her frustration getting the better of her. 'Annie hasn't been seen since yesterday afternoon.'

'What?' Archie stared at her, confused. 'She's been gone for twenty-four hours and no one's reported her missing?'

'They didn't know. It's just been a terrible mix-up. Her mother and her grandmother both thought she was with the other one, and they've only just realised. It's nobody's fault, but she's been gone all night now.' Josephine stopped short, unable to keep her emotions in check for any longer, or to pretend to herself that this was just any child; she was fond of Annie, and now that the practical distraction of finding Archie was gone, she found herself haunted by her last memory of the little girl in the school hall, by the idea that they had all been going blithely about their business, unaware that she needed their help, and most of all by the knowledge that if she had insisted on accompanying Annie to her grandmother's, this would never have happened. 'I'm sorry,' she said, 'but we've lost precious time, haven't we? If she's hurt herself, or—God forbid—if someone's taken her, the hours that we've missed are crucial.'

Archie didn't insult her by trying to deny it. 'How old is Annie?' he asked gently.

'Nearly five. It's her birthday next week.'

'And where was she last seen?'

'At the school playground. It was just after the evacuees arrived.' Prompted by Archie's questions, Josephine outlined the afternoon's events as she remembered them, then explained how the misunderstanding had come about. 'The Ridleys were just trying to help out,' she said. 'They really don't deserve this.'

'Were there any children left on the bus?' Archie asked. 'Is there a chance that Annie could have got mixed up with another group and moved on somewhere else? It was chaos from what I saw in London yesterday, and you've just said that no one here really knew what they were doing.'

Josephine shook her head. 'I don't see how that could have happened. The buses were both empty when they left—we waved them off. One of the drivers is here with his family, though, so you could ask him, just to be sure.'

'Was Annie still there when the buses left?'

Josephine thought about it, trying to clarify the order of events in her own mind. 'I think she'd gone by then, but I honestly couldn't swear to it. You'll have to ask her mother.'

'All right. I'll come with you now.' He turned back to Virginia. 'Will you go and find someone from the Hall and ask them to put a call in to the local station? I think we're going to need some help here, and the less time we waste now, the better.'

She nodded and squeezed his arm, then left immediately to do as he asked, with Teddy and Evie in tow. Josephine took Archie across to the stage area, where she found Margery playing skittles with Noah and the evacuees, while Elsie Gladding was doing her best to reason with her daughter and son-in-law. 'We've wasted enough time already,' Tom Ridley was saying. 'We should be out there looking for her now, not sitting round here waiting for some bloke who doesn't even know the village to tell us what to do. I'm going to get some of the lads and we'll make a start.'

Elsie was obviously relieved when she saw Josephine, but Ridley was looking for a fight, and the sudden presence of Scotland Yard did nothing to calm him down. 'How the hell are you going to find her when you've never been here in your life?' he shouted, his tone pitched somewhere between fury and panic. 'This needs to be done by people who know where to look, people who know my little girl, and we need to get on with it. Standing round talking won't get her back.'

'I don't disagree with you, Mr Ridley,' Archie said calmly. 'The more people you can round up to help, the better, but there needs to be a plan to make sure that whatever resources we *do* have are used to their best effect.'

'Listen to him, Tom,' Kathy pleaded, taking his arm. 'He knows what he's doing.'

He shook her off angrily, but didn't argue, and Archie took advantage of the silence. 'Someone needs to be at home in case Annie comes back. Will you do that, Mrs Ridley?'

'Yes, of course.' Her face brightened, and Josephine hated to see the hope in it. 'She might be there already, Tom, now she's taught us a lesson. We've been out most of the day, after all. She might be sitting on the back step waiting for us.'

It seemed unlikely that Annie would have willingly denied herself the fete that she had been so looking forward to, just to make a point, and Archie was careful not to encourage Mrs Ridley's optimism. 'Someone should be at her grand-mother's house, too,' he said. 'As I understand it, she was supposed to be there last night?'

'That's right.'

'It don't sound like either of you could decide where she should be.'

'Tom!' Kathleen looked at him in disbelief. 'That's not fair.'

'Isn't it?'

'Come on, love,' Elsie said, trying to intervene. 'You're both upset, and we need to—'

'No, Mum. I won't have that.' She rounded on her husband. 'If you hadn't been so late picking us up, we'd have dropped Annie off like I wanted to. If I'm taking some of the blame for this, then so are you.'

'Mr Ridley, perhaps you could go and fetch your friends,' Archie said, before things could get any worse. 'We'll search between the school and your mother-in-law's house, following the route that Annie would have taken. How far is it?'

'A couple of hundred yards, no more.'

'And what else is near the school?'

'Fields, mostly, and some allotments.'

'Those are a priority, too, and we'll need people to go door to door to ask if anyone saw Annie yesterday and get them to check their sheds and outbuildings.'

'What would she be doing in there?'

'She was upset about the evacuees, wasn't she?' Kathleen nodded. 'Well, if she's run away in protest, she might be worried about coming home now in case she's in trouble. The longer she's gone, the harder it will be for her.'

'Of course she's not in trouble! We just want her back home.'

'I know, and the local force will help with the door to door when they get here. The most important thing we can do at the moment is cover as much ground as possible, so go and get your volunteers, Mr Ridley. I'll meet you at the gate.'

Ridley nodded and ran off towards the beer stall, which was becoming increasingly rowdy as the day wore on. 'We'll go home and wait, then, if there's nothing else we can do?' Kathleen said, and there was already an empty, defeated note in her voice.

'Thank you, but I just need to check a few details with you before you go. What was Annie wearing yesterday?'

Elsie answered quickly, as if it were the one thing she could do to help. 'A yellow sundress. It's her favourite, and she's growing out of it, really, but she won't give it up, so we have to keep letting it out, don't we, Kathy? And she had a doll with her—a rag doll. I made it for her birthday.'

'Tell me exactly where she was the last time you saw her.'

Funny, Josephine thought, but the simplest of words seemed to have an ominous undertone in the tension of the moment, and she knew the thoughts going through Annie's mother's head as certainly as if they had been spoken aloud. 'She was at the far side of the playground,' Kathy said, making an effort to pull herself together. 'I went to the door of the hall to see her off and try to cheer her up, but she wasn't having any of it. She was pleased to be going, I think—she loves being at Mum's, and helping out in the shop. Anyway, I waited until she got to the road, and I waved but she didn't turn back. She went between two of the cars that were parked along the verge, and I lost sight of her after that, so I went back inside.' She bit her lip, obviously reliving the scene in her mind. 'It was all so normal. I didn't give it a second thought.'

'Were the buses that brought the evacuees still there at that point?'

'Yes, they were parked outside. Some of the volunteers were unloading food and stuff.'

'But Annie didn't go anywhere near them?'

'No.'

'And can you think of anywhere else she might have gone? Any friends she sometimes stayed with? Other relatives in the village?'

Kathy shook her head again. 'No, she only ever went to Mum's, and she doesn't start school until next week. She was so excited about it.'

She covered her eyes, and Elsie tried to comfort her. 'It's all right, love, we'll find her, I promise. She's probably waiting at home, like you said.'

'We'll need a photograph of Annie, Mrs Ridley. Do you have one I could borrow?'

'Why do you need a photograph? Everyone round here knows her.'

Archie paused, and Josephine knew that he was trying to find a gentle way of making her face the reality of the situation. 'We might need to look further afield if we can't find her here. Don't give up hope, though. We'll do all we can to find Annie, and it's a small village. As you say, most people know her, and that's in our favour. Now, I must go and see how your husband's getting on.' He drew Josephine to one side before he left. 'Will you try and find that bus driver for me? I need you to double-check that those buses were empty when they left Polstead.'

'Yes, of course. Is there anything else we can do? Can we come and help you look for her?'

'It would be better if you stayed here and talked to anyone who was at the school yesterday. We need to build up a picture of where Annie went after her mother lost sight of her, and the smallest detail might be useful. Keys to the school, too—that's a priority, just in case Annie hid somewhere there as a prank that backfired. Someone will need to search the premises.'

'The headmistress was here earlier. I'll try and find her, too—or sort something out with Stephen and Hilary. They'll know where she lives.'

'Thanks, Josephine. Ask her to meet me at the school as soon as possible. Now, I'd better go, but I'll come and find you later to let you know what's happening.' When he glanced back at Kathy, there was a sadness in his eyes that went deeper than professional concern, and Josephine realised how much his new responsibilities to Virginia and her children had already changed him. 'These next few hours are going to be hard for the family,' he said. 'Let's just hope we can bring them some good news.'

He left for the entrance gate, and Josephine turned to Kathleen and Elsie, trying to think of something that might bring them comfort. 'Archie knows what he's doing,' she said, falling back on the one thing that she could be sure of. 'Trust him to do his best for you, and everyone else here—we'll all do whatever it takes.'

'Thank you, but Tom's right, isn't he? This *is* my fault. I've let Annie down. Why didn't I let you take her over to the shop when you offered yesterday? She'd have been safe with you.'

There was no easy answer to that, even if Kathy had been in the mood to hear one, and Josephine was glad when Elsie stepped in before her silence became awkward. 'Let me have the other kids,' she said, gesturing to the evacuees. 'They'll be fine with me at the shop for a bit.'

'And they won't be with me, you mean?'

'What? No, of course not. That's not what I meant, but the last thing you—'

Kathy rounded on her mother. 'They're my responsibility, and I'm perfectly capable of looking after them. Just let me get on with it and stop interfering. Don't you realise that's why we're in this mess?'

Elsie flinched, as if she'd been slapped. 'I was only trying to help,' she said, turning desperately to Josephine.

'I know you were, and she didn't mean it,' Josephine said. 'She's just lashing out because she's frightened. Try not to take it to heart.'

She squeezed Elsie's hand, wanting to take the sting out of Kathy's words, but there was no comforting her as she watched her daughter gather together the evacuees and head for home across the park.

10

On the rare occasions that Penrose had experienced a crime in a place he knew personally, he was invariably struck by how it changed in the light of an investigation, and today—although a crime had yet to be proven—was no different. He had been to Polstead a handful of times to visit Josephine, but he saw the village now with new eyes, and felt another atmosphere altogether in its peaceful lanes; everywhere he looked he found a threat to a little girl who was not yet five, and an almost insurmountable challenge to their efforts to find her. The cool, green patches of woodland that stretched out on all sides were suddenly dense and impenetrable; the attractive, well cared for cottages were watchful and secretive; and the pond at the foot of the hill—a picturesque meeting place, so often surrounded by families and small children at play—was transformed into something far more perilous, wide and unfathomable, a magnet for anyone lost in the dark. He wanted to ask how deep it was, but Tom Ridley was already on the edge, his mood brittle and volatile, and Penrose didn't want to say anything that might dash the hopes which were so important to the energy of the search. Privately, though, he feared the worst: if nothing was found tonight, the pond would have to be dragged in the morning.

The nights had begun to pull in and the sun would go down at eight o'clock, which gave them four or five hours of daylight. There was a sense of urgency as Ridley led the way up Polstead Hill, followed by a group of twenty or thirty men in various states of sobriety; what they lacked in clear think-ing, they made up for with good intentions, and Penrose was glad of the determination that he saw in their faces. Most of the villagers were obviously at the fete, but those who weren't came to their front doors to see what was happening, and occasionally one of the men peeled off to visit a house or gather some support from a neighbour. It wasn't quite the methodical door-to-door approach that Penrose would have liked, but he didn't blame them; in their position, he would have done exactly the same, and something more organised could be arranged when the local force got here. The priority now was to cover as much ground as possible.

They got to the green, which was deserted except for a small group of regulars outside the Cock Inn, waiting for the pub to open its doors for the evening shift. 'Is that your mother-in-law's house?' Penrose asked, gesturing towards the small village stores which stood at one corner of the green. Ridley nodded. 'And the school? Where is that from here?'

'It's on the Heath road, just out of sight round that corner.'

He pointed diagonally across the green, and Penrose didn't know whether to be heartened or concerned by the short dis-tance that Annie would have had to walk to get from one place to the other: on the one hand, apart from a brief stretch of road, there were no obvious hazards where she might have come to harm; on the other, it made the mystery of her disap-pearance even more bewildering, and suggested that she had either decided to make a detour for herself, or that someone had taken her. In the comings and goings of the evacuation, the latter possibility would have been less conspicuous than usual, and although he guessed that most people had collected their evacuees on foot, her mother had said that there were cars parked all along the verge; if Annie had got into one of them, it would have been very easy for the driver to continue on the road out of the village without even being noticed. The green itself was overlooked by houses on all three sides, although the pub would have been shut at the time in question. If Annie had got as far as that, there was a good chance that someone might have noticed her—but he doubted that she had. It seemed inexplicable that she could vanish in the few yards between there and the shop.

'It's no distance at all, is it?' Ridley said, his anger with his wife apparently gone, replaced by a despondency at the task ahead. 'I shouldn't have been so hard on Kathy. I'd have let Annie go on her own, too, if it had been down to me.'

'I'm sure she'll be pleased to hear that, Mr Ridley. It's important that you stick together through something like this.' It wouldn't be the first time that Penrose had seen a couple torn apart by the loss of a child, and this was the beginning of what might turn out to be a very long nightmare for the Ridley family. 'Let's get started,' he said, trying to sound more optimistic than he felt. 'There's plenty of daylight left.'

'What do you want us to do?'

Quickly, Penrose divided the men and issued his instructions until the immediate vicinity was covered. One group was dispatched to check the gardens and outbuildings around the green; another took charge of the footpaths and lanes that stretched away from the heart of the village; and the final party, including Annie's father, spread out in a line to comb the ground as far as the school playground. 'Don't forget to call her name while you're looking,' he said. 'I'm going to check her grandmother's house and the area around it. We'll regroup at the school, and make a plan there for the fields and allotments in the other direction.'

The men seemed heartened by a new sense of purpose, and Penrose left them to their work, confident that they would be both vigilant and efficient. He turned his attention to the tiny redbrick cottage that housed the village shop, noticing that Annie's grandmother didn't seem to have arrived back from the fete yet. The front door opened onto a narrow lane, which led down past a pair of terraced cottages and then seemed to fizzle out in a scruff of brambles and trees; in the distance, he could hear the faint trickle of water from a brook. He tried the shop door without success, then opened a small gate and followed the garden path round to the back of the cottage, calling Annie's name as he did so. The garden was bigger than he expected, out of proportion to the house itself, but he saw instantly that it was far too well-kept to offer many hiding places for a little girl. Neat flower borders, generously stocked with marigolds and shrub roses, surrounded two rectangles of lawn, and the path that separated them led down to a small wooden table and two chairs, perfectly positioned to catch the evening sun. A box of toys sat under the table, waiting, Penrose guessed, for Annie's next visit, and he found the sight almost unbearably poignant. He shook himself, irritated by his own response to something so innocent: realistic expectations were one thing, but it was far too early to be quite so downbeat about Annie's chances; for the Ridleys' sake, if nothing else, he needed to rid himself of this dreadful sense of foreboding.

There were two brick-built outbuildings, one a lavatory and the other a shed containing basic tools and a stack of coal, but both were otherwise empty. For a moment, his heart lifted when he saw the hen house at the bottom of the garden: if he were a runaway child, wanting to make a point without going too far to do it, that might have been exactly the sort of refuge to tempt him, but as he pushed open the door, overpowered by the stifling heat and smell of hot straw, the only things there to object to his intrusion were half a dozen disgruntled chickens.

Disappointed, he walked back to the house and peered through the back window. The kitchen parlour was small to account for the business side of the premises, and what little space there was was taken up in part by boxes and unloaded stock, but it looked comfortable and well lived in; if pressed to describe the life it suggested, content and self-contained would have been the words that sprang to mind.

'Can I help you?'

Penrose turned round and found an elderly woman looking at him over the hedge from the next garden. Her eyes, like her voice, were suspicious, and not without justification, Penrose thought: if she had been watching him for some time, his actions would have been unsettling, particularly if she wasn't aware of what had happened to Annie. She repeated her question, this time with less bravado, and he tried to reassure her. 'My name is Penrose, and I'm a Detective Chief Inspector with Scotland Yard, although I'm not here officially today. I'm a friend of Miss Tey's, from Larkspur Cottage.' The name brought a nod of recognition and a slight softening in her expression, but still she looked bewildered. 'I was at the fete just now when Mr and Mrs Ridley realised that Annie has gone missing,' he continued. 'I've been helping to organise a search around the places she was last seen, and—'

'Annie? Missing?' The woman stared at him in horror, and for a moment Penrose thought that she was going to faint, but she recovered herself quickly. 'Are you sure it's Annie?'

'I'm afraid so.'

'But she was here yesterday. Full of it, she was.'

'When was that, Mrs . . . ?'

'Chilver. Winnie Chilver, and it's Miss.'

'*Miss* Chilver—I'm sorry. When did you last see Annie?'

'Yesterday morning, it was—about eleven o'clock, I suppose, because Cyril had already been off up the allotments for a couple of hours. She was here at the shop with her mother. They were going over to the school to take one of the children, weren't they?'

'Yes, that's right,' Penrose said, disappointed that there was no new information to be had. 'Well, she was on her way back here shortly afterwards to spend the night with her grandmother, but she didn't arrive.'

'And you've only just realised that?' The words weren't meant to be as accusing as they sounded, but Penrose couldn't help wondering how often the Ridley family would have to endure the same question, corroborating their sense of guilt and responsibility each time. 'Poor Elsie,' Winnie Chilver said, shaking her head. 'Where is she? Out looking?'

'She's on her way back from the fete, just in case Annie comes here.'

'She loved that child to bits.'

'We're very much hoping to find Annie safe and well,' Penrose said emphatically, relieved that Mrs Gladding wasn't here to notice the doom-laden past tense. 'She was upset about the evacuees, apparently, so it might just be that she ran away to make a point and is now too frightened of being in trouble to come home. That's why we're looking in all the gardens nearby and asking people to check their sheds.'

It sounded pathetically tame, he thought, rather as if it were a cat that had gone missing and not a child, but Winnie Chilver seemed to think it was a reasonable request. 'I'll go and have a look,' she said, 'unless you want to do it yourself?'

'Whichever you prefer,' Penrose said.

'All right, you do it. I'll go and put the kettle on for when Elsie gets back. This must have been a terrible shock for her, and she'll need to keep her strength up for Kathy's sake. Do you want some tea?'

'No, I've got to get on, but thank you.'

131

Miss Chilver turned back to her own house. As she walked up the path, Penrose noticed the old cricket bat in her hand that had been hidden by the hedge; clearly, she had been ready to give her neighbour's intruder as good as she got, and he smiled at the thought, in spite of the circumstances. If that sort of spirit was common in the village, they might just find Annie after all.

He made short work of the Chilver sheds, then took advantage of the empty house next door to scout out its garden, too. When he had finished, he walked down to the end of the lane and examined the thicket, calling Annie's name as he did so, but there was nothing to raise his suspicions, and the fields and footpath beyond it were far too big a job for now, when there were still places closer to home that had precedence, so he retraced his footsteps back towards the shop, conscious that the other men would be getting near the school by now. Winnie Chilver was standing at her garden gate, waiting for her neighbour to arrive, and he paused to have another word with her. 'You've got a good view of the green from here,' he said. 'I don't suppose you noticed Annie later on, did you? Or anything else out of the ordinary?'

She shook her head sadly. 'No, I didn't. I waved to her when she was leaving with her mother, but that was the last time I saw her, and I was here most of the day yesterday, on and off, watching everything that was going on.'

'You mentioned allotments—are they the ones behind the school?'

'That's right. Cyril—that's my brother—he spends most of his time up there. Why?'

'It's somewhere else that Annie might have run off to. We're trying to cover as much ground as possible. Do you think your brother might be able to round up a few volunteers to help us search there? We need as many people as we can get while the light's still on our side.'

'I'm sure he'll do what he can.' She nodded back down the lane and Penrose turned to see a battered old Ford bumping over the potholes. 'That's him now.' She walked over to meet the van, calling out to her brother through the open window as he pulled in tight to the hedge opposite their house. 'Little Annie's run off, Cyril. This gentleman here is from the police. You haven't seen her, have you?'

He shook his head, but didn't speak until the engine was off. 'No, I haven't.' He looked warily at Penrose, as if a uniform might have made him more inclined to trust what his sister was saying. 'We've been busy with the fete all day—too busy to notice who else was there, really. What's she run off for?'

'It wasn't at the fete, Cyril,' Winnie said, ignoring his question. 'It was yesterday, when all them other kids turned up. They haven't seen her since then.' There was a pause while he got out of the car, wincing with the effort as he straightened his legs, and Penrose guessed that the first-place rosettes that were pinned to his blazer had been hard earned over months of physical work. He had obviously made an effort with his clothes for the fete, but he looked uncomfortable in them and the dirt under his fingernails gave away where he would rather be. 'Well?' Winnie demanded impatiently. 'Did you see Annie yesterday? You were up the allotment for most of the day, and she was there at the school with her mother.'

'No, I didn't see her,' he said, taking a pipe out of his pocket.

'Are you sure? Think, Cyril!'

Penrose was beginning to understand why Cyril might want to spend long hours in the peace of an allotment, and he cut in before any more time was wasted. 'Your sister said that you might be able to organise some volunteers to help us look for Annie—we need people to check their sheds, that sort of thing, just to make sure she's not hiding or lying hurt somewhere. Would that be possible?'

'Course it would. We'd be glad to help, wouldn't we, Win? Let me get changed and I'll meet you up there. Several of 'em were still at the fete when I left, but the pub'll be open soon, so they'll be on their way back right enough.'

'Thank you, Mr Chilver. I appreciate it.'

He went into the house without another word, and Penrose was about to take his leave when he noticed that Winnie Chilver seemed distracted. 'Is everything all right?' he asked. 'Have you thought of something that might help?'

'I'm not sure. It's probably nothing, but . . .'

She tailed off, biting her lip, and Penrose couldn't keep the hope out of his voice. 'Anything might be useful, no matter how irrelevant or inconsequential it seems.'

'Well, it's what you said about things being out of the ordinary. It was all a bit like that yesterday, but I did notice something that seemed strange. Not at the time, mind you, but after the fete today. It was the Herrons, you see.'

She stopped, as if everything were suddenly explained, and Penrose nudged her gently to continue. 'Who are the Herrons?'

'Course, you're not from round here. Silly of me. They live at Black Bryony, on the way out of the village. Lillian and Florence, and their brother, Edmund. Lived here all their lives, they have.'

'And what was strange about them?'

'Well, I saw them yesterday in their car, driving back home from the school hall, and I could have sworn that they had *two* little girls with them.'

'Was one of them Annie?'

'That I couldn't say.'

'Then what was strange? Surely they were just collecting their evacuees?'

'Yes, except they've only got one girl. She was with them at the fete today, but Mrs Lampton said they wouldn't take her brother, or anyone else for that matter. He's had to go to Miss Tey and her friend.'

Suddenly, Penrose wished that he had had more time to ask Josephine about Noah and his sister. 'Are you sure there were *two* girls in the car?' he asked.

'Well, if you're asking me to swear to it, I couldn't go that far. But I'm fairly sure it's what I saw. The little dark-haired girl, she was on Florrie's knee in the back, and I could see her properly because she was on this side as the car went past. But I'm sure as they went down the hill that there was another little head next to her. I probably wouldn't have given it another thought, but now what you've said about Annie . . .'

'Thank you, Miss Chilver. You've been very helpful.'

He walked away, deep in thought, and almost bumped into Annie's grandmother as she hurried round the corner at the end of the lane. 'Have you brought some news?' she asked breathlessly, and Penrose could see that she didn't know whether to hope for or fear it. When he shook his head, her face settled into a kind of blank disappointment, and he could see that she had been crying. 'I'm sorry, no. I wanted to check your garden to make sure that she hadn't come back here. I thought you might be back to ask, but . . .'

'I would have been, but everyone kept stopping me, wanting to know what was happening. They've all been very kind, asking how they can help, but I don't know what to say to them.'

'Well, the search is underway now, and I'm expecting the local police to be here at any moment, so we'll be able to cover more ground. I'll be asking them to devote as much manpower to this as possible.'

'To find Annie, or to catch whoever took her?' It was a direct question, and it disarmed Penrose. 'That's what you're thinking, isn't it? I can see it all over your face. One night, yes—she might have run off and thought about teaching us a lesson—but we're heading for two now, aren't we? And I'll tell you something—she wouldn't have missed that fete for the world.'

'Don't give up hope, Mrs Gladding,' Penrose said gently. 'We'll do everything we can, I promise.'

11

As soon as news of Annie's disappearance began to spread, the fete wound down, deflating like a punctured balloon as any vestige of holiday spirit left with the search party. Stalls were packed away, or in some cases merely abandoned, as the urgency of the situation dawned on the villagers, most of whom respected the Ridleys and had a soft spot for their daughter. There was a quiet determination to help, Josephine noticed, a united effort that was different from yesterday's endeavour in one very important respect: today, it came not from a sense of duty, but from the heart, from a shared realisation that the possible outcome was too sad to contemplate. Today, it was personal.

'Can you believe Mrs Humphreys?' Hilary said, catching up with Josephine by the redundant carousel, its circle of horses now poignantly silent and still. 'She's taken me to task for cancelling the fancy dress competition because her daughter will be too old to enter next year and this is her last chance. The gall of the woman! I'm afraid my reply contained a very specific instruction.'

'Have you seen your nice Mr Davis recently?' Josephine asked, too cynical to be surprised by someone's single-mindedness. 'Archie wanted me to check with him that the buses were empty when he left here yesterday, but I haven't been able to find him.'

'I think he's gone home,' Hilary said. 'They were thinking about leaving when he was introducing me to his family, and that was a good hour ago. The wife didn't seem in a very good mood, and it was all a bit awkward.' She frowned. 'So Archie thinks that Annie might have gone off on the bus by mistake? Wouldn't we know about that by now?'

'I suppose so, but I think he's just trying to cover all possibilities. We've lost so much time already.'

Hilary made a face. 'I don't even want to think about that. Out all night with no one even realising that she's missing? And those terrible storms we've been having . . .' She shuddered, and pulled herself together. 'But the Tiptree people will know where to find Mr Davis, and they're still here. It's very thoughtful of them, actually—they've offered to help Miss Bloomfield . . .'

'Oh, that's the other thing. Archie needs the school to be opened so they can look for Annie there.'

'One step ahead of you. That's what I was about to say— Miss Bloomfield's already gone over with the keys, and she's arranging hot drinks and sandwiches for the search party. They're taking the things over now in the Tiptree van. Everyone's mucking in.'

'That is kind of them.'

'I think everyone just wants to do *something*. There must be several parents here today who are thinking there but for the grace of God, me among them.'

It didn't take much to imagine how they must feel. She and Marta had only been responsible for Noah for five minutes, and she doubted that they would ever truly know him, but already she was conscious that they thought differently about things, ever mindful of his happiness, and the fear she had experienced only that morning at waking to find him gone still left her cold. Hilary was about to say something else when the grace of God arrived in the more tangible form of Stephen. 'I've just spoken to the police,' he said, 'and they're going straight to the green. They're sending what resources they can, but they didn't sound very optimistic. We're very lucky that Penrose is here—if anything about this can be described as lucky. I don't know how long he'll be able to stay and help us, but at least he can set us on the right track.'

'And who knows, this might all be over much sooner than we think,' Hilary said, a forced brightness in her voice.

Stephen looked graver than ever, as if each strained note of optimism had a direct and damaging effect on his belief in a positive outcome, and Josephine was relieved not to have any deep faith to try and reconcile with the situation they found themselves in. 'The timing is ironic, isn't it?' he said quietly. 'Annie's disappearance coinciding with this sudden flood of youth into the village, almost as if somebody's taunting us with what we might have lost. And cruel on the Ridleys, of course. Very cruel. Sometimes, I do wonder.'

Hilary took his arm and they set out for the village, while Josephine went to find Marta. 'I'm sorry I've been so long,' she said, 'but Archie gave me some things to do and I had to talk to Elsie.'

'It's all right. I've only just got here myself. I've been with Virginia, and she's offered to look after Noah at the Hall for a while if we want to go and join the search. I thought we probably would?'

Josephine nodded. 'There must be something we can do. Archie asked me to stay and talk to people about yesterday in case something useful crops up, but everyone's gone into the village now, so we might as well join them. Let's go and fetch Noah and say goodbye to Margery.'

The number of children in Margery's care had grown in their absence, gathered together in a small group by the Gospel Oak. The children seemed transfixed by a man in a top hat and tails, who had arranged five apples on a tree stump in front of him, and was encouraging his audience to choose the one that had the shilling in it. After much coaxing, a girl in the front row pointed to the apple in the middle, and the man cut it open in front of her. There was nothing inside, so he gave the fruit to her to eat and moved on to another guess, repeating the process until only one apple remained. By now, the children were clamouring to take part, and there was a roar of excitement as the showman held it up for them all to see, then cut theatrically into it, revealing a bright silver shilling embedded deeply in its core. 'I'm not sure about the trick, but the showmanship is wonderful,' Marta said, waving to Noah, whose face was radiant with excitement as he joined the other children to get a closer look at the treasure. 'There won't be many apples left on our tree now he's seen that.'

Margery pulled herself away from the group as soon as she saw them. 'I thought a bit of sleight of hand might be in order for the children,' she said. 'While they're concentrating on this, they won't notice how worried the grown-ups suddenly look. Is there any news?'

'I'm afraid not,' Josephine said. 'We've just come to fetch Noah and drop him off at the Hall, then we're going over to the school to see if we can help.'

'Good. We'll come with you and lend a hand. Phil's got a few of his friends together to help, too. Come and meet him.'

To Josephine's surprise, Margery led them over to the magician himself. 'Marta, Josephine—this is my brother, Philip Allingham. Phil, these are the friends I told you about.'

Margery's brother removed his hat, and although his thin, chiselled face was very different from his sister's, Josephine saw the resemblance instantly in the beautiful deep brown eyes and ready smile. 'You're quite an entertainer,' Marta said admiringly. 'Where did you learn that?'

'I've been with the fairs for years now,' Phil said, 'and once a grafter, always a grafter. I can turn my hand to most things, really, but fortune telling is my strength. That, and character reading.' He turned to Josephine, peering at her intently. 'Your chin, for example—it shows you've got an inventive streak, but your eyes are suspicious. You seldom see the best in people.'

Margery shook her head, laughing. 'Don't be taken in by that for a moment,' she said. 'I told him you were a detective novelist. Inventive chins and suspicious eyes go with the territory.'

'Ah, but that doesn't mean it isn't true.' He winked at Noah, and turned to go. 'I'll get the boys rounded up and we'll see you in the village,' he called back over his shoulder. 'We'll find that little girl, don't you worry. We don't hold a grudge.'

It was an odd thing to say, but he was gone before Josephine could question it. She noticed that Noah was suddenly looking at them with a new respect, and wondered if Margery and her family could possibly get any more interesting. 'He's an extraordinary man, my little brother,' Margery said, reading her face so adeptly that Josephine guessed the talent ran in the Allingham genes. 'He left a London office at twenty-one to join the fair, and he hasn't looked back since. I was tempted to go with him for a while. He wrote a book about it a few years ago—it was quite a hit, got him some talks with the BBC, that sort of thing.'

Intrigued, Josephine listened, remembering scenes and characters in one of Margery's books that she had always believed to be solely a product of the writer's vivid imagination. 'Do you see much of him?' she asked.

'Oh, he turns up whenever he needs somewhere to store his things or his girls, then we lend him a fiver and he's on his way again.'

'And the "boys" he's gone to fetch?'

'The gypsies in the wood. That's who he came here to see. He's got contacts all over the country.' She stubbed out her cigarette and brushed down her skirt, as if she meant business. 'Right, let's go and find this little girl, shall we? You lead the way.'

When they got to the heart of the village, Josephine realised just how badly she had been hoping that someone would greet them with good news, but uniformed police officers were knocking on doors and searching the hedgerows, their faces set and earnest, and as soon as she got out of the car, she could hear Annie's name being called in all directions; to her ears, the cries sounded desperate now rather than hopeful. Inside the school hall, the scene was a faded parody of the day before, and Josephine guessed that she was not the only one who would gladly have welcomed back yesterday's exuberant chaos instead of this subdued, dejected sense of calm. They were quickly roped into making sandwiches, and whenever she saw someone who had been there for the evacuation, she asked every question she could think of, hoping to have the smallest piece of information to pass on to Archie, but the response was always the same: no one had seen Annie after she left the building, and no one had any idea where she might have gone. It was as if she had simply vanished into thin air, the unwitting subject of one of Phil's magic tricks.

'I'm going to see if I can find Archie,' she said to Marta, when there was a lull in people taking a break for refreshments. 'I'll go mad if I stay in here much longer. There must be something more useful we can do than butter bread. I hope this isn't a taste of things to come when the war starts.' She wrapped up a sandwich for Archie and took it outside. The light was beginning to fade now that the sun had gone down behind the trees, and she found him ordering cars to be brought forward onto the playground, ready to shine their headlamps onto the nearby fields as darkness fell.

'Anything to buy ourselves just a little more time,' he said, accepting the sandwich gratefully. 'Bugger the blackout.'

'Have you found anything at all?' she asked.

He shook his head. 'No, nothing—not a single trace of her. No clothes, no sightings, no illuminating witness statements, and certainly no Annie. What about you? Any luck with the bus driver?'

'No, I'm sorry. He'd already left the fete, but I've spoken to his boss and he'll be at work all day on Monday. I've got a telephone number for the factory if you want to speak to him there, but you'll have to keep trying until you catch him between deliveries.'

'Wonderful, thank you. I dare say it'll be a waste of time, but I've got to the stage where I'm crossing things off rather than hoping to strike lucky.'

'Is it that bad?'

'Honestly? I'm expecting the worst. I was hopeful to begin with, even with the loss of time, but we've covered a lot of ground now, thanks to all the people who've turned out to help, and we're still no further on than we were at four o'clock.'

'What happens next? Will you be allowed to stay and help?'

'Certainly tomorrow. After that, the Chief Constable here is very happy for me to be involved, but I might have to do it from London. I've got an unsolved murder case in a block of flats, and resources are tight, as you can imagine.' He finished the sandwich and lit a cigarette. 'While you're here, tell me about the family that's taken Noah's sister in.'

'The Herrons? What do you want to know?'

'Were you there when they collected her?'

'Yes. There was a scene, because Noah didn't want to be separated from her.'

'And they only took one child?'

'That's right. They were very firm about it.'

'You're sure?'

'What are you getting at?' Josephine listened as Archie explained what he had been told. 'Well, they certainly only took one child officially. One of them stayed to do the paperwork while the other took Betty out to the car. Their brother was waiting, apparently. I can't speak for what happened once they were outside, but there's certainly been no evidence of anything to the contrary from what I've seen since.'

'Thank you.'

Josephine was quiet for a moment, thinking the matter over. 'I suppose that's what happens now, isn't it? We all start looking at each other differently. Never in a million years would I have thought you'd be asking me about the Herrons.'

'Well, the woman was probably mistaken, and that's the other thing to expect—sightings of Annie all over the place. That's why I hate these cases so much—there's never enough time or manpower to cover everything, but you feel obliged to chase up even the unlikeliest of leads. There's always this nagging suspicion at the back of your mind that you're going to ignore the tiny bit of information that makes a difference.'

'If you do want any more background on the Herrons, Margery's known the family since their younger days.' She smiled. 'Actually, they interest me, so you must promise to share anything you find out. It might come in useful if I need more than gentle persuasion to get them to let Noah see his sister.'

'I'm sure Margery's tales are fascinating, but there's so much to do. I might drop in and see the Herrons, though, just to check. Where's the house?'

'Not far from the cottage. On the left-hand side of Marten's Lane as you're leaving the village.'

'Right. I'll see what time I have.'

'Can we help again tomorrow? What will you be doing?'

He hesitated, obviously trying to spare her feelings for a child she was fond of, but there was no gentle way of telling the truth. 'Dragging the pond at first light, and bringing the dogs in. We'll move the search over to the woods and park-land around the church—and yes, help would be gratefully received. It's a big area to cover.'

'All right, we'll be there. If I don't see you again tonight, try and get some rest.'

She kissed him and went back to the hall, where things were beginning to wind down. 'Anything positive to end the day on?' Margery asked, handing her a cup of coffee.

'No, I'm afraid not—and knowing Archie as well as I do, I feel even more pessimistic. He's always the glass-half-full type until there's a reason not to be. He has to be in his job, otherwise I don't know how he'd do it.'

'Yes, it must be very difficult for the real detectives,' Margery said with a smile. 'Much safer to stick with the ones we make up.' She paused, then lowered her voice. 'Has Noah ever been in trouble with the police? I'm sorry—that must seem like an odd question.'

'It does rather. Why do you ask?'

'Just curiosity, really. I couldn't help noticing that when you came over with Mr Penrose at the fete this afternoon, Noah went so pale that I thought he was going to pass out. Then he hid behind a tree until your friend had gone. It seemed an odd reaction, but I'm probably reading too much into it. No reason that Noah would even *know* he's a policeman, I suppose. He certainly doesn't look like one.'

'I'm not sure I can answer your question. We know so lit-tle about Noah apart from where he lives.' Josephine thought about it, tempted to dismiss the idea, but Margery was a very shrewd judge of character. 'Noah's a bit of a mystery to us at the moment,' she admitted, 'but it's still early days.'

'Yes, it is. I dare say we'll all be a lot wiser before too long.' She opened her handbag and took out a card. 'That's my telephone number. Will you let me know what happens with little Annie?'

'Yes, of course.'

'And you must come and visit us soon, but in the meantime, if I can be of any help, just ask.' Josephine thanked her, and wrote her own number down on a scrap of paper. 'Now, I'd better go and find Phil so he can take me home,' Margery said. 'Pip will be thinking that the judging was a very tough call to take this long.'

Marta and Josephine stayed for another hour to help with the clearing up, and by the time they walked back to the car on the green, darkness had engulfed the village, stamping its own note of hopelessness on what had already been a desolate day. If anything, the heat was more oppressive now than it had been earlier, and Josephine doubted that the night would pass without more thunder. Lanterns and torches moved around the village, carried by unseen hands like flickering fireflies, evoking a childlike sense of wonder that could not have been more at odds with the reality of the night. Occasionally, Annie's name echoed in the air, but it was called less often now, as if hope of finding her alive had disappeared with the light. As they drove to the Hall to fetch Noah, all Josephine could think about was Kathy Ridley, waiting at home for news, without even the distraction of doing something practical to comfort her. The hours must seem endless, she thought, surrounded by reminders of her daughter, and tormented by the same pitiless questions. Where was Annie, and what should she have done to protect her?

12

Lillian had just settled down with her book when she heard a knock at the door. She took her glasses off and listened, waiting to see if it would come again or if she had been mistaken, but there it was, polite and insistent, the worst sort of caller at any hour, let alone at ten o'clock at night. In normal times, she would have been tempted to ignore it when they were all at home; Ned was in his study, and Florrie had gone upstairs to put Betty to bed, so there was no chance of an emergency that needed her attention. But these were *not* normal times, and if Florrie was trying to get an over-excited child off to sleep, she wouldn't be pleased to have her efforts undone so soon by a thoughtless caller. With a sigh, Lillian put her unfinished, ill-fated book on the arm of the chair and went out into the hallway. If it was those women about Betty's brother again, she would have something to say about it.

'I'll get it,' she called softly to Florrie as she passed the bottom of the staircase.

Her sister's voice drifted back down in response, an indignant, stifled whisper. 'Just get rid of them, whoever it is. We don't want visitors at this hour.'

They kept their father's old walking cane in an umbrella stand by the front door, its solid silver top offering a suitably robust response to a potential intruder. She had no idea why they did it—whether they wanted them or not, visitors hardly ever came—but, like many things in their lives, it was a habit that remained unquestioned, and tonight, for the first time, she held the cane in her hand as she opened the door.

The man was a stranger, but everything she needed to know was in his hand, and she felt the first prickle of fear under her skin as she read the warrant card that he held up for her inspection. 'My name is Detective Chief Inspector Penrose,' he said, and his voice was warm and distinctive, somehow making a generality intimate to her, like the smoothest of wireless announcers; already, she distrusted it. 'I'm very sorry to disturb you at such a late hour, Miss Herron, but it is important.'

She opened the door wider, allowing the light from the hallway to reach his face. 'You're right, Chief Inspector—it *is* late. How can we help you?'

'A local child has gone missing, and we're conducting some general door-to-door enquiries to see if anyone has any information that might help.'

'And yet you know my name, so your call can't be *that* general.'

He smiled, and she didn't know whether to be gratified by the wary respect in his eyes, or to fear it. 'The child's name is Annie Ridley,' he said. 'Do you know her?'

'The girl from the shop? Mrs Gladding's granddaughter?'

'That's right.'

'I know her by sight, nothing more.' There was a silence as he waited for her to add something, and she tried to second-guess what he was expecting; curiosity seemed the most natural approach. 'When did she go missing?' she asked.

'Yesterday, from the school playground. It was while the host families were collecting their evacuees, which is why I've come to see you. I gather you were there to collect Betty Stebbing?'

'That's correct. She's upstairs—safe and well, in case you were wondering.' That was a mistake. The sarcastic inflection that she had given the words was uncalled for, and he was too intelligent not to recognise a defensiveness beneath the aggression.

'I'm glad to hear it—but no, I wasn't wondering. It's *Annie's* safety that concerns me.' He smiled again, reassuringly this time, and Lillian couldn't help thinking that he had the poise of an actor, an ability to adapt to whatever direction the conversation took—except this actor wrote his own script, and that made him dangerous. 'I understand that there was a certain amount of confusion over how many evacuees you were going to take in,' he said.

'Not really. Mrs Lampton may have been confused, but we were certainly not. We took the single girl that we had agreed to take, nothing more, nothing less. Her brother was never our responsibility.'

'Quite. And you brought Betty back here in your car?'

'Yes, of course.'

'Straight here? You didn't call in anywhere, or give any of the other children a lift home?'

'No, we had quite enough on our hands with one.'

'Did you see Annie while you were at the school?'

She hesitated, sure that she hadn't, but using the opportunity to consider what he might be trying to get at. 'No, I can't say I remember seeing her, but that doesn't mean she wasn't there. There were lots of children milling around, and I didn't really pay much attention.'

'Perhaps your sister might remember more clearly?'

'I doubt it—she left the hall before I did—but I'll ask her when she's finished with Betty. The child still hasn't settled properly, and Florence is having to spend a lot of time with her.'

'Might I have a word with your brother, Miss Herron? I understand that he was outside in the car, waiting for you, and there's a chance that he might have seen something that could help us.'

Lillian tightened her grip on the handle of the cane, surprised to find that she suddenly required it for support. 'You've obviously been doing a lot of understanding, Chief Inspector, but I'm afraid that's out of the question at this time of night. My brother's health is unreliable, and he needs his sleep. You're very welcome to come back tomorrow and speak to him, but I would consider it a courtesy if you could telephone first.'

'Yes, of course. Once again, I'm sorry to have disturbed you, but just to be clear, you didn't have any other child with you in the car yesterday, no matter how fleetingly?'

'Absolutely not.'

'Thank you. Goodnight, Miss Herron. I'll telephone you in the morning.'

She watched him go, a lantern clanking at his side, casting a bouncing light onto the path in front of him. Florence came downstairs, clutching the doll that she had given to Betty to play with; Lillian found the image disconcerting, an untimely reminder of the child her sister had been—prone to hysterics and always on the edge of a tantrum. 'Who was it?' Florrie demanded accusingly, as if the visit had been entirely Lillian's doing. 'What did he want?'

'It was the police. A child has gone missing.'

The words echoed around the hallway, spilling out over the carpet and filling the room like a physical, suffocating presence. Lillian clutched at the banister to steady herself, disorientated by the way in which the phrase contracted time, confusing then and now. Suddenly, she was a child again, and it took Florrie's absurdly oblivious question to bring her back to the present. 'What's that got to do with us?'

'I don't know, but reading between the lines, someone seems to have told the police that we had another child with us in the car yesterday.'

'And we all know who. Why would she do that?'

'I don't know, Florrie, but he came here specifically to ask us, and he's coming back tomorrow to speak to Ned.'

'Well, that sounds much more sensible. I don't know what people are thinking of, turning up unannounced at all hours of the night. If he comes in the morning, I'll make some of those macaroons that Edmund likes so much.'

Where was Ned yesterday lunchtime? Why did he need to go out on his own in the car? Why was he so late picking us up? For a moment, Lillian really believed that she had spoken her suspicions aloud, so frustrated was she by her sister's naivety. She looked at Florrie, straightening the doll's clothes and caressing her hair, and longed to shake her into some sort of reality, but she also knew the importance of keeping the peace. 'That would be lovely, dear,' she said, too tired to do anything else. 'I'm sure the policeman would appreciate it.'

13

It was late when they got back to the cottage, and Marta and Josephine were dead on their feet. They had managed to rouse Noah from a deep sleep at the Hall for long enough to get him into the car and home to his own bed, but even the fresh night air couldn't wake him sufficiently to ask too many questions, and they were grateful for the peace. He crawled willingly between the sheets, exhausted from the restlessness of the night before and the excitement of the day. Marta stayed to tuck him in while Josephine went next door to pour them both a drink. She stoked up the range, more for comfort than for warmth, and lit all the lamps downstairs, keen to dispel the desolate feeling that often occurs when tiredness collides with a lack of hope. Instantly, as the soft yellow light fell on everything that was familiar and precious, the night seemed less bleak, and she was glad to pull the comforts of the room around her.

She turned the wireless on low, wondering what had happened in the world while their minds were on the crisis closer to home. The BBC hadn't wasted any time in abandoning its advertised schedules, making a nonsense of the current *Radio Times*, and she was greeted by the sort of undemanding, familiar music that might be easily interrupted in the event of a news announcement. It was harmless enough at this time of night, but she couldn't help thinking that the war would barely have begun before someone told Sandy MacPherson what to do with his organ.

Marta came out of the study and closed the door softly behind her. 'He's dead to the world,' she said. 'It's nice to see him like that. He looks so young.'

'Good. I hate to think of someone his age having to be the man of the house already. There's plenty of time for that.' She handed Marta her wine and stood the rest of the bottle on the range to warm. 'Is he all right after what's happened, do you think? He seemed to take it in his stride, but I never really know what's going on in his head, and today can't have been easy, especially after all the disruption of leaving home. God forbid, but it could have been his sister who went missing.'

'Don't think that hasn't occurred to him. He woke up long enough to ask me if he could help with the search tomorrow because he'd want people to look for Betty if she got lost.'

'And what did you say?'

'That he can, as long as he promises to stay close to us.' Marta smiled. 'Apart from anything else, I couldn't think what we might do with him if I said no—and I think it will be good for him. It'll make him feel part of the village.'

'What a strange way to settle in.' She sipped her drink thoughtfully. 'Margery asked me something about Noah today. It seemed odd at the time, but it makes more sense in hindsight.' She told Marta about the reaction to Archie that Margery had observed. 'Thinking about it, he didn't want to meet him earlier in the day either, did he?'

Marta seemed sceptical. 'No, but look how much we're asking of him—of all those kids, actually. What must it feel like to come here from London? There's not one tiny familiar thing about it—a completely different way of life, different houses, different people with strange accents, even different air to breathe. I'm not surprised that Noah doesn't want to meet one more person than he has to.'

153

'Yes, that's true. I'm probably just feeling guilty that *I* didn't notice how upset Noah seemed. I was too absorbed in what had happened to Annie.'

'Well, it's hardly been a normal day. I think we can forgive ourselves for being distracted, and we'll make it up to Noah. He's a good kid, and I'm sure we'll find out more about him when he starts to trust us. I hope we get to meet his mother one day.' She clapped her hand to her forehead. 'Fuck, we forgot to put his letter in the post. I feel terrible now. She'll be waiting by the letterbox every day for some news, and she won't even know where he is.' Marta got up to fetch the envelope from her bag. 'Now she won't hear anything until Tuesday.'

Strange, Josephine thought, that they should so readily be creating a picture for themselves of a family they didn't know at all, based on some carefully polished shoes and Noah's obvious affection for his mother. She hoped their life at home was as secure and loving as the note that she had found with his belongings suggested. 'We'll have to post it in the morning, on our way to the Hall,' she said. 'Leave it by the door so we don't forget again. Did you find out anything more about him this morning, when you were getting him ready? I haven't had a chance to ask you.'

'Nothing much, really. He mentioned a couple of friends from school that he misses—their parents have kept them in London, apparently, and he wishes he'd been able to stay, too. He said he was worried about what might happen to his mum now that she was on her own.'

'Did he mention his father at all? I know he said he was gone—do you think he meant called up?'

Marta shrugged. 'I don't know and I didn't like to ask too many questions, not on his first day.' She drained her glass and refilled it. 'I wish we hadn't forgotten that bloody letter, though.'

'Perhaps the Herrons will mention him. I bet they posted theirs.'

'Yes, I suppose they might have done, if only to complain about him being a nuisance. Still, at least that would let her know that he's arrived safely somewhere.'

'I wonder if Archie went to see them,' Josephine said. 'They must have made a very sharp exit from the fete. I didn't see them for dust once the stalls had packed up, and I was hoping to get a better look at the fossil-collecting brother.'

'We'll have to call on them with Noah, and that reminds me—I've left their cakes in the car, with those things that Hilary sent for Noah.'

'All that can wait until the morning.'

'Are you hungry? I could make us an omelette or something.'

Josephine shook her head. 'I don't really want anything. I keep thinking about Annie. The later it gets, the less likely it seems that she'll be found safe and well. This is the second night now.'

'Do you think someone's taken her? It's hard to believe that she would stay away deliberately for as long as this. I remember having tantrums with my parents when I was little, and I ran away a couple of times, but I could never hold my nerve for more than an hour or so.'

'And even harder to believe that she's lost. Annie knows this village like the back of her hand. She treats every nook and cranny of it like a playground, and people see her in the shop all the time. If she'd been found locally, they'd know exactly where to take her.' She sighed, depressed by the short-ening odds on bad news.

'Come here,' Marta said, making more room on the sofa, and then, as Josephine hesitated: 'It's all right. Noah's sound asleep, and that bed from the vicarage creaks so loudly that we'd hear a flea moving on it. We'll know if he gets up.' Happy to be convinced, Josephine curled up in Marta's arms, relieved not to be on her own with the sadness, at least for a few more days. The midnight news began, and they listened to Chamberlain's latest appeal to German reason, and what felt like an equally futile attempt to find new hope in peace moves from Mussolini. 'I wish they'd just get on with it now we've come this far,' Marta said. 'It's agony, all this waiting around for something to happen. Don't they realise that the rest of the country has already fired the starting gun? It's ridiculous that we're all getting on with it while the politicians are holding out for the drop of a handkerchief.'

It seemed that the cabinet agreed with her, at least. The newsreader reported vicious arguments in parliament, with threats of a sit-down strike until war was declared, and Josephine was glad when the broadcast came to a close. Marta reached across to switch the wireless off, and they sat together in the quiet of the room, enjoying the gentle crackle of the fire and the fragile illusion that nothing outside could touch them. 'This might be our last night of peace,' Josephine said softly. 'Why does it feel like anything but?'

They were both drifting off to sleep when the telephone rang, shrill and intrusive in the silence. Josephine scrambled to answer it before the noise could wake Noah. 'Perhaps there's some news,' she said. 'Please God, let it be good for a change.' She picked up the receiver, hoping to hear Archie's voice, but all that greeted her was a terrible crackling on the line. 'Hello? Who is this? I'm sorry, I can't hear you. Can you speak up?' When the voice came again, it was distant and vaguely familiar. 'Yes, of course,' Josephine said, and Marta looked curiously at her, detecting the strained politeness in her voice. 'Just one moment. I'll get her for you. It's for you,' she said, passing the receiver over. 'Alfred Hitchcock.'

'At this time of night?'

'I suppose it's the middle of the afternoon in Hollywood.'

The presence of the film director—albeit at a distance of thousands of miles—made the night seem more surreal than ever, and Josephine listened carefully, trying to piece together the whole conversation from Marta's rather stilted side of it. 'Did he really say that?' Marta asked. 'So what does he want instead?' The question triggered a lengthy monologue, and when Marta finally spoke again, her tone hovered between frustration and weary resignation. 'Yes, I understand. We don't really have any choice, do we?' There was another long pause, and then the conversation was brought to a close. 'Yes, yes of course. I'll see you both then.'

She put the receiver down. 'What was that all about?' Josephine asked.

'Selznick's rejected the treatment for the film,' Marta said, her head in her hands. 'He said that he's bought *Rebecca*, and he intends to make *Rebecca*, just as Daphne du Maurier wrote it. Hitch is furious.'

'I can imagine, but you've said all along that the book was in danger of being lost.' She smiled. 'I didn't hear you say "I told you so", though. Pity. I'd like to have witnessed that.'

'Believe me, he didn't need any more provocation. Poor Alma—she must be having a terrible time trying to soothe his ego through this one. From what he said, Selznick didn't mince his words. He called Hitch's version vulgar and distorted.'

'Is that fair?'

'Probably. He's certainly swamped a lot of its tension with old-fashioned movie scenes, which is strange, really. The book might almost have been tailor-made for him. Anyway, Selznick's sent him back to the drawing board, so it's war between those two already. If this is what it's going to be like, I wish I'd never taken the job.'

'But this will be a good thing in the long run, surely? I know it means extra work for you now, but it sounds as if you'll end up with a better film, and it might do Hitch-cock good to work for someone who stands up to him.' Two years on, Josephine was still smarting from the changes that the director had made to her own novel in bringing it to the screen, and she spoke with feeling. 'I know I'm biased, but I'm just pleased for Daphne du Maurier. After what he did to *Jamaica Inn* . . .'

'Josephine, that's not everything. I really don't know how to tell you this, but I've got to leave earlier than planned.'

'What?' Josephine's heart sank and she looked warily at Marta, a note of challenge in her voice. 'How much earlier?'

'They want me to fly on Thursday instead of Sunday.'

'Well, it could be worse, I suppose.' Josephine was disappointed, but the expression on Marta's face had suggested a more imminent departure, and the prospect of a few more days together came as a relief. 'At least we'll be able to get Noah settled.'

'But there are some things that Hitch wants me to do in London first. That will take a couple of days, then I'll go on to Southampton for the flight. I don't have everything I need here, so I've got to fit in a trip to Cambridge as well. I'll have to leave tomorrow. I'm so sorry.'

Josephine stared at her in disbelief. 'You're planning to leave tomorrow and we've been sitting here discussing the finer points of a bloody film adaptation?' In her anger, she had raised her voice, and she knew it would be impossible to say all she had to say calmly. 'Come outside,' she whispered. 'We can't have this conversation with Noah in the next room.'

She led the way out to the garden and Marta followed, infuriating Josephine still more by stopping on the way to find her cigarettes. The bench by the climbing rose was usually where they sat for some peace at the end of the day; tonight, in the darkness, her mood was as thunderous as the air, and she turned on Marta as soon as she sat down. 'Have you forgotten what we did yesterday? We've got a young boy asleep in there and we promised him a home until Hilary can get him settled. He's troubled and he's lonely and he's angry, and I can't believe you're thinking of leaving all that to me.'

'I know it's not ideal, and I know you did it for me—'

'You're absolutely right it's not ideal. We'd *never* have taken Noah if we'd known you wouldn't be here to see it through. Didn't it occur to you to say no to Hitchcock?'

'I can't say no, Josephine. This is a crisis.'

'No, Marta—an impending war and a missing child, *that's* a crisis. How *dare* you call what's going on between two middle-aged men with more money than sense a war, even as a joke.'

'All right, that was a poor choice of words, but you know what I mean.'

'I'm not sure I do.' Josephine took a breath, knowing that if she were to change Marta's mind and avoid the sudden departure that frightened her so much, reason would get her further than resentment. 'Can't you call them back and explain what's happened?' she asked. 'It's all very well carrying on as normal if you're thousands of miles away, where reality can't touch you, but we're at war here, or as good as, and suddenly everybody's got responsibilities that they weren't expecting. Surely even the Hitchcocks would understand that?'

'There is another way round it,' Marta suggested tentatively. 'You could come with me—to London, at least. We could spend some time together there, perhaps even take Noah to see his mother and let her know he's all right.'

'And take him straight back to the place he's just been sent away from? Don't be so ridiculous. What would that do to his head?' Josephine sighed, resigned now to the inevitability of Marta's change of plan. 'Anyway, this village has got its own grief at the moment, and I can't just walk away from it if there's the slightest chance that I can help. I thought we both felt that way. What happened to being rooted here? Did you mean *anything* you said yesterday?'

'Of course I did. A few extra days doesn't change any of that.'

There was no conviction in her tone, and Josephine could see how guilty Marta felt. Now that the shock of Hitchcock's summons had subsided a little, she understood the dilemma and sympathised, even if the responsibilities she was being left with terrified her—but the row had also taught her something about her own motivations. 'You're right,' she said. 'I did do this for you, because I knew how important it was to you, but I did it for Noah, too. He needs someone on his side, and if you have to go, he'll just have to make do with me.'

At least Marta knew better than to promise to make it up to her. 'I've got to go and pack,' she said, standing up with a sigh.

'Of course you have.'

'Are you coming inside? It feels like rain.'

'No, not yet. I'm too angry.'

Josephine watched Marta as she followed the path back to the cottage, and saw the fleeting sliver of light as the door opened and then closed again. She waited for a lamp to appear in the room upstairs, feeling more lonely now than she ever had before Marta came into her life. In her head, she was already composing the letters she would write while her lover was away, trying to do justice to everything that Marta meant to her, but the simple fact was that she loved her, and would miss her desperately, and there was no point in complicating that with clever words. Somewhere in the woods behind the cottage, she heard the cry of a fox, deceptively close in the darkness, and as Marta had predicted, the first drops of rain began to fall. She thought of Annie, dreading the search tomorrow and afraid of what they might find, but reminded, too, that life was short and unpredictable. Reluctant now to waste more time, Josephine got up and went inside to make her peace with Marta. There would be plenty of nights to spend on her own, but she would be foolish to let this be one of them.

14

Cyril sheltered in his shed for a while, until it became obvious that the rain wasn't going to stop any time soon. He listened as it pounded on the roof, thinking—as he always did—that there were few things more comforting than the sound of rain when you were warm and dry. It took him straight back to being a kid, when he and Winnie had hidden in the attic, waiting for the drink to wear off and their father to forget why he had ever wanted to hurt them. Staying out of sight was something they'd learnt early.

Tonight, he was especially glad of the storm. It cleansed the earth and took the tension from the air, even if it couldn't begin to wash away the sorrows of the day. With a heavy heart, he thought back to the Ridley girl's face in the school hall; she had looked so sad and mistrustful, as if the weight of the world were on those tiny shoulders, and he had tried to cheer her up. He hadn't told Winnie about stopping to play with Annie while he was dropping off the jumble; she had caught him off guard this afternoon, and to admit to the lie now would make it worse; Win would only worry, and—with the police around—it didn't do to confuse things. Still thinking about Annie, he took an old oilskin off the hook by the door and put it on, then locked the shed and headed home. Several men were still out and about, drifting off gradually to their own firesides, to their wives and children, and Cyril imagined that a few of the village kids would get a tighter hug tonight. There but for the grace. He was a great believer in fate.

His boots were heavy with mud, and he was bone tired. The excitement of the last couple of days had given him more energy than he'd had in years, but the search had taken the last of it, and now it was as much as he could do to put one foot in front of the other. By the time he had crossed the green, the bottoms of his trousers were soaking wet and rain trickled down the back of his neck, making him shiver. He checked his van, then let himself quietly into the cottage, hoping that Winnie wouldn't be awake to plague him with questions about the search or grumble about the water on the carpet, but the parlour was dark and mercifully peaceful, and she had obviously stoked up the fire for him before going to bed. She could be thoughtful like that, in spite of everything, and she had always been good to him. They'd had their ups and downs over the years, but he didn't know what he'd do without her.

Quietly, he pulled one of the dining chairs closer to the warmth of the stove and sat down to untie his boots. 'Was it you, Cyril?' He jumped up and turned round to find Winnie sitting in her usual chair in the corner of the room. She leant forward and lit the lamp, and he saw her face framed in a pool of yellow light. 'Was it you who took little Annie? Tell me the truth, or I swear to God I'll go to the police myself.'

Cyril sat down again and waited for his heart to stop pounding. He had never been able to lie to his sister. 'No, Win,' he said, when he trusted his voice to be strong enough. 'Of course it wasn't me.'

15

It had been the longest night of her life, of that there was no doubt, but at last the sky was beginning to change colour. Kathy Ridley got up from her kitchen table and poured away another cup of tea, trying to find some hope in the start of a new day. In truth, she had no idea what to feel: the butterflies and nausea that had been with her since that terrible moment of realisation yesterday afternoon were stronger than ever on an empty stomach, but the emotions that went with them had changed as time went on: her anger at the thought that Annie might have run away was quickly replaced by fear of an accident, and now the idea of someone having hurt her had taken root, bewildering and all-consuming in its horror. Common to them all, though, and hardest to bear, was the certainty that she had failed to protect what she loved most in all the world.

As the light strengthened, bringing more definition to the familiar trees and outbuildings that surrounded the farmhouse, she moved quietly from room to room, blowing out the candles that she had lit in every window to guide Annie home, and vowing to herself that she would light them every night until her daughter came back to her. The search had been called off just after midnight, when the rain set in, but Tom had refused to stop looking, returning home briefly to change his wet clothes, then going straight back out to the fields around the school. He had hardly spoken a word to her, except to report that there was no news, and she feared what this might do to them, but there was no room in her troubled mind at the moment for anyone but Annie. She had spent the long hours of waiting in a painful contemplation of every possibility, rewriting her daughter's absence with varying degrees of plausibility: perhaps she had been taken from the road by a passing car, or run over and left in a ditch; perhaps she *had* run away, and had got herself lost in the woods at night; perhaps she had been struck by lightning or trapped under a fallen tree, and was lying somewhere waiting to be found, thinking that they had forgotten her. Like every child who was loved unquestioningly from the moment she was born, Annie had always taken it for granted that her parents could do anything; whatever trouble she was in, she wouldn't understand why Mummy hadn't come to rescue her.

There was a noise in the yard outside and Kathy rushed to the back door and tore it open, longing to find Tom there with their daughter in his arms. A police car was parked outside the barn, and her heart raced again as she waited to see if it had brought Annie home, but there was no little girl in the back seat, and when the policemen got out, their expressions were fixed and unreadable. 'Mrs Ridley?' one of them asked, and she nodded. 'There's no news, I'm afraid,' he said, anticipating her obvious question. 'We're here to search the farm and the outbuildings.'

'I did that yesterday, when I got back,' she said. 'Annie loved playing hide and seek, you see, so I tried all the usual places. We don't let her go in some of the barns, obviously, 'cause there's stuff in there that she might hurt herself on, but I looked everywhere yesterday, just in case.' She hesitated, aware that the policeman had begun to look at her with something like pity in his eyes. 'It gave me something to do while I was waiting for her to come home,' she added, as defiantly as she could manage, 'so you don't have to waste your time here.

There must be other places in the village that you haven't tried yet.'

'There are, and we won't leave anything to chance, I promise. All the same, we'd like to look again here if you don't mind, just to be sure.' Despite the phrasing, it was a statement of fact, not a request for permission, and Kathy nodded, helpless to do anything else. She watched as another car turned into the yard, and then another, and suddenly the police seemed to be everywhere, turning out the sheds and searching behind rusted old farming equipment, scouring the thickets and ditches that bordered their home. Their thoroughness should have been reassuring, but she took no comfort from it; inexplicably, she found it threatening, something that she couldn't bear to witness, so she went back inside, concerned that the evacuees would be awake by now and frightened by what was happening in this strange, new world they had been brought to.

It was wrong of her to resent them, but there was only one child that she should be worrying about, one child that she wanted to see, and she was glad to find the others still asleep. Perhaps her mother was right after all; they would be better off with someone else. Deep down, she blamed them for Annie's disappearance, and it would only be a matter of time before her resentment started to show; if they had never arrived in the village, her daughter would be safely tucked up in bed. She closed the door quietly on them and walked along the landing to her own room, where the upstairs windows gave her a better view of what was going on outside. She watched as four policemen moved methodically down the rows of cherry trees that stretched as far as the eye could see; in the other direction, nearer the heart of the village, men were walking in a line across a field, spaced carefully apart like beaters at a pheasant shoot, and the sight was so bizarre that she had to close her eyes and look again before she could believe that it was real. How could all these people be searching ditches and woods and farmland for her little girl? And why wasn't she out there with them? It was kind of everyone to want to help, and she was grateful to them, but there was no way that she was staying at home today.

She couldn't go into Annie's room, not yet. Other than a cursory glance to make sure that Annie wasn't hiding there, she had spent the night avoiding it, convincing herself that if she left it untouched, her daughter would be back to reclaim it and they could pick up where they had left off, as if nothing untoward had happened. She was glad that she had put the others all in together, that a desire to soothe Annie's ruffled feathers had stopped her from letting a stranger sleep in her daughter's bed, but now she wondered if there hadn't been something more prophetic in the decision, some sort of mother's intuition that the room must be left untouched, just in case it was all she had left.

The thought frightened her and she tried to shake it off, but it was still there, at her shoulder, as she went downstairs to get breakfast ready for the children. She glanced up as she was filling the kettle and saw Tom walking slowly across the yard to the house. It was obvious from the slope of his shoulders that he hadn't found his little girl; he looked defeated and broken, years older than when he had left for the fete. She waited for him to come in, not trusting herself to say or do the right thing in front of the strangers outside, worried that her husband still blamed her for the confusion of the day before. He closed the door behind him, but still he didn't speak, and she looked anxiously at his ashen face. 'What is it, Tom?' she asked, torn between wanting and dreading his answer. 'Say something, please. You're frightening me now.'

'They're dragging the pond.'

Four words, just four words, but Kathy felt the ground shift beneath her feet. She opened her mouth to respond, but her voice and mind let her down. In the silence, Tom walked past her and up the stairs; she let him go, rooted to the spot for what might have been minutes or hours. Eventually, she was brought to her senses by a sound that was completely new to her—mournful and insistent and not entirely of this world, worse even than the most tormented cries of an animal in pain. She found Tom in Annie's bedroom, punching her pillow and sobbing with a violence of which she would never have thought him capable. She went to him and he clung to her, uttering sounds that made no sense, uniting them with the raw, terrible energy that racked his body and now hers. This must be what it means to break down, she thought, and it shook her to the core, not just because she had never seen him like this, but because—until now—she had believed with every fibre of her being that they would find their daughter alive.

'She did know we loved her, didn't she?' he said as she held him, and Kathy no longer had the strength or the conviction to argue with the finality of the words.

'Of course she did, love,' she said. 'Of course she did.'

Noah's presence on Sunday morning made Marta's departure an oddly formal one, and Josephine couldn't decide whether that was a blessing or a curse. As she stood at the cottage gate, watching the car disappear up the grass track to the road, it was hard to believe that Marta was on her way to another continent rather than simply popping out for milk.

Her absence, and the thought of another long search for Annie, made the day a dismal prospect, but she tried to make the best of it for Noah's sake. They opened the suitcase that Hilary had packed for him, and Josephine let him choose the clothes that he wanted to wear, then sent him next door to change while she cleared away the breakfast things. A dispirited BBC announcer had picked up where she left him the night before. The news was a doom-laden countdown to Chamberlain's eleven o'clock ultimatum; with only three hours to go, the outcome seemed inevitable, and Josephine switched the wireless off and took a cup of tea out to the sun.

She wandered round the garden, thinking about Marta as she absentmindedly deadheaded the flowers that her lover had planted, then rescued the flourishing runner bean plants that had taken a battering during last night's storm. The garden was Marta's sanctuary, and her gift to Josephine. After three years of hard work, nurturing and shaping the wilderness that they had inherited, there wasn't an inch of it that didn't carry its own character and beauty, and Josephine couldn't think of anything that brought her more joy. Every year, she looked forward to the surprises of a new season: the ancient varieties of snowdrop that Marta had collected, subtly different in ways that Josephine had never noticed; the daffodils and bluebells that ushered in spring, a natural extension of the fields and woodland that surrounded the cottage; the explosion of peonies, lupins and roses that scented their summers, the fiery red and yellow dahlias that would continue long into the autumn. The garden had always been nothing short of a miracle to Josephine, a celebration of their love; now, it was more important than ever, keeping Marta close as the long weeks of separation stretched out in front of her.

Noah seemed to be taking his time, so she went inside to see what he was up to. 'How are the new clothes?' she called, with a cursory knock on the study door. She had obviously surprised him, because he hurriedly threw the blanket across the bed and stood staring at her, as if there were something he didn't want her to see. 'Is everything all right?' she asked. He nodded, looking more guilty than ever. 'What's in the bed, Noah?'

'Nothing.' The lump beneath the sheets gave the lie to his answer, and she looked at him, giving him the chance to change his mind. 'It's just my pyjamas,' he said eventually.

'All right, but don't leave them there. Give them to me and I'll fold them up for you.'

Reluctantly, he pulled back the sheets and Josephine realised instantly what was wrong. Noah's pyjama trousers were soaking wet, and a smell of urine rose up from the bed. 'I'm sorry,' he said. 'I didn't mean to do it.'

He obviously thought she was going to be angry with him. 'Of course you didn't,' she said, adopting a bright and breezy tone to show that she meant it, 'and it really doesn't matter. It's just an accident. We can soon clean it up. Come here.' He did as he was told and she gave him a hug. 'If it happens again, you must promise to tell me and we'll sort it out together. Is that a deal?' Noah nodded. 'Good. We'll get these sheets in the wash, but first let me look at you.' She held him at arm's length and nodded approvingly at his choice of clothes for the day—a long-sleeve, button-down shirt in a bright shade of blue, and some navy shorts. 'You look very smart,' she said, 'but we'll have to do something about those sleeves. They're far too long for you.' She tried rolling them up, but there was too much material. 'I'll have to cut them off and hem them. Let me get my sewing basket. I won't be a minute.' She went next door and found some pins and a pair of scissors. 'It won't be up to your mother's standards, I'm afraid, but I'll do my best. Come here so I can measure them.' Noah hesitated, staring at the scissors in her hand. 'It's all right—I'm not that bad, I promise.' She took a step towards him, but stopped instantly when Noah let out a piercing scream and threw himself onto the bed, scrabbling into the corner to get as far away from her as possible. 'Noah, what on earth's the matter?'

'Get away from me!'

'All right, all right—but I'm not going to hurt you.' Josephine stood back and put the scissors down on her desk, shocked by the expression of pure fear on the boy's face. She waited while he calmed down, then sat on the edge of the bed, careful not to get too close. 'Why are you so frightened?' she asked gently, and then, when there was no answer: 'Listen, I have no idea what's wrong, Noah, but I swear to you that no harm will come to you while you're here. You're safe with me, and I know it's asking a lot when you've only just got here, but you have to trust me.' She held out her hand as if she were coaxing a frightened animal, trying to analyse the expression on Noah's face; as well as his obvious distress, she could detect a desperate wish to believe her, and in the end, the latter won out. He allowed himself to be drawn towards her and she held him tight, resisting the temptation to ask the myriad questions that were running through her head. 'You can tell me anything,' she said, hoping that she was up to dealing with whatever that might be, 'but I'm not going to force you into it. I know we don't know each other very well yet, and this is all so strange for you, but I'm here if you need me. Will you remember that?' He nodded, and didn't pull away. 'Now— shall we find another shirt for you to wear, or will you let me deal with this one?'

'I want this one.'

'All right. Take it off and I'll have a guess at the sleeves.' Josephine busied herself with collecting the soiled sheets, occasionally casting surreptitious glances at Noah as he changed his shirt. The only explanation that she could think of for his reaction was that someone had hurt him, but there were no bruises or scars on his body to suggest the abuse that she had feared. Still trying to make sense of what had happened, she took the shirt next door to deal with and put the scissors firmly out of sight, then found some clean sheets and put the others in the wash, ready for the following day. 'Try this for size,' she said, and was pleased to see that she'd guessed well. 'Perfect, and I've been thinking—as Marta's had to go away for a bit, how would you like to move upstairs and have your own room? We could fill it with some of the books and toys that Mrs Lampton sent, and the bed's a lot more comfortable. What do you say?'

She was touched by his enthusiasm, and as they went upstairs and set about changing the room that had never been Marta's into something more suitable for Noah, he seemed to shake off whatever dark associations had ambushed him downstairs. By the time they were ready to walk into the village, he was as happy as Josephine had seen him, and she questioned for a moment the wisdom of subjecting him to the sadness of Annie's search when he obviously had troubles of his own, but he seemed as eager to take part as Marta had said he was, so she decided to play it by ear.

The green was quiet when they got there, with the search today focused elsewhere. Josephine posted the note to Noah's mother in the letterbox by the shop, then knocked at Elsie's back door, keen to hear the latest news and offer her support. There was no answer, and she guessed that Elsie was either with her daughter or out with one of the search parties, so she left her a note and moved on. As she came back round the house, she found Winnie Chilver standing at her front gate, and passed the time of day with her. 'And how are you, young man?' Winnie asked, when they had exchanged the usual remarks about the sadness of Annie's disappearance.

'All right, thank you.'

'And your sister? How is she getting on.'

'Okay, I think.'

'Are you sure?'

'Betty's fine, Miss Chilver,' Josephine reiterated. 'Why shouldn't she be?'

'Oh, no reason, but I know who I'd rather be staying with in their position.' She smiled, and ruffled Noah's hair. 'You got the long straw. See you make the most of it, and keep an eye out for your sister.'

Irritated, Josephine nodded to her and led Noah away before he took on yet more worries. Coming so soon after what Archie had said to her the night before, Winnie Chilver's words intrigued her, and she wondered what the issue was between her and the Herrons; she must remember to mention the brief conversation to Archie when she saw him during the search.

As it turned out, they met sooner than she had anticipated. She walked down Polstead Hill, telling Noah stories about the village as they went, and stopped short when she got to the tiny bridge at the bottom of the road. She had forgotten what Archie had told her, but clearly the dragging of the village pond was already underway, and it was a sombre sight. There was a rowing boat in the middle of the water, moving slowly from one bank to the other, and every now and again it stopped to haul up a large, three-pronged grappling hook, which was examined carefully by the two men on board and then thrown back in.

'What are they doing?' Noah asked.

'Looking for something that might help us find Annie,' Josephine said after a brief pause, satisfied that it wasn't exactly a lie.

As they watched, the boat stopped again, and she waited with bated breath while the men strained every sinew to raise the hook to the surface; to her relief, whatever came with it was quickly dismissed, and the menacing object was cast once again into the water. It took a long time for the rope to stop uncoiling, and Josephine wasn't surprised; the pond—which looked so harmless on a normal day—was deceptively deep, and she knew that it had claimed its fair share of victims, including Thomas Corder, brother of the village's famous murderer, who had fallen through the ice on his birthday back in the early 1800s. A crowd was gathered on the northern side of the pool, away from where the police had stationed themselves, and Josephine was struck by the expectant silence of the scene; it was as if the village were holding a collective breath, and it gave the gentle sound of the oars making contact with the water an uncharacteristically ominous quality. 'Come on,' she said to Noah, wanting to move him on before the boat stopped again. 'We mustn't get in the way, and it's time we were at the Hall for the search.'

He looked as if he would have liked to stay, but followed her without an argument. They got to the junction, and just as she was debating whether or not to take the longer route, which didn't skirt the pond, she heard Archie's voice calling her name. He broke off from his colleagues and ran over to them, and Josephine looked at Noah, curious to see how he would react after Margery's observations. He seemed apprehensive, but there were no convenient trees to hide behind, so he contented himself with sticking close to her side. 'I'm glad I've seen you,' Archie said. 'Can I have a word?'

'Of course, but first you've got to meet Noah. I wanted to introduce you at the fete yesterday, but we lost our chance with everything else that was going on.' Josephine knew how single-minded Archie was when he was working, and she hoped that by drawing his attention to Noah, she might encourage him to temper anything that he was about to share with her to suit the ears of a ten-year-old.

'Hello, Noah. Are you settling in all right?'

Noah nodded, but wouldn't meet Archie's eye. 'He's a bit shy,' Josephine explained, 'but we've got his room set up this morning, and now we're off to the Hall to see what we can do to help. You are still searching up there today?'

'Yes, in a while. Is Marta not with you?'

'Marta's had to go,' she said. 'Blame Alfred Hitchcock, but it's a long story and not something you've got time for now. What did you want to talk to me about?'

Archie looked awkwardly at Noah. 'Do you see those flowers?' Josephine asked, pointing to an obliging patch of dandelions and poppies in the hedgerow. 'Go and pick some for me while I talk to Archie, and we can give them to Mrs Lampton as a thank you for your clothes.' Noah ran off, happy to be gone, and she turned back to Archie. 'What's happened?' she asked.

'We've found something,' he said, and Josephine's heart sank. 'Mrs Gladding said that Annie had a doll with her, one that she'd made for her birthday.'

'That's right. A rag doll.'

'Did you see it?'

'Yes. Annie showed it to me in the shop. Is that what you've found?'

'We've found *a* doll. It was in the pond. The boys brought it up just now, and I was about to take it to the Ridleys to see if they can identify it.'

'But you want me to look at it now?'

'Would you? I'd like to be forewarned, but I'll understand if you'd rather not.'

'Of course I'd rather not, but I'll do it if it helps. If it *is* Annie's . . .' She tailed off, unable to bring herself to finish the sentence.

'It's not conclusive, obviously, but the possibilities that it raises are concerning. Thank you, Josephine. I'll only be a minute.'

He went back to the edge of the pond and returned with a small cardboard box. 'All right?' he asked, and she nodded.

The doll was smaller than she remembered, but its yellow dress—similar to the one that Annie had been wearing—was familiar. Josephine had assumed that she would be able to tell one way or the other as soon as Archie lifted the lid, but now her memory played tricks on her and she hesitated, knowing how important it was that she answered truthfully. 'I'm not sure,' she said, sensing Archie's impatience with her. 'I remembered Annie's doll as having lighter hair, but this one's been in the water, so that might explain why it looks darker.' She sighed, frustrated with herself. 'I'm sorry, Archie, but I really can't be sure. If you pressed me, I'd say that the doll I saw had blue eyes like this, but I couldn't swear to it, and this matters too much to tell you what I *think* I can remember. I'm not sure I can help. You'll have to ask her parents—or Elsie, of course. She'll know better than anyone, but she's not at home at the moment.'

'All right. I'll go over to the farm now. There are some awkward questions I've got to ask, and I can't put them off any longer.'

'Why awkward? You surely don't think that they had anything to do with this?'

'I'm trying to keep an open mind, but the first rule in something like this is always to clear the ground under your feet, as difficult as that might be.'

Josephine wanted to argue, but she knew better than to tell Archie how to do his job; she had tried that in the past, and it had never ended well. 'Did you pay a call to the Herrons?' she asked instead.

'Yes, but I didn't get over the threshold. I'm supposed to be going back today to talk to the brother, but this has rather thrown things.' He tapped the box, and Josephine looked again at the sad little figure, but the more she studied it, the more she doubted herself, and she was glad when Archie put it away. 'I'm sorry about Marta,' he said.

'Yes, so am I.'

'How long will you stay now?'

'I don't know. Until Hilary's found somewhere for Noah, obviously, but I don't feel as though I can leave before we know what's happened to Annie. What about you and Virginia?'

'I'm certainly staying until tomorrow. Virginia's going back today with the children. Teddy's got to get ready for school.'

'I'm sorry I didn't see more of her.'

'So am I—but hopefully there'll be plenty of time for you to get to know each other.' At last, he smiled. 'I've got to go.

I'll try to catch up with you later to let you know what the Ridleys say about this.'

'I wish I could have helped.'

'Don't worry about it. I probably shouldn't have asked.'

He turned back to the pond, and Josephine waved to Noah, who handed her an impressive bunch of weeds. They turned left, leaving the melancholy of the pond behind them, and followed the road to Bell's Corner, then cut across gently sloping grazing land to the church. For the first time this side of summer, the chill of the night had refused to be chased away by a weakening sun, and Josephine stopped to put on the cardigan that she had been carrying, hoping that Noah was warm enough. She watched as he chased rabbits and collected the first young conkers to fall, gleefully accepting of the changes in the year that made her so wistful about the death of another summer. It was such an adult thing to want to recapture what was lost, she thought; children had no patience with that sort of futility. More than anything, though, she was pleased to see that the terrified little boy cowering on the bed had gone, at least for now; it was an image that she would find very hard to forget.

The church bells were ringing, calling the village to the morning service, and Hilary waved and beckoned them over. 'This is a nice surprise,' she said. 'We don't often see you here on a Sunday morning—still, this is hardly a normal Sunday, is it?'

Josephine wasn't sure if she was referring to Annie or the imminent announcement of war, but in either case the answer was the same. 'No, I don't suppose it is.' She winked at Noah, and he handed over the flowers.

'Are those for me? Thank you, Noah. That's very sweet of you.' Suddenly there were tears in Hilary's eyes, and she smiled apologetically at Josephine. 'Seeing him in that outfit has just about finished me off—it only seems five minutes since Benjamin was that age, and now he's wearing a uniform.'

'He's gone already?'

'Later today. He's so grown up, Josephine. I don't know where the time went.' She took a handkerchief out of her bag and blew her nose. 'I woke up this morning to the sound of five little strangers running round the rectory, and before I came to my senses, I honestly thought that I was ten years younger and back to my own kids' childhood again—and do you know, just for a moment, I was *so* happy. I really can't start letting those thoughts in, or I don't know where I'll be.'

'It's a difficult time.'

'Yes, it is, although I'm ashamed at myself for complaining when I think of what Mrs Ridley must be going through. Have you heard anything?'

'No, not really,' Josephine said, deciding that it wouldn't be right to mention the doll before Archie had talked to Annie's parents. 'We were hoping to help with the search today. Marta's had to go to London.'

'Then you can both keep me company. That pew feels very draughty at times.'

Josephine was about to explain that they hadn't really intended to go to church when she caught sight of the Herron sisters joining the congregation. Betty was with them, wearing a dress so horribly old-fashioned that it might have been from Florence's own childhood, and Noah seemed keen to see his sister, so they followed Hilary down the nave and seated themselves in the pew nearest the lectern. There was a forlorn atmosphere in the church, despite a good turnout, and Josephine looked round at the haggard, sleep-robbed faces of the men who had been searching for Annie long into the night. Stephen had set up a wireless in the pulpit, ready for the Prime Minister's announcement, but the war seemed to have been relegated to second billing in most people's minds, and she noticed how few of them had remembered to bring their gas masks, herself included.

She admired Stephen's optimistic spirit, but 'All Things Bright and Beautiful' seemed a rather hollow choice of opening hymn for that particular morning; had she been in charge, she would have stuck to the big patriotic numbers, something that didn't have an irony in nearly every line. What the music lacked, though, Stephen's sermon more than made up for—a sensitive, heartfelt expression of hope and determination, moving in its simplicity, and somehow relevant to both the wider world and the village's own personal crisis. At a quarter past eleven, when the vicar finished his prayers and moved across to switch on the wireless, there was a sense of unity and togetherness amongst those present that Josephine was comforted to be part of.

The wireless crackled into life as the sound of Bow Bells was faded out, replaced by Chamberlain's announcement from the Cabinet Room in Downing Street. As inevitable as it was, and as long as it had been expected, the formal declaration of war was so at odds with the peace of this sunlit country church that it felt strangely insubstantial, and Josephine could see that she wasn't the only one who was struggling to grasp the reality of how much things had changed in just a few minutes. Quietly, Hilary took her hand.

Chamberlain concluded his speech with a certainty that right would prevail, then gave way to a BBC announcer, but what followed was just as chilling to Josephine as the Prime Minister's own words. '*All cinemas, theatres and places of entertainment are to be closed immediately until further notice,*' the announcer declared. '*Sports gatherings and all gatherings for the purposes of amusement, whether outdoor or indoor, which involve large numbers congregating together, are prohibited until further notice. This refers especially to gatherings for purposes of entertainment, but people are earnestly requested not to crowd together unnecessarily in any circumstances. Churches and other places of public worship will not be closed.'*

In that moment, it finally dawned on Josephine that the danger and restrictions which they had all been talking about were just the beginning. Her life would be changed beyond recognition by what had just happened: the theatre was gone, and much of her livelihood with it; all the simple routines that she took for granted, the pleasures that shaped and enriched her life, would have to change; the people she loved would inevitably scatter, kept apart not just by government regulations but by the new duties and priorities that filled their days. It was impossible to say how long this would go on, but— whether it was months or years—that time could never be reclaimed. She was forty-three, already an age when days felt less throwaway than before, and passed more quickly; now, with her father growing older, and her current separation from Marta, she found she already resented what was being taken from her. As selfish as it was, she felt cheated—cheated, and afraid.

Stephen got up to switch the wireless off, and his face was grave when he returned to the lectern. 'Most of us believed that this would never happen again,' he said, and there was a restrained anger in his voice that Josephine had never heard there before, the emotion of a parent and not a parson. 'Many of us fought to make sure that it wouldn't, and there are names on the memorial outside of fathers and husbands and sons who sacrificed much more to make that promise real and tangible.' He paused, and in the silence, Josephine heard one or two stifled sobs from the rows behind. 'The temptation today is to feel betrayed—at least, that's how *I* feel, as if all our resolve and good intentions were nothing more than a childish fantasy, adequate for storybooks, but having no place in the rational world of men. And yet we must try to rise above that, for the sake of each other, and for the family among us which is currently experiencing the sort of anxiety and fear that we can only begin to imagine. This is not a time for cynicism or for surrender; in war, or in the more immediate crisis that our village is currently facing. On both fronts, I share Mr Chamberlain's faith in you, and in the fundamental humanity that our society rests on. I know that you will all play your part, with calmness and with courage.'

17

Maggie Lucas woke early on Sunday morning, cursing a day that would bring her no post. She still had very little knowledge of where Angela was, and no idea at all who was looking after her. A basic announcement had been posted on the school gates the day before, confirming that the children had arrived safely at their various destinations in Suffolk and Essex, but she had never heard of any of the villages that were listed, and although it was meant to be reassuring, the statement's guarded formality made her daughter feel more lost to her than ever. There was nothing else she could do except wait for a postcard and hope that the family was kind.

She rattled round the house for a while, tidying rooms that didn't need to be tidied, then ate her breakfast alone at the kitchen table. When the single plate and cup had been washed and stacked in the drainer, she sat down with a magazine, a luxury that she had often longed to have time for, but it was impossible to concentrate, so she busied herself in selecting a small pile of toys and books that Angie would be pleased to have as soon as she knew where to send them. It took no time at all, and as the rest of the day stretched out ahead of her, blank and meaningless without her family, Maggie began to wonder what on earth she would do with herself while she wasn't a wife or a mother. They would send her mad, these four walls, if there was nothing to bring them to life, and suddenly, in spite of how worried she was about him, she envied Bob his call-up: at least he wouldn't have to live with the silence of an empty house.

In the end, she couldn't stand it any longer. It was a beautiful day, filled with sunshine that had lost the fierceness of high summer, so she changed into something decent and went out for a walk, trying to find a blessing in the fact that she wouldn't have to scrub the front step half as often now that hers were the only shoes traipsing across it. The street was oddly normal after the disarming stillness of the house, and Maggie could detect the beginnings of Sunday lunch on the air as she walked to the top of the road, where a group of her neighbours was huddled around a car, listening intently to the radio. As she drew closer, she was conscious of the same voice coming from nearly every house, drifting out to her through the open windows in grave, stilted phrases that she didn't want to hear. She knew what it was and she knew what it meant, but it frightened her more than she cared to admit, and when someone called after her to confirm that they were finally at war, she pretended not to hear and walked on.

She headed for Victoria Park, retracing her footsteps to happier Sundays without really being conscious of what she was doing. The flower stall on the corner of Temple Street was up and running, with bucketfuls of dazzling roses and chrysanthemums spilling out across the pavement, a carpet of vibrant colour that had stopped Angie in her tracks whenever they walked this way and invariably cost her father a shilling or two. She had always taken ages to choose, Maggie remembered, but the flower seller had been patient with her, often throwing in a few extra stems if it was near the end of his day. This morning, trade was even brisker than usual and several of the people waiting to be served were in uniform; suddenly, everywhere she looked, it had become a time to say goodbye.

The park came as a sudden surprise of green amid the noisy, crowded streets, a little bit of countryside held hostage by the town. It delighted her, as it always did, and for a moment her mood lifted as she dared to believe that the world was as unchanged as this haven made it seem. She wandered between the shrubberies and formal gardens, losing all track of time until she found herself at the bandstand with its canvas chairs set out in a half-circle, ready for the afternoon performance. An image of Angie ambushed her without warning, dancing in a sunlit patch of grass as the Guards band played something from Gilbert and Sullivan. Maggie closed her eyes, picturing the sheer joy on her daughter's face, the point of her foot in the tiny white shoes and the way she had stopped so shyly when she realised that the audience was watching her rather than the musicians. The memory was too painful and she opened her eyes again, horrified to realise that she was behaving as if Angela had died, already accepting that this searing sense of loss would be permanent.

She looked at her watch, disappointed to see that barely an hour had passed since she left the house, and wondering how long it would be before the war delivered something more dangerous than boredom and a lack of purpose. As if someone up there could read her thoughts, an unfamiliar noise cut through the day, a persistent wailing and moaning that rose steadily in pitch and gradually fell away, only to rise again, echoing eerily across the city. The noise continued relentlessly, until it occurred to Maggie that the sounds of the bombs actually falling could scarcely be more disturbing.

All around her, people in the street stopped dead in their tracks, staring stupidly at each other as if they didn't know what it was, as if they hadn't been warned of this a thousand times or more in the last few months. There was a collective hush around her, an unspoken consensus that to make the first move or even to acknowledge the sound of the siren would be to admit the reality of the danger. Then a man's voice over to her right broke the silence, putting into words what everyone else was surely thinking: 'Christ, Hitler didn't waste much time, did he?' The atmosphere changed in an instant, but as Maggie stared at the mixture of panic and fear in the eyes of those who were closest, all she felt was a flood of relief: if Angie was safe from all this, then she could put up with the separation, no matter how long it lasted; she could put up with anything as long as she knew that one day they would be together again. Thank God, she thought, as she joined the crowds hurrying to the nearest shelter. Thank God that we've done the right thing.

18

When Penrose arrived at the Ridleys' farm, the local police were packing up, ready to leave. As he got out of the car and looked round at the yard, one of the officers approached him, careful to avoid the puddles from the overnight rain, and Penrose introduced himself. 'Have you found anything?' he asked.

'No, sir, I'm afraid not. A few toys scattered around the place, but just what you'd expect from a family. No sign of little Annie, though, and nothing to suggest that she's come to any harm—not here, at least.'

'Do you know the family?' Penrose asked, noticing the familiarity in the other man's tone.

'I've had a few drinks with Tom in my time, especially in the winter, when the pheasant season starts.'

'You live here?'

'I'm over at Bower House Tye now—that's where the wife's from—but I come back for the shoot when I can. Tom's one of the regular beaters, too, so we sink a pint or two at the end of the day, just like our fathers did—thick as thieves, they were. They're both gone now.'

'And what's Mr Ridley like?'

There was no disguising the reason for the question, but if the sergeant felt a conflict of loyalties between his job and his friend, he didn't show it. 'Tom's a good man,' he said. 'He works hard for his family. I'm not saying that he doesn't lose his temper now and again—he can be hot-headed, just like his father was. But I'll tell you this, sir—he worshipped that little girl. Carted her everywhere, he did.' He shook his head, not immune to the sense of disbelief which was beginning to replace the initial shock of Annie's disappearance amongst those who knew her. 'I hope to God she's all right, for all their sakes.'

'So do I, Sergeant. Thank you for your help. If you're done here, we're moving up to the area around the church and the Hall. Go there next, would you?'

'Right away, sir. The gypsies are there at the moment.'

'So I gather. Some of them helped with the search last night.'

'Do you want us to have a word with them?'

'All right, but general enquiries only. We don't want more trouble than we've already got, and I'm assuming you haven't got any reason to suspect a connection with Annie's disappearance?' Except age-old prejudice, he added under his breath.

'No, sir.'

'Then keep it civil.' Penrose waited until the police cars had left the yard, then walked up to the house. In the distance, he could see another gang of local men stretched out across fields laid bare by the harvest, scouring the ground with sticks. There should have been nothing strange about men on the land round here, especially at this time of year, but still it seemed wrong, a travesty of the village's natural rhythms and essential character.

The back door opened before he had a chance to knock, and Ridley looked startled to see him. 'I was just going out again,' he said.

Penrose noticed that his voice was gruff and hoarse from shouting his daughter's name. He had watched him with concern the night before, soaked to the skin and bitterly cold, refusing to go home even when darkness and the weather meant that staying out could be of little practical use. 'I'd be grateful if you'd wait,' he said. 'I'd like to talk to you both.'

'Have you found her?' Annie's mother joined her husband in the doorway, looking drawn and pale.

'No, Mrs Ridley, I'm afraid not.'

'But you've found something. I can see it in your face.'

'Can I come in?' She nodded, and they both stood aside to let him pass. The kitchen was homely and untidy, scattered here and there with a child's belongings, things that Penrose guessed were currently a torment to them.

'Sorry, I haven't cleared the kids' breakfast away yet,' Kathy Ridley said, collecting up some dishes.

'Having other people's children here must be hard for you at the moment.'

'It is, but none of this is their fault. They're out with my mother now. Please, sit down.'

He took the nearest chair, and found himself opposite a photograph of Annie that stood in pride of place on the dresser. Another frame stood empty next to it, and he wondered if it usually held the photograph that she had selected to give him; the heavy, black border seemed ominous, and he looked quickly away, before they could guess what he was thinking. 'We've found a doll,' he explained gently, moving a little brown jug of milk to the side and placing the box on the table. 'Your mother said that Annie had one with her on Friday when she went missing. I'd like you to look at this and tell me if it's hers.'

She nodded, obviously frightened now. 'Where did you find it?'

'It was in the village pond.'

'Oh no.'

Kathy Ridley grabbed at the back of the chair, and her husband stepped forward to support her. 'Sit down, love. This might not be anything to do with Annie.'

Penrose waited patiently for her to compose herself, feeling like an intruder. The couple's suffering was tangible, and—as detached as he had to remain—he found it impossible not to be affected by it. It was the only part of his job that he hated, this obligation to analyse the body language of people who were so obviously grieving, teasing at every word they spoke in case it carried some sort of subtext, and he was glad when Ridley turned to him almost as a challenge. 'Come on, then. Let's see it.'

He slid the box across the table and Ridley took it, staring anxiously at his wife as he opened it for her to examine. 'It isn't Annie's,' she said without a moment's hesitation, choking back a sob of relief. 'Thank God, it isn't hers.'

'You're sure?' Penrose asked, concerned that she might have seen only what she wanted to see. 'Look very carefully, Mrs Ridley.'

'I don't have to look any more. I know that doll's not Annie's. The one Mum made for her had blue buttons and lighter hair. And this isn't new, you can see that. It's been loved by somebody—but *not* by my daughter.'

Penrose took the box back. 'So what happens now?' Ridley demanded. 'Shouldn't we get back out there and keep looking?'

'We need to widen the search, and look for Annie further afield. Do you have the photograph I asked for, Mrs Ridley?'

'Yes, I've got it here.' She got up and took the picture from behind some cups on the dresser. 'Is it all right? It's the most recent one we've got.'

Penrose looked down at the image of Annie on her father's shoulders. 'It's perfect, thank you. I'll take good care of it.

Now, we've covered most of the village itself, so we need to—'

'But you're not going to stop looking here, surely?' Ridley interrupted him. 'What if we've missed something? We can go out again, can't we, perhaps get more people this time.'

Penrose recognised the desperation to do *something*, to cover the same ground and clutch at straws because it was preferable to admitting that the task might actually be never-ending. 'We *are* going to search the school and the immediate area again later today,' he said, 'but this time we'll bring in some dogs to try and pick up Annie's scent.'

'You should have done that yesterday, before the rain. There won't be any trace of her now, will there?'

Penrose bit his tongue, resisting the temptation to point out that there had been rain the night before, too, so even yesterday would have been too late; there was no good to come from reminding the Ridleys that their daughter had been gone for twenty-four hours before she was missed. 'These things take time to organise and I agree that's frustrating, but while there's the slightest chance that it might be of use, I'd like to try it.' He turned to Annie's mother. 'Do you have an item of clothing that she's worn recently?'

He didn't need to explain why. 'I'll fetch you something. I've just been sorting the laundry, ready for tomorrow, but Annie's things are still upstairs in the basket. I couldn't bring myself to wash them, just in case it's—'

She stopped abruptly, unable to say the words 'in case it's all I have'. 'It would be better to have something that hasn't mixed with your clothes,' Penrose said. 'Perhaps her pillow-case? I'll come with you, if I may. I'd like to see Annie's room.'

'What for?' Ridley demanded, his patience running out. 'Why waste time on that? If she was in her bloody room, we wouldn't be doing any of this.'

'I'll show you up.' Mrs Ridley put a hand on her husband's shoulder, then led Penrose upstairs. 'Don't mind Tom,' she said. 'He blames himself. We both do.'

Annie's room was at the end of the landing—small, but with an uninterrupted view of the farm, and filled with morning sunlight. Her mother stripped the pillow of its cover while Penrose looked round as discreetly as possible, quickly establishing that there was nothing there to help him. 'Bring her back to us,' Kathy Ridley said, handing him what he had asked for. 'Please bring her back.'

'I'll do everything I can,' he promised. 'You have my word.'

Back downstairs, Ridley was pacing up and down the room like a prisoner in the condemned cell. 'Is that it?' he asked. 'Can I go and look for my daughter now?'

'Just a couple more questions,' Penrose said firmly, and something in his manner had the desired effect: Ridley sat down, and didn't argue. 'Can either of you think of anyone who might have taken Annie? Any family or friends who might be involved in her disappearance, for whatever reason? Anyone in the village? Please think carefully.'

'No, there's no one.' Annie's mother stared at him, genuinely bewildered by the question and why he was asking it. 'I can't believe *anyone* would hurt her. Why would they do that to a little girl?'

There were too many answers to that, and Penrose moved on. 'You were late getting to the school on Friday, Mr Ridley— why was that?'

'I was working.'

'Here at the farm?' He hesitated, then shook his head, and Penrose noticed his wife looking at him curiously. 'So where were you?'

'I drove over to Tiptree,' Ridley admitted. 'They buy our fruit, but we've been having a bit of trouble with them this year and I went over to get it sorted, once and for all.'

'You promised me you'd let that go, Tom.'

'How could I? It's our biggest income, Kathy—we can't afford to lose it just because Maitland thinks he can use this war to drive our prices down.'

'Maitland?' Penrose queried.

'Henry Maitland. He's the foreman at the factory.'

'So he can confirm you went to see him?'

Again, Ridley shook his head. 'He wasn't there. They told me he was at Colchester Station, helping out with the evacuees, so I just came back again. It was a waste of time.'

'Did you go straight to the school when you got back here?'

'Yes, I was late enough as it was.'

'So the last time you saw Annie was before you left for Tiptree?'

'At breakfast, yes.' He closed his eyes, either to hold on to that last image of his daughter, or to ease the agony that came with it. 'She was sulking about us taking someone in, and complaining about her porridge.'

'But there was nothing else troubling her, as far as you know? No arguments in the family? She hadn't been told off for anything recently?'

The realisation that no one was above suspicion seemed to dawn on them both at the same time, but it was Mrs Ridley who spoke up. 'Do you know what's been going through my mind since yesterday?' she asked. 'I keep thinking of everything I'd give up just to have Annie walk through that door— my life and Tom's, our marriage, our home, everything that means something to me, just to know that she's all right. God forgive me, but I even started bargaining with Annie—let her be hurt, but not dead. Whatever's wrong with her, we can fix it—just don't let her die. Do you have *any* idea what it's like to hope that your daughter gets hurt simply because it's not the worst thing that can happen?'

'No, I don't.'

'Then don't you dare come round here and say that Tom or I would harm a hair on her head. Get out there and find her, because we'll cope with anything once she's back.' She took her husband's hand, a united front for the first time. 'You keep looking for Annie, because that's what *we're* going to do—and we'll search for her like she's alive until someone can prove to us different.'

19

Marta arrived in London just after lunch. Liverpool Street was busy, with several platforms still devoted to the mass exodus of children from the city, but the railway staff seemed remarkably cheerful, and—had she not read about it in the newspapers— Marta would never have guessed that this time last week they were on the verge of a strike. There was a long queue for taxis, but she passed the time by eavesdropping on the couple in front of her, who had been caught up in a false air-raid alarm set off by a civilian plane from France; sirens had caused panic across the country, apparently, and Marta hoped that Josephine had been spared the worry. Polstead had its fair share of concerns at the moment, without being troubled by Hitler.

Even so, she wished she were back there. Feeling desperately lonely, she put her hand in her pocket for the note that Josephine had given her as she left, and found with it the scrap of paper on which she had scribbled down Noah's address. It had seemed unlikely that she would need it at the time, but now she was here and at a loose end, she was tempted to use it. The forgotten letter still preyed on her conscience, and there was nothing on Hitch's list that she could do on a Sunday; by the time she got to the front of the queue, she had made up her mind. 'The Athenaeum Hotel, please,' she said, 'but I need to stop off somewhere on the way. Can we go via Castlefrank House on Hoxton Street?'

'Bit of a contrast, Miss, if you don't mind me saying. I don't often go from Hoxton to Piccadilly in the same fare.'

'I imagine we're all getting used to new things,' Marta said, and her tone did the trick: she was left to pass the rest of the journey in silence. 'Wait for me here, will you?' she asked, when the car pulled over by the Gaumont cinema on Hoxton Street. 'I won't be long.'

'Be as long as you like,' the driver said, pulling yesterday's newspaper out from under his seat. 'It's your money.'

Marta waited to cross the road as a large army lorry drove past, with men sitting on kitbags in the back, all looking impossibly youthful. They smiled and whistled when they saw her, and she smiled back, suddenly reminded of the autumn of 1914, when she had waved someone off who had never returned. With a horrible sense of déjà vu, she shook the memory off and headed for the block of flats that stood a few yards further down the street. There was no access to the building from the front, so she pushed open a wrought-iron gate and followed a path round to the back to try her luck there. The flats had been built around a single, uninspiring courtyard, with a couple of poorly tended borders and some exhausted-looking plane trees that were no match for the predominance of concrete. With the noise of the traffic cut out, the area was unexpectedly quiet, and Marta was struck by how strange it was not to see children playing outside on a Sunday afternoon. She looked up to the building, and realised that she was being watched from more than one of the windows; when a door opened over to her left, she was surprised to see that the person on his way out was a policeman.

'Can I help you, love?' he asked. 'You look like you're lost.'

'Is it that obvious? I'm after Flat 33.'

'That'll be on the third floor. Next staircase along, I think.'

'Thank you. You've saved me a lot of time.'

'Happy to help.'

There was no lift, and Marta paused to get her breath back before knocking on the Stebbings' door. When there was no reply, she tried again, then took a pen out of her pocket to leave a note; she was disappointed not to meet Noah's mother, but at least she could put her mind at rest and let her know that her children were safe. She put the note through the letter-box and turned to go, but stopped when she heard a noise from inside the flat, as if someone had dropped a cup and saucer. This time, she knocked less politely. 'Mrs Stebbing? I'm sorry to disturb you, but it's about your son.'

The door opened with a swiftness that took Marta by surprise, though she didn't have to ask again to know that she had found Noah and Betty's mother: the resemblance—particularly with her daughter—was striking. The woman stared at her visitor with an odd expression on her face, a mixture of fear and curiosity. 'Who are you?' she asked guardedly. 'What's up with Noah?'

'Nothing's up with him. I'm sorry, I didn't mean to alarm you—just the opposite, in fact. My name is Marta Fox, and I'm from a village in Suffolk called Polstead. I wanted to let you know that Noah has arrived there safe and well, and that a friend and I are looking after him.'

'So what are you doing here?'

It was a good question, and one that Marta was beginning to ask herself. There seemed little point in complicating things by trying to explain her part-time connection with Suffolk, or the fact that Noah was soon to be moved somewhere else: she could already see that she wasn't at all Mrs Stebbing's idea of the homely, country woman who should be caring for her children. 'I'm working here for a couple of days, so I thought I'd come and tell you in person,' she explained. 'I guessed you'd want to know as soon as possible that Noah is all right. Betty, too—she's staying with a family close by.'

'They've split 'em up?'

'I'm afraid so, but we'll make sure they spend plenty of time together.'

'Is everything all right, Maureen?'

Marta turned round. She hadn't heard the door open in the flat across the hallway, but two women were standing there, obviously a mother and daughter. It was the younger of the two who had spoken, and there was a wariness in her voice that bordered on hostility. As feeble as it seemed, Marta suddenly felt intimidated. 'I'd better leave you in peace,' she said. 'Would you like me to give Noah a message for you?'

Maureen Stebbing hesitated, and Marta suspected that the words that came out of her mouth were not the ones she wanted to say, nor the ones she might have used had they not had company. 'Tell him to keep his head down,' she said, with another glance over at her neighbours. 'And tell him not to cause any trouble.'

Marta nodded and went downstairs, wishing she hadn't come. She might have eased her conscience, but she had paid for that with her own peace of mind, and now she couldn't get the visit out of her head. It had been stupid of her to think that she might sit down with Noah's mother and talk about a boy she barely knew; her intentions had been good, but she hadn't taken into account the lingering resentment that surrounded the evacuation plans, or the fears and worries of people who had no choice but to stay in London, separated from their children. It had been incredibly insensitive of her—and yet, and yet . . . In spite of all her reasoning, there was something that bothered her about Noah's mother; she had seemed frightened, for herself as well as for her son, and Marta recognised that in another woman. As she left the building, she wondered if the absent Mr Stebbing was handy with his fists.

Lost in her thoughts, she took a wrong turning and had to retrace her footsteps. It was just as well that she did, or Maureen Stebbing would have missed her. 'I'm glad I've caught you,' she said, her tone completely different. 'What must you think of me? It's just that this is all so new. It's such a shock, and there's no one to tell you what to do. Noah wasn't even supposed to be going away, but then it seemed like the only way to keep him safe.' Her words came out in a rush, a far cry from the tight-lipped woman who had greeted her upstairs. In the sunlight, Marta could see that she had a bruise on her throat.

'Mrs Stebbing, is everything all right?'

'Yes, or at least it will be, but I *do* miss them—that's what I want you to tell them. I should be looking after Noah, not the other way round, but tell him how much I love him. Betty, too. You'll take care of them, won't you?'

Marta nodded, feeling more guilty than ever for what she had left Josephine to deal with on her own. She was about to ask Maureen Stebbing what she had meant by Noah looking after her when a police car pulled up behind her illegally parked taxi, and the driver wound his window down impatiently and shouted across the street. 'Are we going any time soon? I can't stay here all day.'

Marta nodded and turned back to say goodbye to Noah's mother, but Mrs Stebbing had already gone back inside.

20

Florence Herron was the complete opposite of her sister, in looks and in the welcome she gave him. Penrose was ushered straight through to the kitchen when he eventually arrived at Black Bryony, and there were no recriminations for the fact that he had forgotten to telephone ahead as promised. 'You'll have some tea?' she asked, clearing a chair for him.

He was about to refuse, when he saw that everything was set out ready, almost as if his visit had been looked forward to. 'Thank you. Tea would be lovely.'

'Splendid. I'll do a tray. Edmund will want something by now. My sister said you wanted to talk to him about this business in the village.'

The phrase was strikingly vague for the seriousness of the situation, and Penrose wondered if his visit from the night before had been played down, or if the younger Miss Herron was one of those people who disliked their lives to be touched by any sort of unpleasantness. 'To you both, actually,' he said. 'I'll try not to take up too much of your time, but I'd like to confirm some details about Friday afternoon.'

'My time isn't important at all, but I'm sure that Edmund will appreciate your consideration. Now, sit down a minute while I boil the kettle.'

Penrose did as he was invited, and took the opportunity to look around the room. The kitchen was at the back of the house, a comparatively recent extension on what he guessed was an eighteenth-century original. Last night, in the dark, he hadn't appreciated quite how elegant the house was: its attractive facade—red brick in Flemish bond—had a town-house feel, utterly out of character with the cottages and farmhouses that were more typical of the village; its out-of-the-way location contributed to the impression of a building set down in the wrong place. 'Is this your family home?' he asked.

'Yes, for three generations. Daddy was the doctor here, and his father before him. My parents loved this house. We couldn't think of letting it go.'

'But your brother hasn't followed in your father's footsteps? Professionally speaking, I mean.'

'No. He could have done—he was certainly bright enough—but he doesn't have Daddy's way with people. The village *loved* my father.' She spoke with pride as well as affection, and Penrose couldn't help but think that there was something childlike about her. 'Edmund's is a more insular nature, I suppose,' she added. 'He has his academic studies, and a quiet life suits him.'

'And his health.' She looked at him curiously. 'Your sister mentioned that his health was unreliable when I was here yesterday.'

'Did she?' She took the kettle from the range and warmed the pot, then spooned tea into it from a caddy on the mantelpiece. There was a row of identical tins alongside it, Penrose noticed, each with a different, handwritten label: 'Doctor'; 'Coalman'; 'Staff'; 'Groceries', all the things for which money needed to be carefully set aside. In spite of the substantial house, the Herrons were obviously not rich. 'My sister isn't very tolerant of the frailties of age, I'm afraid,' Florence said. 'She resents them in herself and scorns them in others. And the last few days have been difficult for her.'

'Difficult?'

'The certainty of another war brings back the losses of the last one, don't you think? Lillian's husband was killed at Gallipoli.'

'I'm sorry to hear that. I didn't realise she'd been married. The name . . .'

'Oh, we've always been known as the Herron sisters and we always will be. Lillian gave up calling herself by her married name soon after she moved back here.'

'And your brother? Did he fight?'

'Yes, he was with the Suffolk at Ypres. He doesn't talk about it much, though. Would you be a dear and carry the tray?'

'Of course.' She led the way up the stairs, taking her time and using the banisters for support, and Penrose could hear her wheezing from the effort of the climb. He took advantage of their slow progress to take in as much as he could of the living arrangements. The house was tall but narrow, with two generous rooms on each floor, one on either side of the staircase, and a bathroom over the kitchen at the back. Helpfully, all the doors were open to throw light onto the landings, and he glanced through each one as he passed, having a strange sense of moving back in time with each level: downstairs, the rooms were comfortable and contemporary, but the first-floor bedrooms were depressingly Victorian, with heavy furniture and flocked wallpaper, and even the room now given over to a little girl was filled with toys from a different age. 'How is your evacuee settling in?' he asked, and Florence stopped to get her breath back before she answered him.

'It's a joy to have her. She's a dear little thing, the spitting image of our youngest sister.' She looked at him, anticipating his question. 'Rosemary died when she was four,' she explained. 'Diphtheria. It broke my mother's heart, and she never really got over it. They tried for another child, but it wasn't to be. Mummy was in her forties by then, and she couldn't carry another pregnancy full term. In the end, the grief of it killed her, and Daddy blamed himself—he was such a good doctor, but he couldn't save his own little girl, or the wife he loved.' She sighed heavily, and Penrose tried to imagine what it must be like to live your whole life in a house that carried such difficult memories. 'We did our best to make it up to Mummy, but you don't understand at that age, do you? It's not simply a matter of replacing what's been lost. We ended up making things worse.'

There was a noise from upstairs, a chair being scraped across the floor, and it drew Florence back from the past with a start. 'We mustn't keep Edmund waiting,' she said. 'He was anxious enough about your visit, and I don't want to unsettle him.'

The attic rooms were light compared to the rest of the house, and the bedroom to the right almost monastic in its simplicity. By contrast, everything that gave substance to Edmund Herron's personality was gathered around him in his study, defining his life like the concentric circles of a tree. The room was packed with curiosities, more like a museum than a domestic space, and Penrose found it easy to believe that Herron had spent most of his life in this room; at first glance, he was easy to miss among its debris. The longest wall was lined entirely with books, double-stacked on the shelves and spilling over into piles on the floor. Elsewhere, glass cases dominated the room, filled with an impressive collection of fossils that would not have been out of place in the Natural History Museum; they ranged from the small-scale molluscs, ammonites and sharks' teeth that most people collected as a child, to larger skeletal remains, mostly of birds, that Penrose suspected were rare and valuable. Individually, many of the fossils were things of great beauty, but they were amassed in a way that struck him as obsessive, and he wondered if Herron went to the effort of looking for the specimens himself, or simply paid for the rewards of other people's work. Either way, he seemed to be involved in a lengthy monograph on the subject: a stack of typed manuscript pages sat on the corner of his desk, kept in check by the jaw bone from some large, long-extinct mammal.

Florence made the introductions, and Penrose—still holding the tea tray—felt himself at a disadvantage, but the other man made no effort to get up or offer his hand. Instead, he sat at his desk and barely lifted his head, responding to his sister with little more than a grunt of acknowledgement. He was either painfully shy or painfully rude; Penrose was inclined towards the latter, although he was willing to give Herron the benefit of the doubt. 'Thank you for agreeing to see me,' he said, with a politeness that stopped just short of sarcasm. 'I can see you're engrossed in your work, so I'll try not to take too much of your time.'

Herron stood up without a word and walked over to the window, staring down into the garden with his hands shoved deep into the pockets of a shapeless cardigan. Irritated, Penrose looked round for somewhere to get rid of the tray, and Florence obliged by removing a fold-out table from the side of the desk, obviously stored there for the purpose. She poured the tea and put a biscuit on each saucer, then took her brother his cup first. He put it down, untouched, on the windowsill, and shrugged his shoulders, as if denying knowledge of a question that had yet to be asked; it was a repeated, uncontrolled gesture, and Penrose was intrigued by the anxiety it suggested. He decided to make his questions as direct as possible. 'Was there another child in the car when you picked up Betty Stebbing on Friday afternoon?'

Herron turned sharply, looking at his sister as if she had somehow deceived him. 'One of the village children has gone missing,' Florence said, and Penrose realised that no one had explained the reason for his visit. 'The Chief Inspector is trying to find her.'

'Why have you come here?' The words were indistinct, mumbled through a thick, chevron moustache, but the curiosity sounded genuine.

'We have a witness who says that Annie Ridley was in your car after you'd been to collect Betty, Mr Herron. Is that true?'

Herron cleared his throat but it was his sister who answered. 'No, it most certainly isn't! I've never heard such nonsense. Who told you that?' When Penrose remained silent, she added: 'Well, I think we can all guess who told you, but she's wrong. Tell him, Edmund.'

Herron seemed too dazed to speak, so Penrose prompted him with another question. 'What time did you arrive at the school?'

'I'm not sure. Two o'clock, perhaps later.'

'And you stayed in the car while your sisters went inside?'

'Yes.' Herron nodded, shrugging his shoulders more often now, in a way that jarred disconcertingly with the emphasis of his answer.

'Were the two buses still in the car park?'

'I think so.'

'And did you see Annie?'

'No. I don't even know the girl. Why are you asking me this?'

He was becoming increasingly agitated, Penrose noticed. 'Did you talk to any child at the school on Friday, other than the one you were collecting?'

'No! Please, just leave me alone.'

He stepped back, retreating towards the corner of the room as if the words were a physical threat, and Florence put a hand on Penrose's arm. 'Let's go downstairs, Chief Inspector. I can answer the rest of your questions. Edmund needs his peace.'

Penrose ignored her, and took Annie's photograph from his inside pocket. 'Just one more question,' he said, holding the picture up and moving closer to Herron so that he could see it properly. 'Are you sure you don't know this child? Her parents are living through hell at the moment, wondering what's happened to her. They just want her back. If you can help them, now is the time to do it.'

'Get out!' Herron reached for an ammonite from one of the bookshelves and made as if to throw it at them. 'You're just as bad as my father, tormenting me like this, but I haven't done anything wrong this time, so just go.'

'This time?'

'Leave me alone!'

Florence ushered Penrose from the room, closing the door behind her. 'Why did your brother react like that?' he asked, struck by the difference between the two family accounts that he had heard of Dr Herron's character. 'What did he mean by not doing anything wrong *this* time?'

He could see that she was upset, but she brushed away the question. 'Edmund and Daddy didn't always see eye to eye. It's harder to be son to a successful father, don't you think? There's so much to live up to. And I can't say I blame him for being a little upset by your questions. Perhaps you should think more carefully before you make unsubstantiated accusations based on lies.'

There was no doubt in his mind that she knew who had claimed to see Annie in their car, and he wondered why there seemed to be bad blood between the Herrons and Winnie

Chilver. 'I'm sorry to have caused your brother such distress,' he said, 'but it wasn't an accusation, simply a question that you were asked to clear up.'

'Well, I trust that we *have* cleared it up, and I don't want to hear any more about it. I'm sorry about the Ridley girl, but it's got nothing to do with us.'

They descended the rest of the staircase in silence, and Penrose decided to push his luck. 'Would you mind if I looked round your garden?' he asked. 'We've been checking sheds and outbuildings, just in case Annie ran away and has hurt herself somehow.'

'Do you think she's still alive?'

'I hope so. We're doing everything we can to find her.'

'Then be my guest in the garden. My sister's out there somewhere with Betty, so please try not to alarm her.'

Penrose assumed she meant Betty, although with a family that seemed so highly strung it was hard to be sure. He thanked her, apologised again for the intrusion, and left the house via the back door. There was a car parked on the gravel drive to the side of the house and he took a detour to examine it, but found nothing of interest inside. The garden was long and narrow, south-facing and divided unobtrusively into several distinct sections—formal and natural, light and shade. There was a small terrace, then steps leading down to a lawn bordered by mature shrubs. A rug was laid out on the grass, scattered with books and one or two toys, and the woman he had spoken to at the door the night before was playing with a little dark-haired girl just beyond it, gently pulling her back each time she strayed towards the bottom of the garden. 'Good afternoon, Miss Herron,' Penrose said, realising that he still didn't know her married name. She turned without a smile, leading him to assume that her hostility the night before had been less about the hour than a general dislike of visitors, particularly if they came with a warrant card. Not for the first time, he found himself wondering if the Herrons had something to hide. 'Your sister gave me permission to look round your garden, so I hope I'm not disturbing you.'

'Not at all, Chief Inspector, although we make sure to clear away all traces of the children we abduct, so you're probably wasting your time.'

She stared at him, and he was surprised to see a faint glimmer of amusement in her eyes along with the defiance. 'Thank you for your frankness,' he said, returning her mockery in kind, 'but it's virtually impossible to remove *every* trace, so if it's all the same to you, I'll look anyway.'

She waved him on his way, and he found it curious that she hadn't asked for news about Annie, although perhaps the very fact of his presence here told her that the child was still missing. The lawn sloped gently down to a stream, which he assumed marked the boundary of the Herrons' property, and it didn't take him long to establish that he was on a wild goose chase.

'No revelations?' Lillian Herron had followed him down, and stood watching him from the shade of the apple trees.

'I'm afraid not, other than to confirm what a beautiful garden you have. It's a lovely spot. I can see why your family has such strong roots here.'

'Can you? Sometimes I wonder. It's such a lot of work.' She turned and walked back up the lawn, and Penrose followed her. 'The garden alone is more than we can cope with, and the house is becoming a liability as we get older. It'll be the death of us all.'

'Don't you have help?' Penrose asked, remembering the tea caddy on the mantelpiece.

'No, not any more, and even if we did, they'd be off to war now, leaving us high and dry, so it's just as well that we've learnt to manage. No, we'll just have to struggle on, won't we, Betty?' She ruffled the little girl's hair affectionately. 'Have you spoken to Edmund?'

The question was casually put, but Penrose thought he detected a tightness in her voice that betrayed her interest in his answer. 'Briefly, yes. Forgive me for saying so, but your brother seems haunted by something. What is it?'

She looked away, staring down the garden and avoiding his eye. 'We're all haunted by something, aren't we? Especially today. Now, if you'll excuse me, I need to take this little one in to Florrie for her bath.'

'Yes, of course.'

He helped her to gather up the toys from the rug, noticing that their story for the afternoon had been *Little Red Riding Hood*—Perrault's version, without the happy ending. It seemed an insensitive choice when the village was in mourning for its innocence, and she must have seen the expression on his face as she took the book from him. 'Sometimes it does a child good to be scared, Chief Inspector,' she said. 'Otherwise they go around thinking that nothing can ever happen to them—and we all know that's not true, don't we?'

21

Noah still had the energy to want to play when they got back to the cottage, so Josephine gave him something to eat and sent him outside, with strict instructions not to leave the garden. As fruitless as it had been in offering any clue to Annie's whereabouts, the search had been an unsettling, bewildering experience which left her struggling to make sense of the fact that someone as vital and full of life as the Ridleys' daughter could suddenly disappear from the face of the earth; it made her want to keep Noah close, and she felt more acutely than ever the emptiness of the cottage without Marta.

When the telephone rang, it was a welcome distraction, and she grabbed the receiver, hoping to hear Marta's voice. 'Josephine? It's Margery here. I've been thinking about that little girl all day and I wondered if you'd had any news?'

'No, nothing,' Josephine said, trying not to sound too disappointed by the caller. 'The whole village has been out looking again today, but she's vanished without a trace. They found a doll that wasn't hers, then we all got worked up over a bit of lace caught in the branches of a tree, but Annie wasn't wearing lace, so we're no further on than when you left us last night.'

Margery sighed. 'I'm so sorry. Her poor parents must be beside themselves.'

'Yes, they are.' Josephine remembered the silence that had fallen across the search party when Tom and Kathy Ridley came out to join them, partly from respect, partly from empathy, but mostly because there was simply nothing to say that might do justice to their sorrow. They already looked like ghosts, she thought, as if the prospect of a world without Annie was draining the life from them. 'I honestly don't know how they've got the strength to put one foot in front of the other.'

'I suppose they've got to stay positive. The alternative is too awful to consider.'

'Yes, it is.'

'Listen, I hope you won't think this trivial at such a terrible time, but I've been speaking to Jessie Bacon today. She's a neighbour of mine, but she was also Dr Salter's housekeeper for donkey's years, and she remembers the Herrons *very* well. In fact, she reminded me of something that I'd quite forgotten.'

'Go on.'

'I can't go into it now. All hell is breaking loose here. We've got a troubled evacuee who won't settle, and it turns out that three of the mothers are pregnant. I must either be very unworldly or very stupid, because I'm afraid that simply never occurred to me. Anyway, I wondered if you and Marta would like to come to lunch tomorrow, and we can talk about it then? And bring Noah, obviously. There are plenty of children here for him to knock about with.'

'Marta's gone to Hollywood,' Josephine said, wondering how something so dismal could sound so glamorous. 'That's a long story, too, but Noah and I would love to come.' It was selfish of her, but she craved a break from the sadness in the village that was seeping into her soul, and she was curious to see the house that Margery had talked so much about. 'Thank you. A jaunt will be a treat for us both, especially if there's some gossip at the end of it.'

'Splendid. Shall we say midday? Park in the square and walk along to the house from there. It's only a hundred yards or so. You can't miss it.'

'All right, I'll see you then—and good luck with your expectant mothers.'

Margery groaned and hung up, and Josephine went to the window to check that Noah was all right, just as the telephone rang again. This time, it was Marta. 'I feel like I've been gone for days,' she said. 'I can't believe how much has happened since I left. Are you all right?'

'Yes, we're fine, but it's been a very strange day. Who'd have thought that the announcement of another war wouldn't be the main topic of conversation?'

'I suppose that's comforting, in a funny sort of way—one little girl, eclipsing the world's troubles. Is there any news about Annie?'

'No, nothing.' She told Marta about the search and the various false alarms. 'Archie's going to call in later if he has time. It wasn't quite the weekend off he was hoping for, and I think he's going back to London tomorrow. How are things down there?'

'Organised chaos. They're still shipping the kids out, and we've had our first air raid—everyone running for cover from a perfectly harmless French plane. Bodes well, doesn't it?' She laughed softly, a sound so close and so familiar that Josephine could almost fool herself into believing that her lover was in the room. 'I have got something to tell you though—I've met Noah's mother.'

'You went to their flat?'

'I couldn't resist it. I wanted to let her know that he was safe, and it was just a stone's throw from Liverpool Street . . .'

'You mean you were dying to see what she was like and grabbed the first chance to find out.'

'That's another way of looking at it, I suppose.'

'And? What is she like?'

Marta paused, and Josephine waited impatiently. 'Frightened, I think. Frightened, and missing her children.'

'You mean frightened of the war?'

'I'm not sure that *is* what I mean. It felt much closer to home, and she was so wary and suspicious . . .'

'She would be, with a stranger on her doorstep out of the blue.'

'Yes, but it was more than that. She's got a bruise on her throat.'

'So someone's hurt her?'

'That's what I assumed.'

'Noah's father?'

'Perhaps. Or another bloke who's come along to fill the gap. How would we know? There was definitely something going on, though, and the women across the hallway knew exactly what it was. It was as if they didn't want her to talk to anyone. She had to follow me downstairs to tell me that she loved her children.'

'How odd.' Josephine hesitated, wondering whether she should give Marta even more to worry about, but it wasn't right to keep things from her, particularly things that supported her suspicions. 'I had a bit of a scene with Noah this morning,' she admitted, then recounted what had happened with the scissors. 'He was absolutely petrified, and my only thought was that he's used to someone hurting him.'

'Is he all right now?'

'Yes, it's as if it never happened—but it makes sense after what you've just told me.'

'She said something strange, too. Something like "I should be looking after him, not the other way round".'

'Perhaps Noah's been sticking up for her.'

'We've got to do something, Josephine.'

'Like what? We've got no idea what we're dealing with.'

'I know, but perhaps Noah will talk to you when he knows you a bit better.'

Josephine was sceptical. 'Perhaps, but that sort of trust doesn't come overnight. And even if he does—what do we do then? Break the family up? Go in all guns blazing?'

She heard Marta sigh. 'You're right, of course you are. It's just that I saw myself in her, I suppose—tied to a bastard with nowhere to turn. I remember what that was like.'

'I know you do.' Josephine knew better than to tell Marta not to get involved with something she felt so deeply about, and in spite of her caution, she wasn't happy about doing nothing either. She thought about Noah's arrival in the village, which suddenly made more sense. 'That might explain why Noah's here in the first place,' she said. 'He had no paperwork—no label or postcard, and it was almost as if he'd been sent at the last minute. Perhaps his mother saw her chance to keep him safe—not from the bombs, but from whatever's going on at home.'

'That adds up. Do you think I should go and see her again?'

'Honestly? No, I don't. For a start, I don't think it will get you anywhere, but selfishly I'd rather you kept yourself safe. It's bad enough that you've got to be in London with all hell about to break loose. Please don't put yourself in danger by travelling any more than you have to. Promise me you'll be careful.'

'All right, I promise, but see what you can get out of Noah. Did you hear Chamberlain's speech?'

'Yes. Believe it or not, we went to church this morning. Stephen set the wireless up at the altar. Everyone thought that he was very good—Chamberlain, that is, not Stephen. Personally, I thought he just sounded like the archetypal family doctor, giving you the bad news you knew already. But it seemed to do the trick—there was a lot of talk afterwards about really *showing* Hitler, and all being in the same boat.'

'It's a bit of a blow about the theatres and cinemas, though.'

'Yes, even Cromwell didn't manage that. I half hoped it might affect your departure, but I suppose Mr Hitchcock has got plenty of American cinemas to make his movies for.'

'I miss you, Josephine.'

'I miss you too. Will you call again tomorrow?'

'Yes, of course. Give Noah a kiss goodnight for me, and tell him his mother misses him and sends her love.'

'I will. I love you.'

'I love you, too.'

She let Noah stay up for longer than she should have, then tucked him up in his new bedroom with a bird book that had caught his attention and the news from home. His face lit up when she gave him his mother's message, but he didn't say anything that brokered an opportunity for questions, and in any case, she was reluctant to fill his head with dark thoughts before he went to sleep. She made a simple supper for later, then settled down with a book in the study that was now her own again. By nine o'clock, she had almost given up on Archie when she heard the sound of a car outside and a soft knock at the door. 'I hope it's not too late?' he said. 'I was intending to come here straight after I'd been to see the Herrons, but I went back to the Hall to change and there was some trouble kicking off in the woods.'

'*More* trouble?'

'I'm afraid so. Some of the locals had got it into their heads that the gypsy camp was the obvious place to look for a missing child, and they weren't very subtle about it.'

'Is everyone all right?'

'Yes, it soon fizzled out, but it's just a shame that it had to happen at all. They've been camping there peacefully every summer for years, apparently, but the minute something goes wrong, it's always the stranger's fault.'

'You might as well get used to that from now on,' Josephine said wryly. 'Have you eaten?'

'No, but don't go to any trouble.'

'It's just soup and a sandwich. Sit down while I go and get it.' When she got back, she found the wine already poured and looked approvingly at the label. 'You didn't get that from Elsie Gladding.'

'No, I'll be sorry to leave the Hall's cellars behind.'

'So you are going back to London tomorrow?'

'Via Tiptree, yes. I want to talk to that bus driver. It's the only thing I can think of that's left to do. We've searched the whole village now, dragged the pond, and I can't imagine there's anyone locally who hasn't heard about Annie's disappearance, so the chances of someone coming forward here with information are virtually non-existent.'

'What about further afield?'

'I'm afraid that's what we're looking at. Appeals in the newspaper and that sort of thing, perhaps a motorist who was passing through the village and might have seen something, but it's too long now, Josephine—far too long. So forgive me if I clutch at bus drivers who just might have driven Annie away by mistake and taken her to another part of the country.'

'You don't suspect him of abducting her deliberately?'

'Should I? You've met him.'

'He was very obliging, but so was Crippen.' She smiled, then spoke more seriously. 'I was thinking just before you arrived—it's hard to know what to hope for now. Annie back safe and well, obviously—but if that's not an option, what would I want in her parents' position? To know the worst, so I could mourn her properly, or to have some sliver of hope to cling to, no matter how unrealistic, even if it means never knowing what really happened? I honestly don't know which I'd find harder to bear.'

He refilled their glasses, and by unspoken agreement, they talked of more trivial things while they ate. 'What did you make of the Herrons?' Josephine asked, when she had cleared the supper things away.

'I've absolutely no idea. I'm pretty sure they're not involved in Annie's disappearance, but you'd go a long way to find three more damaged people under the same roof.'

'Do you think it was the war that took its toll on him?' Josephine asked, when Archie had finished telling her about the scene in Herron's study.

'I'm sure the war played its part, but that doesn't explain why his sisters are peculiar as well. I got the impression that it was more personal than that. The house doesn't seem to have shaken off the past, if you know what I mean.'

'They rarely do, in my experience. Just look at this one. But I might be able to shed some light on the Herrons after tomorrow. Margery's invited me to lunch and she knows someone who goes way back with them. I'll let you know if it's more than just interesting gossip.'

'Please do.'

'I'm not sure I'll be taking Noah round there in a hurry to look at the fossils, though. Did you see Betty? I don't like the sound of her being caught up in that sort of atmosphere.'

'She seemed fine. Happily playing in the garden and oblivious to everything.'

'That's a relief.'

'How well do you know Winnie Chilver?'

'Only to pass the time of day with.'

'There's definitely bad blood between her and the Herrons, and I wondered what it might be?'

'She had a snipe at them earlier too, when I saw her in the village, but Noah was with me and I didn't want him to worry about his sister, so I'm afraid I snubbed her. I wish I hadn't now.'

'But you haven't heard anything else on the grapevine?'

'No. Her brother grows prize-winning vegetables, but I don't think the Herrons have put up a fight in that department.'

Archie stared into the fire, deep in thought, and Josephine watched him, noticing how tired he looked, how different from the carefree man she had been so happy to see at the fete. 'You'll be glad to get back to Virginia,' she said. 'This has taken its toll, hasn't it? It's not just a case—not when a child is involved.'

'I have been missing her,' he admitted, 'which is ridiculous when she only left this morning.'

'I know how that feels.'

'Of course you do. And the kids, too. I've found myself wanting to give Teddy and Evie a hug for most of the day. On the other hand, I'm loath to leave. I want to see this through, and there couldn't be more of a contrast between Annie's disappearance and the case I've got to go back to.'

'What is it? Can you tell me?'

'A murder in Hoxton. The victim was a rent collector.'

'Not very popular, then?'

'No, not even with his widow. He was a nasty piece of work, from what I've heard. She made it perfectly clear that she was glad to see the back of him.'

'Suspiciously so?'

Archie smiled. 'No, she has an alibi—a factory job, with plenty of people to swear she was on shift. We're pretty sure he was killed by someone at Castlefrank House, but they're thick as thieves and not saying a word. All we've got to go on is the rent book to show where he'd been and the pair of scissors that somebody stabbed him with—and to be honest, we're lucky to have those. I'm surprised that whoever did it left the murder weapon behind.'

Josephine stared at him. 'Castlefrank House?'

'Yes—it's a block of flats off the main street. That's where Clifford was collecting the rents. Someone found him dead in a stairwell.' Josephine opened her mouth to tell Archie that Castlefrank House was where Noah lived, but something stopped her from mentioning the coincidence; instinctively, for reasons she was reluctant to admit, even to herself, she didn't want him to connect the two. 'I know I shouldn't say this,' he added guiltily, 'but from what I know of the man so far, I really don't give a damn who killed him, and I resent spending time on that when I could still be searching for Annie.' His resentment showed in the way he stubbed out his cigarette, barely half smoked. 'Are you all right, Josephine? You look worried. I didn't mean to shock you by telling you how I felt.'

She laughed—an awkward, nervous sound that she tried to rein in. 'Of course you haven't shocked me. I'd feel exactly the same in your position. No, I was just thinking about how awful it would be to leave this world with so little sorrow behind you. What would that say about your life?'

'And yet here I am, grieving prematurely for a little girl I never met. I don't know which is less professional, but I think I need some sleep.'

As much as she'd enjoyed his company, Josephine was relieved when Archie left. His car was barely out of earshot when she picked up the telephone and asked for the Athenaeum Hotel, leaving a message for Marta to call at her earliest convenience. She went to bed, troubled by all that had happened, and tossed and turned as the thunder returned once more, rumbling in the distance like a barrel rolled across a wooden floor. Eventually she slept, and in her dreams she heard Annie crying to be found—a mournful, desperate sound, close and insistent, yet no matter how hard she searched, the little girl was always out of reach. When she woke, on the verge of tears herself, the crying continued, and she realised that it wasn't Annie, and it wasn't a dream.

She grabbed her dressing gown and went next door to comfort Noah. He clung to her as he had earlier, but in the unforgiving darkness, his fears took longer to subside. 'What is it?' Josephine asked softly. 'Did you have a bad dream?' He shook his head, and she tried again. 'Noah, did something happen before you left home? Something that frightened you? I won't tell anyone, I promise, but if you're worried about anything at all, you'll feel better if you don't keep it to yourself.' It was a hollow argument, and one that she doubted a child would fall for; sure enough, Noah kept his counsel, but he didn't deny the truth of what she said, and—when he eventually fell asleep in her arms—Josephine found no comfort in the silence of the night.

22

The long spell of good fortune that had confined rain to the night-time hours and left the days warm and dry was threatening to come to an end, and Penrose drove through the gates of Wilkin & Sons Ltd under a slate-grey sky as heavy as his mood. He was later than he had intended, having spent the morning on a last visit to the Ridleys, convincing them that his return to London didn't signal a halt to the search for their daughter. The hours in between his visits had whittled away at their determination, he noticed, and he couldn't help but feel that a lot of the hope now left to them had been bundled up and driven away with him; the sight of Mrs Ridley in his rear-view mirror, standing lost and alone in the yard, was something that he wouldn't easily forget. He had spoken at length with the man who was overseeing the case in his absence, a detective inspector from Ipswich whom he had met before in Suffolk, and who had impressed him on another case. To his relief, Alan Donovan seemed as motivated by the Ridleys' situation as he was, and promised to keep him informed while he was away.

The Tiptree factory and its associated buildings made up a sizeable part of the modest Essex village, and it was little wonder that the name was more widely known now as a brand than as a place in its own right. The site had the feel of a self-contained community: a handsome old farmhouse, surrounded by purpose-built sheds and machine rooms, with a concert hall, a billiard room and various other facilities for the staff. The company's success was evident in the amount of surrounding land it had bought over the years: rows of workers' cottages spilled out from the centre in neat terraces, given names like 'Cherry Chase' or 'Damson Gardens', and the houses were generously proportioned and well-kept. If first impressions were anything to go by, the firm was obviously a good employer, and cared about the people who worked for it.

He announced himself at the timekeeper's lodge, and asked for Henry Maitland or Ronald Davis. Davis was still out on a delivery, but Maitland responded quickly to the secretary's call. He was a tall, fair-haired man with glasses, in his mid-thirties and more studious than Penrose had expected. 'I'll take the Chief Inspector to my office, Miss Barnard,' he said. 'Let me know when Davis comes in.'

'I never knew you made so many different products,' Penrose said, as he was led briskly through a packing room, where men in flat caps and waistcoats were loading an assortment of jars into wooden crates.

'We try new items every year, alongside our signature lines,' Maitland said enthusiastically, picking a jar of grapefruit marmalade off a shelf as he passed and handing it to his visitor. 'This is one of our newest. It never pays to stand still.'

It had been a mistake to show any interest. Penrose was treated to a detailed account of the firm's success, as well as a detour to the boiling room, where a row of women were sorting fruit into the pans. The room was hot and noisy, filled with the intense, sweet smell of strawberries, and—as impatient as he was to get on—Penrose couldn't help but be impressed by the scale of the operation. He resisted the temptation to ask more questions, though, and was relieved to get to Maitland's office in the extension built onto the farmhouse.

Maitland shut the door and offered Penrose the seat on the other side of his desk. 'Can I ask why you want to talk to Davis?' he said, without any further preamble. 'I know it's about this missing child, but why him?'

'Because I understand that your firm undertook a lot of the transport for Friday's evacuation, and that Mr Davis was at the school in Polstead at or around the time that Annie went missing. I'd like to clarify some of the timings, and find out if there's the slightest chance that Annie got on the bus and was accidentally taken away from the village.'

'So you don't suspect him of any wrongdoing?' Penrose didn't answer immediately, and Maitland was quick to fill the silence. 'I have the reputation of the firm to consider, Chief Inspector, so I'd be grateful for your frankness.'

'I've no reason to suspect that Mr Davis played any deliberate part in this, but a little girl has vanished without trace, so I want to see if either of you can help me piece together the events of that day. The slightest detail might be of use, and—'

'Me? You want to ask *me*?' He stared across the desk at Penrose, a note of panic in his voice. 'I really don't see how I can help you. I wasn't anywhere near Polstead on Friday.'

'I'm not saying you were, Mr Maitland, but you are connected with the missing girl's family through your work, and Tom Ridley says that he came to see you on Friday morning with regard to a dispute about the fruit that he supplies to you. He tells me that you weren't here, but I would be grateful if someone from your company could confirm that Mr Ridley made that visit.'

'Oh, yes—yes, I see. Well, my secretary did leave a note to say that Ridley had been, but if you want something more specific, ask at the lodge on your way out. We log all our visitors, so Miss Barnard will be able to give you an exact time.'

'Thank you. Do you know Annie Ridley?'

Once again, the straightforward enquiry seemed to bring a disproportionate response, which intrigued Penrose. 'As I said,

I'm not very familiar with Polstead,' Maitland insisted, 'and I spent all day Friday at Colchester Station, dealing with the evacuees there. Hundreds of children came and went that day.'

It wasn't what he had asked, so Penrose repeated the question. 'Just generally,' he clarified. 'I understand that you didn't see her on Friday, but I wondered if you'd ever met her during your dealings with her father.'

Reluctantly, Maitland nodded. 'Yes, I've met her once or twice. I have a daughter, Cissy, who's roughly the same age, and they've played together at the company functions— Christmas parties, the annual Harvest Home, that sort of thing. All our farmers and their families are invited, the Ridleys included.' He lowered his gaze, and Penrose waited for him to express his concern for Annie, which had been notable by its absence, but Maitland surprised him. 'Can I tell you something in confidence?'

'I can't promise to keep it confidential, especially if it has a direct bearing on the case, but I'll do my best.'

'I have my own suspicions about Davis. I have done since I heard what had happened.'

And yet you haven't come forward, Penrose thought cynically. 'So what do you suspect?' he asked. 'And why?'

'He was very late getting back here on Friday, and he wouldn't give me a satisfactory explanation. The buses were supposed to be returned to the hire firm by five o'clock, but when I got back here from Colchester at half past six or thereabouts, Davis and the bus had only just arrived.'

'You said yourself that hundreds of children were involved—wasn't it unlikely that the day would run to time?'

'That's true, but he left Colchester Station bang on schedule with the last group of children. He was a bit late getting back from Polstead, admittedly—he said he'd had to give them a hand settling in—but we made up for it with a very swift turnaround, so I don't understand what the delay was. Davis is one of our most efficient delivery men.' He said it almost grudgingly, and Penrose wondered why he bore the driver such animosity. 'Anyway, I was angry that he'd wasted more time by coming back here rather than taking the bus straight to the hire firm. We had to pay for an extra day, which was a little galling when you consider what we were doing. I had a good mind to dock it from his wages.'

'Did you ask him why he came back here?'

'Yes, although I didn't really need to. I could see for myself what he was doing. When I got here, Davis was scrubbing that bus from top to bottom.' Maitland leant forward, allowing the possible significance of the words to sink in. 'Now why would that be necessary?'

'I dare say you asked him.'

'Yes, and he came out with some nonsense about the kids being travel sick.'

'Surely that's possible? Likely, even.'

'I suppose so.' He paused, an actor giving his best line the respect it deserved. 'Except that the sleeve of his shirt was covered in blood. He said he'd cut himself on a packing crate, but I doubt that. I think *blood* was what he was scrubbing from those seats.'

'That's a very serious allegation, Mr Maitland.'

'And one which I'd like you to investigate—but please, keep my name out of it. He's not someone I'd want to get on the wrong side of.'

From the little that Penrose had already been told, Maitland seemed to have a knack of getting on the wrong side of people. 'Are you saying he's a violent man?'

'That's for you to establish. But on Friday, when I confronted him, he looked at my daughter and said something about keeping an eye on your kids because anything can happen when your back's turned. Quite frankly, Chief Inspector, I found that faintly threatening.'

There was a knock at the door, and Miss Barnard put her head round. 'Ron's just back, Mr Maitland. Do you want me to bring him here?'

'No, I'll come out,' Penrose said before Maitland could answer; he wanted to speak to the driver on his own. 'Thank you for your time, Mr Maitland. You've been very helpful.' It was quite a skill to dismiss a man in his own office, but Penrose had perfected it over the years and it served him well now. He left Henry Maitland half sitting, half standing at his desk, and the look of uncertainty on his face was satisfying.

The weather had improved by the time he got outside. In the car park, Davis was loading crates onto a lorry with another man, ready for his next delivery. Penrose introduced himself, sparing him the embarrassment of a warrant card, and asked if there was somewhere they could talk. 'My house is nearby and I'm due a break,' Davis said, with no hint of reluctance. 'Come back there with me while I fetch something to eat.' He turned to his colleague. 'Get on with this while I'm gone, Pete. I won't be more than half an hour. Cheese and pickle do you?'

Pete grinned and nodded, and Penrose followed Davis across the car park and through a gate into Cherry Chase. 'Have you worked for the firm long?' he asked.

'Since I was a boy. Growing up round here, it's the obvious choice.'

The company's houses were just as attractive close up as they had seemed from a distance, bigger and of a better standard than most factory workers' homes. 'It seems like a decent place to work,' Penrose said.

'You'll not find better. If you work hard and you're loyal, they look after you for life.' He gestured to the row of cottages as they passed. 'A lot of us served in the war, and Mr Wilkin let our families live here rent free if we enlisted voluntarily. You don't get chucked out when you're old, either. Some of the longest serving employees keep their cottages to see out their days in, and they don't pay a penny. The firm does it to mark special days or celebrations—my parents were chosen on old Mrs Wilkin's ninetieth birthday. She was a wonderful woman, you know—it was her recipe that started all this, made in her own kitchen back there at the farmhouse.'

It was noticeable that while Maitland had talked about the firm's business achievements, Davis talked about the people; there was a genuine warmth in his voice when he spoke of his company, a pride to be working for them, and Penrose liked him all the more for it, in spite of what he had come here to discuss. They turned in at a gate in the middle of the terrace, and Davis let himself in, calling his wife's name as he led his visitor down a narrow hallway and through to a small, sunny kitchen. Joan Davis was younger than her husband by a good ten years, and would have been beautiful had she not looked so drained and exhausted. 'Where's Charlie?' Davis asked.

'Outside. I was just about to give him his lunch.'

Penrose glanced out of the kitchen window, and saw a boy of about twelve sitting in a wheelchair under the cherry trees at the bottom of the garden. 'Good. I don't want him to know about any of this. We'll talk in here.'

Joan Davis took that as her signal to leave them to it. She picked up a tray, and Davis opened the back door for her. 'Your sandwiches are on the side,' she said. 'Don't forget them.'

Penrose waited for the door to close behind her, then said: 'It's about what happened on Friday.'

'Course it is. I heard about the girl going missing. Have you found her yet?'

It was impossible to know whether he meant alive or dead. 'No, I'm afraid not. To be honest, Mr Davis, it's as if she's vanished into thin air, which is why it's so important for me to build a picture of exactly what was going on at Polstead school when you dropped the evacuees off.'

'Ask me anything you want. If I can help, I'd be delighted to.'

'Thank you. What time did you get there?'

'Just before one. There'd been a mix-up, because they were expecting us earlier, but Polstead was the second drop-off of the day. We'd already been to Manningtree, and then we had to go back to Colchester and load them up again.'

'And how long were you in Polstead?'

'Longer than we meant to be. We had to keep them on the bus for a bit, because there were far more than they thought they were getting, and the vicar's wife wanted to make sure there hadn't been a mistake.' He smiled, and shook his head. 'To be honest, I felt sorry for her—she was doing her best, but she'd been landed in it, just like the rest of them, so we stayed to help out. We were supposed to have a break before the final delivery, but we worked through that instead of going straight back to the station. I suppose we were there a couple of hours in total. That didn't suit them back at base with the clipboards, but it was our time we were using. Nobody died.' He flushed, horrified by what he had said. 'I'm sorry. That wasn't . . .'

'It's fine, Mr Davis. I know what you meant. When you left Polstead school, were the buses empty?'

'Yes, of course they were.'

'*Completely* empty? You checked?'

'I had a quick look up and down the aisles to make sure that no one had left anything behind.'

'And the driver of the other bus did the same?'

'No, I checked both of them. Harry's a good driver, but I was in charge and I didn't want anything to go wrong on my watch.'

Penrose pushed the photograph of Annie across the kitchen counter. 'I realise what a difficult question this is, when you were ferrying so many children and time was of the essence, but did you notice her while you were in Polstead?'

He watched Davis's expression closely, but there was no sign of recognition, only an intense sadness. 'Her poor parents. They farm for us, I hear?' Penrose nodded. 'Then I've probably seen her at some do or other, but I don't remember. And I certainly didn't notice her on Friday.'

'You were late back on Friday evening, and . . .'

Davis scoffed. 'I wondered if we'd get to that. Call me stupid, but I doubted even Maitland could stoop as low as scoring points off something like this.'

'Scoring points in what way?'

'What did he tell you? That I was covered in blood and washing away the evidence?'

'What's your version of events, Mr Davis?'

'The one I gave to him. The bus needed cleaning because at least three kids were sick on it. And I cut myself on a packing crate—look.' He held out his right arm, and Penrose studied the cut, a couple of inches long and just beginning to heal. 'I'd give you the shirt, but it's Monday, and it'll be on the line by now. If you don't believe me, though, ask the Polstead woman—she was there when it happened, and she helped me clean it up.'

'I do believe you, but I'm curious to know why Mr Maitland would want to incriminate you, unless he believed what he was saying.'

'Same reason I'd want to incriminate him, I suppose. We don't get on, and perhaps if a kid had gone missing from

Colchester Station on Friday and there was the slightest chance he could have done it, I'd have found something dodgy on him, too.'

'But why?'

'It's private. Do I have to tell you?'

Penrose hesitated, torn between honesty and finding out what he wanted to know. 'Could it possibly be relevant to Annie's disappearance?' he asked, and Davis shook his head. 'Then no, you're not obliged to answer, but tell me this—did you threaten Mr Maitland's daughter?'

'*What?*'

He looked genuinely bewildered, and Penrose explained. 'Did you advise Mr Maitland to keep an eye on his daughter because anything could happen to her?'

'That's not what I meant, and he knows damned well it isn't.'

'So what did you mean?'

Davis stared down the garden to where his wife was patiently helping their son to eat something, and the silence stretched out until Penrose thought that he was going to refuse to answer. 'Charlie hasn't always been like this,' he said eventually. 'There was a time not so long back when he'd wear me out before breakfast—and I don't mean in the way he does now. He was so full of life, so curious about everything— but that all changed eighteen months ago, when he had an accident.'

'What happened?'

'He got run over, just outside the factory. Joan used to work there, too—she was a secretary, and that's how we met. She was kind to me when my first wife died, and things sort of went from there. I knew she was too young for me, really, but I was lonely and it seemed too good to be true.' He laughed bitterly. 'And it was, of course. We were all right for a bit, but then she took up with Henry Maitland. She was with him when that car hit Charlie—working late, if you know what I mean. She should have been taking care of our son, but she only had eyes for her fancy man, and Charlie ran off while she wasn't looking. It wasn't the driver's fault—there was nothing he could have done.'

'I'm so sorry.'

Davis shrugged. 'What can you do? He'll never walk again, though—and that's what I meant. Take your eyes off your kids for a second, and everything changes—but it was aimed at Maitland, and certainly not at his daughter.'

'What about the affair?' Penrose asked, understanding why Davis would resent Maitland so bitterly, but struggling to find a reciprocal grievance.

'It stopped there and then, but Joan's never forgiven herself. I think she was going to run off with him, you know—in his own selfish way, I reckon Maitland loved her. He certainly didn't take kindly to the fact that she ended it and stayed with us, although he's too stupid to see that it was out of guilt and nothing to do with love. He thinks I won, but the way I see it, there weren't any winners. Except little Cissy, perhaps—she's still got a mummy and daddy, and kids need that, don't they?'

If he'd had time, Penrose would happily have returned to Maitland's office and made things even more uncomfortable for him, but that was a luxury he couldn't indulge in when he was due back in London. 'Does Mrs Maitland know all this?' he asked, as Davis showed him to the door.

'I don't know. That's their business. She certainly hasn't heard it from me, but she was looking daggers at Joan during that fete. We had to come away. I couldn't put Charlie through that—I don't want him ever to know the truth about his mother and why he's the way he is. He's had enough to cope with, and hate eats away at you.'

'Thank you for your frankness, Mr Davis. You have my word that none of this will go any further.'

'That's decent of you, but you can't keep a thing like that private, not when it happens at work. Everyone knows what went on. We've just got to try and make the best of it.'

He shut the door and Penrose walked away, shaken by the unseen crises in everyday lives that his job often forced him to expose. When he got back to his car, he was surprised to find a note on the windscreen, with an urgent message to call a number that he didn't recognise, and an invitation to do so from the timekeeper's lodge. 'Are you sure?' he asked in astonishment, when the operator had put him through. 'Yes, yes of course—do it straight away. Keep trying, and I'll be with you as soon as I can.'

23

Josephine enjoyed the drive to Tolleshunt D'Arcy almost as much as Noah did. He insisted on bringing his bird book with him, and although the confirmed sightings along the way consisted of nothing more unusual than pheasants, a kestrel and a couple of magpies, they were exciting enough to him and Josephine was just pleased to see him happy. She had spoken to Marta earlier that morning, sharing her concerns about Noah's distress and the murder that had taken place where he lived. In the cold light of day, her conviction that the two were somehow linked wasn't as compelling as it had seemed the night before, but Marta took it seriously enough. In the end, Josephine agreed to discuss things obliquely with Noah when a suitable chance arose, if only to stop Marta from heading back to Hoxton to have a heart-to-heart with his mother.

They crossed the county border into Essex, making good time in the old Austin Chummy that Josephine had inherited along with the cottage. The secretive pleasures of Suffolk's lush, scented lanes soon gave way to the showier landmarks of Britain's oldest city, looking particularly impressive against the morning's brooding skies. She took a detour through Colchester's pretty town centre, showing Noah the Roman walls, priory ruins and castle keep, then pulled over in the high street to check the map and mark the route out for him to follow. As they ticked off the miles and the lyrical village names that punctuated their journey—Oxley Green, Layer de la Haye, Salcott-cum-Virley—Josephine toyed with the idea of setting a book in this part of the world, but village mysteries were too close to home for the time being, and she put the thought reluctantly to one side.

Tolleshunt D'Arcy began to be signposted, and it wasn't long before they could see its outskirts up ahead across the fields, a pencil line of attractive pink and white cottages that grew steadily broader, spilling out into a bustling centre. By comparison with Polstead, Margery's village was practically cosmopolitan, boasting a newsagent, a butcher and a baker, as well as a general stores. There was a tricycle parked outside the post office, which had the bowed, small-paned windows of a Victorian sweet shop, and at the forge, a man in a goatskin apron was busy shoeing a black and white horse—a scene which must have remained unchanged for a hundred years or more. The 'square' that Margery had mentioned was in fact a triangle, a meeting point of three roads with a maypole at its centre, topped with a weathercock and flanked by a pair of small trees. One of the roads led to Tiptree, Josephine noticed, and she wondered how Archie was getting on.

She parked near a pub called the Queen's Head, which was set back from the road in its own yard, and chose the route that led further into the village, remembering that D'Arcy House was central. She saw it almost immediately, not just because it was close, as Margery had said, but because it dominated the street, like a duchess at a garden party. 'Is that where we're going?' Noah asked, looking uneasily at the imposing Queen Anne facade, and Josephine nodded, knowing exactly how he felt.

'It certainly is. Crime obviously does pay, so remind me to work harder when we get home, will you?'

The sun came out as they approached, drawing the warmth from the soft red brick and making the house sparkle. There was a meadow directly opposite, and Josephine wondered if that was where they held the cricket match that Margery had talked so much about. D'Arcy House opened right onto a busy main street and the pavement was narrow, forcing them into the road a couple of times to avoid an open casement. Josephine glanced through the windows as she passed, eventually coming face to face with Margery, sitting at her typewriter with a cigarette in her mouth. She waved when she saw them and got up straight away, stretching and rubbing her neck as though she had been at work for some time. 'I've been trying to earn my afternoon off before you got here,' she said, joining them at the window.

'That's very diligent of you.'

'Yes, I know. It comes from being born into a fiction factory, I suppose—you don't want to let the side down.' She stubbed out the cigarette in an ashtray that was already on the windowsill, and Josephine guessed that she often stood here, watching the world go by. 'I worked out recently that I've written more than eight million words since I was seventeen, not counting the ones that haven't been sold, and *still* I worry that my publisher might think me difficult.'

Josephine smiled. 'Do you? I *hope* mine will. Is it another Campion?'

'No, we're having a break from each other. This one's a serial for America. It's nearly done, thank God—at least I thought it was, but they cabled first thing this morning to ask me very politely if it might include a war background.' She raised her eyes to the heavens.

'Hasn't it occurred to them that you might like to escape from it for a bit? You *and* your readers. I think we'll all need that before long.'

'Nothing new there. The whole of life is about escape, don't you think?' Margery's warm, musical voice took the edge off the sentiment, but Josephine couldn't help wondering what this middle-class, successful woman—apparently happily married and at the centre of village life—could possibly want to escape from. 'Hello, young man,' Margery said to Noah. 'Have you worked out how my brother did that trick yet?' He shook his head shyly. 'Well, I might show you later, when we've had lunch. Come to the door and I'll let you in.'

She ushered them into a hallway that smelt of freshly polished oak, pausing to chat with a couple of passers-by before she closed the door behind them. 'I used to hate this house being on the road,' she admitted, 'but now, when I sit in the dining room with the window open, I know everyone who goes by and they all know me. I'm not sure if the war's made me sentimental already, but I'm starting to find that remarkably heartening.'

Josephine felt much the same about a cottage at the end of a footpath, miles from anyone, but the differences between them only made Margery's company more interesting to her. Architecturally, D'Arcy House was less straightforward on the inside than it had seemed from the road. The front rooms were spacious and lived up to their exquisite facade, with panelled walls and high ceilings; the back of the house was much older—the sort of rambling building that disorientates a stranger with stairs, landings, and endless nooks and crannies. A plump, attractive woman of around Margery's age came down the passageway from the kitchen, wiping her hands on a tea towel. 'I thought I heard the door,' she said, in a pleasant country accent. 'Don't know why we bother having a bell with you at that window all day.'

Margery accepted her teasing good-naturedly. 'Noah, this is Christine,' she said. 'She looks after us all, and she's got some friends for you to meet—and a very good lunch in store. We'll see you in a bit.' Christine held out her hand and Noah followed her happily through to the kitchen. 'We've got five evacuees,' Margery explained, 'and Chrissie's been marvellous with them, so Noah's in safe hands. She's marvellous with everyone, actually, especially me. I don't know what I'd do without her. I thought we'd have lunch in the garden if the weather holds?'

'That sounds lovely.'

'Good. Come through to the bar first, and I'll make us a drink.'

Josephine assumed it was a turn of phrase, a glorified description for a tray of decanters on a sideboard, but she was wrong. One of the smaller downstairs rooms at the heart of the house had been transformed into a proper bar, complete with a serving counter, benches around the walls, and even a shove ha'penny board installed in the corner. Tankards hung from heavy timber beams above a cool flagstone floor, and the overall effect was not unlike walking into a small country pub. 'This is wonderful,' Josephine said, looking at the eclectic collection of cartoons on the walls.

'It's fun, isn't it? And very popular with our friends. I sometimes feel I've missed my vocation as a landlady.' She nodded to the drawings. 'That's a rogues' gallery of some of our regulars. Pip drew a lot of them.'

'So I see. He's very good.' Josephine examined the sketches more closely, wondering why—in an abundance of images, drawn with humour and affection—she couldn't see any of Margery.

'He's a graphic artist by trade. He does most of my book jackets, and this one here'—she pointed to a charcoal sketch of a bespectacled man in tails—'is by Grog, another friend of ours. This is Albert Campion himself, of course. Now, what can I get you?'

Josephine asked for a gin and tonic, and Margery poured the same for herself. 'Let's take these outside,' she said. 'Come on, Brock.' A young collie dog got up lazily from a blanket in the hallway and trailed at Margery's heels as she led the way through to the garden. 'His mother surprised us with a litter of fourteen a few years back,' she explained. 'Strictly speaking, he belongs to my sister Joyce, but she's just joined the Wrens, so we're looking after him.'

From what Margery had said at the fete, Josephine was anticipating a glorious garden, but the reality exceeded her expectations. 'I don't think even Mr Chilver could improve on this,' she said, looking admiringly at the neatly cut lawn and flourishing borders, stocked with a variety of flowers and mature shrubs. Like the house, the garden managed to be both gracious and beautiful without a hint of ostentation, and the somewhat haphazard planting—neat lines of runner beans sitting next to a stunning display of yellow lilies, a threadbare grass path lined with fan-shaped apple trees—only added to its charm. 'It's a proper garden, if that doesn't sound too ridiculous. It doesn't need rosettes.'

'No, I know exactly what you mean, and that's probably because it's always been tended by proper gardeners—no landscape artists or designers, just people who know what they like and what they don't. I've always found it a sanctuary, in good times and bad. I came out here yesterday after the announcement, and just sat under the laburnum for a bit, waiting for a comforting thought.'

'And did it come?'

Margery considered her answer. 'Clarity came, I suppose—a sense that this is where our philosophy has led us. This is what comes of not interfering when you see something horrible happening, even if it isn't your business.' They sat down at a table on the terrace by a large Victorian conservatory that reminded Josephine of exotic hothouses on country estates. 'Then I thought to myself, whatever happens—*whatever* happens—we must never go pretending that things were going well before the war. There's been a growing sense of dissatisfaction in most of our generation for some time, don't you think?'

'Yes, I do.'

'We were disillusioned early, and we've come to maturity without a faith, but it seems criminally silly that we should have to find it in another war.'

Her words brought back the despair and emptiness that events in Polstead had partially eclipsed for Josephine. Over their drinks, she brought Margery up to date with what little news there was of Annie. 'With every day that goes by, it gets harder and harder to hope for a happy ending, and I know Archie fears the worst, even though he's determined to do everything he can.'

'What do *you* think happened to her?'

Josephine hesitated. Her mind had been going over and over the possibilities from the moment she knew that Annie was missing, but a direct question helped to crystallise her thoughts. 'I think someone picked her up on the main road,' she said. 'Normally, an unfamiliar car would be an event in Polstead, but not on Friday, when there were people coming from other villages to collect their evacuees and everyone's attention was elsewhere.'

'An *un*familiar car? You don't suspect anyone closer to home?'

'You sound disappointed.'

Margery laughed. 'You're right, of course. The writer in me doesn't want an open-ended narrative, and a puzzle's only as good as its solution.' She thought for a moment, then added more seriously: 'Actually, it's not just the writer. If Annie got into a stranger's car, the chances of anyone finding her are so small. She could be anywhere in the country, and how would you cope with that if you were her parents?'

'I can't begin to imagine, but I'm not sure it's worse than finding the answer on your doorstep. The idea that someone you knew and probably trusted had hurt your child must be unbearable, too. You'd always be thinking that you should have seen what the culprit was really like and done more to protect what you loved.' The Ridleys felt that anyway, she thought; it was written all over their faces, clear in everything they said. There was a clamour at the back door, interrupting Josephine, and she watched as Christine led Noah and the other children down to the bottom of the garden, where they spread a blanket out on the lawn and proceeded to unpack a picnic. 'Either way, it's a terrible situation,' she sighed, turning back to Margery. 'The whole village will be scarred by it.'

'Is Annie the sort of child who'd go with a stranger?'

'Oh yes. She was naturally curious—that's one of the things I loved about her. She was always up for an adventure.' The past tense hung in the air between them; sadly, Josephine didn't try to correct it. 'There was a rumour that she'd been seen in the Herrons' car,' she added, hoping to raise the subject that had brought her here. 'Winnie Chilver—the sister, if you remember—told Archie that she'd seen Betty *and* Annie being driven away from the school hall, but he doesn't think there's any truth in it.'

'Really? Now that *is* intriguing, and it ties in with what I wanted to tell you.'

'Yes, you said you'd been delving.'

'Not intentionally, although I'm not saying I'm above that sort of thing. No, it was all to do with the garden. I called in on Jessie yesterday afternoon to see some snaps of the old house. I told you she worked for Dr Salter?'

'You said she was his housekeeper.'

'That's right. Extraordinary woman—she used to help him out with minor operations. You'll meet many a man in

Tolleshunt D'Arcy who's had a tooth pulled by Jessie Bacon. Anyway, I was telling her about the problems I'm having with the gardener, and I happened to mention Mr Chilver and his dahlias—and she reminded me that he used to work for the Herrons when he was younger. They both did, actually. Winnie was their housemaid, so she and Jessie were often thrown together when their families socialised, and they knew each other quite well.'

'How interesting—that can't have been an easy household, if the behaviour I've seen is anything to go by. And once a servant, always a servant, I suppose. No wonder she resents them if that's how they treat her.'

'There's a bit more to it than that.'

'They were sacked?' Josephine guessed. 'There's obviously some bad blood between them, and that would explain it.'

'No, they weren't sacked. On the contrary, in fact. Winnie was set up in a cottage in the village, if you know what I mean.'

'I'm not sure that I do,' Josephine admitted.

'Well, according to Jessie, Winnie was *very* close to Dr Herron. His poor wife was in delicate health, she says, and it seems he looked elsewhere for his home comforts—so when Winnie left their service, they looked after her. Still do, I gather. She's got the house for life. There was some talk at the time about her coming into some money from an aunt who died, but Jessie says that's nonsense.'

'And the Herrons did that to buy her silence?'

Margery shrugged. 'That's what I assumed, although I'm afraid I couldn't get Jessie to do anything as vulgar as spell it out.'

'But that doesn't really make sense,' Josephine said, having thought about it for a moment. 'Why would Winnie Chilver bite the hand that feeds?'

'I don't know. Mr Chilver stayed on as gardener for a while after his sister left, but—'

'Marge? Marge!' The voice came from inside the house, and Margery looked round impatiently. 'That's Pip. He's on shift in the Warden's Post. I hope nothing terrible has happened. Sitting out here with you, I'd quite forgotten there was a war on.'

'Marge? Oh, there you are . . .'

'Exactly where I said I was going to be. Is it an air raid?'

'What? Oh no, it's nothing like that. I almost wish it were—we're prepared for that.'

'Then what are you doing out here? You're not supposed to leave the telephone. Josephine, meet my husband, Philip Youngman Carter. Pip, this is Josephine Tey.'

Pip was tall, with dark, receding hair and a thin face, and he reminded Josephine of a more serious Noël Coward. 'Delighted to meet you,' he said, 'and I'm sorry to interrupt with so little ceremony, but I need Margery to come inside for a moment. Miss Page from White House Farm is here and she's brought the child back with her.'

'What *is* she thinking of?' Margery snapped. 'She can't do that. We're not *Exchange and Mart*.' She turned to Josephine. 'This is the evacuee I told you about who won't settle.'

'It's more than that, apparently,' Pip insisted. 'The girl has barely eaten a thing since she arrived and she cries all the time. She keeps saying that she doesn't belong here and she wants to go back because her mother and father will be missing her.'

'Her and thousands of others,' Margery said, but there was sympathy in her voice.

'Miss Page won't go until she's seen you. As far as she's concerned, you're the billeting officer and it's up to you to sort this out. She's happy to take one of ours instead, but she says she doesn't see why she should have to worry herself sick about a child that isn't even hers. Between you and me, she's got a point—the girl looks awful.'

'Angela, isn't it?'

'Something like that.'

'Go and get Christine to take her outside with the rest of the children—if anyone can calm her down, it's Chrissie. Will you excuse me for a minute, Josephine?'

'Yes, of course. Is there anything I can do to help?'

'It doesn't sound as if there's much that either of us can do. I'll probably have to get in touch with the girl's school if it really is as bad as all that, and they'll let the parents know, but I'll try not to be long and then we can have some lunch.' She downed her drink and stood up. 'And to think I used to worry that village life wasn't adventurous enough!'

Josephine turned her chair slightly to follow Pip's progress as he walked quickly across the lawn and took Christine back into the house. Noah seemed to have palled up with a boy of around his own age, and she watched as they talked and laughed together, hoping that there wouldn't be any trouble. The picnic seemed to be going well, and it was all that she could do to stop herself from going over and helping herself to a sandwich. Instead, she sipped her gin and thought about what Margery had told her. It was none of her business, but the Herrons fascinated her, particularly since Archie had told her about his second visit to Black Bryony. The threat of a scandal never entirely went away, she thought, and shame was a powerful motive, especially in a close-knit community like Polstead, but still she could see no connection with Annie's disappearance.

The sound of a child crying broke the peace of the afternoon, and everyone turned to look at the new arrival, Josephine included. Christine had Angela in her arms, but none of her attempts to soothe or distract her seemed to be working, and the little girl continued to sob and beat her fists in frustration against Christine's shoulder. The long-suffering housekeeper transferred her from one arm to the other, dislodging the sun-hat that she had been wearing in the process, and Josephine stared in shock at the child's red, tear-stained face, which tracked every moment of her fear and distress. It was a pitiful sight, and Josephine got slowly to her feet, unable to think of a time when she had felt more relief, or more joy. She looked again to make sure, disorientated by the discord between her emotions and the girl's obvious pain, but there was no doubt about it. 'Annie!' she called, hurrying across the lawn. 'Annie! Thank God.'

Christine turned to her in surprise. 'It's Angela, Miss,' she said, obviously embarrassed to have to correct one of Margery's guests. 'Her name's Angela, and she's . . .'

Whatever she was about to say was lost in the scream of recognition that came from the child in her arms. Annie stretched out her hands to Josephine and struggled violently to be put down; confused, Christine obliged her. 'I'm so sorry,' Josephine said, conscious that her own tears must look even more out of place than Annie's. 'This will seem very strange and please don't ask me how it's happened, but this child's name is Annie, not Angela. She's the girl who's been missing from my village for several days now, and we'd just about given up hope of finding her.' Annie was clinging to her legs, not remotely interested in explanations when all she wanted was a hug from someone she knew, and Josephine scooped her up and held her tight. 'Annie, we've all been so worried about you. How on earth did you end up here? Your mummy and daddy have been looking everywhere for you. They'll be so pleased to have you home.'

She didn't say anything, but there would be plenty of time for explanations when she was back where she belonged.

Josephine noticed Noah watching them and beckoned him over. 'This is Annie,' she said.

'You found her?'

There was a look of admiration on his face that Josephine didn't really feel was merited by the stroke of luck that had brought Annie to her, but still she was touched by it. 'Isn't that wonderful news? Finish your picnic while I go inside and let everyone know what's happened, and then we can take her home.'

Christine gave Josephine directions to the dining room, but the voices would have led her there anyway: Margery's was patient, if a little weary, while her visitor sounded indignant and at her wits' end. They both stopped short when they saw Josephine standing in the doorway, holding a child who was now the very picture of contentment. 'I'm sorry to interrupt,' she said, 'but there's obviously been a terrible misunderstanding. I don't know who Angela is, but this little girl's name is Annie Ridley, and she's from Polstead, not London.'

'This is Annie?' Margery said, her tone hovering somewhere between astonishment and delight. 'How simply marvellous! Annie, you have no idea how pleased I am to meet you.'

'But she came from *London*,' Miss Page insisted, still struggling to catch up with events. 'She was on the bus from the station, and she was wearing this.' She rummaged in her handbag and took out one of the familiar evacuation labels. 'I brought it with me so you'd have her details. This makes no sense. Why would a child from Polstead need to be evacuated?'

Josephine smiled apologetically. 'She wasn't supposed to be. She was telling the truth when she said that she didn't belong with you and she shouldn't be there—but how were you to know? It's only what thousands of children are saying at the moment.' She took the label, remembering that afternoon in the school hall, when Annie had been sulking and impossible to pacify. 'Did you find this, sweetheart?' she asked gently, but Annie shook her head. 'Are you sure? I saw you playing with one of these. You're not in trouble, I promise, but we need to understand what happened so that we can put everything right.' Annie hesitated, obviously deciding whether or not to trust her. 'You did find it, didn't you?'

'Yes.'

'In the school hall?' Again, she shook her head. 'Where then?'

'In the playground, on the floor.'

'So where's Angela?' Miss Page demanded. 'I've written to her parents, telling them that she arrived safely. What on earth will they think?' She turned accusingly to Annie. 'Why didn't you tell me who you really were? Do you have any idea what trouble you might have caused?'

Annie hid her face and Josephine tried to calm the situation, but Margery got there first. 'I'm sure she's very sorry, and we'll clear up all the misunderstandings right away, but the important thing is to let Annie's family know that she's all right and get her home to them.'

'Can I use your telephone?' Josephine asked.

'Yes, of course. We'll give you some peace and quiet—you might be able to get more from our little wanderer here if it's just the two of you.' She ruffled Annie's hair. 'Would you like something to eat, sweet pea? I know where there's a very nice chocolate cake.'

Margery ushered Pip and Miss Page from the room, and Josephine sat down at the desk with Annie on her lap, grateful for her friend's diplomacy. She understood the anger that Annie's deception had caused, and feared that the same might be true in some corners of Polstead once the relief of her safe return had passed, but she had no doubt that her parents would forgive their daughter anything to have her home safe and sound, and they were Josephine's priority. As far as she knew, the Ridleys didn't have a telephone so she called Elsie Gladding at the shop, but the line was engaged. Frustrated, she picked up the receiver again and asked for Wilkin & Sons, hoping to catch Archie before he left for London. The woman who answered told her that his car was still in the car park, and promised to get a message to him, so Josephine left Margery's number and a request for him to call, deflated at having such good news to deliver and no one to deliver it to. She picked up the misleading luggage label and thought about what Miss Page had said, wondering if she should call Hilary to find out where the real Angela Lucas had been billeted, but it didn't seem right to talk to anyone else in the village before the Ridleys knew that Annie was safe, so she tried Elsie again without success, then put the receiver firmly back in its cradle to wait for Archie.

As Margery had said, their dining room had been completely taken over by the war. The room was elegantly furnished with good quality, interesting antiques, and there was still a hint of domesticity in the books and scraps of sewing that littered the surfaces, but otherwise it was a sober reminder of the times they were facing: a wall map of Europe had been pinned above the desk, and the shutters were standing by the windows, ready for the blackout; gumboots and gas-proof suits made of oiled cloth filled the room with an overpowering smell of poultices; and the wall behind her was lined with boxes of medical equipment—bandages and packets of lint, bottles of Dettol and sal volatile that reminded Josephine of her time as a VAD during the last war. The wireless was on low in the background, and in the corner nearest the door, buckets and shovels stood by for use in the event of incendiaries. Wherever she looked, there was an ominous sign of this strange new world that no one wanted to get used to, and when the telephone rang, she half expected to hear that enemy planes were approaching the coast.

'This is Detective Chief Inspector Penrose. I've been asked to ring this number.'

Stupidly, she had forgotten to leave her name. 'Archie, it's me. I'm at Margery's house, and Annie's all right.'

'Are you sure?' he asked, and she could hear the disbelief in his voice.

'Yes, she's here with me now. It's all been an awful mistake. She picked up another child's evacuation label, and somehow got herself billeted to Tolleshunt D'Arcy. She's too upset for me to probe much at the minute, but I suspect you were right all along—I think she got on the bus out of defiance, and ended up having a much bigger adventure than she meant to. She was so frightened and upset when I first saw her, and I'm guessing that the longer she pretended to be someone else, the harder it was for her to tell the truth. I've been telephoning Elsie so that she can let the Ridleys know, but I haven't got through yet. You're happy for me to do that? I don't want them to wait a minute longer than they have to.'

'Yes, yes of course—do it straight away. Keep trying, and I'll be with you as soon as I can.'

'All right. It's D'Arcy House, on the main street. You can't miss it.'

This time, the phone at the village shop rang and rang, and Josephine was just beginning to think that she had missed Elsie when she answered, slightly breathless, as if she had been outside; for once, the hope in her voice wasn't a torment to Josephine. 'Elsie, it's Josephine Tey. I've got some marvellous news for you. I've found Annie, and she's absolutely fine.' There was a long silence on the line, and eventually Josephine realised that Elsie was quietly weeping; she let her cry, getting all the guilt and tension of the last few days out of her system, and allowed herself to acknowledge properly for the first time that the whole village, herself included, had believed in their hearts that Annie was dead. 'I'll explain properly when I see you, but—'

'Is she *really* all right? I don't care about anything else as long as I know that.'

'Yes, she's been well looked after and she's right here with me now. You can ask her yourself.' Josephine held the phone to Annie's ear so that she could say hello to her grandmother. 'We're in Tolleshunt D'Arcy,' she added, explaining as succinctly as she could what had happened with the luggage label, 'so not far away at all. I'll bring her back to the farm in a little while. Will you let Kathy and Tom know?'

'Yes, of course. I'll go over there right now and tell them. So you'll bring her home to us this afternoon?'

'We'll leave as soon as I've spoken to Mr Penrose. He'll take care of anything that needs to be done on the official side, and then we'll be on our way. In the meantime, I think Annie's going to have a large slice of chocolate cake.'

Margery arrived on cue with a tray just as Josephine was hanging up. 'I'm assuming you'll want to get this little girl home as soon as possible, so I've brought us our own picnic. I don't see why the kids should have all the fun, and we can do lunch properly another time.'

'That's very kind of you. I've just spoken to Annie's grandmother, and they can't wait to have her back.'

'The best telephone call you've ever made?'

'Without a doubt.'

'I don't want to put a dampener on things, but I promised Miss Page that we'd get to the bottom of the situation. I think she honestly believes that the police are going to arrest her for abduction at any minute.'

'Archie's on his way here now, as it happens, but I don't think he's got his eye on Miss Page. I was just about to phone Hilary Lampton to find out where Angela Lucas is. If her mother received two cards in the post this morning, she must be very confused by now.'

'Good idea. I'll go and get the tea—unless you'd prefer another gin?'

'No, tea would be lovely. Is Noah all right?'

'Absolutely fine—and quite a natural at croquet, it would appear.'

Hilary answered straight away, and the Polstead grapevine had obviously been working overtime. 'Josephine! What wonderful news. Stephen's just told me. He bumped into Miss Bloomfield, who'd just met Elsie on her way to the farm. I really couldn't be happier.' So much for the Ridleys being the first to hear the news, Josephine thought wryly. 'Bit of a gaffe with the labels, I understand?' Hilary continued. 'Quite frankly, I think it's a miracle that a damned sight more of this hasn't gone on.'

'That's why I'm phoning,' Josephine said, when she could get a word in. 'Are you able to let me know who Angela Lucas is staying with? She's the girl whose label Annie picked up, and we're keen to make sure that her mother has the right information.'

'Yes, of course. Hang on a minute while I go and get the book.' Josephine helped herself to a slice of chicken and ham pie while she waited, realising suddenly how hungry she was. Hilary was gone for a while, and when she picked up the receiver again, she sounded confused. 'That's very odd. I don't have any record of an Angela Lucas being billeted with us. She was on our original list, but she never arrived on the day—several of them didn't, if you remember, but that rather paled into insignificance compared with all those who arrived without warning. The official lists turned out to be bloody useless.'

'But Angela must have been there, otherwise how would Annie have picked up her label?'

'Oh yes, I see what you mean. That *is* puzzling. Let me check again.' There was a silence and Josephine waited impatiently, beginning to sense that something was wrong. 'No, she's definitely not in Polstead. Do you want me to get in touch with the office at Hadleigh, just in case? They'll have lists for the whole district.'

'Would you? And call me back as soon as you know. I'm on Tolleshunt D'Arcy 241.'

'Any luck?' Margery asked, returning with the tea.

'Not yet, I'm afraid.' Josephine glanced down at Annie, reluctant to say anything that might upset her, but the little girl was fast asleep in her arms. 'There's no record of an Angela Lucas in Polstead. Hilary's checking the area for me, but if the label was in Polstead, then surely Angela should be?'

'You'd have thought so, wouldn't you? Unless the labels were mixed up at school, of course, before the kids even left London.'

'Some sort of prank, you mean? Girls messing about?'

'I wasn't thinking of anything as deliberate as that, but you're right. A practical joke *is* a possibility, in which case we're looking for the proverbial needle.' They stared at each other, and Josephine didn't know whether to feel alarmed or reassured by the fact that Margery was obviously as concerned as she was. 'Let me just double-check the Tolleshunt D'Arcy lists,' she offered. 'It would be embarrassing to find that she's been safely here all the time, and yours truly as the billeting officer didn't realise it.' She shuffled the paperwork on her desk. 'No,' she said eventually, with a sigh. 'She's not with us. I'll phone our district office, too, as soon as your friend has rung back.' She brightened, trying to stay positive. 'I'm sure we're reading far too much into this. There's probably a very innocent explanation.'

'Perhaps,' Josephine said, struggling to share her optimism, 'but you and I make a living out of solving puzzles, so don't you find it odd that neither of us can come up with one?'

24

Penrose had made many difficult house calls in his time, break-ing the news to grief-stricken parents that their child had been killed or abused; he had also taken the brunt of a family's anger at the lack of progress on an investigation, where a body had yet to be found or insufficient evidence existed to convict a prime suspect—but his visit to Bob and Margaret Lucas was set to be a first. Never before had he gone so empty-handed, not even knowing for sure if a crime had been committed, or if their child's disappearance was down to a bureaucratic error in the evacuation procedure that would come to light in due course. The situation wasn't of his making, but still he felt responsible: the Lucases would no doubt already be feeling the loss of their daughter, no matter how sensible it had been to send her away, and they deserved more from him than the sketchy list of possibilities that he had to offer.

He had gone straight to the Yard on his return from Essex, hoping that some of the checks he had put in place from Tolleshunt D'Arcy would have paid dividends, but every enquiry so far had led to a dead end. Over the weekend, there had been a few reports of evacuees destined for East Anglia ending up in Plymouth or Blackpool, so there was still a chance that Angela would be found in somebody's records as they moved their search further afield, but such extreme cases were few and far between, and privately Penrose agreed with Josephine and Margery: the label suggested that Angela had, however briefly, been in Polstead, or had disappeared on her way there, and if that assumption proved to be correct, then all the hopelessness that had begun to dominate their search for Annie Ridley was as easily passed from one child to another as that small, misleading piece of identification had been.

On the spur of the moment, he decided to take a female police officer with him. If his worst fears turned out to be justified, then the family would need support, and Lillian Wyles had twenty years of experience on the force, as well as the sort of sensitivity and no-nonsense kindness that made her a natural friend to people facing the darkest time of their lives. Penrose respected her abilities, and the quiet, determined way in which she had faced down the widespread prejudice that challenged any woman who attempted a police career with so few role models to learn from, and he was pleased to have her with him.

It was four o'clock in the afternoon when they arrived at the Lucases' address, a time when residential streets like this would normally be teeming with children just home from school. Today, they were eerily empty: no ball games were underway and no friends had gathered together outside the corner shop; the chalk-marked pavements up and down the road were gradually fading, with no one left to play hopscotch. Penrose parked the car outside number forty, noting the silence and the twitch of a net curtain on either side, and knocked firmly at the door.

Margaret Lucas was a young woman—twenty-five at the most, Penrose guessed. She looked tired when she answered the door, and her make-up was a half-hearted affair: lipstick and powder, but nothing more, as if she had realised that there was really no point by the time she got to her eyes. She looked curiously at WPC Wyles, but it was hard to say if it was a uniform at her door that was the issue, or the fact that a woman was wearing it. 'We're here about your daughter, Mrs Lucas,' Penrose said, when he had introduced them both.

'Angie? Why? What's the matter? Has something happened to her?'

'We're not sure, but there are some concerns that we'd like to discuss with you.'

He was aware of the answer's inadequacy even before he saw the confusion on her face. 'You'd better come in.'

She stood aside to let them pass. The front door opened straight into the sitting room, with a small kitchen beyond that, and there was the smell of burnt toast in the air. A clothes horse had been set up by the radiator, and Penrose's heart contracted when he saw the rows of little dresses and cardigans that had been lovingly hung out to dry. Wyles caught his eye and looked away. 'I'm sorry about the laundry, but the weather was a bit iffy today so I've kept it in here,' Mrs Lucas explained. 'I thought Angie would want something a bit warmer now the summer's over. She couldn't take much with her, you see, and to be honest, I wanted to keep busy. It's been so quiet since she left.'

The whole house had that routine, aimless tidiness of someone with too little to do: magazines perfectly aligned in a rack; tins stacked neatly on a shelf; no crockery left dirty on the side to deal with later. 'Is your husband due home soon?' Penrose asked.

'Bob? No, he's been called up, so it's just me here. What's all this about?'

'I'm afraid that your daughter hasn't arrived at her evacuation post, Mrs Lucas. We're worried that—'

She held up her hand to stop him, laughing with relief. 'No, no—it's so kind of you to come, but Angie's perfectly safe. The card came this morning. Honestly, I don't think I've ever been so pleased to hear the postman.' She put her hand to her chest, and breathed out heavily. 'God, you frightened the life out of me for a minute there. It's been bad enough having to wait all weekend, but it was worth it when that dropped through the letterbox.' Penrose glanced over to the postcard, propped up in pride of place by the clock on the mantelpiece, where Mrs Lucas could see it whenever she passed through the room or sat listening to the wireless. 'It's a farm she's gone to—she'll like that. She loves flowers and animals—well, they all do at that age, don't they, and we could never really give her a pet here. And I thought they sounded kind—that's the main thing. She's missing us, apparently—a bit slow to settle. I know I shouldn't be, but I was pleased to hear that. You want them to be happy, of course you do, but you want to be missed, too, don't you? Is that selfish of me?'

She looked to the other woman in the room as the person who would understand, and Wyles shook her head. 'No, of course not. It's perfectly natural under the circumstances. I'm sure most parents feel the same way.'

Maggie Lucas seemed grateful for the reassurance, and Penrose stepped in quickly, before the illusion of all being well could take root. 'I'm afraid that postcard was referring to another child,' he said gently. 'There's been a misunderstanding.'

'What sort of misunderstanding?' She snapped the words, her voice suddenly a higher pitch.

'At some point in her journey on Friday, your daughter lost her identification label and it was picked up by another girl. That girl was mistakenly taken to a village called Tolleshunt D'Arcy as an evacuee . . .'

'No, that can't be right.' She snatched the card from the mantelpiece and thrust it at them. 'Look—it says Angela. There's her name. Are you telling me that was a lie?'

'The card was sent in good faith,' Penrose insisted, 'but because Annie arrived wearing Angela's label, everyone assumed that's who she was. There was no reason to believe anything else.'

'So why didn't she tell them, this Annie? Why did she pretend to be someone she wasn't?'

That was a more difficult question to answer, and Penrose could only repeat what little information he and Josephine had managed to glean so far from a frightened child. 'Annie was angry with her parents, so she thought she'd run away to teach them a lesson. She found Angela's label in the school playground where the evacuees were dropped off, and she hid under a seat on one of the buses. When the bus went back to Colchester Station to pick up more children, Annie was still on board, and she got mixed up with the next batch of evacuees to be delivered. I can only assume that she thought she'd be in trouble, and the longer she kept up the pretence, the harder it was to tell the truth.'

'So she's wasted all this time playing games, when my Angie could be anywhere?'

'I'm afraid so. Her parents thought that *she* was the one who was missing, and we've been searching for her ever since, but she was found this morning, safe and well.'

'Angie's been gone since Friday? That's three days, and me and her father didn't even know anything was wrong. We could have been looking for her.' The shock had finally caught up with her and her legs buckled, as if she were about to faint. Wyles moved forward quickly to support her, and led her over to a chair, then went next door to fetch a glass of water. 'This can't be happening,' Mrs Lucas said, waving the water aside. 'Please tell me none of this is real. How can she be here with me one minute, then vanished into thin air the next? Why don't they *know* where she is? There must be records and systems.'

'There are. We're checking everything that we can at the moment, and we certainly haven't given up hope of finding Angela somewhere else in the country, safe and well. It's a huge operation, and mistakes are bound to be made—but, as you say, we've lost some time over the weekend, so I'd rather cover every possibility, just to be on the safe side. What was Angela wearing when she left?'

'Her school uniform. She loves school—it's as much as I can do to get her to change out of it when she gets home. Red and grey, it is.'

'Did she have anything with lace on it?'

'Lace? On a school uniform? No, of course not.'

'And did she have a doll with her, Mrs Lucas?'

'Polly, yes. They were only allowed to take one, so she went with her favourite. I've got some others to send on, though.' She nodded to a box on the side table, and Penrose saw that it was already addressed to a farm in Tolleshunt D'Arcy. 'I thought that having some familiar things would cheer her up.'

'And what sort of doll is Polly?'

'A rag doll, with blue eyes and black hair. She's a bit worse for wear now—Angie carts her everywhere.'

Penrose heard Kathleen Ridley's voice as clearly as if she were in the room: *It's been loved by somebody* . . . 'I have to tell you that a doll like that has been found in Polstead,' he said quietly.

'Well, then—Angie *must* have got there, mustn't she? Why aren't you looking for her?'

'We have searched the village extensively.'

'But for this other girl, not for Angie.'

Penrose hesitated. How could you tell a mother that—in practical terms—it mattered little who they were looking for? The results, or rather the lack of them, were the same. 'We *will* be going back there now to look at things again,' he promised. 'Some of the teachers at Angela's school are still in Polstead, so we'll talk to them first and try to establish when and where she was last seen.'

'She was with one of them the last time I saw her,' Margaret Lucas said. 'At least, I assume he was one of her teachers. He was with the school party, and he was being ever so kind to her.'

'Where was this?'

'On the platform at Liverpool Street. I know they said we weren't supposed to go, but I couldn't just leave her at the school.'

'You didn't recognise this man?'

'No, but he seemed to know Angie—that's why I thought he must be a teacher. He had a bag of sweets with him, and he was wiping her face with a handkerchief. She'd been crying, you see. She was upset when she left.'

'What did he look like?'

'He was an older man. Dark hair, greying a bit, and smart—he was wearing a suit.'

'Would you know him again?'

'Yes, I think so.'

'And did he get on the train with Angela?'

'I didn't see her go. There was some trouble in the crowd, so I looked over to see what was going on. Just a few seconds it must have been, but when I looked back at the train, Angie was gone, and Lizzie, too.'

'Lizzie?'

'Another girl from the school. They'd been paired off in the line, so at least she had a friend.' She clenched her fists in her lap, trying to control her emotions. 'They *said* she'd be safe, and that's all we wanted. They said if we let her go, she'd be looked after until it was all right to come back. Why did we trust them? What can Hitler throw at us that's worse than this?' Penrose tried to think of an answer that didn't sound trite or dismissive, but his imagination failed him. 'She wouldn't eat her breakfast that day,' Mrs Lucas continued, reliving in her mind the last hours she had spent with her daughter. 'She went away hungry, and I'll never forgive myself for that. She left here thinking that she'd done something wrong, that we didn't love her any more, and we should have tried harder to make her understand, but we thought we'd have time to do that when this was all over. Now, if something's happened to her, we'll never have the chance to put things right, will we?'

She broke down, and Penrose waited until the first wave of grief had passed, trying to imagine what it was like to believe that your child had died doubting your love. 'Mrs Lucas,' he said, experiencing a depressing sense of déjà vu, 'I can't change anything that's happened up to now, but you have my word that we will do everything humanly possible to find your daughter.'

She nodded, but he could see that she wasn't remotely comforted, let alone convinced. 'I'll need to tell my husband what's happened,' she said, wiping her eyes.

'Yes, of course. If you give me his regiment, I can arrange for you to speak to him.'

'I want to go there.'

'To his regiment? I'm not sure if—'

'No, to the village where Angela went.'

The request took him by surprise, although it shouldn't have done, and his response was clumsy. 'There's no need—'

'That's not for you to say. If my daughter's missing, I want to be doing something to find her. She's only gone in the first place because I trusted someone else to look after her, and I'm not making the same mistake again.'

Penrose nodded. 'Is there someone who could come with you? Someone to be with you now for support?'

'My sister, if she can get time off work. She only lives in the next street. I'll go round and ask her in a bit.'

'Very well. We'll bring a car to collect you both first thing in the morning.'

25

Winnie heard the click of the front gate as she was sweeping the hearth rug, and wondered where the week had gone. She went to the window and watched as Florence Herron walked up the garden path for their regular appointment, her basket on her arm, her head held high—every inch the bountiful lady taking pity on a faithful old retainer. It was the image she liked to project, and—for the sake of what it brought her—Winnie was happy to collude in the deception. Respect was everything to the Herron children, just as it had been to their father, and it had cost them dear to hold on to it. She craned her neck to see to the end of the lane; sure enough, the car was parked in its usual position at the side of the green, Master Edmund behind the wheel. Funny, after all these years, that she should still think of him as the boy he had been back then, and she tutted to herself, irritated by her own deference. One of these days, she'd march up to that car and call him out, if only to see the fear on his face, but today wasn't the day to make a scene; today, she'd let him hide behind his sister.

Florence had brought the child with her, brandished at her side like a trophy, and Winnie wondered why she had bothered. It was the first time that she had been close enough to the Herrons' evacuee to see her properly, and the resemblance to poor little Rosemary took her breath away. Florence knocked at the door, and Winnie made her wait, as she always did. Her days of answering bells, of being constantly at someone's beck and call, were long gone, and she enjoyed this small sliver of power almost as much as the bigger hold that she had over the family. It was childish, perhaps, but she didn't care; she'd had to grow up before her time, and there was no one left who would dare begrudge her a chance to claw back some of what was lost. The knock came again, less imperious this time, and she smiled when she heard it, a sure sign that Florence was irritated.

She sauntered to answer it, trying to look welcoming for the little girl's sake. 'I'm sorry to have kept you waiting,' she said. 'I was out in the garden.'

'Of course you were.'

There was a silence as the two women took stock of each other. 'You'd better come in,' Winnie said eventually. 'I wasn't expecting such pleasant company today.' She looked down at the child, still a little disconcerted by her dark chocolate hair and hazel eyes; the dress looked familiar, too, and with a start, she realised that the Herrons had put the poor little soul in the clothes of their dead sibling; she could all but smell the mothballs. 'It's Betty, isn't it?' she said. 'I met your brother yesterday, and he seems like a very fine chap. Such a shame you couldn't be with him. Brothers and sisters should stick together.' She looked meaningfully at Florence, then turned back to Betty. 'Would you like a glass of milk?'

Betty nodded, and Florence put a hand protectively on her shoulder. 'I thought I'd bring her with me today, just to let you know she's safe and well. I know how concerned you can be for a child's welfare, and I wouldn't want you to worry unnecessarily.'

Winnie ignored the sarcasm and showed her visitors into the parlour. Even though she came here as the weaker party, Florence always managed to flaunt her disdain for the house; without waiting to be asked, she sat down at the table, positioning herself on the very edge of the chair, as if too much contact with the fabric of the Chilvers' life would somehow diminish her. Winnie saw her eyes flick dismissively round the room, falling in turn on the shapeless, worn cushions and threadbare carpet, on the curtains that were past their best. She went through to the scullery to get Betty's milk, ashamed by the way in which Florence always managed to make her pick unhappily at the scab of her own existence, finding fault with things that at any other time were enough.

She returned with a single glass, and if Florence noticed her lack of hospitality, she chose not to mention it. The basket of cakes and pies—the thoughtful reason for her visit, as far as any neighbours were concerned—had been laid out on the table, and Betty was sent to sit quietly in the corner while the old adversaries turned to face each other. 'I must admit, I hesitated over coming here today,' Florence said. 'If you insist on spreading lies about my family, I really don't know why we should feel obliged to continue with this arrangement.'

It wasn't so much the words that angered Winnie as the arrogance with which they were spoken. She looked at Florence's petulant face, remembering how much she had hated her as a child. Lillian had been the clever one, detached enough to stay out of trouble, and Edmund had been too cowed by his father to have much of a personality at all; but Florence had always had a sense of entitlement, couched in a calculating humility, that made Winnie see red, and nothing had changed over the years. She retaliated instantly, without stopping to consider the long game that Florence might be playing in making such a provocative remark. 'We'll continue it because I know what's buried in your garden. *I* get to say when it stops, not you.'

She held out her hand, and Florence took an envelope from the basket and handed it over. Slowly and deliberately, Winnie counted the money out onto the table, knowing how deeply this suggestion of mistrust offended her visitor. Florence glared at her. 'Daddy would be so disappointed to know that you're just a grubby little liar after all,' she said.

Winnie paused, taking a breath before she answered. 'You're still jealous, aren't you? Even after all these years. You can't bear the thought that your precious father took Cyril and me on to give us a chance.'

'Only because you fluttered those slutty eyelashes at him.'

'Is that the best you can do?' Winnie smiled. 'I've lived with that slur for fifty years or more, and it hasn't troubled me, although it's disrespectful to him. Your father loved your mother. If you'd had parents like mine and Cyril's, you'd appreciate that, not tarnish it with lies to cover up something far worse.'

'Well, I don't want any more lies from you, either, or there'll be consequences—for us all.'

Florence stood up to go, but Winnie put a hand on her arm. 'Are you *sure* they were lies? *Really* sure, I mean. You know what your brother is capable of, and once you've taken one child, it's not hard to take another.'

'That was different. He was a child himself, we all were. He didn't understand what he was doing.'

'But still a child died.' Winnie had scored a hit, and she hammered it home. 'Do you know where Edmund was when the girl went missing?'

She could tell by the expression on Florence's face that her lack of an answer troubled her, but doubt only made the younger Herron sister more aggressive. 'I could ask you the very same thing,' she countered.

'What do you mean?'

'I remember the way that Cyril looked at my little sister when he worked for us. I didn't know what it meant then, but I do now. Nothing was too much trouble for him, was it? He looked after Rosie for hours in the garden while Mummy was too ill, showed her all the pretty flowers, let her go in that shed of his when it rained . . .'

'Where's the harm in that? Your parents—'

'Were grateful, yes—that's the irony of it all.' She went over to Betty and stroked her hair. 'I walked in on them once, you know. It was the most beautiful summer's day—so hot, and not a cloud in the sky. I couldn't work out why Rosie wouldn't want to be outside with us, so I went looking for her.'

Winnie stood up. 'I think you should go.'

'He hadn't shut the door properly, silly man.' Florence laughed, a hollow, awkward sound, and it was as much as Winnie could do not to strike her. 'It was stifling in there, and it smelt of tobacco. I can never smell a pipe now without being taken instantly back to that day. Rosie was on your brother's lap, and he was jiggling her up and down, moving her closer to him. She thought it was a terrific game—smiling away, she was. He had his hand on her thigh—I can see it now. Those rough, calloused fingers looked so odd against her young skin, so big and dirty, and the expression on his face was . . .' She shuddered. 'Well, I don't think I've ever seen anyone look so *loving*, but it was a different sort of love to the way that our parents looked at us. I understood that, even then.' She pulled herself out of her reverie, and looked directly at Winnie. 'So how do you know it wasn't Cyril? Have you asked him?'

Winnie hesitated. To say that she had would be to admit her doubts, and yet she had known that Cyril's answer was the truth. 'He'd never do that to the Ridley family,' she said, sticking to words that she could trust her voice to speak with conviction. 'Cyril would never touch a hair on that little girl's head.'

Florence smiled, and the ground shifted beneath Winnie's feet, although she didn't know why. 'Annie Ridley isn't missing, though,' Florence said, after a long pause.

'What?'

'I saw Mrs Gladding just now, on my way here. They got Annie back today. That woman from Larkspur Cottage found her in another batch of evacuees. It's all been a dreadful mistake.'

'Thank God.' The relief was almost too much for Winnie, and she struggled to keep it in check. 'Well, then, what are you—'

'No, it's another girl who's gone missing, one of the children from London. A stranger. *That's* who you need to ask your brother about.' She glared at Winnie, with genuine hate in her eyes. 'Who knows where Cyril was on Friday afternoon, or how many children there have been over the years? He travelled round quite a bit, didn't he, when he was younger—a jobbing gardener, always on his own? So yes, I'm calling an end to this arrangement here and now. I've had enough of putting money in a pot on the mantelpiece for the likes of you.'

'The likes of us? How dare you. You're talking nonsense, and none of it changes what we both *know* to be true.' It was bluff on either side: they both felt in their hearts what their brothers were capable of, and they would go to any lengths to protect them; it was the one thing they had in common, that and the memory of a day, fifty years ago, when a child had died and a family had conspired to cover it up rather than face the shame. 'You wouldn't risk it,' she said.

'Try me.'

In the heat of the argument, Winnie hadn't heard Cyril coming home, and she jumped when he opened the door. 'What's going on, Win?' he asked warily, trailing dirt across the carpet she'd just cleaned. Before she could stop herself, she looked at his hands, imagined them touching a child. 'Win, what have you done?' he repeated. She opened her mouth to answer, but he had already noticed the girl in the corner. 'Rosie?' he said. 'Rosie, is that you?'

'Her name's Betty, Cyril,' Winnie snapped, desperate to banish the expression of rapture on his face. 'Don't be daft. Rosie's dead.'

'Spitting image, isn't she, Mr Chilver?' Florence said, and there was a note of triumph in her voice. 'I wondered if you'd notice the resemblance.'

She picked up the empty basket and held her hand out to Betty. Winnie watched them leave. In that moment, with a certainty that was almost restful, she knew exactly what she had to do.

26

Lillian had begun to crave this moment of the day more than any other, the half to three quarters of an hour when Florence went up to check on Betty, then busied herself with her nightly routines, locking the doors and fastening the downstairs windows, making sure that the fire was safe and taking a bedtime drink to their brother's study. She found herself hurrying through her supper so that she was ready to turn in as soon as Florrie made a move, alert to the first yawn or lull in conversation, eagerly sneaking up the stairs to make the most of the precious minutes in which the room was hers and not theirs, in which the room was quiet. Sometimes, she thought it was the only thing that kept her sane.

Tonight she appreciated the peace more than ever. Florrie had come home from the Chilvers in a terrible mood, huffing and puffing about her row with Winnie, slamming pans down in the kitchen and even snapping at Betty when she wouldn't clear her plate. From what Lillian could glean, the conversation had consisted of threats on either side that were too dangerous ever to carry out, but she made the right noises as Florrie vented her indignation throughout the evening, returning to the subject whenever a new angle on the well-worn themes occurred to her. Now, Lillian put the subject from her mind as she pushed the door to and climbed into bed. She sipped her cocoa while it was still hot, then picked up *Middlemarch* and flicked back through the last few pages, trying to remember where she had left Dorothea the night before.

In no time at all, her sister's chores were over. 'Well, she's nicely settled for the night,' Florrie said, sinking heavily down at the dressing table. 'At least she's not restless like she was when she first got here. I think we're making some progress with her, don't you?' Lillian didn't reply, and Florence swung theatrically round on her stool to look at her. 'Oh, you're reading again, dear. Sorry. I won't interrupt.' If Lillian had the chance to spend half as much time with her books as her sister seemed to think she did, she would be the most well-read woman in Suffolk. She gritted her teeth and said nothing as Florence turned back to the mirror and opened a pot of face cream, sighing heavily every few seconds in a way that made it impossible for Lillian to concentrate. She looked up, distracted, as Florrie had intended her to be, and caught her sister's eagle eye in the mirror. 'The cheek of the woman, though,' Florence said, seizing her opportunity. 'Fancy suggesting that Edmund was somehow involved. It's a disgrace.'

Lillian gave up and put her book down. 'But we don't know where he was, do we?' she pointed out, her irritation making her speak more provocatively than she would usually have done. 'The fact is, if the police came here tonight and asked us to give Ned an alibi for the hour after those buses rolled into the village, we simply couldn't do it. We *would* do it, but it would be a lie. So in that sense, Winnie Chilver was absolutely right.'

'Nonsense, dear. You're talking as if we're in one of those sordid little detective novels. I don't know what you can be thinking of, suggesting that our brother needs an alibi.'

'But he might—and sordid or not, we'd do well to agree on it now, while we've still got the chance to confer.'

'I'm sure there's a perfectly innocent explanation.' Florrie pursed her lips in a tight line, signalling an end to the conversation that she had begun.

'Wouldn't it be easier just to ask him where he was? At least we'd be forewarned. I don't know why you insist on treating him with kid gloves like you do. He's not a child, but you're harder on Betty than you are on Ned.'

Her voice had risen slightly in her frustration, and Florrie put a finger to her lips. 'He mustn't hear us talking like this. And as for asking him, I don't want to confront him like that. He'll think we don't trust him, and you know how volatile he is at the moment. This business has really upset him. It's brought everything flooding back, and I'm worried that he might do something silly if we put any sort of pressure on him.'

'That's ridiculous. He hasn't got the guts.'

'He told me only yesterday that he'd be better off dead, that he was no use to us at all. It was after that policeman left. Edmund was beside himself. *You* didn't see him, but I did, so don't you dare provoke him.' She put the face cream down decisively on the dressing table, and went over to pull down her sheets. 'No, we need to tread carefully with him—trust me on that. We need to show him how much we love him.'

In the room above, Lillian could hear Ned pacing up and down, punctuating their conversation with slow, deliberate footsteps. 'It's silly not to have a plan, though,' she reiterated. 'Just suppose that Winnie Chilver actually does what she says she's going to do—what then? She knows exactly where that baby is buried. It wouldn't take them long to find it if she's inclined to help them out.' She paused, considering for the first time what had always been too horrific to contemplate; until now, though, the house had felt unassailable, their own private fortress. 'We could move it,' she suggested tentatively. 'Ned would have to do it, but that would solve all our problems.'

Florrie stared at her in horror. 'Are you out of your mind?' she asked. 'Yes, the Chilver woman knows, but that makes her complicit, so she's not going to say anything. She's got too much to lose. Anyway, they're not looking for a—'

She was interrupted by a noise from above, a slammed door followed by footsteps coming down the stairs. 'That's Ned,' Lillian said redundantly, as it was hardly likely to be anybody else. 'What on earth is he up to now?'

'I don't know, but I hope he doesn't wake Betty.' They both listened as the footsteps passed their door. 'Perhaps he's getting himself a hot drink,' Florrie whispered.

'But you took him one.'

'Then perhaps he needs another. It might help him sleep.' She threw off her bedcovers and reached for her dressing gown. 'I'll go and make it for him.'

Lillian caught her arm. 'Wait—I think I heard the back door. He's going outside.' Sure enough, the gravel at the side of the house gave their brother away and Lillian listened in vain for the sound of the car starting up. Suddenly, her sister's words of warning about Ned's state of mind seemed less melodramatic than before. 'We'll have to go and look for him,' she said.

They went downstairs as quickly and quietly as possible, and Lillian led the way through to the kitchen. Florrie went over to light a lamp, but Lillian stopped her, wanting to see out into the night. 'Listen.'

She identified the noise, even before a pitiless moon drew her attention towards the bottom of the garden. It was the sound of a spade hitting the earth—a sharp, hard, metallic sound that seemed to resonate straight from her dreams. Lillian closed her eyes, but not before the image of her brother was firmly lodged in her mind: silhouetted in the moonlight, just beyond the orchard; transposed across the memories of that younger boy, but rooted in the same desperation, the same fear and guilt.

'Lillian, we've got to do something.' Florence's voice was hysterical, and she tugged at her sister's sleeve like a child. 'We've got to stop him, before someone sees what he's doing.'

Lillian hesitated, unable to move from the spot, even if she had wanted to. She watched as the glint of the spade rose and fell repeatedly, overcome by a sense of relief that this really might be it; that Ned, for all his recklessness, might actually be doing the sanest thing that any of them had attempted in fifty years. Eventually, though, an instinct for self-preservation won through. Fuelled by Florrie's panic, she took an old coat off the hook on the back door and went outside to reason with her brother. 'Ned,' she called, as she hurried down the garden. 'Ned, please—don't do this. It won't do any good.'

He took no notice at first, but as she got closer to him, she saw him throw the spade to one side and fall to his knees. The grave was shallower than she remembered it, and for a moment she thought that he had abandoned his task too soon, but then she saw it—fleetingly, before a cloud covered the moon: the corner of a blanket.

Gently, Lillian put a hand on Ned's shoulder and let him weep. She glanced up at the window of her old room and saw Betty staring down at her, framed in the light from the landing, balancing on the same chair to watch that she herself had used when she was a child. It was like coming face to face with her own past, and for one ridiculous moment, she almost believed that she could go back and change things. When Ned was quieter, she led him back to the house for Florrie to fuss over, then returned to the garden to put things right as best she could until the morning.

27

Josephine's status within the village had shifted subtly from celebrity to heroine overnight, no matter how accidental her discovery had been. The transformation came with welcome material gains—a hamper from the village shop, an enormous basket of the season's last cherries, an open invitation from the landlady at the Cock Inn—but nothing compared to the moment when Annie was finally reunited with her family. Josephine didn't know how long the Ridleys had been waiting at the gate, but they were there when her car turned into the farmyard late on Monday afternoon, and the joy on their faces was something that she would never forget. It had made her more conscious than ever of how quickly things could change: at the same time as she was charged with setting the Ridleys' world to rights, Archie would be destroying the foundations of another family's happiness, and she felt desperately sorry for his side of the bargain. Her emotions had made her reckless: it wasn't hard to guess Noah's thoughts as he watched Kathy Ridley take her child in her arms, and Josephine found herself telling him that he would see his own mother soon; it was a promise that nagged at her for the rest of the evening.

She woke on Tuesday morning with a depressing lack of purpose, and realised how much the collective search for Annie had distracted her from Marta's absence. Noah had had another restless night, so she let him sleep late and settled down at her desk to write some letters, but she hadn't got far when Hilary arrived with the latest reward for her efforts.

'I'm not interrupting, am I?' she asked, placing some flowers and a bottle of Burgundy from the vicarage cellars on the dining table.

'Not really. I was just writing to Marta before she flies out, but I'll have to stop in a minute for Noah. I haven't decided what we're going to do today yet.'

'Exhausting, isn't it? I'm taking two of mine into Bury later, while they're still letting us put petrol in the car. I've got to do some shopping, and I thought I could wear them out with a spin round the Abbey Gardens before they have to knuckle down at school. Noah can come with us, if you like. He might enjoy that.'

'Yes, I think he would. We went through Colchester yesterday, and he's been plaguing me ever since for stories about Roman soldiers. Medieval monks will make a nice change, if it's not too much trouble?'

'No, the more, the merrier. And it will ease my conscience for forcing him on you in the first place.' There was no mention of the promised new home for Noah, but Josephine didn't press the point; she was enjoying his company, and the idea of being on her own wasn't something she relished.

'I'll have to get him ready, though, and I don't want to hold you up.'

'You won't. We're not going until this afternoon. Drop him off at the vicarage in a couple of hours, and he can have his lunch with us.'

'All right. Have you got time for coffee?'

It was a rhetorical question. She had never known the vicar's wife to refuse hospitality, and today was no different. 'Gasping. I'd love a cup. Thank you.'

Hilary removed her gloves and made herself at home while Josephine put the kettle on. 'Have you heard from Benjamin since he left?' she asked.

'No, not yet. He'll have a lot to think about, I suppose.' She sighed heavily. 'I might as well get used to worrying about where he is and what he's doing. This isn't going to be over any time soon. I still have to pinch myself that it's happening at all. It's hard to believe that we're actually at war when everything in the village is normal—well, normal in that respect, at least.' She took the vase that Josephine had filled with water and began to arrange the gladioli she had brought. 'Is there any news on the other girl? I'm sorry I couldn't help more yesterday.'

'You saved time by ruling things out, even if it wasn't the answer we were all hoping for. No, I only spoke to Archie very briefly last night, but he's coming back here today with Angela's mother. She insisted on coming, and Archie wants to question the teachers who are staying at the Hall. Apparently, the last sighting of Angela was with one of them at Liverpool Street.'

'Oh? Do you know which one?'

It was an odd question, Josephine thought. 'No, I've no idea.'

'But Archie doesn't think that this teacher is *responsible* for Angela's disappearance?'

'I don't know. As I said, I didn't speak to him for long because Noah was calling me, so he didn't go into any detail.' She took the coffee pot to the table and opened the almond biscuits from Elsie Gladding's hamper. 'It's not impossible, surely?'

'Of course not. It just seems very hard to stomach, someone in a position of trust like that.'

That was true, but there was more to it than that. Hilary seemed flustered, just as she had when the school parties first arrived, and Josephine was curious. 'You *do* know one of the teachers who brought them here, don't you?' she said, deciding that they had been friends for too long to beat about the bush. 'Who is he?' Hilary denied it again, less convincingly than ever, and Josephine was astonished to see that there were tears in her eyes. 'Whatever's the matter?' she asked.

'Nothing. I'm just being silly.'

'I doubt that.'

Hilary attempted a smile. 'It's Benjamin's going away, I suppose. It's brought it all back, and to see Andrew so suddenly in the village, just out of the blue like that.'

'Andrew?'

'Yes, that's the teacher's name. Andrew Madden.'

'And who is he to you?'

She hesitated, apparently weighing up whether or not to answer, then said: 'He's Benjamin's father.' It was the last thing that Josephine had expected to hear, and it took her a moment to digest the information. 'See, I've shocked you, haven't I?' Hilary continued, misconstruing her silence. 'Please, Josephine, you mustn't say anything. However badly you think of me, you must promise to keep this to yourself.'

'Of course I will, and I don't think badly of you at all. I'm just trying to catch up.'

Hilary shrugged her shoulders. 'Well, I might as well tell you now I've started. Stephen's been so good, but you have no idea how I've longed to have another woman to talk to all these years.'

'Stephen knows?'

'Yes, of course.' She took a deep breath and pulled herself together. 'I told you where we met, didn't I?'

'At a hostel in London. You were doing charity work, and Stephen was the curate.'

'It's funny how everyone assumes that, even though I've never actually said it. It *was* a hostel for unmarried mothers, that's true enough, but I wasn't helping the charity. The charity was helping me.' Josephine listened as Hilary rewrote her past, conscious that—as unexpected as the revelations were—something about them made perfect sense. The Lamptons' marriage had always seemed to her so deeply rooted; their bond had an unbreakable quality that often comes from having had to fight together to keep it, and she recognised it from her own relationship with Marta. 'I was sixteen, and I got pregnant by one of my teachers—by Andrew,' Hilary continued. 'It was such a shock to my parents, and my father wouldn't have anything to do with me, so I ended up in a hostel in a part of London where nobody would know who I was. Stephen was a curate doing pastoral work there, and we fell in love. He asked me to marry him, and offered to bring Benjamin up as his own child. I refused him at first, not because I didn't want to marry him, but because I knew what it would do to his career—and I was right. He always wanted the challenges of a city parish, but the church in its wisdom needed to punish him for his choices, and he wouldn't take no for an answer, no matter how often I said it. That's how we came to be here. Stephen gave up everything for me.'

'I don't think he'd put it quite like that.'

'Of course he wouldn't, and I love him for it. It's worked, too—we've both had more happiness from each other and from our family than anyone has a right to hope for. Stephen doesn't regret it for a minute—not now, anyway, although it was hard at first. He's come to see that people need him every bit as much in their own way here as they would do in a city. It's not a soft life, just because it's beautiful. That's why I can't let this get out, Josephine—you see that, don't you? I wouldn't want him to lose their respect because of my shame. Never in a million years did I think it would follow me here.'

'Did Andrew recognise you?'

'Yes, I think so. I certainly knew him instantly, but we haven't spoken. I think he's as keen to avoid me as I am to steer clear of him. I never told anyone but Stephen who the father was, so Andrew didn't lose anything by it. It would do neither of us any good to rake it all up again.'

'Then why are you so worried?'

'Because of everything that's going on here. Secrets are vulnerable when people's lives are under scrutiny, and you've just said yourself that Archie wants to question the teachers. God knows what will come out, whether it's relevant or not, and you know what people are like. The slightest whiff of a scandal around Andrew and young girls and they'll lynch him—and it wasn't like that, Josephine, it really wasn't. I was as much to blame as he was.' Josephine had mixed feelings about that, but she kept her silence. 'I can't have Stephen mixed up in all that. God knows, it's hard enough to earn your place here when you're an outsider—you can testify to that.'

'I certainly can, although finding a lost child can take years off the process.'

Hilary smiled. 'I'll let Stephen know. He'll be so glad I've told you—and it's a great relief to me.'

She didn't sound like someone whose burden had been lifted, and Josephine wondered if, in spite of her protestations, Hilary was genuinely troubled by the thought that Andrew might be involved in Angela's disappearance. 'There's something else, isn't there?' she prompted gently. 'What is it?'

'It's stupid after everything I've said, but I can't get it out of my mind that I should tell Andrew about Benjamin. His own flesh and blood is off to war. Doesn't he have a right to know that?'

'You'd risk it all coming out.'

'Yes, I know, but that doesn't mean it isn't the right thing to do.'

'It's only right if there's a point to it, and what *would* be the point?' She and Marta had had a similar discussion the night before, wondering how best to deal with the possible connection between the Stebbings and their murdered rent collector. 'I can't see that anyone would benefit from it, not even Andrew. This will be hard enough for you and Stephen. Don't make it worse.'

Hilary nodded, and this time she did breathe a sigh of relief. 'You're right, of course you are. Thank you, I appreciate it.' She wiped her eyes and stood up. 'Right, battle face back on. I'll see you with Noah in an hour or so.'

Josephine was still thinking about Hilary long after she had dropped Noah off and doubled back into the village to post her letters. The war might not have arrived yet on their shores, but there was no question that its shadow was already here, distorting everything in its wake, adding a destructive, febrile element to every human emotion. It was as if a storm had come, bringing things to the surface that had remained hidden for years, and Josephine couldn't help but wonder if any of them would remain untouched by it.

She parked on the village green, pulling up a few yards from a black Daimler and two marked police cars. Angela's mother had obviously arrived from London with Archie, and the vehicles struck a sombre note in an otherwise gentle scene. A small crowd had gathered outside the shop, and everyone was looking across the green to the school, suggesting that the party had gone there as its first port of call. Josephine put her letters in the box, then went over to join Elsie and her daughter, pleased to see that Annie looked happy and relaxed after her self-inflicted ordeal. Kathy, on the other hand, still wore the strain of the last few days in the bags under her eyes and the haunted expression that had not entirely left her;

perhaps it was Josephine's imagination, but she seemed to be holding her daughter just a little more tightly than usual. 'Has Mrs Lucas been here long?' she asked.

'About half an hour,' Elsie said. 'Your friend brought her, with a police woman, and she's got someone else with her— looks like her sister.'

'And they're at the school?'

Kathy nodded. 'They went straight there.'

No sooner had she answered than the party came back into view. Archie and his colleague flanked two women, one with her arm around the other. The woman being comforted was young and slim, with fair hair; Josephine couldn't see the expression on her face, but she could tell from her body language that she was completely lost—in need of support, almost, to put one foot in front of the other. She saw Archie point down the hill towards the pond, and guessed that was where they were heading next.

'I should go and talk to her,' Kathy said. 'Look at her— she's got no hope left.'

'I don't know if that's a good idea, love,' Elsie said cautiously.

'But I know how she feels, Mum, and who else here can say that? She mustn't give up, and I want to help. We've been so lucky.'

'I know we have, and that's why I don't think it's a good idea to . . .'

But Kathy wasn't listening. She walked up to meet Mrs Lucas, and the group was close enough now for Josephine to see how uncomfortable Archie looked at her approach. 'Mrs Ridley, perhaps this isn't the time,' he said, his voice carrying the same note of warning as Elsie Gladding's, but expressed more forcefully.

Kathy waved his objection away. 'I won't keep you long, and I know you've got to get on, but I wanted to say how sorry I am for what you're going through—we all are. We nearly went out of our minds when it was us, so if there's anything we can do to help, please come and ask.'

Mrs Lucas looked blankly at her, and it was left to her sister to answer. 'Thank you. We appreciate that, don't we, Maggie? Everyone's been so kind.'

'So it was your daughter who took Angie's label?' Mrs Lucas asked.

'Annie, yes.' Kathy glanced back to the shop, where Annie was sitting on the grass outside, pulling the petals off a buttercup. 'I'm sorry for the misunderstanding, but you mustn't give up hope, you really mustn't.'

Before anyone realised what was happening, Maggie Lucas wrenched herself away from her sister and went over to Annie, yanking her to her feet. 'Why didn't you tell someone who you were?' she shouted, shaking her until Annie began to cry. 'Angie's been gone for days because of you, you selfish little liar. We could have been looking for her, but we didn't even know she was missing. Now she's been out there in the dark night after night, and she *hates* the dark. If anything has happened to her, it'll be your fault.'

She lost control completely, with desperate, choking sobs that cut through the stunned silence, and it was left to Archie to intervene. He led her gently away, back to her sister, and Kathy tried to calm Annie down. She was white with shock, and her hands trembled as she stroked her little girl's hair. 'Take them home,' Josephine said to Elsie. 'I know Kathy meant well, but it's too soon for her to be around all these reminders—she's still in shock herself. And Annie needs to be somewhere safe. Go and look after your family. I'll watch the shop while you're gone.'

Elsie squeezed her hand gratefully. 'Thank you. I'll be as quick as I can. Help yourself to anything you want, and just lock up if you have to go. The keys are in the till.'

'Take as long as you need. Noah's gone out for the afternoon, so I'm not in any hurry.' Josephine headed towards the shop, noticing that Winnie Chilver had come out from her front garden to see what was going on. 'So that's the mother?' she said, emotion bringing a tremor to the Suffolk accent. 'That's the woman who's lost her little girl?'

'Mrs Lucas, yes.'

'Must be terrible, not knowing what's happened to her.'

'Yes, it must.' Variations on that thought had been circling Polstead for days now, but there was something different in the way that Winnie spoke, a deep-seated regret that made Josephine wonder if she'd known losses of her own.

'I'd have liked a child, I don't mind admitting it,' Winnie said, answering the unspoken question. 'I've often wondered what it would have been like, that bond with a little one, but at least I've saved myself the pain of it. It's not right, what she's going through.' The last words were spoken more decisively, and she walked after Maggie Lucas without waiting for Josephine to say anything. 'Inspector,' she called, and Archie looked round in surprise.

'Yes, Miss Chilver? What can I do for you?'

'There's something I need to say, something that might help you.'

Maggie Lucas had been standing with her sister, set apart from everyone else as Archie gave her the time she needed to compose herself; now, she turned round and stared at the newcomer, clutching at the first straw of hope that had been offered to her. 'What do you know?' she asked.

It was clear from the frown on Archie's face that he would have preferred to hear whatever Winnie had to say in private, but there was no going back now that she'd started. 'You need to talk to the Herrons again,' she said, and her voice was clear and suddenly strong for her age. 'If they won't tell you what's in their garden, you need to look for it. About halfway down, by the apple trees. And neither of those women know where their brother was on Friday.'

28

Penrose arranged for Maggie Lucas and her sister to wait at Polstead Hall for news, leaving Wyles to look after them there. He telephoned his colleague in Ipswich, asking for a forensics team to be put on standby in case they were needed, then headed out to Black Bryony with one of the other police cars for support. The house was quiet when they arrived. The Herrons' car was in the drive, parked where it had been on his last visit, but there was no answer at the front door, so he followed the herringbone path round to the back of the house and stood in the shade of a large cedar tree, looking down the garden that he had searched only two days before. Clearly something had gone on in that short space of time: today, he didn't even have to leave the terrace to see that the earth had been disturbed in the exact spot that Winnie Chilver had mentioned.

He hammered on the back door, worried now that he had left it too late, that some vital piece of evidence had been removed thanks to his failure to take an elderly woman seriously. Eventually, Florence came to the door, scowling at the noise. 'I need to speak to Mr Herron,' Penrose said. 'Is he at home?'

'No, he's not.'

It was obviously a lie, but Penrose was saved the trouble of challenging it.

'Let him in, Florrie. I want to talk to him as much as he wants to talk to me.'

'But Edmund—'

'Let him in.' Edmund Herron spoke with a calm authority, seemingly a different man from the one Penrose had interviewed on Sunday. 'Come through to the sitting room.' Lillian Herron was standing on the first-floor landing at the door to the child's bedroom, but she made no move to come down; Florence followed Penrose and her brother across the hallway, but the door was firmly closed before she could join them. 'My sisters mean well,' Edmund said, 'but they've protected me for too long. It's time this was out in the open, while they've still got some life left to live.'

Penrose took the chair to the left of the fireplace, with a view through French windows to the lawn and trees beyond. 'I've been told that there's something buried in your garden,' he said, taking advantage of the fact that his host seemed in the mood for candour. 'The implication was that it's a child. Is that true?'

'A baby, yes. It's perfectly true. I killed her, and I buried her there myself.'

'When was this?'

'Fifty years ago, almost to the day.'

'I must warn you, Mr Herron—this is a very serious situation. You have the right to do this at a police station if you would prefer, under caution and with legal advice.'

'No, this can't go on. I'll do whatever you need me to do officially, but I want to tell you everything here and now, so that I can't lose my nerve like I have so often in the past. It's time.'

Penrose nodded. 'Thank you. Whose baby is it?'

'I honestly don't know. I've never known who she was. We called her Phoebe, my sisters and I, but that wasn't her real name.'

'So how did she come to be in your garden?'

'I took her. I was only twelve, and the girls were a couple of years younger. We didn't know what we were doing.' He must have seen the scepticism in Penrose's face, because he added: 'All right, we *knew*, but we didn't really understand the seriousness of it. It was just a game—and a well-intentioned game, at that.'

'Where did you take her from?'

'The gypsy camp in the woods a bit further up the lane. They came every year, and still do.'

'They're here now.'

'Yes, I know, but back then the folk at the Hall weren't as happy for gypsies to set up on their land as they are now, so they camped here or in Dollops Wood. They had work in the fields, picking cherries or helping with the harvest. They stayed for the fair, then went on their way.'

'Why would you take a child from them, Mr Herron? In what way was that "well-intentioned"?'

He had allowed his sarcasm to get the better of him, and for the first time Herron seemed defensive. 'I know how this will sound, but we took her for our mother. Our sister had died three years before of diphtheria, and my parents never really got over it. They longed for another child.'

'Yes, your sister told me.'

'Did she? Then she probably told you how unhappy my mother was, how ill she made herself through pregnancy after pregnancy, only to lose the child each time. I loved my mother, Chief Inspector. We all did, but she was never the same after Rosie died. We wanted to make her smile again, and we knew even at that young age that only another child could do that. Selfishly, we wanted our mother back, happy and kind and loving like she was before.'

'So you decided to steal a baby for her?'

'No, it was never as calculating as that. We were out playing in the woods one day, like we always did.' He sighed heavily, and touched a finger to the bridge of his glasses. 'None of us spoke about it, but we spent less and less time at home. My parents were always in mourning. Each room became a tiny mausoleum to the children they'd lost—clothes that were bought in readiness but never worn, dolls that were supposed to compensate for the babies that never came. We hated those dolls, you know—they were a constant reminder that we weren't enough. We used to have mock funerals for them in the back garden. It was all so innocent, until one day it wasn't.'

He had wandered from the point, but the emerging picture of the Herrons' childhood began to make sense of something that Penrose had previously found incomprehensible; at least he knew now why they had stayed at the house, why they were still—in some respects—the children they had been, sticking together no matter what instead of carving out lives of their own. 'You were telling me about that day,' he prompted gently.

'Yes, of course. Well, whenever we were in the woods, we always used to dare each other to go right up to the camp, and I was braver than the other two. One day, I found Phoebe in a beautiful carved crib outside one of the caravans. There was no one about—absolutely nobody—and suddenly it seemed so obvious, as though we'd been meant to find her. At least, that's what I told myself. I picked her up and took her to show my sisters. One of them—I honestly can't remember which—said we should take her to Mummy, and that's what we did. It seemed so easy. She didn't even cry.'

'How did the baby die?'

Herron took a long time to respond, and the obvious relief that had made his answers up to now so full and fluent began to desert him as he approached the most painful part of his story. 'We smuggled her into the house and up to the nursery,' he said eventually, 'but my mother was resting and we weren't allowed to disturb her. My father was always very strict about that.' He stopped again, and Penrose noticed the disconcerting shrug of the shoulders that had been absent up to now. 'Then the baby started to cry, and we didn't know what to do. We didn't want anyone to know about her until we gave her to my mother—it was our precious gift to her, you see—so Lillian tried rocking her like she'd seen my mother doing with Rosie, but that didn't work. There was a blanket box in the nursery, so in the end I put her in there. Lillian didn't want me to, but I didn't know what else to do. It was entirely my decision, nothing to do with my sisters.' Herron had avoided Penrose's eye for most of the conversation, staring into the distance, but now he bowed his head and his words were muffled. 'The baby must have suffocated, because the next time we saw her she was dead.'

Penrose gave him a moment, and then asked: 'Whose decision was it to keep this quiet and bury her here?'

'My father's. He made me do it to teach me a lesson. He stood over me in the pouring rain while I was digging the grave, and he beat me every time I stopped.' Herron took a handkerchief from his pocket and wiped his eyes; his face was bright red from the shame, which seemed to have bypassed mere memory and acquired again the urgency of the moment. 'She was so cold when I put her in the earth, and he told me to cover her up, but I just couldn't do it. I couldn't bring myself to put soil on something so defenceless, so he grabbed me by the neck and forced me to my knees and made me scrabble at the dirt with my hands until it was done.'

Penrose had to keep reminding himself that he wasn't judging the man sitting in front of him, but the twelve-year-old boy he had been. 'That seems very cruel,' he said.

'He was ashamed of me. The shame was worse for him, I think, than the fact of the baby's death. He didn't seem to care much about that once he knew she was only a gypsy.'

'*Only* a gypsy? But your father was a medical man. Surely every life should have mattered to him?'

'You'd think so, wouldn't you, but as far as I know there isn't a cure yet for bigotry or prejudice. It's why I could never follow in his footsteps, even though he wanted me to. I couldn't choose a profession that helps some people and not others.' His reasoning was similar to Penrose's own decision to turn his back on his medical training, and he respected Herron for it. 'And as it turned out, he was right to be relieved. There was a bit of fuss when the baby first went missing, but the police hated the gypsies and they didn't put themselves out looking for her. Nobody did. There was nothing like the searches that have been going on here, and someone even put a rumour about that they'd killed her themselves. Everyone soon forgot about it, even before the camp moved on somewhere else. At least my mother never knew, thank God. She would have cared, whoever the baby was. It would have killed her. It nearly killed me.'

Penrose believed him. 'But Winnie Chilver knew? How?'

'Oh yes. Winnie and her brother both knew. Winnie was our maid and Cyril did gardens for lots of people all over the county, us included—he was quite sought after, in his own way. They were both there that day. It was Winnie who found the baby in the nursery and took her to my father, and it didn't take him long to get me to own up. Winnie tried to make out I'd hurt Phoebe deliberately, because she had some bruises on her skin, but I swear I didn't. They must have been from the box we put her in, but I don't think Winnie believed that.'

'Did the Chilvers blackmail your family?'

Herron nodded. 'I'm not sure they'd call it that, but my father panicked and the Chilvers didn't argue when he offered to look after them financially. We took the arrangement on after he died—an unlucky inheritance, you might say.'

'I need to establish that what you've told me is the truth, and I should have a search warrant to dig in your garden . . .'

'Do it, please. I want this over. I want to pay for what I did—properly, through the law. It can't be worse than the punishment I've been inflicting on myself for all these years.'

Penrose was glad to have his permission, but he wondered if Edmund Herron realised how deeply his sisters would be implicated in whatever was found in the garden; the lives they had left to live were no longer necessarily their own. 'Were you trying to remove the body yourself last night?' he asked. 'I see that the ground has already been disturbed.'

'I don't know what I was doing, if I'm honest. I just know that I wanted it all to stop, one way or another. This missing girl has brought everything back.' And they hadn't even started on that yet, Penrose thought, but he needed to see for himself what was here before he moved on with his questioning. 'Do you want me to come with you?' Herron asked.

'No. Please wait in the house with your sisters.'

He looked relieved and Penrose went out into the hallway, narrowly missing Florence, who had obviously been listening at the door and was scuttling back to the kitchen. He left one officer in the house to keep an eye on its occupants and sent the others out to the car to fetch the equipment they needed, then led the way down the garden. 'Careful how you go,' he said, when they were ready to dig, 'and let me know as soon as you find something.'

The Herrons were together in the kitchen when Penrose got back to the house; Florence was fussing round her brother with tea that he obviously didn't want. In the end, he brushed her aside and took a bottle of Scotch from a cupboard. He waved a glass at Penrose, who shook his head. 'Where were you between noon and two o'clock on Friday afternoon?' he asked.

'He was here, with us,' Florence said immediately, glancing at her sister. 'Then we all went to the school together to collect Betty.'

'Where is Betty now?'

'In the dining room, reading,' Lillian said. 'There are no windows to the back there. We thought that might be wise as you seem hell-bent on destroying our garden.'

'Thank you, that's thoughtful of you. Now, Mr Herron— we know you weren't at home at the time I mentioned, so where were you?'

'I really do object to your calling us liars in our own kitchen,' Florence said. 'As I said—'

'Stop it, Florrie,' Edmund said. 'You've always been a terrible liar, and as I wasn't doing anything wrong on Friday, there's really no need to make things worse. Unless you think I *did* abduct that girl?'

'No, of course not, dear.'

She seemed comforted by his reassurance all the same, and Herron smiled sadly. 'See what suspicion does? I've only got myself to blame, I suppose. I was in the woods by the Hall on Friday.'

'What on earth were you doing there?'

Florence Herron seemed to have temporarily taken over the questioning. Penrose frowned at her, but let the question stand as the one he had been about to ask. 'The gypsies are there. It's fifty years since I stole one of their children, and it occurred to me that time was running out. There might be parents there who have been tormented for most of their lives by not knowing what happened to the child they loved, parents who haven't got long left themselves. I wanted to bring them some peace.'

'You were going to confess?' Florence said, with horror in her voice. 'Without telling us what you were doing? Don't you think we had a right to be consulted?'

'You didn't even remember it was the anniversary, did you?' Herron asked, and she shook her head. 'I know you've stood by me, both of you, and I'm grateful. But you're not haunted by this in the way that I am. It doesn't live with you like it lives with me. That's why I went—to exorcise *my* ghosts, not yours. But you needn't worry. I couldn't do it. Rather predictably, I didn't have the guts.' He turned back to Penrose. 'I'm a coward, Chief Inspector, but I'm not evil. I had nothing to do with that girl's disappearance at the weekend. I swear it.'

Penrose believed him. There was a knock at the door and he got up to speak to his colleague, but Lillian Herron called him out. 'Bring the man in, Chief Inspector. Surely we have the right to hear what's been found in our garden?'

'Very well.'

He turned to the officer, who nodded confirmation. 'We've found the baby where you told us to dig, sir. It's wrapped in a blanket and we haven't disturbed it any more than we could help.'

'But you've seen enough to be able to say for certain that it's a baby?'

'Oh yes, no doubt about it—but there's more than one body, sir.'

'What?'

'We dug to the left and right of the original spot, because we found other bits of clothing that obviously didn't belong with the baby. That's when we found two more.'

Penrose stared at him. Suddenly, Lillian laughed, and the noise sounded horribly out of place in the tense atmosphere of the kitchen. 'I'm sorry,' she said, 'that was wrong of me, but I've just realised what you've found. They're dolls, Chief Inspector. We buried them when we were children. I can even tell you their names. I know how awful that sounds in light of what's happened since, but they're not the sinister discovery you think they are.'

'Constable?'

'No, sir, I'm afraid these aren't dolls. The bodies on either side are obviously older—toddlers, I'd say.'

'No.'

The word was spoken as a whisper, then repeated as a scream. Edmund Herron's composure had deserted him, and he became once again the angry, frightened man who had driven them from his study on Sunday afternoon. 'Keep everyone in here,' Penrose said to the constable. 'I need to see this for myself.'

He walked down the garden to examine the wide but shallow grave that his colleagues had uncovered, and saw instantly that there was no mistake. The blanket hid the sadness of the baby's death, and while he knew he should reach down and lift the corner to look properly at what was beneath, he couldn't bring himself to do it. The bones on either side were more exposed, partially covered by fragments of cloth, and he guessed that each skeleton belonged to an infant of around three or four, positioned like a guard of honour to the pitiful form in the middle. None of the bodies was recent, and only when he realised that all three must be roughly contemporary with each other did he acknowledge the complex blend of relief and disappointment that he was still no closer to finding Angela Lucas—relief, disappointment, and now anger that he couldn't put a name to any of the children buried here; they were owed that, at the very least.

Deep in thought, he walked slowly back to the house, trying to reconcile the conflicting certainties in his mind: on the one hand, he was sure that the Herrons' shock was genuine; on the other, he found it hard to believe that anyone could have two bodies in their garden that they weren't aware of—and two was just what they knew about at the moment; there was plenty of ground left to search.

'This is down to him, you know,' Florence said, as soon as Penrose re-entered the kitchen. She had obviously worked herself up into a state of indignation in his absence, while Edmund and Lillian simply looked haunted. 'That's why she's so keen to lay the blame at Edmund's door. She's trying to protect *him*.'

'Who, Miss Herron? Who is this down to?'

'Cyril Chilver. Winnie's brother.'

'Why do you say that?' he asked doubtfully.

'Because he had access to the garden all those years ago. He drove all over the place in that old van of his, and he . . . well, he . . .'

She faltered, leaving the explanation to Lillian. 'What Florence is trying to say is that Cyril Chilver formed a very unhealthy attachment to Rosie, our youngest sister—and for all we know, to a lot of other children, too.'

'You knew this, but you didn't say anything about it?'

'We were young ourselves, Chief Inspector. How were we supposed to understand something like that?'

'But you've had plenty of time to reflect on it since, yet still you've kept your silence—to protect your own secret, I suppose? Each of your families had something on the other, but the evidence swung rather more in the Chilvers' favour.'

'You can't afford to rule out what we're saying, though, surely? We might not have evidence, but you've got to agree that it makes sense? Up on those allotments on Friday, walking back and forth across the playground every day . . .'

'And even his sister thinks it was him,' Florence added. 'Just look in her eyes when you ask her.'

Penrose cast his mind back to Saturday night, and the wholehearted way in which Chilver had taken part in the search. The Herrons' accusations seemed unlikely, but Lillian was right—he couldn't afford to ignore it. Edmund Herron had been very quiet, overshadowed once again by his sisters, but he spoke now with a strength that surprised them all. 'I don't know about the Chilvers, but I do know that I had nothing to do with what you've found in that garden, except for the death I've already confessed to. You won't get me to admit to anything else.'

Penrose stood up. 'That's good enough for me. We'll stick to what we know—for now, at least.' He cautioned Herron and nodded to the constable to take him outside to the car. 'And I'd like you both to come to the station as well and answer some more questions.'

To his surprise, neither sister objected. 'And the Chilvers?' Florence demanded. 'Are you going to do anything about them?'

'I'm going to speak to them now, but think about what it means if you're right. If Cyril Chilver is responsible for Angela Lucas's disappearance and the other bodies in your garden, not to mention any number of children in between, don't you wish you'd stopped him by telling the truth? Your brother's finally had the courage to do the right thing, but it's years too late. Just think how many lives you could have saved.'

He could see that the words had hit home, with Lillian at least. 'What about Betty?' Florence asked, and the hypocrisy of her concern riled Penrose so much that it was as much as he could do to remain civil.

'I'll make sure she's looked after,' he said, and went to fetch the child, glad to have the Herrons out of his sight.

29

Josephine's first hour as shopkeeper was a busy one, but most of her customers were primarily interested in gossip, so she had nothing more taxing to do than weigh out pear drops and toffees from a kaleidoscope of tall jars, and assure Mrs Bumpstead that the eggs were today's. She had often stood on the other side of the counter, chatting about births and deaths, village events, newcomers and minor scandals, all the glue that kept the community together, but today there was only one topic of conversation, and she found it extraordinary that so many people seemed to have known from the outset that Edmund Herron was responsible for Angela's disappearance—which rather begged the question why they hadn't been more helpful on Saturday. She was as shocked as everyone by Winnie's revelation, though, and she longed to hear from Archie and find out if there was any truth in it.

There was a mid-afternoon lull in trade, so she went through to the back to put the kettle on and feed the shop's cat, who was almost as spoilt as Annie, in spite of Elsie's protestations that she only kept him there for the mice. Her thoughts turned to the Ridleys, and she wondered how deeply affected Annie would be by what had just happened; Kathy had been hasty in approaching the other girl's mother, but it had been well meant and Josephine could understand her motives, just as she could understand why Maggie Lucas would feel so angry and unforgiving towards Annie. It was an impossible situation, and there was only one thing that could make it right, but that seemed less likely now with every passing hour.

The shop was still quiet when the tea was made, so she took it out to the bench at the front to drink in the afternoon sun. She had hoped that Winnie Chilver might be standing at her gate, ready to answer the hundred and one questions that Josephine had about her past involvement with the Herrons, but there was no sign of her, so she contented herself with the sweet, lilting call of a willow warbler, and hoped that Noah was having a nice time. Before long, the birdsong was interspersed with voices from the house next door—muffled, but unmistakably raised in anger. Josephine listened, wondering if Cyril was annoyed by what his sister had started. If Margery's information was correct, then Winnie's accusation would surely put their home in jeopardy; from a selfish point of view, she would have been wise to keep her counsel. The voices continued off and on for a couple of minutes, then fell silent.

Almost immediately, the front door opened and slammed as Cyril Chilver left the house. He strode down the path, fit and youthful as always, although today his energy seemed fuelled by rage. Josephine watched as he crossed the lane to his van and got in, then drove past her towards the green and off in the direction of the allotments. Something in his expression troubled her and she looked back to the house, wondering if she should make sure that his sister was all right. If they had had the row that Josephine suspected, Winnie was bound to be upset.

She took her cup back inside, found the keys in the till and locked the shop up while she popped next door to check that all was well. There was no answer to her first knock, so she tried again, then went round the back to try her luck there. The cottage was small, and it seemed ominously quiet for a house that she knew was occupied. Worried now, she peered through the back windows and called Winnie's name, but the only reward for her efforts was an empty silence. The back door was open, and Josephine stepped into a tiny kitchen which smelt of beef and onions. Two dinner plates sat ready to be washed on the draining board, and there was a loaf of bread on the side, with three slices cut but not eaten. 'Miss Chilver?' she called again. 'It's Josephine Tey. Are you all right?'

There was no response, so she ventured further into the house, and immediately understood why. Winnie Chilver lay on the floor in her parlour, her pose graceless and undignified. The hearth rug was rucked up, and at first Josephine thought that she had tripped and hit her head, but when she got closer, she saw that Winnie had been hit across the face with the poker that lay at her side. Her eyes were half closed, and there was blood drying around her nose and mouth, staining the cotton of her housecoat and blending with the loud, floral pattern in an absurd parody of her brother's triumphs. The sight sickened Josephine, but she overcame her repugnance to bend low over Winnie's face, hoping to hear a breath and feeling at the same time for a pulse; the woman's wrist was painfully thin, emphasising the fragility of her age. Josephine failed to see how her body could have withstood the shock, but miraculously the pulse was there, faint but defiant. 'I'm going to get help,' she said, hoping that Winnie could hear her. 'I won't be long, I promise.'

She hurried next door to telephone first for an ambulance, and then for the police, having no idea of how to contact Archie. When she returned to Winnie's side, she feared that even the few minutes that she had been gone might have been too long, but the pulse was still there, if a little weaker than before. She found a blanket to keep Winnie warm, then held her hand while she waited impatiently for the ambulance to arrive. Her breathing was shallow and laboured, but still she wanted to speak. 'Don't try to talk,' Josephine said, as Winnie's lips moved in silent agitation, forming words that her body would not let her say. 'You need to save your strength, and there'll be plenty of time to talk later.'

Somehow, Winnie summoned up the energy to shake her head, and Josephine knew that she was right: it was a cruel miracle that she had survived this long. 'What is it?' she asked, keen to do anything that would make the inevitable as peaceful as possible.

She lowered her head again to listen, feeling Winnie clutching at her hand in her desperation to make herself heard. Her voice was rasping, but distinct enough for Josephine to make sense of the few words she could utter. 'Cyril,' Winnie said. 'Cyril, not Edmund. All of it. The baby, too.'

Josephine repeated everything to show that she had heard and understood, and instantly Winnie was calmer; a couple of minutes later, just as the ambulance was drawing up outside, she was gone.

Josephine let the driver in and explained everything as fully as she could, then left him to tend to the body and walked out into the sunshine for a moment to wait for the police, shocked and saddened by what had happened, and desperate for some time to herself to make sense of Winnie's final words. To her surprise and immense relief, she saw Archie's car draw up at the end of the lane with Betty in the back seat.

'What on earth's going on?' he asked, getting out and running over to her. 'Are you all right?'

'Yes, but you need to find Cyril Chilver. He's killed his sister.'

'*What?*'

'I think he's responsible for Angela, too.' She brought Archie up to date quickly and succinctly, repeating Winnie's words verbatim.

'So the Herrons were right,' he said. 'Why the hell didn't they speak up sooner?'

'You know what Winnie meant?'

'Yes, I do. Listen, I'm going to try the allotments to see if I can find Chilver. Send the police car straight up there when it gets here. And it's a long story, but you'll have to take Betty for now. The Herrons are in no position to be looking after a child.'

Josephine went with him back to his car and held out her hand for Betty, who looked frightened and bewildered to have been removed yet again from what she was used to. 'You're going to stay with your brother from now on,' she said, determined to keep the promise, no matter how rash it seemed. 'Now come with me. I've got the keys to the sweet shop.'

30

Penrose smelt the smoke as soon as he got out of his car. Cyril Chilver was having a bonfire.

Another police car pulled up behind him, and he gave his instructions quickly. 'That's the allotment we're after,' he said, pointing to the plume of grey. 'One of you go round to the left and approach it from that way, the other come with me. Our priorities are to put that fire out and get him into custody. He's obviously looking to destroy some evidence, but who knows what his game is after that. He could have gone anywhere in that van, so it seems to me he's got a plan—unless he really is deluded enough to think that he can get away with this. Are there more men on their way?'

'Yes, sir.'

'Good. Let's get on with it.'

He saw little point in attempting to surprise Chilver. His patch was on the nearside of the allotments, and there was no reliable cover to be had from the vegetable plots and sporadic outbuildings that backed onto it, so he took the most direct route, retracing his footsteps from Saturday night, when the man he was now looking for had been his guide. To his relief, Chilver was still there, sitting on a bench in front of his shed, staring out across the flower beds and partially harvested crops, to all intents and purposes as if this were any other day. He glanced from left to right as Penrose and his colleagues approached, but made no attempt to move.

However difficult or painful an investigation had been, Penrose always relished this moment, when a suspect had been tracked down and it was up to him to get to the truth through a process of logical, methodical questioning. Today, he realised as soon as he was in speaking distance that he didn't want to know. Chilver disgusted him, and he found it impossible to put his personal feelings to one side and acquire the sort of detachment that made him so good at his job. To his shame, he had already judged the man in front of him, and for the first time in his life, he had to force himself to give someone the opportunity to tell his side of the story. It showed in the tone of his opening question, and he made no attempt to rein himself in. 'Your sister's been assaulted, but you know that, don't you? She's dead, Mr Chilver.'

There was no response, not even the subtlest shift of expression. The bonfire had obviously been burning for some time, and it had lost the fierce intensity of its early heat. The police constable who had accompanied Penrose fetched water from a nearby rain barrel and doused the flames easily, then stamped out the last remaining flickers of defiance. Chilver watched him intently, but didn't try to stop him.

'I suppose that was her punishment for what she told me about the Herrons,' Penrose continued. 'She didn't know what she was doing, though, did she? She thought it was just the baby. She had no idea until you told her in your rage that there were other bodies, that she was unwittingly leading us to you. Or did she know all along, and simply decide that you had to be stopped?' Still Chilver ignored him. There was a thermos flask on the bench next to him, and he filled a tin mug from it and took a sip. 'Who are the children buried at Black Bryony?' Penrose asked. 'We know about the baby, but the others you killed and took there—where did they come from? Where are the parents who've been missing them all these years?'

Chilver shrugged. 'Does it matter?'

'Of course it matters!' Penrose checked himself, refusing to allow Chilver to provoke him. 'You killed the baby, too, didn't you? Edmund Herron was telling the truth when he said he didn't hurt her—but you did. Your sister told us that before she died.'

For the first time, Penrose detected a reaction. A hint of surprise and annoyance passed across Cyril Chilver's face when he realised that Winnie had betrayed him, or perhaps it was simply an acknowledgement of the fact that he couldn't control everything after all. He topped up his mug, using the distraction to compose himself, then lifted the flask and waved it at his visitor. Sickened, Penrose shook his head. 'I don't want to drink with you, Mr Chilver.'

He shrugged. 'Suit yourself. So Winnie told you that, and you believed her?'

'Why would she lie?'

Chilver just smiled, waiting for Penrose to catch up. 'What would I be doing in a nursery?' he asked, when he saw that the penny had dropped. 'I can't remember setting foot in that house in all the years I worked there.'

You didn't need to, Penrose thought cynically; you had all you needed in the garden. 'Are you saying that your sister did it?' he clarified. 'But why?'

'For the money, of course. She saw the chance to gain from that boy's mistake, and she took it. She hated those Herron children. Spoilt rotten, she always said, and we've lived well enough from it all these years.' His demeanour changed again, and he glared at Penrose. 'But *I* wouldn't touch a baby. What do you think I am?'

Penrose couldn't quite believe that Chilver honestly believed himself to be in the right. 'I don't want to understand you,' he said, losing his patience. 'I don't want to give you the satisfaction of thinking about you very much at all, actually. It's your victims who interest me, and I just want to know the truth—for them, and for their families. Where is Angela Lucas?'

'Where she'll be looked after.'

'Is she dead?' Frustrated by a long silence, Penrose pulled one of the canes from a row of peas and used it to rake through the ashes of the bonfire. The flames had done their work efficiently, but not everything had been destroyed, and Penrose had to steel himself when he saw the charred remnants of a child's haversack, the buttons from a mackintosh. 'You must have done it as soon as she got off the bus,' he said, piecing things together for his own sake. 'All those children milling round, bewildered and far from home—you couldn't stop yourself. Did you plan it, I wonder, or just strike lucky? Angela probably didn't even make it into the school hall, did she? I suppose you took her to see your pretty flowers, and she was happy to go with you. Her mother said she loved flowers, but then all children do. It's magic when you're that age, somewhere like this.' He gestured towards the dahlia bed, knowing that he would never be able to look at that flower again without feeling sick to his stomach. 'Her mother is beside herself with grief and worry. I don't suppose there's any point in my asking you to give her some peace?'

Penrose walked up to the bench, knowing that to prolong this was futile. Chilver watched him, occasionally taking a sip from his mug. 'It must have been very confusing for you when we all started looking for Annie. No wonder you were so willing to help. Were you laughing at us behind our backs?

The police, your friends in the village—all searching for the wrong girl. You must have been dying to share the joke with someone.' He paused, trying to reconcile himself to the fact that he would never have an answer to the question he was about to ask. 'How many have there been, Mr Chilver?'

'That's for me and them to know,' he said, reaching again for his flask. 'No one else.'

His words were slurred, his movements slow and clumsy, and suddenly Penrose realised what he was doing. He moved forward and knocked the cup from Chilver's hand. 'Oh no you don't,' he said, hauling the man to his feet and pushing him back against the shed. 'We're not doing this your way. You'll pay for what you've done, and I'm not going to let you take the coward's way out. What's in that flask?' He picked the thermos up to sniff it, and his relief at finding it still more than half full was almost overwhelming; it was doubtful that Chilver could have drunk a fatal amount of whatever sedative he had chosen, but Penrose was furious with himself for giving the man the slightest opportunity to escape justice, and he couldn't control his temper. 'Where is she?' he shouted, taking Chilver by the collar and slamming him hard against the side of the shed. Out of the corner of his eye, he noticed that his colleagues had turned their backs, happy to collude in whatever methods he chose to adopt. 'Tell me what you've done with her. Is she here?' Chilver's eyes looked fleetingly down to the left, an involuntary movement which he was quick to correct, but Penrose noticed it, and knew with a heart-rending certainty what he would find in that patch of earth next to the shed, a patch that was strangely bare by comparison with the abundance of growth in every other part of the allotment. 'I'll find her if it's the last thing I do,' he said, allowing his hand to tighten for a few seconds around Chilver's throat. 'And I swear I'll wipe every inch of you from this soil and from this village.'

He let go reluctantly. 'Cyril Chilver, I'm arresting you on suspicion of the murder of Winnie Chilver and the abduction of Angela Lucas.' When he had read him his rights, he beckoned to the nearest officer. 'Get him to a hospital, and for God's sake keep him conscious. I want him fit to stand trial.'

'Yes, sir.'

'And ask the station to send forensics here first, not to the other address I gave them. That can wait.'

Chilver was taken away, and Penrose turned back to the shed, where he presumed Angela had been killed. It smelt of the shallots that were hanging in bunches to dry, but there was also a strong scent of tobacco from the bottles of insecticide that lined the shelves, and Penrose thanked his lucky stars that Chilver had been too much of a coward to use those to harm himself rather than a sedative. Standing at the door, his eye fell on a small square box, the kind that held a child's gas mask. He put on his gloves and picked it up, and the smell of rubber hit him as soon as he opened it, but it was the piece of paper taped to the inside of the box that took his attention, a note to Angela from her mother, explaining how important it was that she wore the mask whenever she was told to, written with such love and care that he had to stop reading before he got to the end.

He put the box down, and opened the drawers in a small chest that stood in the corner. Most of them were full of seed packets and garden paraphernalia—twine and secateurs, labels for seedlings and some old brushes—but the bottom drawer held a random collection of objects, innocent enough individually, but damning in light of what he now knew. Penrose cast his eye over the assortment of buttons, hair clips and tiny shoes, but something else stopped him in his tracks: a brown luggage label, identical to the one that Annie had picked up from the playground, except the name on this one was Lizzie Buckle. He remembered what Mrs Lucas had said to him the day before—as a comfort, or so she had thought at the time: at least Angela was with a friend.

31

It was a beautiful evening, but the faint smell of smoke still hung on the air as Josephine walked across the green and up Heath Road to the school. The events of the afternoon were the talk of the village, and a few people had gathered at the edge of the allotments, watching as the area was transformed into a scene of unimaginable horror. Four police cars, including Archie's, were parked on the playground in front of the school hall, and a mortuary van stood in wait at a discreet distance. The allotments had been roped off, and a uniformed policeman was guarding the path that wove down through the plots, while others busied themselves around the area that had belonged to Cyril Chilver.

Archie stood at one end of the patch, directing everything and conferring with a scene of crime officer, and if Josephine hadn't been so concerned for him, nothing in the world could have persuaded her to attend this sombre vigil. He had returned briefly to the shop, officially to use the telephone, but she knew him well enough to realise that what he had actually needed was a moment apart from his colleagues to come to terms with what he had discovered and to steel himself for the task ahead, a moment to react to these terrible deaths personally instead of professionally. When he left her to go to the Hall and speak with Angela's mother, she could see that he had been crying.

There was no sign of Mrs Lucas, and Josephine guessed that she had decided to wait where she was for news rather than put herself through this ordeal, perhaps wisely counselled by her sister. Stephen Lampton was talking to one of the policemen, but she could see now that most of the other villagers present were men who had been turned away from their allotments while the search was going on. Out of respect, or perhaps out of shock and bewilderment at the darkness that had flourished unseen at its heart, Polstead had stayed away. Stephen raised his hand when he saw her, and it occurred to Josephine that the challenges of a city parish were nothing compared to the task he had ahead of him in rebuilding this community, already fractured before the war could do its worst.

The atmosphere amongst those gathered on either side of the rope was brittle and melancholy, and as the instruction to dig was given, a silence descended on the scene, broken only by the evening cry of a blackbird and the harsh, relentless sound of shovels cutting through earth. Those who weren't clustered around the area of soil next to the shed began to clear the rest of Chilver's allotment, and there was something about the methodical destruction of all this growth that was symbolic as well as practical: as Josephine watched the men tearing up the flowers that Chilver had nurtured and tended, the message was as clear as if his victims had screamed it aloud; that order and beauty were not to be trusted, that at a time when everyone feared the incomer, it was in the familiarity of home that the real threat lay.

She stood apart from Stephen and the others, focusing not on the dig but on Archie, and finding all she needed to know in the series of emotions that passed across his face. He stared resolutely down at the ground, his face pale and set, barely blinking as his colleagues shifted spadeful after spadeful of earth. She saw him frown and hold out his hand to halt the digging, then crouch down and reach forward to touch something. Fleetingly, he closed his eyes and bowed his head, and when he stood again, it was with a new sense of purpose. He gave a nod to the police photographer who had been waiting on the sidelines to be called, and as he turned and looked briefly over in her direction, she saw the sorrow in his eyes and knew that he had found what he was looking for.

She walked away, too saddened to watch any more, and waited by Archie's car, knowing that he would want to take the news to Angela's mother as soon as possible. 'Are you all right?' she asked, when he came out to join her.

'Not really, no.'

'Sorry. It was a stupid question.'

He leant against the bonnet and pressed his fingers to his eyes, as if he could wipe out what he had just seen. 'There are two girls there,' he said quietly.

'*Two?*' Josephine stared at him in horror, unable to believe what she was hearing.

'I found another label in the shed that belonged to Angela's friend. I didn't tell you earlier because I didn't want it to be true, but I'm afraid it is. Now I've got to find another set of parents who may or may not have guessed that something's wrong. It feels as though this will never end.'

'How much do you think his sister knew about what he'd been doing?' Josephine asked, voicing the question that had been troubling her since Winnie's death.

'That's one of the things we'll never know now,' Archie said, 'although I think Chilver was telling the truth about the baby. God, how I hate the not knowing.' He pulled himself together, and attempted a smile. 'Thanks for coming here. You've no idea how much it helped. Now, I'd better get to the Hall and tell Mrs Lucas that we've found her daughter. I've done this so many times, but it never gets any easier.'

'I suppose that's as it should be,' Josephine said.

Archie nodded. 'She'll be forever wondering what went on in that shed, and no one can help her with that. She'll have to identify Angela's body, too. I wish her husband were here with her, but at least she's got her sister. They seem very close.'

'And then are you going back to London?'

'Yes, until I'm needed here again. I want to go home, if I'm honest. I want to be with Virginia, and hug Evie, and argue with Teddy about what he can and can't take back to school with him. Will you be all right?'

'Of course I will,' she said, a little too brightly. 'I'll have plenty to keep me busy once I collect Betty from Elsie's, starting with where she's going to sleep. That cottage is getting smaller by the day.'

'And Marta? Have you heard from her?'

'Briefly, last night. I phoned to tell her about Annie, but we couldn't speak for long because she was expecting a call from Hitchcock. She'll probably phone tonight—we've got a lot to catch up on.'

She had never really been able to fool Archie, and now was no different. 'The world's a bloody awful place, Josephine, so don't choose to be lonely. She's not going until Thursday, is she?'

'No, why?'

He smiled, properly this time, and opened the car door. 'Because it gives you plenty of time to pack. Virginia tells me that California is always at its best in September.'

32

Marta had still not returned her call, and by eleven o'clock on Wednesday morning, Josephine was getting worried. In the end, she telephoned the hotel again.

'I'm afraid Miss Fox has already left,' the receptionist said. 'She checked out first thing this morning.'

'Checked out? Are you sure?'

'Yes, madam, perfectly sure,' he said, sounding faintly affronted at the sleight on his competence. 'I dealt with her bill myself.'

'But she was supposed to be with you until tomorrow.'

'Yes, I'm aware of that, and she was very apologetic about having to leave early, but I gather it couldn't be helped.'

His tone implied that the subject was closed, and Josephine thanked him and hung up, wondering where Marta could be. It was unlike her not to keep in touch, even when Hitchcock was running her ragged, and Josephine couldn't believe that she would change her flight details without saying anything. She tried Marta's number in Cambridge, just in case she had forgotten something and had had to go home, but there was no answer there, either, and by then she had run out of ideas. There was nothing for it but to wait.

Frustrated, she went to the window and watched as Noah showed Betty the garden, absentmindedly scratching his midge bites while he took her round the vegetable patch, just as Marta had taken him. She would miss them when she left, but she was pleased with the arrangements that she had made for them; they would be happy and cared for, and after the last few days, that sort of reassurance was more precious than ever.

She went upstairs to change into something cooler, and heard the sound of a car coming down the track towards the cottage. It was a taxi, and she waited for the first glimpse of her visitor, scarcely daring to hope. When Marta got out, she hurried down the stairs and flung open the front door. 'You have no idea how I've been longing to see you,' she said. 'I spoke to the hotel and they said you'd checked out. I began to think you'd already left the country.'

'Without telling you? No, I tried calling you first thing, but your line was engaged for ages.'

'Sorry, I was speaking to Margery.'

'Then I realised that I was wasting precious time, and anyway, I wanted to be with you, not just speak to you, so I got the first train to Ipswich and came straight here. Where's Noah? Is it safe to give you a kiss?'

'He's in the garden with Betty.'

'Betty?' Marta looked surprised but pleased. 'So the harridans have finally relented.'

'It's a long story, but yes—to that, and the kiss.'

They went inside, then Marta went out to see Noah and Betty while Josephine made some coffee. She took it out to the bench, thinking about how much had changed in the few days since she and Marta last sat here together, and remembering how unsettled she had felt. 'Those two seem very happy,' Marta said, coming over to join her.

'They do, don't they? Noah's better by the day. We had dry sheets and no nightmares for the first time last night. I think being with Betty has made all the difference.'

'So what's the long story with the Herrons?'

Josephine told her everything as succinctly as possible, not wanting to revisit the darkness that had kept her awake for most of the night. 'I haven't spoken to Archie since he left,' she said, 'so I have no idea what will happen to Florence and Lillian—or even Edmund, for that matter, if it was actually Winnie Chilver who killed that baby—but I think we can safely say that Betty won't be going back to Black Bryony any time soon.'

Marta lit a cigarette, obviously trying to take in everything that had happened in her absence. 'I've got a confession to make,' she said eventually. 'I went to see Noah's mother again last night.'

'Why doesn't that surprise me? Although I thought we agreed to leave things . . .'

'Yes, I know we did, but you needn't worry. She wasn't in, or at least she wasn't answering the door, so it was all a bit of an anti-climax.'

'What were you hoping for by going to see her?'

'I've been asking myself that.' Marta poured the coffee while she thought about the answer. 'I wanted to help her, I suppose. I wanted to tell her that if someone was hurting her, then I understood what that was like.'

Josephine took her hand, wishing as she had a thousand times before that Marta didn't understand those things quite so well. 'Well, I don't think it was her husband,' she said. 'Noah was actually quite happy to talk about his father once I got round to asking him. He *has* signed up, and he went as soon as he could. Noah hasn't seen him for a couple of months, so he certainly wasn't responsible for that bruise you saw. But he also told me that someone his mother didn't like was bothering her, and he wished she weren't on her own.'

'*Was* bothering her? So that could have been the rent collector?'

'Yes, I suppose so. Or someone else entirely.'

'I think she killed him, though, don't you? I think he was threatening her for money or for sex, and she defended herself. That would explain everything—her behaviour when I visited her last time, and how frightened you said Noah was, the fact that someone had been violent towards her. We know that the man was stabbed with tailor's scissors, which she would have had . . .' She stopped when she saw the frown on Josephine's face. 'I know what you're thinking, and you're right. I'm creating some sort of fantasy detective novel, where I confront Noah's mother about the crime and she confesses on the spot, then I make everything right for the whole family. It's ridiculous.'

Josephine laughed. 'That's not what I was thinking, and of course it isn't ridiculous to want to help, but my scenario's slightly different from yours.'

'Go on.'

'Noah wasn't supposed to be evacuated, was he? He wasn't on the list, and he didn't have a label or any other paperwork.'

'So?'

'I think his mother saw her chance to get him away safely, so she took it.'

'You think *Noah* was in danger?'

'Yes, but not in the way you mean. It might have been Noah who killed the rent collector.' Marta stared at Josephine in astonishment. 'I think that's what she meant when she told you that *she* should be looking after *him* and not the other way round. The note he had with him could be read that way, too—I had another look at it.'

'But do you think someone as young as Noah would even be capable of that?'

'If he was frightened enough for his mother, yes.'

Marta stared across the garden at the two children. 'I don't want to believe it,' she said.

'Then don't. That's the beauty of not knowing.' The words brought back Archie's frustration from the day before, but in this case, Josephine disagreed with him. It was better for them, and probably better for Noah, if she and Marta remained blissfully ignorant of what had gone on.

'Has Archie said anything about his investigation?'

'No, he's been a bit busy on other things, and I haven't asked him. I'd rather not discuss it. I hate keeping things from him.' There had been times in the past when both she and Marta had made bad decisions about what Archie should or shouldn't know, and she didn't want to repeat her mistakes.

'Has Hilary found anywhere else for Noah and Betty to go?' Marta asked.

'No, but I have. Margery's offered to take them. That's why I had to speak to her this morning.'

'And she can take them both?'

'Yes. The woman who had Annie by mistake felt so bad about bringing her back that she took two of Margery's evacuees to make up for it, so there's a vacancy at D'Arcy House. They'll have a fantastic time there. Noah and Margery already get on like a house on fire. I'm driving them over on Friday morning, then heading straight back to Scotland.'

'On Friday? I didn't think you'd be going quite so soon. I was tempted to change my flight back to Sunday and tell Hitch to like it or lump it.'

'That would have been nice, but I've got to go.' Marta looked down, dejected, and Josephine tenderly brushed a lock of hair back from her face. 'There's a lot to sort out if I'm going to join you in America next week.'

7 SEPTEMBER 1940

It was a quarter to five when the sirens wailed, and Maggie was on her way home from a Saturday afternoon at the pictures with her sister. A few minutes later, she heard the planes grinding overhead—hundreds of them darkening the brilliant blue skies—and the bombs started to rain down, savage and relentless in their onslaught, tearing buildings apart all around them.

'So this is what we've been waiting for,' Jenny said, with panic and awe in her voice. 'Come on, sis—we'd better get to the shelter.'

She grabbed Maggie's hand and headed for the nearby underground. A huge pall of smoke rose up ahead, with scores of smaller fires breaking out in all directions, and Maggie could hear the crackle of flames and clanging of bells as every fire engine in the city seemed bound for the East End. Beneath her feet, the pavements were already covered with the fine, frosty glitter of powdered glass.

She hesitated at the entrance to the shelter, shoved and jostled by the people behind her, and Jenny turned round in frustration. 'What are you doing, Mags? They're not messing about now.'

'I know they're not.' Small fires grew bigger as she watched, others died down only to break out elsewhere, and the danger grew more imminent every second, but still Maggie hesitated.

'You want to be with her, don't you?' Jenny raised her voice to be heard above the chaos and pulled Maggie into a shop doorway, away from the crowds. 'You want to be with Angie.'

'I've tried, Jen. I've tried so hard.'

'I know you have.'

'I thought it would get easier, you know—when they hanged him, or when the first Christmas was over, or the first birthday. They say those things all help, but none of them do.'

Jenny pulled Maggie close, tears streaming down her face. 'What am I going to do without my little sister?'

'You're not going to stop me?'

'Since when have I ever been able to do that?' She held Maggie's face in her hands. 'I was there with you, remember? I know you died the day they found her.'

'Look after Bob for me.'

'We will, I promise.'

'And don't tell him what I've done.'

Another wave of planes was on its way, swarming like bees in blind fury. Under a flame-red sky, Maggie turned and walked back down the open street towards them.

ACKNOWLEDGEMENTS

Among the hundreds of accounts of the mass evacuation that took place across Britain in September 1939, none is more vivid than Margery Allingham's in *The Oaken Heart*, her biography of a village at war. As much as I love Allingham's fiction, this has long been my favourite of her books, and she emerges from it not only as a remarkable writer, but as a woman of extraordinary courage, humour and humanity. 'I was rather nervous about its local reception,' she wrote to a reader in 1941, 'but to my intense relief they have taken it in exactly the spirit in which it was written. They are very grand people, very genuine and very 'true' in every way. Now that I'm living virtually alone with them I realise that more and more.' Those 'grand, true' people have been a huge inspiration for this novel, and anyone interested in getting to know them better should look out the splendid Golden Duck edition of *The Oaken Heart*.

I'm deeply indebted to Julia Jones for her extensive work around the Allingham family, and especially for her balanced, insightful account of Margery's life and work in *The Adventures of Margery Allingham*, one of the finest biographies I've ever read. In quoting one of Margery's letters, that book also made it very easy to find a title for my own. Tey and Allingham were fans of each other's writing, but—to my knowledge—they never met in real life; I wouldn't be at all surprised, though, if they were to team up again one day, a little further down the road of this series.

I'm also grateful for the help and support of The Margery Allingham Society, and in particular to Catherine Cooke and Chris Seymour for tracking down Margery's telephone number at D'Arcy House with detective work of which Albert Campion himself would have been proud. You can find out more about the Society and Margery's life and work at www.margeryallingham.org.uk.

Years later, Tolleshunt D'Arcy was the backdrop for the murders at White House Farm, just outside the village; thanks to Carol Ann Lee, whose meticulously researched book on the subject reveals a house with a fascinating past and provided the name of the family who lived there at the outbreak of war.

The history of the Wilkin family is comprehensively documented by Maura Benham in *The Story of Tiptree Jam*, and brought vividly to life in the museum at the firm's home in Tiptree (which, as you would expect, also has a very fine tea room).

As she has so often, the late and much-missed Irene Cranwell helped to steer this book with the stories she left behind; if she hadn't hated her dollies enough to bury them in her garden, *Dear Little Corpses* might have taken a very different direction. And my thanks to Chris Jennings, who, in Tweeting a photograph of his mum, Valerie, as a young evacuee with lovingly polished shoes, unwittingly taught me so much about the emotions of the parents left behind to worry.

My editor, Walter Donohue, has been a friend to Josephine and to me from the very beginning, and I appreciate his subtle and sensitive contribution to the life of these novels more than I can say. With each new book, I grow more grateful to the extraordinary team at Faber who give this series everything they've got, and to my friend and agent, Veronique Baxter, and her colleagues, Sara Langham and Nicky Lund at David Higham Associates. Huge thanks, too, to Grainne Fox and Fletcher & Company and to all at Crooked Lane Books for looking after Josephine in the US. The kindness and patience of everyone who waited for the book through a difficult time has meant the world to me.

It's been lovely to take Josephine back to Polstead, and I hope that those who live there now will forgive me for adding features to what is already a beautiful village. Writing about Suffolk could not have come at a better moment, allowing me, in the saddest of days, to remember and celebrate the happiest of childhoods and the wonderful parents who made anything and everything possible.

And finally to Mandy, also a Suffolk girl: thank you for reminding me every single day that there's joy and beauty in being a grown-up, too.